WORLD WAR ZERO

A SWAG TALES PAPERBACK

First published as Marah Chase and the Conqueror's Tomb in the United Kingdom and United States by Pegasus books in 2019

This edition published as World War Zero in the United Kingdom and United States in 2022.

This edition published by Swag Tales, Glasgow, G40 4TR.

Cover design by Jay Stringer.

Book formatted in Affinity Publisher.

Standard Paperback Edition ISBN: 978-1-9168923-6-1

Ebook Edition ISBN: 978-1-9168923-7-8

<u>The Eoin Miller Trilogy</u>
Old Gold
Runaway Town
Lost City
<u>The Sam Ireland Mysteries</u>
Ways to Die in Glasgow
How to Kill Friend and Implicate People
<u>The Marah Chase Thrillers</u>
World War Zero
End of Eden
<u>Stand-Alone Novels</u>
Don't Tell a Soul
Roll With It

"An archeologist and a spy walk into a bar . . ."

ONE

M arah Chase tried to kick-start the engine of her stolen motorcycle.
Once.

Twice.

No dice.

She checked for bullet holes, not expecting to run out of fuel so soon. Of all the vehicles she could have taken, she managed to pick the one with only half a tank. Chase added this to a growing list of problems, which so far included:

Being out of food.

Being out of water.

Being in the middle of the Syrian desert.

And—this was her personal favorite—being chased by armed mercenaries.

It was fair to say that things hadn't gone according to plan. And, like most missions, this was mostly because she didn't *have* a plan. Chase had set off across the sand on a stolen bike, with nothing more than a half-baked notion and a sense of direction.

She squeezed her left arm gingerly, where a deep cut was covered with a makeshift bandage. The blood was now sticking to the inside of her jacket. Her throat burned with each breath. Exhaustion was making her nauseaous. Chase turned in her seat to look back the way she had come.

The mercenaries were still in pursuit, their vehicles throwing up a dust cloud as they moved in from the north. Some were firing automatic weapons into the air, and one of them was holding a digital camera. With their heads covered in dark cloth and the black flags waving from their vehicles, they claimed affiliation with ISIL, but that was a cover. Al-Salif, under the leadership of Ayman Musab Faraj, was a criminal organization using people's fears of Islam as a disguise.

Each time they destroyed a temple or statue, the value of the remaining items rose. Ayman Musab Faraj was rumored to have one of the finest collections in the world.

Chase touched her side, feeling the bulge beneath the leather, where her messenger bag was protected from the elements. There was a statue inside. Priceless. The last piece of a Palmyra temple that had been destroyed during the civil war. Al-Salif wanted it back.

Chase would rather have died than hand it over.

Of course, that wasn't her preferred option.

A large swell of fear bubbled up from her gut. But that was fine. Fear was good. Fear was part of the human immune system, the antibody to complacency. Cold, honest, logical. The real heart of fight or flight was a process of elimination. First things first: She could rule out fight. Chase was outnumbered, outmuscled, and outgunned. Any direct confrontation would end badly. Flight? She made one last attempt at starting the bike, and this time the engine turned over. She felt the machine start to shake and rattle.

It would soon die.

A second dust cloud was closing in now from the west, heralded by the sound of more engines. A jeep crested a rise. Standing on the back, towering over the driver, were two figures dressed in the fatigues of the Syrian military. Two guns were trained on Chase, waiting until they were within range. They were risking a run into occupied territory to make a grab for her.

Chase breathed in. The fear whispered.

There was another way to fly.

She headed straight for the government jeep, weaving from side to side to avoid the bullets and getting low to the gas tank, making herself a small target. Chase knew they wanted to avoid a direct hit if they could. They wanted her alive. A political prisoner. An example to others in her trade.

Once she was close to the jeep, she banked into a sharp circle and accelerated into the curve. She let the back wheel whip around, fighting for purchase, kicking up a large dust cloud. Chase rolled off the bike and used the cloud as cover. She flattened herself to the ground and watched as the two vehicles collided, and heard the universal language of surprised grunts. The bike skidded away across the desert floor.

As the dust and sand in the air began to thin out, Chase could see that the two armed men had climbed down from the jeep and started to walk toward the bike. That left just the driver. He had a size advantage. Chase would only get one shot.

She took a quick glance to the north and saw that Al-Salif were getting close. They could see her. It looked like they were shouting out warnings, a brief moment of cooperation between two enemy forces. But they weren't near enough to get the message across.

Chase climbed to her feet and walked around the side of the jeep. She grabbed the driver by the lapels and prepared to try to heave him out of his seat, but she could tell she didn't have the strength to pull his weight. He was going to have to do the work. She leaned forward and winked, then blew him a kiss. He shifted his weight and moved toward her, and that gave Chase the start she needed. She pulled him clear of the jeep and kicked him in the face, hopefully stunning him for long enough to get away.

She climbed into the seat just as the two armed men turned around. When they saw her, they started to shout unholy things about her mother and raised their guns.

Okay, *now* they were ready to shoot her.

Chase put the jeep into gear and floored the pedal. The jeep lurched forward. She aimed at the two men, who were polite enough to stand close together, and felt the bone-breaking thud as she drove through them. One fell away to the side, but the other fell toward her. He smacked his head onto the hood of the jeep but managed to grab hold and climb forward.

Chase spun the jeep around to head back in the direction she'd been going. She could hear shouting now, and revving engines, as Al-Salif closed in. They got within range, and bullets hit the back of the jeep, while the guy on the hood shook his head, gaining focus. He raised his gun and pointed it at Chase's face. She tugged left on the wheel, then right. The guy didn't shake loose, but he couldn't hold the gun steady. He pulled the trigger, and shots flew into the air. Chase heard another volley of bullets from behind, hitting the flatbed of the jeep and coming in her direction.

She leaned to the side, out of the way, as the windshield exploded. The guy on the hood took the hits, his face turning into raw mince as he slid off the side.

Chase looked behind again and saw that two Al-Salif jeeps were close, one on each side of her jeep, and three motorcyclists were coming up between them. With the pedal of her own vehicle floored, she was staying just out of reach, but if she slowed down for any reason they'd be on her. And the bullets weren't all that bothered by the distance between them. Another spray of ammunition lined the floor of the jeep behind her seat. She pulled left on the wheel and felt something hot burn past her right shoulder as a bullet ripped through the seat.

Chase was all out of luck on this one.

The next round would hit her.

TWO

Travelling through Syria was never easy.

Chase had been three times since the civil war, and each trip had been difficult. None of them had gone this badly wrong.

This time, Chase had been joined by Ryan Wallace, an old university friend who worked in the same trade. Relic runners. Treasure hunters. Grave robbers. Whatever. The black market for antiquities had been growing since the invasion of Iraq and the Arab Spring. The ancient world was being crushed by wars, bombs, and climate change. Thrown into this mix were local amateur archeologists, people digging up their own country for items to sell, raising money to feed their families. Chase and Wallace were part of an elite inner circle of experienced professionals, known on the circuit as relic runners or gold dogs. They could name their price, with bored billionaires and corporations willing to pay through the nose to secure historical items for private collections. The higher the risk, the higher the reward. And it didn't come any riskier than Syria.

Coming in had been the easy part. Smuggling was another growth industry, made up of a network of people who would sail up and down the Euphrates, carrying refugees into Turkey. Wallace had hired one of these sailors to get them in, and taking the river allowed them to keep a distance from the cities, seeing the reality of modern Syria.

For Chase, this was important. She didn't want to see the faces or hear the voices. She was stealing their history, but the alternative was to let it be lost.

In Palmyra, Chase and Wallace had come across an Al-Salif camp. The group had destroyed many of the ancient monuments, including the Lion of Al-lāt, a statue that had stood for more than two thousand years. They'd been digging deeper, as if excavating for something specific.

When Chase had tried to get a closer look at what they were doing, she'd become separated from Wallace. The mercenaries captured him, and everything had gone wrong from there. The only blessing was the statue she now carried beneath her jacket. A small stone lion, similar to the famous old Al-lāt version, but with wings folded against it's side.

It was the last of its kind.

Now it was three days later. Chase was in the south of the country, with no backup and no supplies, save the stolen jeep. Handing the statue back wasn't an option. Al-Salif were after her as much as the relic now. People in her line of work had been going missing in this region for years.

Two months previous, Ayman Musab Faraj had beheaded an archeologist who refused to say where he'd hidden some relics. Three months before that, Al-Salif had dragged a British news reporter from her convoy and beheaded her on camera. They'd uploaded the video to YouTube, and her family had seen it on the internet before the British government had time to contact them. The reporter had been one of the first to break the news of the damage Al-Salif were doing to Palmyra.

Whichever way she looked at it, Chase was at the top of their shit list. And she wouldn't be any safer in government hands. The Syrian authorities made a harsh example of people caught smuggling artifacts. They had no support from international law because, well, they were international criminals. Not considered any better than the terrorists and mercenaries.

She turned back to face the horizon. In the distance she could make out the dark shape of Golan Heights. It was contested land, currently split between Syria and Israel. Much of that area was held by the opposition fighters. Western forces had a presence there. It was an open secret that the CIA had been training many of said opposition groups, including some who used to be affiliated with Al-Qaeda. The civil war had made for some very uneasy alliances. Neither Al-Salif nor the Syrian army would follow her up into opposition territory.

More important, Golan Heights had been Wallace's plan B. The north was the quickest way in and out of Palmyra, but the south was the safest. They'd gone with speed as plan A, but Wallace never entered a country without a backup option. There was a case full of supplies hidden near the Israeli border.

If Chase could get to it, she'd be in the clear.

She breathed in and closed her eyes for a second, listening to the voice of fear.

Flight is still the best option.

It's not that they're chasing you.

It's that they can shoot you.

Your next problem is the bullets.

There was a bag on the passenger seat. Chase started to rummage through it while keeping one hand on the wheel. Her fist closed around magazines for automatic rifles, then some papers and, finally, something useful.

A grenade.

Chase held the explosive up above her and heard gears change on the chasing vehicles. She turned to see that they'd slowed down a little, and the next volley of gunfire wasn't coming. She pulled the pin with her teeth, then twisted in the seat and threw the grenade back toward her pursuers in an underarm lob.

The two jeeps swerved in opposite directions, leaving a large space between them where the grenade fell. The explosion sent dirt and rock flying into the air, knocking two of the motorcyclists from their rides. Chase heard screams. The jeep to the left had swerved far enough away, but the one on the right was caught by the blast and tipped over, sending its occupants sprawling to the dirt.

No time for guilt; keep moving.

The jeep on the left was still behind her, and there was still one other motorcycle, but they'd lost ground in avoiding the grenade. Chase kept her foot to the floor, and the distance between her and the remaining pursuers grew.

She heard gunfire, but nothing was hitting home.

The surface beneath the wheels started to change, harsh desert giving way to healthier land. Now she could see sparse vegetation and rocks, with compacted dirt replacing the sand. Up ahead was a collection of burned-out single-story buildings and the beginnings of a dirt track running between them. This would have been one of the many farms that once covered this part of Syria.

Before the drought. Before the war. Before the bombs.

Soon she was on pavement.

A road. The engines behind her revved, and Chase heard the occasional bullet hitting the road. This was mostly posturing. As they began the slow climb to the plateau, Al-Salif were starting to fall farther back. Soon they would need to give up the pursuit to avoid running into a battle, but their egos wouldn't let them simply stop. They needed to rattle their sabers for a while longer.

Chase looked back again to see that the soldiers had stopped. They parked their vehicles on the road and stood watching her. One of them was bent down over a small metal object that was catching the sunlight. It looked like a Zippo lighter.

Huh?

That was when Chase noticed a trail of dark liquid running down the road, right to where the soldiers were standing. The fuel gauge was a lot lower than it had been a few minutes ago. One of the bullets must have hit the tank. Chase saw the stooped figure spark the lighter into life and touch the flame to the trail of gas, sending it chasing after her.

Oh, come on, that's not fair.

THREE

The jeep exploded into a fireball as it crested the rise. It rolled on for a few hundred yards before coming to a stop, where it stood burning on the road.

Chase had jumped free in the seconds before the flames caught her, landing on her wounded arm. It took every stubborn inch of her not to scream in pain. *Maybe if I give them my nicest smile,* she thought, *they'll only slightly kill me.*

She reached into the messenger bag and ran her fingers across the surface of the statue. It was cracked, which would reduce the value, but she could still make good with it. The sound of a motorcycle engine filled the air, and Chase turned to see the rider coming up the road. The other soldiers were still hanging back. The rider circled Chase slowly, once, twice, enough to make the point, before stopping before her and killing the engine. She climbed to her knees and put her hands up.

He laughed and climbed off the bike. "Nice try, Chase."

Chase wasn't sure which surprised her more: that he knew her name or that he spoke with a broad Yorkshire accent. There was an automatic rifle slung across his shoulder, but instead he reached inside his sand-coated military fatigues and pulled out a pistol.

He pointed it at Chase's head. "You still have the statue?"

Chase said nothing.

He stepped closer and pressed the gun to her head. "They've found something. A temple, a tomb—I don't know what it is."

Chase blinked. She said, "What?"

"They were digging. The statue, your statue, it came out of this chamber they found, in the ground. They keep saying something, I think it's a name. Aten."

"Aten?"

Chase knew the name. It was a sun god from ancient Egypt. She couldn't think why that would be relevant to an excavation in Palmyra. Or why this guy was telling her about it.

"Another one, too. Saint Mark? I didn't think there were any saints out here."

"There aren't now."

"Something about the 'Old Ones' too. That's a phrase I keep hearing." He turned to look at the other soldiers, starting up the hill toward them, then back to Chase. "Jump me."

"What?"

"I'm SIS, but I can't blow my cover for you. The bike can get you to the border. Jump me, and make it look good.

Chase grabbed his gun hand and pulled the weapon away from her face. She threw herself at him. They hit the ground together.

"Sorry," said Chase, and punched him in the face. He lay still.

Chase climbed to her feet, ignoring the way her knee tried to buckle when she put weight on it, and mounted the motorcycle. She kicked it into life again and roared away. After a minute or so, Chase glanced back. The Brit was standing on the road, staring after her, with the burning jeep beside h im.

When she looked back a second time, he was gone.

Chase relaxed and eased off slightly on the throttle. As the adrenaline of the pursuit wore off, her aches and pains came back into focus. The cut on her arm stung, and now her knee was throbbing. There was a sharp pain in her right shoulder that could be a pulled muscle. It was going to take a month's worth of long baths to get over this one.

Chase took a look around as she rode. The hills and valleys on this high ground were formed by ancient volcanic activity. It was an odd mix of desolate rock and beautiful vegetation. She turned in the direction of a valley to her right and rode down a winding path through a grove of struggling eucalyptus trees. Clearing the grove, she hit the outskirts of a destroyed city.

Quineitra.

Ruined houses lined bulldozed streets, with old rooftops lying flat on the ground like gravestone markers. Mattresses and broken toys littered the broken paths, which were separated from the roads by curbs painted alternately black and white. Closer into the center of the city, a number of buildings were still standing, but not by much. Officially, the town was uninhabited.

Left derelict as a monument to the cost of war. In more recent times, people had started to come back to try to live in the remaining buildings, huddled around fires at night. The city had become a monument of a different kind.

In a large square near the center of the old town, Chase saw a small refugee camp made up of tents and small huts built from the remnants of nearby buildings. The drought had driven people into the cities, and then the war had driven them back out again. They were gathered in the tents. Starved and dirty. The makeshift village reminded her of the stories she'd read about Hoovervilles, shantytowns for people who'd lost everything during the Great Depression. The best thing about being interested in history was that it kept repeating itself. There would always be a second chance to see something.

The residents watched as she rode by.

Nobody called out or begged.

At the end of the village, Chase turned left. She pulled the bike to a stop outside a hospital. It was a large building, with a harsh square design reminiscent of a 1960s British tower block. The windows were burned out, and the front wall was pitted with bullet holes. Chase climbed the front steps and walked in through the charred square hole that had once been the front door. In the abandoned lobby, she moved around the edge of the room, keeping close to the walls to avoid holes in the floor. At the far end, next to another door, was a gap in the wall, down at ankle height. Chase reached inside and closed her hands around the handle of a case. She pulled it out toward her.

The stash was supposed to hold the clothes, money, and fake passports Chase and Wallace needed to get across the border into Israel.

It was empty.

What the hell?

Chase heard the floor creak. She hadn't moved. Someone else was in the room behind her.

"Magic," a familiar Scottish accent said. "It would be nice of you to put your hands in the air and turn around."

Ryan Wallace was standing in the doorway. He was tall and skinny, with a tangle of brown hair that he usually wore gelled but was now damp and matted. He liked to look more like a rock star than an archeologist, and he usually pulled it off. He'd had a growing career with TV documentaries and bestselling books, specializing in ancient Greece, until a scandal effectively killed his academic reputation. He had been proven to have been lying in his academic papers, exaggerating certain finds in order to secure funding. Nobody ended up in their line of work without having had other doors closed on them first.

Magic was his nickname for Chase. Based on an old running joke about the way she insisted her name be pronounced. Marah, rhyming with *Ta Da*.

Wallace was dressed in a clean linen suit that, up until recently, had been in the case. He was pointing a small pistol at Chase. He'd never been comfortable with guns. He held them like someone who'd seen them only in movies. Chase had more experience, had grown up using them on a farm.

But the distance between them negated that. Wallace would have time to fire as many shots as he needed before she could get to him.

"Thought you'd got rid of me?" he said.

"I had no choice."

Chase sounded almost convincing. She nearly had herself fooled. But Wallace wasn't buying it. Al-Salif had caught up with them at on oasis. Chase had seen them first and made a split-second choice, between getting caught with Wallace or making it out on her own.

She'd left him to die.

Now it looked as though he wanted payback.

FOUR

Wallace walked toward her, picking his steps carefully to avoid falling.

"Glad you could make it," he said. "I was worried we might lose out on our investment."

He reached out to touch her side, running his hand up the outside of her jacket, stopping when he could feel the lump he was looking for. He tugged on the jacket's zipper with the same hand and reached inside. He found the messenger bag pressed close to Chase and then pulled a small bundle free.

"Wally, listen, I—"

Chase cut herself off. There hadn't been any other way. Stand or run. The only choice she'd seen was to run. Al-Salif wanted to kill them both anyway. Going back for Wallace would only have gotten her killed.

But how had he made it out?

"Nae bother," Wallace said. "Really, it's fine. I was planning to ditch you anyway. There was only one set of clothes in the case, only a passport for me." He raised his voice. "Wilhelm."

Chase heard the floor creak again. Before she could react, a hand grabbed her shoulder and worked its way around her neck, pulling her up and back. Chase's feet left the floor, and she started to struggle for breath.

Another man stepped in through the doorway behind Wallace. Large, with gorilla-like sloping shoulders that connected to his head with little in the way of a neck in between. He was dressed in faded military clothes.

"I made some new friends in Palmyra," Wallace said. "The brawn here is named Braun. I know, right? That guy behind you is Wilhelm. They've got some questions for you." He turned to Braun. "All yours."

Wallace waved a goodbye at Chase and picked his steps carefully out though the doorway, clutching the package tightly to his side.

Wilhelm's grip around Chase's throat tightened. She curled her right hand into a fist and swung it upward, trying to connect with any part of him. When that failed, she kicked backward, connecting with the inside of Wilhelm's knee and knocking him off balance.

Chase spun free and put her momentum into a second punch, this time connecting with something solid, sending him staggering back. She got a look at him as they separated. He was almost a foot taller than her, but much thinner, built like a mop handle.

Wilhelm shook his head and stepped forward, snarling as he made another grab. Chase swung her right foot, thankful that she was wearing solid desert boots, and connected hard with his groin, following fast with a punch to his face. She heard—and felt—Wilhelm's nose snap. He fell into a ball on the floor, swearing in German.

Chase whirled back to face Braun, but he'd moved surprisingly fast and was already on her. He lifted Chase and threw her against the wall. Stars danced in front of Chase's eyes as her head connected with the solid brick surface. She slid down toward the floor. Braun swung a punch on the way down, and it connected with her stomach, driving out whatever remaining air she had in her lungs.

She flopped forward onto her knees and retched.

He paused to admire his work, and Chase used those seconds to her advantage, lunging forward with the strength she had left, aiming for his knees. But his legs were as hard as steel rods, and Chase crumpled at his feet.

She rolled onto her back and stared up at him, dazed. He had a cruel smile, showing teeth against taut, gray gums. Looked to be enjoying himself.

Braun reached down to grasp her hair. Chase squirmed just beyond his reach and kicked upward with her booted foot, connecting with his jaw. He staggered back but recovered his footing quickly.

Chase rolled onto her side just in time to avoid a vicious kick from the large man. She tried climbing to her feet, but Wilhelm stepped in from behind and took out her weight with a sweep of his foot, knocking her back down. He rolled Chase onto her front, lying facedown on the dusty floor, and then wrapped a handkerchief around her neck and pulled it tight. She kicked but couldn't connect with anything, and she felt the weight of both men pinning down her arms.

A deep, rumbling voice said in German, "Stop fighting."

The weight on her back pushed the air from her, even as the hand-kerchief tightened and she felt her throat grow hot and airless. Chase's ears popped as she gasped, trying to suck in some air. After a moment, everything seemed to slow down. She felt her body growing heavy.

I can't fight.

I can't fly.

As she relaxed, the men on top of her eased off a little. Chase heard, distantly, through all the fog in her ears, the floor creak.

I can fall . . .

She pulled one last spark of energy from somewhere and rolled to the side. The two men had been using their weight to stop her from getting up; they weren't braced to prevent her moving laterally.

There was a loud groaning sound, then a snap, and the floorboards gave way beneath them. Chase had been expecting this. As the ground dropped away, she grabbed for something to hold on to, and her hands found purchase in another crack a few inches from the edge of the new hole. She dug in and hung on, sucking in huge gulps of air to try to get her body going again.

Braun and Wilhelm had no such luck. They had both fallen through to the basement. Chase heard two heavy thuds and at least one bone snapping. If she had anything in her stomach, she might not have been able to keep it down. After another minute of slow, deep breathing, she had enough strength to haul herself up.

Chase looked back over the edge. The basement level was mostly shrouded in darkness, but there was light around the edges from gaps in the walls, and the fresh new hole in the floor was creating a spotlight on the ground below. She could see the two men lying in a heap. Wilhelm's arm was at an unnatural angle; his eyes were open and blinking slowly. Braun was facedown, but his shoulders were moving as he breathed.

Chase called down to them, "At least you're in a hospital."

She walked slowly back around the edge of the room and then out through the entrance, down the steps to the road. The motorcycle lay on its side. Wallace had slashed the tires and opened the tank, spilling the gas out across the asphalt. There was a bottle of water waiting for her next to the wreck. Chase smiled. Despite all the aches and pains and her still-burning lungs, she let out a laugh. He'd expected her to find a way past those guys.

The joke wore thin when she realized she was still three miles from the border checkpoint. She started walking. With each step she had to find a new way to distract herself from the throbbing of her knee, the stabbing pain in her shoulder, and the cut on her arm that felt warm and irritable. And now her throat hurt.

When she walked past the refugee camp, Chase saw children with cracked lips. Dehydration had become one of the biggest killers in Syria. She handed over the water bottle and walked on.

At the checkpoint, she could see soldiers watching her for half a mile as she approached. They didn't make a move to come any closer, even though they could see she was in pain. As she got closer, she saw that they wore reflective sunglasses, hiding their eyes, but she knew they were watching, wondering what this was about.

Without money or identification, Chase was going to need to talk her way across. As she drew nearer to the guards, she started to call out that she was an American and had been attacked and lost her ID. She also added something about a warm bath and hey, does anybody have some dark rum?

Once she was at the crossing, one of the guards stepped forward and lifted the barrier. Nobody made a move to stop her or ask any personal details. Nobody seemed to want to acknowledge she was there, other than to make way for her to cross. She walked the short distance over into Israel. A second barrier was lifted to let her straight through. Chase hesitated for a moment, poised for some kind of inspection.

"They know who you are, Chase."

She turned to face a row of cars that was parked at the curb. A man with thin, sandy-colored hair and a bushy mustache was leaning against a black town car.

He was wearing slacks and a khaki shirt, with his sleeves rolled up. His name was Toby Schlamme. He worked for the Israel Security Agency, better known as Shin Bet.

Chase had met him before. It hadn't gone well.

"Welcome to Israel." He opened the car's back-seat door. "You're under arrest."

MARAH CHASE IN

WORLD WAR ZERO

WRITTEN BY

JAY STRINGER

EDITED BY

STACIA DECKER & KATIE McGUIRE

A SWAG TALES PRODUCTION

FIVE

The cell was hot. It was a narrow, rectangular space, with brick walls painted white and a bench bolted to one side for Chase to sit on. There was a window high up, on the smallest wall, at the end of the bench, with barred windows letting in the afternoon sun. The window was just high enough that prisoners could be allowed to hang themselves, if convenient.

Chase had been driven straight there from the checkpoint. Schlamme had exchanged a few pleasantries with her on the drive but hadn't answered any questions about where they were going or why she was under arrest. His involvement meant it had to be serious.

Chase had been arrested three times in Jerusalem. The most recent run-in with Schlamme had been when she had attempted to excavate beneath the Temple Mount under the cover of darkness. Schlamme had threatened to hold her indefinitely under a variety of anti-terrorism laws. He could still make good on that if he wanted to.

Schlamme had allowed a silent nurse to take a look at Chase's injuries. After she was bandaged up, she had been led to this cell and left alone for hours. The only interruption had been a guard bringing her a large plastic bottle of water and a stale egg sandwich. She stretched out on the bench and tried to sleep.

Chase heard footsteps out in the corridor. Two sets: the heavy, slow boots of the guard, and someone else a little softer. The large metal door by her head opened a few seconds later, and a woman walked in.

She had dark brown hair that didn't look used to the climate, and was wearing a deliberately rumpled suit. Her features were partially covered by sunglasses. She walked with the kind of bored ease that they teach at academies. Chase had never seen anyone looking more like a spook.

Spies didn't try to blend into the crowd in this part of the world. They liked to be seen. You were supposed to know who they were and avoid causing them any trouble. The only question was, which service did she work for?

The spook leaned against the far wall in silence. Chase had received this treatment before. It was a tactic to unsettle her, to make her speak first. That was fine, because she liked to have both the first and the last words in a conversation.

"An archeologist and a spy walk into a bar . . ." Chase left that hanging.

"Archeologist?" the spook said. "Is that what you're calling yourself?"

She spoke with a regionless English accent. Sharp and cool. Not quite money, but someone who'd learned to pass among people who were. Chase's mother had been Glaswegian, and chase inherited her allergy to that kind of accent. If the spook was a Brit, then she was most likely MI6. Or whatever name they were going by that month.

The British security services had been all over the news in the last few months. A former intelligence analyst had leaked classified information to the press. All the main services had been implicated in breaches of privacy. The media were having a field day.

Chase didn't know why an MI6 agent would be visiting her now, so she kept quiet, waiting to see what came next.

The spook pulled a notebook from the inside pocket of her suit jacket. "General Kuzmin called you a grave robber," she said, reading from the pages. "The head of the FBI calls you, and I quote, 'a dirty treasure hunter.' Professor Rabia said you're a mercenary. Zawi Hawass calls you a desecrator. My personal favorite, because I was talking to Mr. Schlamme a few minutes ago, is when he calls you a terrorist. Doesn't sound much like archeology."

Chase sat up and then slouched against the wall. She paused before answering to scratch her nose, trying to find a way of showing she wasn't impressed. "Career advice from someone who has spy tattooed on her forehead?"

The spook smiled. She slipped off her sunglasses. Chase saw attractive, clear blue eyes, running a little to gray at the edges. She looked several years younger than Chase. The type SIS tended to recruit straight out of university. Chase had learned to spot them at Oxford, a certain class of people who were clearly on that career path, whether they knew it or not. Approached on campus one day by a professor, or a stranger in a bland coat, invited to attend a job interview.

"My name's Joanna," the spook said. "Mason."

"You pick that one out yourself, or did it come with the job?"

Mason smiled again, just in the corner of her mouth, and it invited Chase in on the joke. "Are you always this much fun?"

"Usually I let people buy me a drink first."

Chase caught herself. The sensible, grown-up part of her brain said, Don't flirt with the spy. The other part, the one she tended to listen to, said, Well, she's cute.

"How's the archeology working out for you?" Mason asked.

"I admit, things could be going better," Chase said, nodding.

"Do you prefer *relic runner* or *gold dog*?"

"I don't really care."

Mason leaned back against the wall and let the silence stretch out. Chase knew this technique, too. Mason had slipped too easily into bantering with her, and the quiet was a way to take control again.

"Schlamme really doesn't like you." Mason took out a pack of cigarettes and offered one to Chase, who declined. Mason waited until she'd gotten a smoke lit and enjoyed the first drag, then continued. "I think he's inclined to let you disappear for good."

"He wouldn't dare," Chase said with a snort.

"Well, the problem you have is that you're not actually here right now. There's no record of you entering Israel. No paperwork." Mason reached into her suit and pulled out a US passport. She started flicking the pages. "And this is in a hotel safe in Turkey. I should probably hand it over to your embassy, report you missing."

Chase banged her head gently against the wall behind her.

This was a setup.

Chase waved her right hand in front of her face, showing that she was annoyed by the smoke. "What do you want?"

"Well." A smile spread slowly across Mason's face. It wasn't the friendly version she'd given a couple of minutes earlier. "Now that you mention it, there is some work you could do for us."

"No thanks. I've got work," Chase replied.

Mason pushed off from the wall. "So, what's this, your lunch break?"

Chase's reply was subdued. She knew she needed to accept the offer. "Vacation."

Mason banged on the door. They both heard the bolt sliding across on the other side; then the door swung outward, and the guard, a teenager with an automatic weapon over her shoulder and a cell phone in her hand, stepped aside for Mason to leave.

Mason looked down at Chase. "You mentioned a drink?"

SIX

Joanna Mason sat in silence as she drove inland across Israel. The unmarked blue Kia was comfortable, and she was letting Chase decide whether she wanted to talk. Chase slouched down in her seat for the better part of an hour and left Mason to her thoughts.

Mason kept stealing glances over at her companion.

The file on Marah Chase was thick, but Mason liked to go the extra mile. If she planned to pull someone in as an asset, she wanted to know everything about them, and paperwork and reports could do only so much. It paid to speak to people. Chase's old university professors had given Mason useful details.

Troublemaker, one had said, but worth it. Mason could already see the first part of that; she was hoping the second would show itself, and soon. She's a flirt, an old work colleague had told her over a coffee, but it's mostly just a show. She doesn't trust easily, her old solicitor had said, but she's loyal.

Most of the details Mason had gleaned from the conversations had backed up things she could have found in the file, but she'd learned how to pronounce the name. Marah, rhyming with hurrah. Mason had looked it up. A Hebrew word, from Exodus, referring to a well of bitter water the Israelites passed on their way out of Egypt.

Mason tried not to read anything into that.

The telling moment had come in conversation with a BBC producer who had worked with Chase on a couple of documentaries.

"Oh, she'll hate you," the producer had said, as soon as Mason had introduced herself.

"Why?"

"You're one of *them*," he'd said. "Marah likes to needle authority."

Mason remembered the look on Chase's face when she'd introduced herself at the jail and thought back to what the producer had said. Mason could have come at the situation differently. She'd mastered a number of different accents and spoke half a dozen languages. But the best way to win over someone like Marah Chase was to be authentic. And a file couldn't tell you that. It was the kind of information you got only from speaking to people.

In time, Chase might see they were the same.

Chase's father had been a military man, enlisting to escape poverty in rural Washington. Mason's dad was a civil servant in Whitehall but came from a dead industrial town in the Midlands. Chase's mother had been a peace activist from Glasgow, who met her future husband across a picket line at a demonstration against nuclear weapons. Mason's mum was a schoolteacher from Hackney. Mason had the same contempt for the authorities, but somehow, she found herself working with them. Telling herself she was changing the system from within, while her job was to keep the status quo in place.

Chase sniffed the air. "I stink."

"Well, I wasn't going to mention it."

Chase kept a straight face for a few seconds, then cracked a smile. They drove in a relaxed silence for a few miles and watched the scenery pass. The evening sky was a mix of red and orange fading to gray. Skies like this were one of the reasons Mason loved spending time in this part of the world.

London was great. It was home. But scenes like this didn't exist there.

"Did you know him?" Chase asked. "The guy in the news?"

Mason knew who Chase was referring to. Martyn Wood. The officer who'd leaked information to the press. "Yeah. A little."

That was the first real lie she had told Chase. Mason and Wood had been friends, going all the way back to university.

Chase watched Mason's reaction as she asked, "Do you think he was right?"

That wasn't a ball Mason was willing to catch. There wasn't enough time in the world for her to figure out what she felt about her old friend. The pain of his betrayal still hurt, but she had to keep it locked away.

"He agreed to keep the same secrets I did," Mason said. "Signed the same forms."

She hoped she'd masked the tension in her voice.

They'd agreed to keep the same secrets, but some of those secrets were bad. Maybe Martyn had just been braver than she was.

A car had been following them for the past thirty minutes. Mason turned left off the main road, away from the clouds, and headed down into the valley that held the Sea of Galilee. The water stretched out ahead of them, surrounded by vast green fields and small towns. They followed the curve of the freshwater lake, driving through the towns of Capernaum and Ginosar, until Mason could see the city of Tiberias up ahead.

The car was still with them. Hanging back.

Mason drove along route 90, sticking close to the edge of the lake, and pulled into the car park of a hotel. It was a tall, thin building with the name Leonardo painted down the side in red letters. Across the road was a gated area also with the hotel's name on it, leading to a fenced-off section of the beach. There was a glass wall at the rear of the car park, and from the other side came the sounds of people splashing around in a pool.

As she killed the car's engine, Mason watched the tailing driver slow down to confirm she had stopped before passing by the entrance to the car park.

She handed Chase the electronic key to a hotel room. "Room 1016. You'll find fresh clothes. Take a shower and order all the room service."

"All of it?"

"All of it."

"What about you?"

Mason climbed out of the car. She lifted the gun that had been tucked beneath her feet and slipped it into the waistband at the small of her back. "I need to check something out."

Mason set off at something close to a jog. Out on the road, she turned right and headed in the direction the car had driven. The vehicle wasn't anywhere in sight. Their next move would depend on their reason for following. If it was just about following them, the driver would be circling around to find a spot within sight of Mason's car to sit and wait.

If they were here to move on Mason and Chase, the car would be parked a few hotels down, a discreet distance away. They would wait for the cover of darkness, then make their play.

All the hotels were on the same side of the street. Mason crossed over, closer to the water's edge, to get a better vantage point. She spotted the car three buildings down, nestled in the corner of the lot.

She walked to the next building, so she could come up on the car from behind. The next lot was empty, with a low concrete wall separating it from her target. Mason crouched down and made her way along the wall to where she would be in line with the car. She could hear voices talking in German.

That confirmed what she'd suspected.

Mason thought back to what she'd seen on the drive. There had definitely been two of them in front. Had there been a third in the back? She'd never gotten a view of anyone else, but there had been hints of movement in the shadows. Mason needed to plan for three.

Her gun was made of a hard plastic. It wasn't immune to modern airport body scanners but would slip by in checked luggage. It was also designed to be quiet. The mechanism that fired the shot, and the barrel, had been specially designed by MI6 to reduce the gas and pressure. The shots would still be heard, but in the dark city evening, they could be confused with a car door closing.

Mason rose and leveled the gun at the back of the car.

Two men were standing with their backs to her, looking down into the trunk and debating which weapons they needed. Mason considered climbing over the wall and getting in closer, to help control the noise, but she would be trading off the security provided by this small distance. She was the most skilled fighter on her team, but technique was only part of the equation when going up against two heavily muscled men. She stayed alive in the field by making the right choices, and the best option was to take them out from here.

She was taking aim at the bigger of the two when large hands grabbed her wrist and pulled her forward. There was a third man, and he had been crouched on the other side of the wall, matching her position.

He hauled Mason over the concrete, and the momentum allowed him to throw her at the back of the car.

She took the hit on her shoulder, falling to her knees and trying to stop the world from shaking around her.

The gun was gone. Mason couldn't see where it had fallen.

One of the men pulled her up.

Mason saw the knife too late.

SEVEN

Tan Bashir pushed through the pain. The torture was an inconvenience, but it was something he'd been prepared for.

He didn't know where he was.

He was blindfolded.

His lungs burned.

His throat gagged.

He was in total control.

This wasn't his first time being waterboarded. He'd gone through it three times in training and twice in the field. It was one of the reasons he got assignments like this. Everyone had their specialties, and Tan Bashir was good at being tortured.

And, frankly, these Al-Salif guys were amateurs. Bashir felt as though he should offer them advice, but that would mean breaking character.

The aim was to scare the target. Make the body think it's drowning. Push the mind to lose control. A panic attack sets in; the lungs go into overdrive. Before you know it, information is slipping out. Something, anything, whatever they want to hear, whatever makes the water stop.

If water doesn't work, they use fizzy drinks. Coke. Pepsi. Sprite. The carbonation adds a new dimension. If the fizz doesn't work, they use oil, thick and slimy. Gunk that slides down through the nostrils, into the back of throat, and sits there, trying to kill you.

If you hurt someone enough, they'll tell you anything. It doesn't have to be real. Most of the time, the victim starts making things up. The torturer can't really tell the difference. Real information gained under duress looks pretty much the same as fake.

The secret is to build lines of defense in your mind. Pick a piece of information and make it the one thing you absolutely must not give up. Then, when the pain gets to be too much, give it up. That buys a break, a pause while they try to decide if that's what they're after.

They start again, but so do you. Pick another line of defense, another piece of information that you will guard to your last breath. Then cave and reveal it when things get too intense. It doesn't even matter what it is. Never mind what they're asking. Choose to believe they're after this one thing. Convince yourself each time that this is the key detail, build up all your natural defenses around it, and the torturers will start to tire themselves out extracting it from you. They may give in. They may kill you. Either of those options is a win.

Again.

Again.

Reload. Rebuild. Hold onto this one nugget. Put everything you have into holding that line. Then give in.

Again.

Again.

They had his name. They had his rank. They had his inside-leg measurement. He'd told them the first football match he'd been to, and the name of his first crush. There was no longer any secret about his preference for Escape from L.A. over Escape from New York. Personally, he thought coffee was overrated, and now his captors knew it.

Each time they'd gone to work on him, it had taken energy and effort to pull the information out. They were growing tired. Frustration was audible in their voices. Anger. Humiliation. Bashir knew they were getting ready to write the whole thing off and kill him, and then he would have won, and the pain would stop.

And they wouldn't have any of what they wanted.

Bashir had known the risks when he helped Chase escape. He'd known it could blow his cover. The order to capture her had come right from Ayman Musab Faraj. They had failed at every opportunity, and people were already turning on one another, looking for a scapegoat. Bashir would probably have taken the fall even if they hadn't figured out he was there undercover.

And what a time for his cover to blow. He was only a couple of days away from getting the answers he needed.

If Chase hadn't wandered into their camp, if his hand hadn't been forced, he could've been home by the end of the week, catching up on Coronation Street and Doctor Who. Watching Hull City. Enjoying the rain. Oh, man, the rain. It's hard to understand the joy of water falling on your face until you've lived in a desert.

And now it had all been for nothing.

No, not nothing. Even if the only thing he'd done was save Chase's life, just one person, it had been worth it. He told himself that, and he mostly believed it. Mostly. But SIS knew Al-Salif was a cover, and he was there to connect all the dots. Ayman Musab Faraj had been educated at Eton and Oxford and put in time both on Wall Street and at the London Stock Exchange. Prior to the Arab Spring, he'd shown no signs of worshipping any god other than money. Al-Salif's finances were managed in the usual way, filtered through shell corporations and investment funds. But they were going in the wrong direction: Rather than the funds flowing toward the front line, they were heading away. Into private pockets. A significant share of the profits was going completely dark. That is, even the best forensic accountants in the business were losing track of it. It was hidden, with no way of tracking where it ended up.

For an operation on that scale, Faraj had to have some pretty powerful friends. But now, Bashir wouldn't get the chance to find out who they were.

Unless he could turn the tables on these guys. It was rare, but it happened. Sometimes the victim could inspire sympathy in the torturers, and the torturers would start giving up key details without even realizing what they were doing.

The questions came again.

Bashir prepared himself for the next round.

EIGHT

T he first time Chase stepped out of the shower was to answer the door to room service. She wrapped herself in a towel and made polite small talk with the young porter, who spoke in brief bursts of broken English while holding a conversation with her towel and tattoos. He wheeled in two trollies laden with food and alcohol.

The second time was when she heard movement out in the room. She left the water running as cover while she pulled on her bathrobe and inched open the door to look out. Mason was leaning against the wall, breathing heavily. Her shirt was covered in blood.

"Oh, hey." Mason's voice was faint. She sounded woozy. "The food's here."

Chase entered the room and pulled out the chair from the desk. Mason eased down onto it.

"I'm calling a doctor." Chase picked up the phone's receiver off the cradle, but Mason reached out to stop her.

"No doctors. Spy stuff," Mason said. "Get my bag."

On the floor beside the bed were two open suitcases full of new clothes and a small leather satchel. Chase lifted the satchel, and Mason reached out, then tugged on the lining inside. It came away with the sound of Velcro, and Chase saw a small compartment underneath. There was a slim plastic case strapped to the back of the bag, which Chase removed and opened, revealing a first aid kit.

"You'll need to help me," Mason said between gulps.

"Dammit, Mason, I'm an archeologist, not a doctor."

Mason laughed at that, before grimacing.

"What the hell happened?" Chase asked.

Mason managed a shrug. "Just a case of mistaken identity."

"Are they still around?"

"I sorted it."

Chase found a syringe and a bottle of Dilaudid. "Let's do something about the pain first."

"No, no." Mason pushed the drugs away. "I need to be clear while we do this. After that, by all means, dope me the hell up."

Mason started to unbutton her shirt and pulled it out from under the waistband of her trousers. She leaned forward and tried to shrug out of the cloth, but Chase stood up and pulled it the rest of the way off, slowly. She bundled it up and dropped it to the floor at their feet. It might come in handy if they needed extra dressing for the wound. Mason leaned back into the hard wood of the seat. Mason was wearing a simple black bra, and Chase watched her breasts rise and fall in staccato bursts as she sucked in air.

Mason caught the look.

"Concentrate," she said.

"Oh, I was."

A few inches below the bra was a bloody gash. It was at an angle, slicing downward into Mason's side.

"Knife wound," she said.

Mason did most of the work herself. She worked through the pain with a detached efficiency, cleaning the wound with alcohol and directing Chase to apply pressure while they assessed the damage. Mason pulled a small tube out of the kit and handed it to Chase, who unscrewed the cap and then pierced the silver seal. Chase smelled glue immediately. Mason talked her through what to do, and Chase applied the glue over jagged flesh and then applied pressure again by pressing a small gauzelike material to the wound.

"This is like fixing a bike tire," Chase said.

Once the glue was dry, Chase rubbed a pain-relief gel over the area and started to prepare the syringe for an injection of the Dilaudid. Mason took it from her and said, "I'll do that bit myself."

A couple of minutes later, Mason was wearing a clean T-shirt and leaning back on the bed. She sipped from a glass of bourbon. They'd started to pick their way through the food, sampling a bit of everything. The mix of painkillers and alcohol looked to have relaxed Mason, and Chase tried again for information.

"How did you know I was coming across today?"

Mason's voice was a little drowsy. "Had eyes on you in Turkey. You and Ryan Wallace. I wanted to pick you up before Syria but wasn't ready."

That opened up a load of extra questions, but it hadn't been what Chase was getting at. "Okay, but what I meant was how did you know I was coming across here today? It wasn't part of the plan."

"We have a man in Al-Salif."

"The guy who helped me escape."

Mason didn't reply. Chase knew they were skirting around classified information. Had she been picked up because of her information on Al-Salif? That didn't make sense, though, because Mason had wanted to contact her before Syria.

"He talked to me," Chase said. "Told me Al-Salif found something, a tomb or temple. Mentioned some names."

"What names?"

"Aten and Saint Mark."

"Mean anything to you?"

"Sure. A sun god from Egypt, and a christian saint. Also a part of New York that is nowhere near as cool as it used to be. Do they mean anything to you?" When Mason didn't answer, Chase pointed to the wound. "Who were those guys, and why did they stab you?"

Mason relented with a nod. "They go by the name Reinheit Eighteen. White supremacists. Terrorists for hire. They were coming for you at the border, but Schlamme got there first. They were about to try again here." Mason sipped her drink. "I took them out. I've put a call in to Schlamme, and he'll make them disappear."

"But why are they after me?"

Mason pulled the satchel across the bed toward her. "This is where it gets interesting."

NINE

"The short version: Hitler really was obsessed with the occult," Mason said. "Just like in the movies. He sent teams all over the place, looking for all kinds of things. Garden of Eden. Atlantis. A lost valley in Tibet. He actually did send people looking for the ark of the covenant."

"Well, he was crazy."

"Sure. But we were feeding him the information."

"What?"

"The Nazis had us beat. They had more people, more land. We were losing ground across Europe, and your guys weren't in the fight yet." Mason smiled. "It was Ian Fleming's baby. He was in the intelligence division, running disinformation campaigns, circulating false briefings to smoke out Nazi spies. When he learned about Hitler's obsession with the occult, he came up with a false specialist unit, supposedly full of archeologists. Really it was just Fleming and a bunch of academics feeding crazy stories to Hitler. They would publish sexed-up reports, leak information to newspapers. And the Nazis bought it. Believed we were off searching for Excalibur or pieces of the cross, Thor's hammer."

"That's insane."

"Suddenly hollowed-out volcanoes seem tame. The more Hitler bought into it, the more he split his resources. When Rommel was winning in

North Africa, Fleming started cooking up stories about artifacts in Egypt. It tied one hand behind Rommel's back, because each time he wanted to advance in one direction, Hitler would be pulling him in another."

"So he wasn't just crazy—he was an idiot."

"He was a drug addict. True story. Hopped up out of his mind for most of the war. So nobody on our side took this stuff seriously. But then this happened." Mason sifted through the paperwork until she found one file in particular.

The paper had yellowed with age. She handed it to Chase. "And the game got real."

Chase looked at the cover. In block typewriter capitals was the heading. OPERATION: KINGMAKER. Beneath that was a list of names and departments, people who had been included in the circulation of the material. Underneath all of that was a summary of the report.

The Tomb of Alexander the Great.

Chase groaned. "No way."

Alexander the Great, the king who united Europe, Persia, and North Africa, was one of the holy grails of archeology. He showed up in Egyptian hieroglyphs and was referred to in the Quran. Short of finding solid proof of one of the religious figures, like Moses, Jesus, or Muhammad, Alexander was the next best thing.

"Back in 1925," Mason said, "when everyone with a shovel was digging in Egypt, there was an expedition to Alexandria, looking for the tomb. It was led by"—Mason paused to read the name, but Chase knew it was for effect—"Henry Forrester."

Chase let out a sigh that said *of course*.

The universe was handing her a beating today. Henry Forrester had been a rich eccentric who caught the archeology bug, sinking much of his family's fortune into backing his own expeditions into Egypt. When the Carnarvon team uncovered Tutankhamun's tomb, they'd been in direct competition with Forrester, who had been less than a mile down the valley, digging in a different spot. His biggest obsession had been Alexander, and the city he founded in his later years, Alexandria. Toward the end of Forrester's own life, he'd undergone a number of radical conversions, taking up positions diametrically opposed to everything he'd built his life on. He helped the Coptic Orthodox Church establish a diocese in the UK and became an advocate for returning items of antiquity back to the countries they'd come from. More important for Chase, Forrester had set up a foundation that identified promising students from poorer backgrounds and paid for them to study history and archeology. The Forrester Foundation had footed the bill for Chase to travel over from the States and read at Oxford.

Chase had another close connection to Henry Forrester.

"I dated his great-granddaughter," she said. "Zoe Forrester."

Mason smiled. "Let's pretend I didn't know that. So, Fleming came up with the story that Alex found some kind of buried weapon, a relic of mass destruction. He used that to take over the world. Whoever found the tomb would find the weapon and end the war."

"And Hitler bought it?"

"Never made it that far. Forrester got wind of the plan and asked for a meeting with Fleming. There's no record of what they discussed, but whatever it was, it convinced Fleming to scramble a real team and go digging around."

"And?"

"Nothing." Mason shrugged, dropping the paperwork back onto the bed. "Nobody found anything. Forrester refused to help, and after a while it just sounded like the ramblings of an old loony. None of the communications from the original expedition revealed anything. All they found were some pans, statues—"

"And coins," Chase said.

She knew which expedition Mason was talking about. It was an unwritten rule that everyone who received the Forrester grant would do a research project on Alexandria. Chase had chosen to write about two of the cities of famous women, Hypatia and Cleopatra, but she still knew the details of Henry Forrester's excavations.

Mason handed another document to Chase. It was a photocopy of an old page, written in an almost inelligible scrawl. "Recently, part of Forrester's private journal has come to light. It's causing all kinds of trouble."

24th of May, 1925.

This is a difficult situation.

I believe in history. I believe in preserving it, showing it to the world in museums. I've always agreed that those who forget the past are doomed to repeat it. But now I've found something that should stay forgotten. The most important find of my life, of anyone's life, and I wish I hadn't found it.

Alexander is here.

He dug too deep.

I've seen hell.

The secret rests with him, and it must stay buried. I have been entrusted with the key. Without it, nobody can ever find him. But with that, perhaps I bury myself. What good archaeologist chooses to hide the past?

Chase's mouth went dry. She felt a rush of excitement.

"He . . . This is . . ." She paused. "Can't be."

Mason sighed. "And this is where the Visitologists come into it."

Oh, great, Chase thought. Them.

TEN

The Church of Ancient Science had been officially founded in the 1920s as an offshoot from Rosicrucianism, filtered through pulp magazine sensibilities and heavily indebted to the work of H.P Lovecraft. They believed humanity had been mentored by ancient aliens. These aliens would return only when humans had proven themselves ready for the next stage of enlightenment.

For the first five decades of its existence, the Church was seen as a harmless group, showing up at science fiction conventions and staying mostly in the fringes of religious debates. All of that changed with the appointment of a new leader in the 1980s, James Paxton Robinson. He'd invested heavily in glossy television documentaries, news websites, and upgraded the church's image, trying all the time to get rid of the "Visitology" nickname. Robinson also lobbied to have Ancient Science recognized as a religion in America and Europe and to qualify for the tax breaks that came with that status. The influx of cash grew the church grew into a global force with billions of dollars in the bank. In more recent times, the Church had started using that money and clout to campaign for permission to excavate various sites of religious interest, looking for evidence of ancient technology or alien visitation. So far, none of the requests had been granted, but everyone was braced for the day the Church challenged this in court. It wouldn't be hard to argue that their religious beliefs were being discriminated against.

"We've been monitoring them for decades," Mason said. "In the nineties, they started buying out old church buildings around the world, converting them to their own temples, or building new temples next to sites that were important to other religions. Two years ago, they made Alexandria their new home."

She dropped an aerial photo of a church on the bed between them.

"Yeah," Chase had followed that one with interest. "I'm familiar with them."

The Visitologists had made big waves in the local community when they bought up land on three sides of a famous old mosque in the center of Alexandria. They built a skyscraper, which that was now the tallest building in the city, and wanted to use the rest of the land to build research and education facilities. The project had been held up by public objections.

"Sounds like you're already not a fan," Mason said, picking up on Chase's tone.

"Cranks and racists."

"Racists?"

"Ancient aliens, fringe stuff, so much of it boils down to that. Saying the ancient Egyptians couldn't have built the pyramids without help, because the brown people were too primitive. Scratch the surface, you always fins white supremacy involved. Von Däniken's book was edited by a literal Nazi."

"That's interesting," Mason pursed her lips. "I didn't know that it could connect, but we'll get to it in a minute. The mosque started to suffer from structural problems, amid claims the Visitologists had been digging beneath the foundations. Only rumors, so far. Then, about a week ago, the Visitologists applied for permission to dig two more sites, one next to a church and the other across the road from the mosque."

A connection fired in Chase's mind. "Saint Mark."

Mason was caught off guard, her flow interrupted. "What?"

"The church in Alexandria, the one they want to build next to, is it the church of Saint Mark?"

Mason looked down at her notes. "Yes."

Mark was the patron saint of Alexandria. But what would be the connection with an excavation site out in Syria? Chase thought again of the statue she'd rescued. A winged lion. The symbol of Saint Mark.

Mason continued. "They handed in that page from Forrester's journal, along with the documents from Fleming's dossier, to back up their claim."

"How did they get them?"

"No idea on the journal. But the dossier was easy. In your game, put something in the ground and leave it there, it becomes priceless. But in mine, take information and put it in a vault, and it becomes worthless. Most of our secrets from that time are public knowledge now. These files were still there, along with the documents from Fleming's real dig, just waiting for someone to come along and get them."

"The Egyptian authorities will never give permission."

"They already did. They're too scared to deny it and bring about a test case. But the government has imposed certain conditions. One of them is secrecy. The Visitologists can release information to the press if they find anything that ties to their own beliefs, but they're gagged until then. And anything they find will remain the property of Egypt. At the moment, the digs are being carried out undercover, made to look like construction projects for office buildings. That gives us some time."

Chase already had an idea of why Mason was telling her all this, but she asked the question anyway. "Time for what?"

"First, let's say Forrester was right, and the Visitologists find some kind of ancient tech. That's going to piss everyone off. And next thing you know, they'll charge into Jerusalem or Mecca with a backhoe, and we'll have World War Three.

"Second, the far-right are gaining ground at a rate we haven't seen in a hundred years. There are a lot of political parties who would like to lay claim to Alexander's legacy. If any of them had his remains, they could use it as a symbol, give people something to rally behind."

"And that's where your stabby friends come in?"

Mason reached into her bag and pulled out four photographs. The first showed two men standing on a dais. One was short and slight, with an expensive suit and a poised wave. The second was taller, almost gangly, with neatly coiffed yellow hair and a nervous energy that showed even in the still image.

"This was taken nearly ten years ago. On the right is James Robinson, head of the Visitologists. On the left is Adam Parish. American. He was one of the first superstars of the digital right, founded a website called FellowT ravelers.com and made a name for himself on the talk-show circuit. Loved conspiracy theories, hated grammar. Says the Vikings founded America. Got in some trouble when he was linked with Reinheit Eighteen."

Mason held up the second picture. It showed Parish in conversation with two men. Parish was in focus in the middle of the frame, and though the other figures hadn't been caught in any great detail, Chase could see enough to recognize them. One was tall and rail-thin, like a broom handle. The other was smaller and built like a gorilla. Wilhelm and Braun, Wallace's new friends. "Parish dropped off the radar after the story broke," Mason said. "Then three years ago, he showed back up as a Visitologist, claiming to be reborn. Sued the pants off anyone who tried to link him to the old news stories." Mason handed over the third picture: Parish remade, tall, tanned, and athletic, with cropped hair. "He's the head of 'special projects' for the Visitologists, which means he's in charge of all the fuss they're causing. And this all ties in nicely with what you just said, the links between ancient aliens theories and white supremacy. Now I know about that, it doesn't seem like such a big leap to go from R18 to Visitology."

The fourth picture was of a large round table at a banquet or party. On the far side of the table, clearly framed in the photograph, were political figures from Russia and the US. In the foreground, facing away from the lens, were the backs of three men's heads.

"I don't have solid proof," Mason said. "But this was taken at a birthday party for an oil tycoon. Those faces, you can recognize. These guys here?" She pointed to the three heads. "I think that one is James Robinson. That one is Adam Parish. And that one, I'm convinced, is Ayman Musab Faraj."

"The Visitologists and Al-Salif?"

"Right. I can't prove it yet, but I think they're all linked. Al-Salif. Reinheit Eighteen. The Visitologists. Together."

Chase tapped the photograph showing Wilhelm and Braun. "These two attacked me before I crossed the border. They were working with Ryan Wallace."

"I know. Well, I suspected." Mason pulled a UK passport out of her bag. "I lifted Wallace's passport the same time I got yours, and he hasn't been back for it. So whatever he's doing, he's traveling under a different identity, and not one I have on file."

"Ryan's always got backup plans."

"The real question is, when did they get to him? In Syria, or before?"

"You think he was already working with them before we went in?"

"It's a possibility."

"But if they already had him, why go after me? He's the Alexander expert."

"My best guess is they want you for the Forrester connection. Or maybe—" Mason paused.

"Maybe what?"

"If they can't hire you, they want to make sure you don't work for anybody else, either."

Chase leaned back on the bed and sipped her bourbon. "How's your side?"

Mason looked down and touched the T-shirt above where the dressing would be. "Barely feel it now. Cuts always look worse than they are. You should see some of my other scars." Mason left that hanging for a beat and then got back on subject. "I want you to find Alexander before they do.

And the weapon, if there really is one."

Chase gave some side eye. "You can't believe that part."

"What matters is they believe it. But the British government can't interfere with a religion's business without some solid proof. Egypt's hands are tied, and their security services are threadbare since the uprising. You're not tied to either of us; you're independent. You can get in and look around, see if there's anything we need to know about."

"But they know about me. If you're right, and they're all connected, I'll have Al-Salif, the Visitologists, and the Nazis all looking for me."

"Business as usual, for someone like you."

Chase had to give her that one. Avoiding hostiles was part of the job. Granted, not a part she was always very good at. "What if there really is something there?"

"There can't be anything there," Mason said. "Even if there is."

"You want me to destroy it?"

Could Chase do that? Wipe out the most important discovery in history? She'd only just stopped Al-Salif from doing the same thing. Relic running was a mercenary trade. She was an international criminal, selling history off piece by piece. She'd given up any real rights to call herself an archaeologist a long time ago. But still, destroying history?

That would be crossing a line.

"There are bank account details in the safe downstairs," Mason said. "It's in your name and holds two hundred grand. There will be the same amount again once you're done. If you have to go with option two, I can arrange a double payment to ease your conscience." That's a lot of easing.

"And once we're done, I can get you your old life back. A university job, some grants, maybe even a BBC documentary. You'll be legit again."

"And what will you be doing?"

"My job," Mason said, matter-of-fact. "I need to find solid proof of the connections between the Church, Al-Salif, and Reinheit Eighteen. Anything I find will make life easier for both of us." She handed Chase a business card. A law firm. "That's the closest thing to a get-out-of-jail-free card. The firm is a fake, but if you get in trouble with the authorities, hand that over. I'll get an alert. If I can help, I will."

Chase set down the glass on the bedside table and moved closer to Mason.

"So, Jane Bond," Chase said. "How about those scars?"

Mason leaned forward, bringing their lips within a few inches of each other. She reached out with her free hand and pulled loose the belt tied around the waist of Chase's bathrobe, slipping her hand underneath to run her finger over Chase's bare skin. Chase felt her gut grow tight. She flushed warm at the touch.

"You first," Mason said.

ELEVEN

T an Bashir closed his eyes and drifted back into the past, looking for the next detail to build a wall around.

He'd been in junior school when the towers fell. He hadn't really understood the concepts of war or terror, but they had come to define his life. For the kids at school, it didn't matter that he was English. It didn't matter that his older brother had enlisted in the army three days after the attack. It mattered only that he had dark skin and was Muslim.

And none of that had meant a thing when he was old enough to enlist himself. The taunts. The jibes. The playground beatings. None of them had lingered in his mind when he saw his country threatened and his own religion being stolen away from him. He had decided to join the fight.

And now . . .

And now . . .

The torture stopped.

Bashir felt the straps being loosened. His blindfold was removed. There were bright lights overhead, and blotches danced in his vision. After a moment, the lights were switched off, and he heard people leave the room as he blinked away the moving imprint of the fluorescents.

The room around him was dark. Black drapes covered each wall, but from the way sound moved, he got the definite sense that there were walls.

This wasn't one of the tents of the Palmyra camp. He was in a building, perhaps a compound. There was a small table next to the board, with cups and jugs full of liquid. The floor was littered with leftovers from the day's work.

Plastic soda bottles, petrol cans, stained paper towels.

Where was he?

One of the curtains parted.

A man stepped into the room to stand in front of Bashir, carrying a small metal briefcase. He was tall and muscular, white, with tanned features and close-cropped hair. Adam Parish. The Visitologist. That proved a connection between Al-Salif and the Church of Ancient Science. Not that it was going to do Bashir any good.

"You know who I am."

Parish phrased it as a statement rather than as a question.

"Adam Parish," Bashir said, his voice hoarse.

Parish set the case on the table. "And you're MI6?" Bashir said nothing.

"It's okay." Parish pressed the latches on the case. "I know you are. Your eyes. You could maybe play poker before today, but now your emotions are on your face."

Bashir said nothing.

"I've been listening in," Parish said. "Nice game you've been playing. I think you're just looking for an argument on Escape from L.A." He smiled. "But I like your approach. I've never seen anyone hold out like that. My friends tell me you spoke to Marah Chase. They saw you saying something, before she took the gun. What did you tell her?"

Bashir stared back at him.

"Understand," Parish continued, "I'm the reason the torture stopped. I think the least you could do is give me a few answers. Did you tell her about the Aten?"

That was the word he'd been hearing. "I don't know what that is," Bashir said.

Parish lifted the lid. Inside the case were two gloves and an assortment of wires and batteries. "The truth. That's a good start. Can you tell me anything about the Knights of Saint Mark?"

Bashir blinked. "Knights?"

"Two for two. Good. Now, maybe you'll do me a favor and tell me who else knows you're here? Who gave you the mission?"

Bashir started to brace himself for further torture.

He didn't know what form it was going to take, but it was coming, and he needed to be ready.

"What I like about the modern day," Parish said, slipping on the gloves and holding up his hands for Bashir to see the palms, where metal strips ran from a glowing blue disc in the center, up to the tips of the fingers, "is that there's an app for everything. Now, I don't really know how this works. Someone explained it to me, but I just pretended to get it. It's based on something King Solomon used, apparently, if you believe that. The wonk who showed it to me, he poured metal filings out onto a sheet of paper, then ran a magnet beneath it, on the other side. He said, if you control the flow of electricity through the brain, you take away the ability to resist. Once I put this on you, you'll tell us everything we need to know."

"That's impossible," Bashir said, but he could hear the doubt in his own voice.

"There is a downside." Parish pressed buttons on the back of each glove, and an electronic hum filled the air. "Which I guess I should tell you. Health and safety and all that. Anything over three minutes will completely wipe the subject's brain. Scramble them all up. A blank disk."

Parish moved his right hand toward Bashir's head. He paused just long enough to add, "And I never use them for less than three minutes."

Bashir felt the metal touch his forehead. His skull started to vibrate along with the sound. The glove grew warm, and his skin tingled. His vision flashed white. Bashir blinked but couldn't even see his eyelids. This bright glow was filling his mind. He could hear Parish talking, but he sounded distant. Then Bashir heard his own voice starting to answer the questions.

TWELVE

Mason flew into London from Ben Gurion. The plane pulled into Heathrow's Terminal 3 at 11:15, right on time, but they didn't open the doors for twenty minutes. That was the confirmation Mason needed. She'd been made. The crew had received a red flag, and the security teams were waiting on orders. Mason had expected it. She'd traveled back under her own name, to make it easy for them to spot her. It was all part of the game, pretending she had nothing to hide.

Mason joined the queue of confused human traffic as she made her way to the bus and the twenty-minute ride to Terminal 5. She kept an eye out the whole time, looking for the moment they made a move.

Terminal 5 resembled a meatpacking plant at the best of times, but today it was positively Blade Runner–esque. Mason saw the bottleneck of passengers at customs, waiting to walk through three different checkpoints and get their bags scanned. She hoped the security team would pick her up now and let her avoid all the hassle. She didn't know who it would be. The security services were in a state of civil war, after Martyn Wood's leaks had implicated all three of them in illegal activities. The three main agencies— MI5, MI6, and GCHQ—were known as Thames House, Legoland, and the Geeks, respectively. Mason worked for Legoland. If she was picked up by one of her own, they would pull her out of the queue early as a favor. If it was Thames House, they'd let her go through the whole process, just to mess with her.

When the Wood scandal broke, the Foreign and Commonwealth Office had taken the extreme measure of suspending all operations. Almost every member of Mason's department was stood down from active duty and encouraged to take annual leave at the same time. It was an unprecedented move in the history of MI6 and increased the rumors of downsizing. After all, Wood had been from Legoland, and the other agencies sensed blood.

If she was picked up by her own side, it would just be a game of evading the truth and getting back to work. But if she was intercepted by Thames House, she could become a pawn in the bigger game.

Two guards stepped to her as she reached the tail end of the crowd. They gestured for her to follow. Pulling aside the security cordon, they led her down a narrow corridor, where two men in plain suits were waiting to take over.

"Boys." She smiled and pushed her suitcase in their direction. "Make yourself useful."

Mason didn't recognize either man, but that wasn't a problem. Picking her up before the security check meant they were on her side. The suits led her down five flights of stairs and through a door out onto the tarmac. A black car with tinted windows and government plates was waiting. One of the suits opened the rear passenger door and nodded for Mason to get in.

She stooped to look inside and saw Guy Lonnen waiting on the back seat.

"Guy," she said.

"Joanna." His reply was curt and cold, but that passed for friendly in Lonnen's world.

Mason ducked down and slid onto the seat. Her side hurt as she bent down, but she was determined not to let it show. The door closed behind her.

Guy Lonnen was director of intelligence for Legoland. He was a slender man, with fine features and an intellectual poise that was going out of fashion in the intelligence community. Lonnen had recruited Mason out of university. She'd been on the verge of dropping out when he made contact.

All three of the main security services had been keeping tabs on her, and he'd promised to guide her through her last year of studies and into the training school.

Lonnen had done the same for Martyn Wood the year before. He'd played guardian to both Mason and Wood, keeping their careers on track and covering their mistakes. It was no secret that he'd seen them as his projects, hoping that one of them would eventually replace him. Wood and Mason handled Lonnen's attentions differently. Wood liked being the golden boy. He was happy to jump through each hoop on his way to the top. Mason resented being seen as a favorite. She felt judged enough as it was without the added resentments and expectations. While Wood followed Lonnen's guidance and built a career in the intelligence division, Mason had surprised everybody by transferring to the operations team. Lonnen had been disappointed, but he'd continued to watch over her. After Wood's betrayal, she was all he had left.

"How was your holiday?" Lonnen asked.

"It was fine," she said, matching his smile.

The car pulled away. They drove out to a private gate, where a security guard let them pass with a subtle nod at the driver. They turned onto a road that threaded around and between the different areas of the airport, and then to a second gate leading out onto a narrow country lane. After a few miles, Lonnen called for the driver to pull into the lay-by. Mason and Lonnen both climbed out and walked away from the car, out of earshot. Lonnen held his phone down at his side, activating an app that would scramble any listening devices that were locked onto them from a distance.

Lonnen said, "How did it go?"

Mason waited before answering. Even here, in an unplanned spot and away from the car, with Lonnen's app, she was nervous about surveillance. "Chase is on board. I couldn't get Wallace; they got to him up first."

Lonnen nodded, then blew his nose before answering. His perpetual cold was a running joke in the trade—along with his paranoia. "Chase will be a good distraction. Draw them out."

Mason had told Chase as much as was needed but not the whole truth. Lonnen believed the Visitologists had started to infiltrate government positions in both the UK and the US. He went as far to suspect there were moles in MI6. Sending Chase into the field looking for the tomb was a way of smoking out the enemy.

"Think she'll survive?"

Lonnen didn't answer directly. "Adam Parish is flying in now. Private church jet, due to land any time now."

"He's coming here?"

"They say it's to inspect the new building."

The Visitologists were erecting a skyscraper on the south bank of the Thames, near Waterloo Station and only a few hundred yards from the London Eye. It had been a controversial decision, placing their new British headquarters within sight of Big Ben and the Houses of Parliament. But in modern Britain, money was king, and the project had been approved.

"I don't know who else is on the flight," Lonnen continued. "There are too many eyes on me. I haven't been able to get the list." He paused. "When was the last time you saw Schlamme?"

That caught Mason off guard. She blinked a couple of times, tried to second-guess the question before answering. "At the border. Yesterday. He roped Chase in for me. Then held the door open."

"He's missing. Won't be long before someone asks why you were meeting with him."

Missing? Mason felt a moment of guilt. Schlamme had gone out on a limb by helping her. The spy game was even more political than Westminster, and Schlamme had risked exposing himself to enemies within his own side, people who were looking for an excuse to move him on. But he'd known the risks. Just as Mason and Lonnen had when they'd started this game.

"It's coming," Lonnen said. "Whatever they have planned. The security forces are on stand-down. Whitehall has wanted something like this for years, any excuse. The government are debating a new national security bill. Shut down the old agencies and set up a new one that answers directly to the prime minister. No oversight."

"We're not ready for this."

"No." Lonnen wiped his nose a second time. "And I'm being called before the FCO committee."

It was almost unheard of for someone in Lonnen's position to go before a committee. The security services had sacrificial lambs for those occasions. There were levels of protection for the people who did the real work.

"My ties to Martyn have put me in a tight spot," Lonnen said. "Picking you up today was a risk, but it might be the last chance we have to speak for a while. I need to stay squeaky clean."

They had started this private war together, but now Mason was on her own.

THIRTEEN

C hase was being followed. So far, it had been nothing more than the vague feeling of being watched, but it was a sensation she'd learned to trust. When Chase had first started working on the black market, she'd found it to be almost as ruthless as academia. Seasoned professionals would sit back and wait, letting others do the hard work, before stepping in to steal the prize. Chase knew of more than one relic runner who had survived the dangers of Egypt, Iraq, or Syria, only to make it home and be attacked in their apartment. To last for as long as she had, Chase had needed to raise her game. And that included being able to recognize when she'd picked up a tail.

She'd been fine on the flight over to London. Arriving at the airport early, she'd seen Mason boarding the previous flight, and Chase was sure they'd both been in the clear. But spotting someone at Heathrow was virtually impossible. The way they pressed everyone in together, there was no chance to tell who was on your toes by accident and who was trying to keep close. After clearing immigration, Chase had caught the train into Paddington, and it was there that she started to sense the problem. As the crowd thinned out leaving the station and people headed off in different directions, she could feel someone staying with her.

She paused a few times, making a show of checking her phone for directions, and tried to steal a look behind. She didn't spot anyone, but the feeling remained. She walked a couple of miles more than needed, in order to make a big loop and head back toward the station. After checking into a chain hotel across from Hyde Park, Chase took the opportunity to freshen up from the journey before heading out a back door, setting off a fire alarm in the process but, she hoped, losing whoever was on her.

The feeling faded.

The trick had worked.

Now onto business. Chase was playing detective, trying to track down a missing person. The challenge was, he'd been missing for two millennia. Henry Forrester was the best starting point. But if the journal was true, Forrester wouldn't have left clues. This wasn't going to be a treasure hunt, solving riddles left along the way. Forrester wanted Alexander to stay hidden. If he did have anything that showed the location, it was a good guess he would have destroyed it. The Visitologists had his journal, which would have been the natural starting point. The best Chase could do for now was to follow his footsteps.

And, if at all possible, avoid asking Zoe Forrester for help.

How would that conversation go? Hi, Zo, I know we hate each other, but I'm in town. Quick coffee?

Chase's career had gone off track after her split with Zoe, when the Forrester family pressured the board of the foundation to withdraw Chase's funding. Chase was an adult. She didn't blame Zoe for what happened next. It was Chase's own decision to start making money off the black market, and it had been her own damn fool idea to try to smuggle that statue out of China. She only needed to look in the mirror to see who was at fault for throwing away her academic career. But rational thinking went out the window at the thought of meeting her ex after fourteen years.

There were different routes she could take.

The Forrester Foundation had been run by a board of trustees. Two family members sat on the board, but they were a token presence. Most of the work was done by two people.

First was Georgie Turner, a historian and tutor, very well regarded in her field. Turner had been teaching at Oxford during Chase's time and was the woman responsible for identifying the students to receive funding. The second was Tim Barron. Barron was a lawyer. Or solicitor. Chase always struggled to remember the difference. His father had been Henry Forrester's solicitor, and the job had stayed in the family. Barron was in charge of the finances from Forrester's estate and, as a result, also held the purse strings for the foundation.

Long after the Forrester family pulled the plug on supporting Chase, Turner and Barron had worked together to keep money available to her.

Chase had fallen out of touch with Turner but maintained contact with Barron. He wasn't an academic and understood the real world. He'd stepped in and given her legal guidance a few times over the years and bailed her out of an Italian jail after a mix-up involving the Vatican and a bag of bones.

Chase set off across Hyde Park in the direction of Barron's Earl's Court office, where he worked out of a converted town house. There were few things Chase enjoyed more than walking around London in spring. It was warm and sunny, with just enough traces remaining of a crisp winter air to take the edge off the heat. Chase had called ahead, and Barron insisted he would cancel an appointment to make time for her. She presented herself to the receptionist not long after and heard Barron's voice booming out of the office before she'd even finished giving her name.

"Marah, come on in."

Chase turned to see him standing in the doorway. He was short and stocky, with the shoulders of a retired rugby player. He'd played for the Welsh national team in the eighties, before the sport went professional. His voice carried a hint of his Welsh roots when he raised his voice, but the rest of the time he sounded like every other rich lawyer in town. His nose and cheeks were flushed with the red traces of alcohol, and his hair had thinned out since the last time she'd seen him.

Barron pulled her into a hug and then waved for her to take a seat in front of his large desk. Barron had a love of all things American and had a long-standing tradition of redecorating his office each time there was a new president, to match their choices in the Oval Office. Republican or Democrat, it didn't matter. Chase noticed, looking around the large white room, that he hadn't chosen to imitate the current president's golden drapes.

"God, Marah, how long's it been?" Barron asked as he sat.

"Too long."

"You haven't aged a day, and I look ten years older."

Chase grinned. His patter never changed. "We both know that's not true."

"Okay, okay. Seven years older. I agree."

Barron leaned back and called his assistant's name, then asked if Chase would like a drink. He reeled off a list of spirits, but Chase asked for coffee.

Chase didn't want to get straight to the point; it was best to ease Barron in. "How's Maxine doing?"

Barron let loose with his gap-toothed grin. "She's very well. Retired a few years ago and developed a pretty strong interest in baking. There's a new kind of pie or cake waiting for me each day." He patted his belly. "I'm not complaining."

"And Rosie?"

The grin spread even wider. "She made me a grandfather just last month. Mar, you better stop the polite talk, because I warn you, that way lies three hours of me showing baby pictures. How are you? Girl in every port?"

"No, I behave myself these days."

"You never lied to me before." He adopted a mock-serious tone. "No need to start now. I had a young woman in here last week asking all kinds of questions about you. I know a government type when I see one. What are you into?"

Chase paused before answering. Barron was one of the few people she trusted. He looked on her like family. But sometimes family can be the worst at keeping secrets. They think they know what's best for you, up to and including privacy.

Barron read the hesitation and nodded. "I'm still your solicitor; this is confidential."

The assistant came in with a coffee for Chase and something for Barron that certainly contained coffee. Chase set down the drink on the desk and fished around in her messenger bag for the photocopy of Forrester's journal entry. She handed it over to Barron.

"I'm picking up that trail," she said. "Someone's gotten a hold of his journal and is using it to try to find Alexander."

Barron frowned as he read it. "I never managed to track this one." He paused and looked up at Chase, seeing if more explanation was needed. "When I was dividing up Henry's collection, I worked with Georgie to catalog the journals. Henry didn't write them based on years, one after the other. He kept separate books for each subject. So he'd had one on the Parthenon, one on King Tut, one on that lost city he excavated—"

"Amarna."

Chase felt something like a cog turning in her mind. She flashed back to the British spy in Syria and the word he'd given her. Aten. Amarna was the site of an ancient city built by Akhenaten. A Pharaoh of the eighteenth dynasty, he was a controversial figure in Egyptian history. He abandoned the traditional pantheon of gods and demanded the country convert to a new religion: the worship of Aten.

She was looking at two different pieces of a puzzle but didn't know how they fit together.

"Amarna, that's it," Barron said. "He had others, a range of subjects. The Library in Alexandria. I found one on Noah's Ark—I assume he was drunk that day. The one everyone wanted to track down was his Alexander work. We never found it."

"Well, someone has it."

"Quite." Barron stared down at the page in silence for a moment. "Quite."

"Where are the others? The ones you cataloged?"

Barron's eyes dropped to his hands on the desk. He tapped his fingers a couple of times. "They were stolen."

"What?"

"Well, you already know about the troubles we had after his death?"

Chase nodded. "Most of it."

After Forrester had died in the seventies, a civil war had broken out within his family. Forrester's wishes had been that his collection be returned to the countries it had been assembled from. A lot of his large fortune had been spent in his final years on restoration projects for public monuments in London, Alexandria, and New York. He'd also funded the building of Saint Mark's Coptic Church in London. The remainder of his money was supposed to go to the Forrester Foundation, rather than to his family.

The compromise had been for his collection to be split, with half going home on loan to museums in the countries of origin, and half staying on private display in the Forrester Mansion. His money, too, had been divided between the family and the foundation.

"The family made bad investments," Barron continued. "And about five years ago, they lost everything."

"Everything?"

Barron's voice was low. This was clearly a painful memory. "It was quite aggressive, just how fast it happened. It was like the family were being targeted. Each time they moved their assets somewhere else, that company took a hit. The collection was divided between private buyers, and we would use different names, disguise who the items were coming from and keep people from sniffing around for gossip. They sold off the mansion to pay debts, lost their holdings. Georgie and I did our best to repatriate the collection, like the old man wanted, but our hands were tied."

Using different names would explain why Chase hadn't known about the fire sale. Gossip usually traveled fast in her trade, but no word had reached her. "God, how did they take it?"

"Not well. David and Marie both passed within eighteen months, cancer and heart failure, respectively. And Michael . . ." Barron gulped. Sniffed. "He took his own life."

Chase felt as though cold water had been poured into her gut. David and Marie were Zoe's parents. Chase had no real regrets over their passing, because they'd done their best to ruin her life. But Zoe's brother, Michael, had been a very sweet guy. He could always make Chase laugh, no matter what the situation. After things had gone bad between Chase and Zoe, Michael had been the only one to stay in touch. He'd been the one to tell her that Zoe was getting married and the one to call her with gossip when it all fell apart. Somewhere along the way, Chase and Michael had drifted apart. The messages grew less frequent, until they stopped completely, and Chase only occasionally thought about looking him up. Would he still be alive if she'd sent just a few more friendly messages?

Her voice sounded raw as she tried to find something to get the conversation going again. "And the journals?"

"Well, the whole collection was stored in the British Museum while the sales and negotiations were going on. They gave us a storage room in the basement. I'm sure it wasn't for free—they would have been expecting some of the pieces to be lent or donated to them for display—but while it was there, there was a break-in."

"They took the books."

"The books. A few statues and coins. Nothing they could ever hope to sell; everyone would know where they came from."

Chase had been working in the trade for too long to have any illusions about that. Stolen items were bought and sold all the time.

"You said someone was targeting them?" she asked. "The money?"

Barron made a clicking noise with his mouth. He set down the coffee in front of him and leaned back in the chair. "I can't prove this, but I'm convinced. Some of it was umbrella corporations, but some was pretty direct. In each case, it traced back to the Visitologists. They destroyed the Forrester fortune."

FOURTEEN

B arron was a bust. Chase was no closer to finding the Alexander journal, and the Visitologists most likely had the rest of Forrester's collection. She was getting into the game too late.

The next step was to visit Georgie Turner, Chase's mentor in college. She was almost as nervous about seeing her as she was about seeing Zoe. They hadn't parted on good terms.

It was the running theme of Chase's life.

Turner had been retired for five years, but, as with a lot of old academics, that didn't mean she had stopped turning up at her office. Barron said she spent her weekdays in her old workspace at the British Museum, where she mostly read books and offered to give tours to lonely-looking tourists.

Born and raised in Alexandria, Georgette Habib had been one of the first students to benefit from the Forrester Foundation. She'd been flown to England and completed two degrees and a PhD, before writing a biography on Henry Forrester. Somewhere along the way, she had married, divorced, and settled in the country. Her history with the foundation had made her a natural pick to sit on the board and oversee its legacy.

She carried herself more like a musician than a professor, and there had been rumors that she'd had a few affairs with students before and after marrying. Chase had never seen any evidence of that and put it down to people needing to make up dirty gossip about a powerful woman. If there was any favoritism being handed out, it was based on her student's potential, not any extra desires.

Turner had been a big influence on Chase. There had been many more polished and experienced applicants to the foundation, but Turner had seen something in Chase and helped her rewrite her application to get it past the rest of the board. She'd then helped Chase throughout her time at Oxford.

Wallace had been on the same course as Chase but hadn't needed the help of a grant. Still, they had both let Turner down. She hated the relic runner trade and often lent her name to articles condemning the archeologists who worked in it. The last time Chase had spoken to Turner, they had argued about Chase's work. The words had been heated. The kind you can't take back.

Chase held her breath as she knocked on Turner's door, but she was greeted with something approaching a smile. Chase could see Turner was pleased to see her but was also reminded of her anger, and both emotions were fighting for control. Chase offered a hand to shake. Turner paused, then pulled her into a hug. Chase could feel the frailty in her embrace. Turner had always been skinny but was now aging into skeletal.

She wore three woolen cardigans over a faded Rolling Stones T-shirt.

"Marah. Come on."

Turner stepped aside and waved her into the office. Chase had expected it to still be stacked high with papers, trinkets, and books. What she found was a minimalist's dream. There was a worn sofa where the desk used to be, with an easy chair across from it. A laptop was perched on the arm of the chair. Music played at a low volume from the computer. The only other piece of furniture was a modest bookshelf in the corner, with a small and neatly arranged collection.

Turner pointed to the sofa. "Take a seat. It's been, uh, how have you . . . um . . . what . . ." She laughed. "I'll start again. How are you?"

"I'm good, Doc. How are you?"

Turner smiled at the old nickname. "Good," she replied. "Can't complain, anyway. Are you . . . still . . ."

"Yes."

Turner looked down at her feet for a second, and Chase heard a quiet intake of breath. Then the older woman rocked forward on the balls of her feet and looked up again. "Look at me, haven't offered you a drink. What can I get you?"

Chase didn't need another drink, but she'd learned a long time ago to say yes. Turning down an offer, even politely, built up a small wall. Saying yes was a way to ease into conversation. She asked for a coffee.

Turner left the office to fetch drinks from the common room. She came back with a cup of coffee and a fresh smile. Chase wondered if she'd stood outside for a moment and rehearsed it.

"What can I do for you?"

"I wanted to pick your brain about Forrester."

Turner scoffed. "You mean Forrester and Alexander."

Chase could read between the lines. Wallace had already been in touch. She didn't want to tip Turner off that they were in competition. "What do you mean?"

"Ryan Wallace called a couple hours ago, asking the same thing."

"What did you give him?"

"Nothing. I'm not going to help either of you."

Chase put up her hands, acknowledging the point. "I get you. But this one, this is legit. An honest client." Chase embellished the truth a little. "And if I find Alexander, I get my life back. It's my chance to go straight again." Chase hesitated, debating whether or not to play her last card. "The Visitologists are looking for the tomb. And you know what they did to Henry's family."

Turner watched her for a long, silent moment, reading her expression. Then she nodded and stood up, mumbling something Chase couldn't make out. She lifted two large books off a shelf. Chase recognized the look of the spines. They each carried an embossed version of the Forrester Foundation logo, a winged lion.

A winged lion.

How had she not made the connection before? The statue in Syria. The mention of Saint Mark. Alexander's city. What had Forrester known? How was this all connected? And what did it have to do with an eighteenth dynasty pharaoh?

Turner sat down on the sofa next to her and rested one of the books on the arm and the other on her lap.

"First things first," she said, "this is a fool's errand."

"Why?"

"Alexander didn't have a tomb. He had tombs. He was moved at least twice. Maybe three times. His first tomb was in Memphis. After that he was moved to a temporary site in Alexandria, before his final mausoleum was built. When people talk about his tomb, they mean the third one. The Soma. A large building in the center of Alexandria. A site for pilgrimage and worship. But archeologists and grave robbers have been searching the city for two thousand years, the same streets, over and over. If he was going to be found, he already would have been. Alexander isn't there."

FIFTEEN

Mason sat drinking coffee at a pop-up kiosk in the shadow of the London Eye. The Visitologist building was on the other side of Belvedere Road. Towering over its surroundings, the skyscraper had been designed to be the tallest structure on this side of the Thames. A show of strength and wealth. It was a circular structure, with windows alternating between black and blue glass on each floor. The Visitologists wouldn't need to say anything else to announce their presence in London, because their tower would do all the talking. And to be so close to Big Ben and Parliament, sitting on the other side of the river, would tell people that they were there to stay.

From her seat, Mason could see a workman clearing away debris and tools from the ground-floor reception area. The building was close to finished, and the next step would be to bring in interior decorators, probably sparing no expense.

Lonnen had dropped her here in the car. She hadn't gone home first to drop off her suitcase. Luggage could be a good surveillance prop in a city like London. It was a sign that she was either a tourist or traveling for business, and nobody would make her as a tail.

She'd been finishing her first coffee when Parish arrived at the Visitologist building in a private car. He'd been greeted at the entrance by men in suits. No women, Mason had noticed. They'd all donned hard hats and high-visibility jackets before entering the building. She was on her third drink by the time Parish reappeared. She was tired and cranky and needed someone to look at her wound, but Parish was more important. Luckily, she was still technically on leave, so nobody would be expecting her at the office.

Mason had a few hours to play with before anyone would get in touch.

Across the road, Parish shook hands with each of the men and set off toward Westminster Bridge on foot.

As with Chase, Mason knew Parish's file inside-out. Copies of birth records, a family background, his blog posts and newspaper features. And also as she had with Chase, Mason had spoken to people who knew him. Reporters and employers who'd crossed him back in his blogging days. Activists who had fought with him. A couple of schoolteachers, who were confused at how a quiet middle-class kid had turned into such a hateful campaigner.

She'd been given three useful bits of information that hadn't been in the file: Parish was paranoid, he was prone to conspiracy theories, and he liked to walk. His old college professor had told of times Parish would be late to class simply because he preferred walking to getting the bus. He'd never learned to drive but didn't like letting other people have control over where he was going. The private car from the airport was a rare exception. If he was moving around central London, Mason was willing to bet he'd do it on foot.

She let him build up a few hundred yards of a lead before setting off after him. She dragged the suitcase behind her on its wheels and sipped from the cup, doing her best to look like she was in a hurry to get between meetings.

One of the weird quirks of tradecraft was that women had an advantage when it came to surveillance. The subjects were hardwired to suspect men of following them. They would keep a jumpy eye on any male figure who shared the street. But a woman? No. Why would she be a spy?

Parish headed across Westminster Bridge and stopped next to Big Ben. Mason felt a surge of adrenaline as he pulled something out of his pocket. Deep within the building behind the clock tower, the government and opposition MPs would be meeting at this very moment, debating whatever issues were on the list for the day. Mason felt the impulse to rush Parish, on the assumption he was holding a weapon.

After a second's hesitation, she saw Parish raise a phone and take a picture of the clock.

He turned to continue up Great George Street. They walked through the park and across the Mall, with Buckingham Palace sitting to their left. Again, Parish paused to take a picture. Mason fell a little farther back. As much as playing the role of tourist could help in a surveillance detail, it was also useful for the person being tailed. Parish could point the phone at a famous monument but turn the camera around, taking a picture of the people behind him. Mason made sure to keep plenty of bodies between them as Parish started moving again.

Through the other side of Green Park, and across Piccadilly, Mason started to get a feeling for where he was going. She knew the Visitologists had an account with the Dorchester, a famous hotel overlooking Hyde Park. Sometimes, the art of following somebody involved not following them but instead predicting their movements and getting a few steps ahead. It was always a risk, but one that separated the good spies from the bad. Mason turned left. She headed down Piccadilly and turned right into Old Park Lane, then straight up to the Dorchester. She made it to the lobby a few seconds ahead of Parish but made a show of checking through her bags for paperwork, letting him get to the desk before her.

After he checked in, Mason made a quiet deal with the concierge. She handed over one of her get-out-of-jail-free cards, in exchange for a call the second Parish made any kind of move out of his room.

Outside, Mason let them flag down a hack cab for her. Parish might hate to be driven places, but Mason was quite happy to let others do the work.

SIXTEEN

"O kay," Chase said. "Back up a bit. Where was the tomb?"

Turner coughed and started into it. "There are a number of things to understand about Alexandria."

Chase already knew a lot of the city's history, but letting Turner lecture was the best way to get her warmed to the subject.

"We believe there had been towns and villages on that land for thousands of years before Alexander came along," Turner explained. "We know one of them was called Rhacotis. The area may have been holy, the site of some ancient worship, cults we've long forgotten about. There were better sites for Alexander to build his capital, so he must have had a reason to choose that spot. He brought in his favorite architect, Dinocrates, to design a new city. Then we get into a few centuries of war. The Greeks, the Romans, French, Persians, Christians, Muslims —each one took the city at some point and changed the layout. The city expanded outward, and the oldest sections were continually destroyed and rebuilt. On top of all that, there was an earthquake and a tsunami, somewhere around 365 ad. A huge tidal wave destroyed the oldest parts of city."

"We've got maps, though. I've seen them."

"Nothing firsthand. We have accounts written by travelers and artists' impressions of the old city, but the only good maps come from hundreds of years later."

Turner opened the book in her lap.

The title page read, Theories on the tomb of Alexander, by H. S. FORRESTER. Chase noticed an impish smile spread across the old professor's face. Even with her misgivings, this was a clear chance to get back to something she loved. Turner leafed through a few pages until she came across a section of quoted text.

"Okay." She ran a finger across the words as she talked. "This is the Alexander Romance. It's fiction, so we know it's not one hundred percent accurate, but it's the most complete record we have. It mentions a grand altar of Alexander opposite the Pharos."

Chase knew the Pharos was the lighthouse, one of the seven wonders of the ancient world. It had sat on an island, attached to the mainland by a man-made causeway.

Turner flipped a few more pages. "We don't have any accurate pictures of the tomb itself, the Soma. But bear in mind, the mausoleum at Halicarnassus would have been fresh in the memory when they designed the Soma. They would want to create something even more grand."

The Halicarnassus had been the tomb of Mausolus, a ruler who died during Alexander's lifetime, in what was now known as Turkey. Another of the seven ancient wonders, standing close to fifty meters in height, and the origin of the word mausoleum.

For the first time, Chase noticed a glaring omission.

"The Soma wasn't one of the seven wonders," Chase said.

"Right. Which is odd, don't you think? Dinocrates designed the city, the Soma and the lighthouse. He would have designed the tomb with the Halicarnassus monument as the thing to beat. The tomb of the greatest king in history would have been his crowning achievement. For a long time, Forrester was convinced that the Soma was the lighthouse."

Chase prompted Turner. "Did he have any proof?"

"Not really. The historical sources don't agree on much, but they all place the Soma on the mainland. One of the other points of agreement is that the building stood on a crossroads, between the city's two main streets."

Turner flicked to two maps. They each took up a full page. The first was a reproduction of ancient Alexandria. The second showed the city as it was in Forrester's time.

Turner pressed her forefinger to the first map. "This is considered the most accurate map of the ancient city. It was put together by an astronomer named Mahmoud Bey, in 1865. He used the measurements given in old accounts and dug down to find old walls and streets. He found that Alexandria was originally built on a grid system, like New York. He found two stages. The expanded city, and, in black, the original walls of a smaller city."

Turner ran her finger along the page to an intersection of two streets. "The Soma was here, at this junction."

She moved across to the modern map and traced a large circle around a few city blocks. "That main west-to-east street still exists today, under a different name. Most estimates put the Soma around here."

Chase brought up a modern map on her phone and zoomed in on the city, pushing the image around until she found the junction Turner was referring to. The Visitologist headquarters, along with the mosque they had dug beneath, were less than a block away from Turner's finger. A little farther up, maybe half a mile away, was the Coptic church they were digging next to. The church of Saint Mark.

"And people have already tried there?"

Turner nodded. "Hundreds of times. There were legends placing the body in a crypt beneath the mosque, but nothing has ever been found."

"A crypt? So, the body was beneath ground?"

"Bit of both. Most accounts have him placed within a large sarcophagus made of glass or crystal. Several of them refer to the sarcophagus being stored in a subterranean chamber, which was the Macedonian custom, and then carried out for public display, which is more in line with the Egyptian rituals."

"What happened next? I think I remember reading one of the Roman emperors sealed the tomb."

Chase had dropped that in deliberately, knowing she would get a nod of approval from her old mentor. You're never too old to seek a little validation.

"Good memory. Yes, Severus ordered the tomb closed off from the public somewhere around 200 ad. And from there, the Soma starts to vanish from record. There are a few scattered references over the next hundred years, but the building seems to have been wiped off the earth by the start of the fourth century."

"What do you think happened to it?"

"Well, the tsunami was pretty destructive. The wave traveled miles inland, and it took a lot of the older buildings with it. Or it could have been the Christians." Turner shifted a little in her seat. She was a devout Coptic Christian, and as much as she revered history, Chase knew Turner was never comfortable blaming her own religion for some of the darker moments of the past. "Alexander was worshipped as the son of God. There was a large cult surrounding him, and with a little more time it could have flourished into a full-blown religion. That's why the Alexander Romance called it an alter. Before Christ, Alexander worship was the biggest contender to become a new dominant religion. When the city was being converted to

Christianity, there wasn't room for God to have two sons. One of them had to go."

"But if the body was stored beneath ground . . ."

"Even if it was, between earthquakes and natural subsidence, a lot of the remains of the old city are down close to the water table now. If there was a tomb beneath the ground back then, it would have flooded out long ago."

"You said Forrester's original theory was the lighthouse. He had another?"

Turner gave the young smile again. She lifted the second book onto her lap. This one was called The Collected Essays of G. S. Turner. Flicking to a section near the middle, she opened it and pointed to the title: Thoughts on Henry Forrester and Alexander.

"Bear in mind the old man was a bit of a character. Some of his theories were . . ."

"Go on."

"He fought in the First World War. Served with a few Americans and picked up a rumor that the Freemasons in the States had a private collection of maps and designs from the ancient world. He got it into his head that they had Dinocrates's original plan for Alexandria, including the design of the Soma. Henry convinced himself that the Soma was a defining principle behind a lot of classic American architecture. He believed Grant's Tomb was a direct replica. He spent two years in the States, trying to track the collection down."

The tomb of President Ulysses S. Grant was in upper Manhattan. Chase knew Forrester had donated money to its restoration in his later years. Now she knew why. Could it be the modern reproduction of Alexander's tomb?

"Did he find anything?" she asked.

"No. It was a wild-goose chase. But then he adopted another pet idea. His last published theory was that Cleopatra's Needles pointed to the tomb."

Cleopatra's Needles were two obelisks that had stood on the waterfront in Alexandria, outside a temple built by Cleopatra. They had been moved in the 1800s. 'Gifted' to other countries. Or stolen, as most people preferred to say these days.

One of them stood on the banks of the Thames.

The other was in Central Park, behind the Met.

Chase thought to the last time she'd seen it, while scouting out an object she was being paid to steal from a private collection in Manhattan. It was miles away from Grant's tomb, which was further up on the other side of the island. But how hard would it be to argue they were lined up somehow, with one of the obelisk's faces pointing in the direction of the tomb?

This was all getting a little too National Treasure.

"Every ruler back then wanted to associate themselves with Alexander's legacy," Turner continued, "so Forrester suggested the two pillars, the needles, would originally have pointed the way from Cleopatra's temple to the Soma, like a gateway. He thought that if you could figure out the exact position they were in, you would see the way to the tomb."

"Did he ever try it?"

"We don't know. Alexander was his life's work," Turner said. "But one day he just lost interest. Refused to talk about it anymore. I assume he decided, like the rest of us, that there was nothing there to find. He took his secrets with him."

Chase felt the familiar excitement of a very bad idea.

The good news was she had a solid lead now. She knew somewhere specific to look.

The bad news was it would mean speaking to Zoe.

"Doc, did Forrester ever say anything to you about Alexander having a weapon?"

Turner didn't answer right away. She watched Chase in silence for a moment before saying, "No."

"The Visitologists think he had something. They seem to think there's a link between Alexander and the Aten, or Akhenaten. They're convinced there's a weapon, or some ancient technology, in the tomb. I want to find it before they do."

"Akhenaten." Turner sighed. It wasn't a happy sound. "I wish people had never heard that damn name. Thousands of years of brilliant history in my home country, hundreds of kings and queens, philosophers, mathmaticians, and all people ever want to talk about is Akhenaten, or his son." She let out a dark laugh. "Or bloody aliens."

"The old man let it go," Turner said. "And so should you."

"Why?"

"The Soma disappeared from history in the space of a century. Completely. That's not possible. It's certainly not something that happens by accident. Imagine if Buckingham Palace or Big Ben collapsed tomorrow, and then in one hundred years nobody could tell you where they had stood. That would take effort."

"You mean a cover-up?"

Turner nodded. "I think someone wanted the tomb to be lost. And they must have had a good reason."

SEVENTEEN

C hase got the feeling again as she left the museum. The tail was back, never there when she turned around. But she caught sight of the same face twice: a young man, dressed all in black, with stern features and a dark complexion. Chase didn't think he was a day over twenty.

When she looked a third time, the kid was gone, but the feeling remained.

Barron had told her that Zoe ran a specialty bookstore. Turner gave her the name and address. Chase caught the tube to Gloucester Road and took a slow walk down. She took a few random turns as she passed through Queen's Gate and Onslow Gardens. The streets were quiet and residential, lined with private parks and large, white-fronted town houses. It was a chance for her to either spot or lose her follower. The problem was, Chase wasn't all that familiar with the area herself, and soon she had to stop to check for directions on her phone.

Sure, you can navigate across a desert without a map or water, but five minutes in a rich bit of London and you're screwed.

While Chase looked at the map, she almost collided with a middle-aged man standing on the corner. She spotted him at the last second and swerved out of the way, apologizing.

"Quite all right," he said, in an accent that spoke of malts and money.

He was dressed in a tweed suit and carried a newspaper under his arm. Chase bit back on the urge to ask if he knew Mary Poppins and instead inquired after directions to Zoe's shop.

The feeling was gone. It was the relief of turning off a dark street at night to get away from the man half a block behind. Never knowing if that guy would have been a threat or if paranoia had gotten the best of her. Chase always chose to turn off the street.

Zoe's shop took up the ground floor of two buildings, with wide windows set into a green frame. A white sign above the door read Forrester's Books, and gold letters on the awning added, Maps, Prints, First Editions, Rare Finds.

Chase checked the hours on the door and found it would be closing in two minutes. She took a look inside before she made a move. There didn't seem to be any browsing customers. She could see a desk near the door, with paperwork and a phone, but nobody sitting in the chair. Chase pushed in through the door, setting off a quiet electronic beep.

"With you in a minute," a voice called out.

Was it Zoe? Hard to tell. Chase had assumed she would recognize her voice anywhere, but they hadn't spoken in more than a decade, and people change. The accent was different, and the voice carried a cigarette habit, low and cracked.

Chase scoped the place out while she waited. Each wall was lined floor to ceiling with brown wooden bookcases, and the contents were arranged into categories. Chase found the crime section and started looking through first editions. She found half a dozen Lawrence Blocks, and four Chandlers, but only one Hammett. A hardback edition of Red Harvest, and the price was penciled onto the title page at twelve hundred pounds.

Yikes.

Chase heard footsteps on wooden stairs and looked around to place them. One of the bookcases at the rear of the room was lower than the rest, and as she got closer, Chase could see they were hiding a banister to a staircase leading down.

Zoe Forrester was climbing the steps toward her.

"Sorry to keep you waiting, I was cleaning some—" Zoe looked up into Chase's eyes, and her voice cut off. She finished with, "Oh."

The years hadn't treated Zoe badly. There were a few extra creases around her eyes, but burying your parents and brother can do that to you. Her hair was still dark and cut into a ruffled pixie. The one feature Chase had always remembered about Zoe was her eyes. They'd been pure mahogany, with a wit and excitement that could light up a room. They carried none of that as they looked up at Chase now. She wore black-rimmed glasses, which was new, and her dress sense had given way to the kind of tweedy look that she and Chase used to mock at university.

Zoe was wiping her hands with a rag, and a faint smell of paraffin or lighter fluid followed her into the room.

Chase said, "Hi, Zo."

Zoe put up a finger to indicate she needed a moment and went over to the door. She locked it and then turned the sign in the window from Open to Closed. She turned back and said, "What the hell are you doing here?"

Chase hadn't been sure how this would go. How would she react if Zoe had been polite? That was an unknown. But arguing was something she was good at. If they were going to tear chunks out of each other, at least Chase had a fighting chance.

"I'm here regarding Henry," she said.

"Oh." Zoe folded her arms and leaned back against the door. "That's it? Been, what, fourteen years? And you're not even here to talk to me."

"What would that look like, Zoe? What would that conversation be?"

"I think it would start with I'm sorry."

Chase threw up her hands in the air. "I am."

"Say it."

"I'm sorry."

"For?"

All these years later, and Zoe was still impossible.

"For whatever. I'm sorry you were a coward. I'm sorry you were controlled by your parents. I'm sorry you couldn't stand up for yourself or for us."

"That's not—"

Chase wasn't finished. "I'm sorry they pulled my funding. I'm sorry I had to find other ways to pay my way. I'm sorry that ruined my—"

"Okay, enough," Zoe shouted. She stabbed a finger in the air between them, pointing at Chase. "You don't get to play the victim. Everything was down to you. Your control issues, your trust issues. You outed me. To them. That was my choice, not yours. I wasn't ready. I wasn't ready to tell them. You had no right."

"I thought you were used to other people making your choices."

Ouch. Direct hit.

Chase could see that one hurt. Every issue between them boiled down into one line. She took a step back and turned to look at the desk, searching for something to fill the silence.

"That's not fair," Zoe said quietly.

"I know." Chase nodded. It wasn't an apology, but she hoped Zoe would take it as one. She didn't want to have to say she was sorry. She wasn't ready. Even after all this time, her stomach knotted at the thought of it.

Chase changed approach and said what she should have started with.

"I'm sorry about Michael. He was a great guy."

"Yes." Zoe swallowed and sniffed back a tear. "Yeah."

"Look, I didn't come to fight." Chase pulled out the photocopy of Henry Forrester's journal entry and handed it to Zoe. "I need to talk about this."

Zoe took the paper and read it. Chase followed her eyes as they moved across the lines of handwriting. She clearly recognized it. "How'd you get this?"

"I've been hired to find the tomb."

"But this, how did you get this? Did you steal this?"

"Zoe." Chase tried for a calming tone. "You think I'd be here like this if

I could have found the book any other way?"

"No," Zoe choked. "No, I don't."

Zoe's turn for a direct hit.

And the worst part was, she was right. Chase had made no effort to contact Zoe in all this time, and she was only doing it now because of a job. She didn't like letting people in, letting them have control over any part of her emotions. She'd never really understood Zoe, didn't trust the other woman's emotions. Zoe had things that Chase craved—a home, a family—but she still seemed to look elsewhere for validation. Zoe's day could be made or ruined by the attentions of a total stranger. She cared so much about what everyone else thought; she would play roles, perform as different personas for each new person she met. It was exhausting.

When things with Zoe had gone bad, the only way Chase knew to deal was to cut all contact. Avoid the problem until it went away. But then, once you get used to avoiding someone, it's hard to reach out again.

"All this time," Zoe said quietly. "All this time, and you never got in touch. Never called. Never emailed. You know they have email now? Didn't even need to pay for postage or a phone call."

"I'm sorry," Chase said. This time she meant it.

"My family died. My whole family. I could have used you."

Chase wasn't sure how to respond. She touched Zoe's arm but pulled away quickly. Zoe smiled weakly at the gesture and then asked what Chase needed.

Chase gave her an edited version of the story. She mentioned the Visitologists and their application to the Egyptian government. She mentioned being hired to find the tomb before they did but didn't talk about MI6 or Mason.

"I can't change us," Chase said. "I can't change me. But this is important. Look at what Henry says in that journal. If he's right, I need to stop them from finding anything. He'd want me to."

This seemed to be their new pattern, argue then settle, rinse and repeat.

Chase hoped she could get out before the next round started.

"Georgie Turner said Henry took his secrets with him," Chase continued carefully. "Could I take a look in his mausoleum?"

"No," Zoe said. "But we can."

EIGHTEEN

M ason had grown to resent her small apartment on Chalk Farm Road.

There wasn't really anything wrong with the place. It was in a good location, and the rent was affordable on her salary. There were five spacious rooms, and the landlord fixed any issues she had with the plumbing or electrics. In fact, it had seemed like the perfect home when she'd first moved in.

The problem was that coming home reminded Mason of all the things she was failing at.

The fridge was empty and carried a vague rotten smell. The plates and cups were still in the dishwasher. The bins were full, and there wasn't another pickup for ten days. There had been a time when she would have been greeted by her dog, Django, and her fiancé, Sean. He was nice. Clean and honest, and mostly in shape, if she overlooked that his belly would overhang the top of his jeans slightly. She'd never cared about that. But now she came home to an empty apartment.

Django lived with Mason's mother. She was away from home too often to look after the little guy, and he'd stopped seeing her as his main human. And Sean? He'd packed his bags three months ago. Mason had always needed to keep a part of herself cut off, ready to focus on the job. It was hard to emotionally embrace one person when her work required her to pretend to be friendly or attached to any number of arseholes out in the field.

The surprise had been that Sean stuck it out as long as he did. They'd lasted three years as a couple. His proposal had been more of a Band-Aid than anything else, a last attempt to bridge the distance that was growing between them. He'd left on the same morning that Martyn Wood had gone on the run. Her fiancé and her friend, both rejecting her on the same day.

Both sides of Mason's life had collapsed, and she could commit to saving only one of them.

It hadn't even been a choice.

So now she came home to an empty flat and resented it a little more each time.

The place was a reminder that she could topple dictators and fight terrorists, but she couldn't hold an adult life together. She could identify nuclear missiles from satellite photographs but couldn't remember to buy milk and eggs.

Mason dropped her travel bag on the floor, next to another one she'd used two weeks before. She filled the kettle and switched it on to boil. There was a jar of instant coffee in the cupboard. One thing she always managed to remember.

People in the office would sneer.

Instant? I only drink real coffee.

Mason would mutter something about how busy she was and how instant was more convenient. What she would really be thinking was, Come live in the real world.

She stripped off in the bathroom and cleaned her wound. It was sensitive to the touch, and the flesh around the edges was pale and thin. Mason was trained in basic field medicine and had carried out small acts of surgery on herself before. But it was always best to get a doctor or nurse to fix the mess when she got home. Going to hospital wouldn't be an option. Legoland would find out about it. There was an in-house doctor at the office, but he would report the injury.

There was a cash clinic she could go to. A doctor there specialized in off-the-books procedures for criminals and smugglers. She covered the wound again as best she could and then pulled a new shirt out of a bag next to her bed.

The doorbell rang. Mason paused. There was a secured door downstairs, with an electronic lock. Whoever was at her door had made it up without needing to be buzzed in.

Mason stepped quietly over to the door, focusing to listen through the wood.

"It's all right, Mase," a Yorkshire accent said. "It's me." Peter Cullis, director of operations for Legoland.

Her boss.

Mason opened the door and waved Cullis in. He was in his late forties, but the field had taken its toll and he had the bearing of a man ten years older. Silver hair and the pragmatic air of a woodwork teacher. Cullis was one of the few people in the game who Mason could relate to. He'd joined the military to avoid the trap his mining family had fallen into and had transferred to Legoland from the SAS. He'd been a legendary field operative before stepping behind the desk.

Mason turned back toward the kitchen and said, "Coffee?" When Cullis nodded, she followed with, "It'll have to be instant, I'm afraid," and then hated herself a little.

"Too bloody right," Cullis said.

He leaned in the doorway and watched as Mason made the drinks. He nodded a silent thanks when she handed him a cup.

"I see his lordship picked you up."

Mason was used to the tone Cullis took when he spoke of Lonnen. It was a long-standing professional tradition that D-Ops and D-Int would have a tense relationship, but Cullis and Lonnen had taken it to the next level. They flat-out hated each other.

Staff at Legoland fell into two camps: those who sided with Cullis, and those who were loyal to Lonnen. Mason had never picked a side. She liked both men. That didn't stop each of them from nipping at the other like divorced parents when they spoke in front of her.

"Yeah," Mason said. "Saved me from the security queue."

"How was your holiday?"

Mason had expected the question. "It was good," she said.

"Get much sun in Spain?"

He peered at her. Mason had logged that she would be taking two weeks in Barcelona. Cullis had eyes everywhere. The reason she'd flown back in under her own name was because she knew he'd spot her arrival either way.

The only question was, how much did he know?

"I didn't get much time in the sun," she said.

"And how was Turkey?"

There it was. He knew every step she'd taken, but did he know why? Or who she'd met with?

"It was fine," she said, matching his smile.

"Has he got you up to something?" Cullis paused to blow onto the hot liquid. "Something off the books?"

"No."

Mason breezed through the lie without hesitating. She would love to be able to bring Cullis in on the secret. But his fractured relationship with Lonnen would make that a difficult sell, and she still didn't know who could be trusted. There were moles in the company; that was one thing Lonnen was sure of. Trust didn't come easy in the spy business. Everyone is trained to deceive. It becomes second nature.

"Because if he is," Cullis said, "you can tell me. I can protect you from whatever shit he's stirring."

Protect. Yeah, right.

Mason was used to that from both men. Always offering to save or protect her, and usually from something no more threatening than a pile of paperwork.

"I'm fine," she said.

"I hope so." Cullis set down the cup on the counter. "Because we can't have any other surprises. I'm not sure the firm could take it. And the Under Secretary has called you up; you're to go before the committee."

"Me?"

"Your ties to Martyn. This is getting serious, Mase. I think they want sacrifices."

"When?"

Cullis pointed at her coffee. "As soon as that's finished."

NINETEEN

H enry Forrester was interred in Brompton Cemetery. One of the most famous graveyards in London, used in countless films and televisions shows. The Doctor, Sherlock Holmes, and Dracula had all shown up there at some point.

The Forrester family had a modest mausoleum there, but Henry had caused a stink by insisting on having one to himself. He supervised the construction in his later years, making headlines when he tested it out by staying the night there upon completion. I'm going to spend a lot of time here, he'd said to the reporter, so I need to know that I like the neighborhood.

The cemetery was farther down Fulham Road. They could have walked there from the shop, but Zoe wanted to drive. They took her zippy sports car, a red MG, and Chase figured it was just a chance for Zoe to show she was doing fine without her.

Chase was happy to take the car. It would make it easier to lose anyone who might have tailed her to the bookstore on foot.

Zoe made her wait, saying she needed to finish up what she'd been doing. After leading Chase down to a small room in the basement that smelled powerfully of the same substance Zoe had been wiping off her hands earlier, she started stacking books into a box.

"They come to me in all kinds of condition," Zoe said. "The lighter fluid helps with old labels or marks." Once the books were packed, she lifted the box and handed it to Chase. "Make yourself useful."

By the time they hit the road, traffic was congested and the sidewalk was full of people in soccer jerseys, the blue of Chelsea and the red of Liverpool. Zoe explained they were into the last few of weeks of the Premier League season, and both teams were chasing a top four finish, and qualification for the Champions League.

Chase didn't really understand soccer, though she'd tried. When she was at Oxford, she had found it was an unwritten rule in England that you had to have an opinion on football. But Chase couldn't develop any lasting attachments to sports teams. She'd had her heart broken when the Sonics left Seattle and swore she would never love again.

Zoe seemed to be really into soccer now. That was new. She'd hated it when they were at university. Or had it just been that her friends hated it? Chase kept sneaking small glances at Zoe, trying to read the changes in her face. Was this who Zoe had always been? Or was this another persona, a character she'd slipped into for a new social crowd? Had the two of them always been going to grow up to become these two very different people, or had they pushed each other this way?

Chase could see Zoe taking the same furtive glances at her. Chase didn't know what people saw when they looked at her. The years spent out in deserts, digging up history for money? The hurt she kept locked deep down?

Zoe smiled. "The two of us."

They both laughed, and the tension seemed to ease.

Chelsea's home stadium, Stamford Bridge, was next to the cemetery, with a train line running between them. There were police everywhere, directing traffic, and both sets of fans were singing and hurling insults. Zoe pulled into a quiet residential street on the other side of the graveyard from the soccer ground. There were signs up saying that only permit holders could park there, but Zoe said she used to be on Brompton's board of trustees and had a pass for the whole area. A few months earlier, she'd apparently also had a key for the large metal gates. They were too tall for Chase to climb in one shot, but there were red telephone boxes on either side that she could get on top of to make it the rest of the way over the railings. With the heavy police presence, though, they'd need to wait until after the match began.

Zoe smiled and beckoned for Chase to follow her. They walked onto another residential street, this one with an automated gate to keep cars out. At the end of the road, Zoe climbed over a low wall that led to the train line, and Chase followed. They walked a few feet along the grassy bank beside the tracks. Chase looked up at the nearest stand of Stamford Bridge. The sky above it was starting to darken.

Zoe pointed to a window in the wall beside them. There was no glass in the frame, just cardboard.

These were the kinds of moments Chase used to love about Zoe, the version of her that she gave only to Chase. They'd first met in a similar situation. Chase had broken into Rhodes House at Oxford, after dark, to take down the portraits of old straight men and replace them with more diverse portraits of former Oxford students, such as Naomi Wolf, Lucy Banda Sichone, and Oscar Wilde. Zoe had the same idea, but she'd snuck in with copies of Andy Warhol paintings.

Those moments had faded as their relationship ran into trouble. But now, as Chase and Zoe climbed through the window into the dimly lit room beyond, Chase felt a flash of the old excitement.

They found themselves inside a large room. Light spilled in from holes in the ceiling. There were leaves all over the floor and a large furnace set into the wall.

"The old crematorium," Zoe said. "Never used anymore. Chelsea used to complain about the smoke from the chimney blowing across them."

"Looks well kept."

"Kids get in here. Homeless people crank up the furnace in the winter. We've been trying to get it demolished for years, but there's too much paperwork. Brompton's a landmark; it's got all kinds of protection. Even the broken bits."

They pushed out through a cracked wooden door into the corner of the cemetery grounds. The old, weather-beaten headstones spread out ahead of them, beneath the shade of the overhanging trees. The evening shadows were starting to creep across the grass. Chase felt an old familiar dread bubbling away in her gut as they walked between the graves. For all that she'd learned to embrace fear in difficult situations, there was one phobia that wouldn't budge.

Chase was scared of the dark.

She'd been a creative child. Her imagination would run wild. Every shadow a threat, every noise a dread. Her father would read to her every night. After a day working on the farm, he would come and check under the bed for monsters. They would hold hands, and he would whisper that she was safe. Until the night her parents died in a mudslide, and the darkness of the bedroom closed in around her. It still did sometimes. As an adult she'd fought to control it. Get the fear locked down. But we never fully lose the childish parts of ourselves. The problem with an irrational fear is that it's hard to control when it strikes.

Chase had a coping mechanism that usually worked: Ignore the irrational thoughts, and focus on the rational ones. Take whatever she was doing in the moment and whatever was around her, and break that down into its component parts. Touch. Sound. Smell. Chase thought of the grass and dirt beneath her feet. The sounds coming from the soccer stadium. Measuring how long her stride was on each step. And on Forrester's journal, the clue she was looking for.

Zoe, as if sensing the need for a change of mood, nudged Chase. "Remember the time we broke into the zoo?"

Chase felt the rush of youth again. That wasn't an evening she was ever likely to forget. She still wondered if they'd caused the animals any trauma, witnessing what the two humans had gotten up to that night.

Zoe led them first to the family crypt. Chase said a small prayer to whoever listened and touched Michael's name, engraved on the wall. She felt every one of the years that had passed since she'd spoken to him.

Henry Forrester's mausoleum sat on a small hill in the far corner of the cemetery, in the shadow of an electrical substation. It stood a little under twenty feet in height, and Chase could now see a resemblance to the top half of Grant's Tomb. It was circular, with pillars running around the outside, appearing to support the conical roof. The pillars were inscribed with odd markings. They resembled an artist's impression of both Egyptian hieroglyphs and cuneiform, without being an intelligible version of either.

Nobody had ever deciphered their meaning. Forrester had designed the structure himself, and his plans had never been found. Between the mystery of its design and the unknown nature of the glyphs, a number of urban legends had grown up around the tomb in the years since Forrester had been laid to rest.

Some said it was a time machine. Others believed it to be some kind of Masonic temple. Chase had even read an article online that claimed it was an alien spacecraft in disguise.

All Chase knew was that the building was the final resting place of a mischievous old man, and she needed to look inside.

TWENTY

C hase examined the hieroglyphs on the outside of the mausoleum. She had seen them before, but with her extra years of experience now, she had hoped to make sense of them. No dice. Fake glyphs were a staple of pseud-archaeology and fringe theories, but Forrester had always been above that.

There were figures drawn on either side of the large brass door, like sentries watching over the graveyard. One was clearly Anubis, the Egyptian god of the underworld. The other looked to be the Minotaur, the half-man, half-bull of Greek myth. Two different cultures. Chase had no idea what they had in common, except for the mind of a kooky old man.

A winged lion was above the door.

"There it is again," Chase said, more to herself than Zoe.

Zoe smiled. "The winged lion represents Saint Mark."

"Interesting. Mark was credited with taking Christianity to Alexandria."

Zoe snorted softly. "I missed having you around to patronize me."

"Sorry," Chase said. "So, I guess that's why he used it as the symbol for his foundation."

Zoe didn't snort a second time, but her tone suggested one could happen at any moment. "Yes. His real family."

Chase had always felt an edge of resentment from the family about having to share the estate with the Forrester Foundation, but she didn't want to open that can of worms right now. Instead, she focused on the door. Forty years of rain had discolored the metal, with streaks of dirt and mold running down the surface. Most of the urban legends said the key had been lost. It was an intriguing part of the mythos, that nobody could see inside.

Fortunately, it wasn't true.

Zoe handed a large key to Chase. "About the only thing I have left from the old man."

"When was the last time any of you checked inside?" Chase said, running her hand around the doorframe.

"Never, as far as I know."

Chase looked closer. "Someone's been in."

She pointed to the edge of the brass door, where the years of water and dirt had combined to form a small ridge stuck to the granite, creating a seal. There was a telltale gap between the growth and the metal, showing that the door had been opened. She slid the key into the lock and turned. It took some effort. The mechanism opened with a heavy click.

The brass door swung inward, scraping across dirt and moss on the floor.

The inside of the tomb was swamped in darkness. Chase hesitated. She felt around the inside of the doorway for something to grab hold of, and her hand landed on something that had no place being in a tomb.

"No way," she said.

Zoe stepped in close behind her. "What?"

Chase flipped the switch beneath her fingers, and the room was filled with light. Chase laughed. Now she knew why Forrester had built it so close to the electrical substation.

The inside of the tomb was a cramped circular room. Paintings of Alexander—and some of Henry Forrester's other obsessions—were hung on the walls, as well as likenesses of people Chase assumed to be members of the Forrester family. There was a stone plinth in the middle, holding a large, ornate coffin. Behind the coffin, on the wall, was a brass disc, looking down on Forrester's resting place like the sun.

"I wonder if he has a TV in here," Chase said. She stepped into the chamber and felt metal beneath her feet. The floor was made of the same heavy brass as the door and the sun. Holes were drilled through it.

The coffin had a similar seal of mold and dirt to that on the door. Chase put her hands beneath the lip of the lid, ready to lift, but Zoe made a nervous sound of objection. Chase pointed to the edge of the lid, where the seal had clearly been broken, just as it had on the door.

"Someone has already done this," she said.

She lifted the coffin's lid. It was lighter than it looked and didn't take much strength. She paused to look for a second at the desiccated corpse inside, dressed in a three-piece suit, with a fedora beside the head. Forrester had been stylish, even in death. The jacket had been opened.

"I need you to hold the lid," Chase said. Then, when Zoe didn't move, she added, "It's either hold the lid or touch the body."

Zoe hesitated a moment more, then shuffled forward and took the weight. Chase reached into the coffin slowly and patted the suit pockets, then felt inside the jacket. She ran her hands along the side of the coffin and turned over the hat, looking underneath.

Nothing.

Someone had already been here, and they might have found what they were looking for. Zoe lowered the lid back into place, and Chase stepped away while Zoe mumbled some kind of prayer beneath her breath.

Chase looked around the walls again, at the paintings and engravings. The bronze sun stood out. It was set into the wall rather than painted. Chase ran her hand across it and felt a slight movement. She stepped back and thought for a moment, then applied some pressure to the disc. It pressed inward.

A loud clicking sound ran around the edge of the room, like latches being sprung. The metal floor dropped down deeper into the ground, taking Chase and Zoe with it in a free fall. Chase's gut lurched, but she had experience with falling and knew how to control her landing. Zoe had no such practice. They splashed down into a shallow pool of water and hit the metal grille beneath the surface. Chase rolled, letting her arms and legs go limp and taking the impact with no lasting damage. Zoe's impact was much harder, and she called out in pain. Chase looked over at Zoe, who was sniffling away a few tears but waved to say she was okay.

The floor had dropped by about fifteen feet. The plinth in the center of the room turned out to be a large concrete column, so the coffin was still above them. The water at their feet had come up through the holes in the metal floor. The walls were covered with the same markings as the outside of the tomb. There was an alcove ahead of them, in line with the metal disc up above, with a small metal box on one of the shelves.

Chase waded over and picked up the box. Something inside it rattled.

"What is it?" Zoe called out. When Chase didn't answer, Zoe stepped in closer and made a grab for the box. "That's mine. Hey."

"Hang on," Chase said. "This is why I'm here, just one second."

Zoe muttered something under her breath that sounded like "typical." It sounded brattish and mean, another aspect of herself that Zoe kept hidden from most people, and Chase fought the urge to snap back at her. Instead, she stayed calm and smiled.

"I know, it's your family. I just want to get a look, make sense of it."

Zoe glowered but didn't make another attempt to take the box. Chase turned her attention back to the contents. She lifted the lid and found Henry Forrester's journal, along with a few sheets of aged paper. The book was bound in a scratched leather cover with the old man's initials embossed on the front. Flipping through it, Chase saw the same scrawled handwriting as the photocopy. The pages were brown and brittle, and the ink was fading away in places. Two-thirds of the way through, she found the torn stub of the missing page.

The sheets of paper in the box were two maps, both of Alexandria. One was a copy of the Mahmoud Bey map, with extra lines marked across the grid.

The second was more modern. It looked to be some form of official document from the 1920s, showing updates to the sewerage system.

Zoe had apparently waited long enough. She moved forward again, and this time Chase let her have the box's contents. Zoe flipped through the papers, then the book. She pulled out her cell and started snapping pictures.

"Because of the water," Zoe said. "They might get damaged."

It was a good point. Chase looked down at the water and noticed the level had started to rise. That wouldn't be a problem. In fact, it could help. All they needed to do was let the water rise and float. If the level made it high enough, they could reach the door.

That was when a metal grille lowered from the ceiling of the tomb, stopping where the floor had originally been.

They.

Were.

Trapped.

TWENTY-ONE

T he committee convened in the FCO headquarters on King Charles Street. The building was part of the collection of government facilities gathered together between the Houses of Parliament and Trafalgar Square.

Mason had been to the FCO before. Her father's office had been there, and she'd sat doing homework or reading a book in the entryway many times. Since joining the intelligence service, she had been here for meetings, but only ever in a supporting role. She had never been the focus.

Until now.

They had left Mason and Cullis sitting in the hallway for almost two hours. The oldest trick in the book. When they were finally invited inside, they took seats behind a table in a large room lined with brown wooden paneling. Across from them, sitting behind a row of desks, were the two people making up the committee.

An investigation of this size would usually be led by the head of the FCO—the most senior civil servant and de facto head of the security services, who answered directly to the government ministers. The role had been filled for more than a decade by Maureen Porter-Goldman. But MPG, as she was known to everyone in the trade, had been the first head to roll after the leaks. In all the mess that followed, no replacement had yet been appointed. The investigation was instead being run by two people, one from each side of the House of Commons.

Sitting on the right was Camilla Worthington. She'd built a successful career in the Met, hitting every attainment target set by the government and taking a firm stand against corruption and institutional racism. She was being groomed by Labour to run for Mayor of London in the future, and she'd been seen as the best bipartisan appointment.

To the left was Douglas Buchan. He was old money. The Buchan-White family were related to the royal family, and several of them had been members of parliament. For Douglas Buchan, power and authority were birthrights. He'd ditched the double-barrel surname in order to sound more appealing to voters and was a rising star in the Conservative party. This inquiry was his ticket to the top table, and Cullis had warned Mason on the drive over that he would be the biggest challenge.

There was also a young woman sitting off to the side, taking notes. She hadn't been introduced at the start of the meeting, but Mason made a point of walking over and shaking her hand.

"Thank you for coming at such short notice." Worthington's tone was friendly, which made Mason more uncomfortable. "Peter told us you've only just come home from holiday. How was it?"

Mason smiled. It was fake, but she was a pro. "It was great, thanks."

Worthington looked ready to say something else, but Buchan spoke first. "I suggest we get right to it." His tone was harsh initially, but he read the room and softened a little. "To get this finished, that's all. After the messes with Leveson and Chilcot, we've promised to deliver this one on time."

Worthington's attention turned to her notes when Buchan looked to her for support. Mason read a tension between them. They were from different parties, but this felt like something more.

"You understand you're not here under any suspicion, Ms. Mason?" Worthington said. "But you were close to Martyn Wood, so it's important we speak to you, to help us with our inquiries."

Worthington sounded exactly like the ex-cop in the room.

Mason nodded that she understood, and then, remembering the minute-taker, said, "Sure. Whatever I can do."

"How would you describe your relationship with Mr. Wood?" Buchan leaned back in his chair as he asked the question. The leather squeaked.

"We've known each other a long time. He was the year ahead of me at university, and we came to the service through the same way." "Guy Lonnen," Worthington said. It wasn't a question.

"That's right. Guy recruited both of us, so our careers probably look more linked than they are."

"What do you mean by that?" Buchan leaned forward. He circled something in his notes.

"Well, as you said, I'm here because everyone assumes Martyn and I were close, but really we didn't know each other all that well. It's just that our careers look linked, because we have friends in common."

"So you'd describe Guy Lonnen as a friend?"

"I don't see what that—"

Cullis coughed to clear his throat. "Excuse me," he said. "But Joanna isn't used to being in this type of meeting. Could I take a minute to talk to her, maybe help us all get this running a little smoother?"

Worthington nodded at the door behind them. Cullis stood and gestured for Mason to follow him out of the room. In the hallway, he walked a few yards to the next doorway, out of earshot of the committee, then turned back to face Mason.

"Don't go picking any fights in there," he said.

"I'm not trying—"

"The Brass aren't like us. We have rules, they don't. MPG has already gone down. Usually that would be enough, but they're still hunting. I don't know how many heads they want. This isn't about finding out who is to blame. They're interested in who can be blamed." He cocked his head back in the direction of the committee room. "They've never liked our department."

That was true. Department B had always been the black sheep of the intelligence establishment. It's origins had been separate, outside of MI6.

Department B had originally been Churchill's SOE, known as the department of ungentlemanly warfare. Filled with saboteurs, army rats, mercenaries, and criminals doing dirty work during the war, answering directly to Downing Street. Once the war was over, the SOE was folded into MI6 as part of a large reshuffle, but nobody in the intelligence community had ever pretended to be happy with arrangement.

The Department would be an easy sacrificial lamb for the investigation, even though the leaks hadn't come from there. And Mason knew the committee wouldn't be afraid to use that implicit threat to apply pressure.

Cullis gestured to the door. "Let's go get the game over with and play nice, give them what they want."

Cullis walked back toward the room and held the door open for Mason to walk in ahead of him. The atmosphere felt different inside. Buchan's notebook was closed, and he was leaning back in his chair, wearing the kind of smile that can never quite cover a bad mood. Worthington was sitting at attention. Her posture had changed, and it spoke of someone who was taking charge. Mason wondered if they'd had the same talk in there that she and Cullis had outside.

"We apologize if the questions felt like you were being led into anything," Worthington said. "We're really not looking to trip you up. Why don't I take us through this step-by-step, and we'll get wrapped up as quick as we can?"

"Sounds good to us," Cullis said.

"Joanna. I can call you that? Okay. So, were you and Martyn Wood friends?"

"Yes. We used to be."

"Past tense?"

"We were close when we first started. But we drifted apart—different jobs, different lives."

Mason had noticed that Martyn started to talk to her less after Sean entered the picture. She'd tried not to make any assumptions out of that, to give him the benefit of the doubt.

Worthington read her notes and said, "I understand you were engaged until recently."

Mason swallowed back her first angry response and said, "That's correct."

"Did he know what you did for a living?"

"Of course not."

And it destroyed us.

"I ask because Martyn Wood has been featured heavily in the news, so anyone who met him through you would now have an idea of your work."

"Sean and Martyn never met."

It was a lie. Sean and Martyn had met three times. Sean hadn't taken to Martyn. He'd felt her friend was up to something, that he'd wanted something more than friendship. Mason wasn't lying to protect Martyn. She didn't want to drag Sean into all this.

"In all the time you've known Martyn Wood," Worthington continued, "has he ever given any indication that his loyalties lay elsewhere?"

Martyn had released a statement via social media. He'd said he was acting out of loyalty to his country. Patriotism. He'd found proof that the state was overstepping its bounds, he'd said, and the British people needed to be told. But Mason knew it would be far more convenient if there was proof he was acting on behalf of another country, even a terrorist group.

They could fit that to a narrative.

"No," Mason said. "He's always been loyal, that I know of."

"How about his politics?" Worthington asked, writing notes on the previous answer. "Has he ever said anything, or shown you anything, that suggested he might have been at kind of anarchist or had any desire to overthrow the government?"

"Everyone in our job is open to the idea of bringing down governments. That's what you pay us for. But never our own."

Worthington gave a full police smile. Buchan's eyes almost popped out of his head.

Cullis leaned forward and said, "I think we can chalk that one up as a no."

Worthington's smile held in place as she made a further note. "Not just yet." She leaned forward and looked directly at Mason. "That's not really an answer, is it?"

"Okay. No. Martyn's always been about attention to detail. It's why he was such a good analyst. He broke out in a sweat if someone turned up with their laces tied the wrong way. The idea of anarchy, or revolution—that would be his worst nightmare."

"I see. But you're more comfortable with them?"

"You trained me in making a mess."

"And what is it that stops you from taking that too far? What would it take to turn that training on your own side?"

"That's the point of this whole investigation, isn't it? What made Martyn do what he did. I don't know. You'd need to ask him."

"What would make you betray us?"

Mason paused. That caught her cold. In so many ways, she was in the middle of doing exactly that.

Waging a private war, along with Lonnen and Bashir. Suspecting everyone else of being the enemy. What had it taken for her to cross over?

Mason covered for her pause with a smile. "Well, I came pretty close when Bake Off moved to Channel Four," she said. "But other than that, I'm not for turning."

Worthington played that straight. "Quite. Now. How would you describe Martyn's relationship with Guy Lonnen?" There it was.

Mason looked toward Cullis, and he gave a slight nod. They wanted Lonnen's head. She was being invited to throw him under the bus. This was one of those moments she'd always heard about, when you were asked to make a choice between your career and someone else's.

Mason didn't get a chance to answer. A junior staff member entered the room after a knock. He crossed the floor and handed a slip of paper to Buchan, who read it in silence, then looked up at Mason. "You have something called a Ten Twelve?" That was a code number.

Someone had used one of her get-out-of-jail-free cards.

TWENTY-TWO

C hase and Zoe both tried using their phones. There was no signal. The water was rising fast, up to their waists now. At the current rate, Chase knew it would only be a couple of minutes before their feet left the floor, and then they'd be carried upward toward the metal grille.

Chase didn't want it to get that far. She knew they stood a better chance while they were on solid ground. Once that was taken away, they had no control over the situation. She tried one more time to get a call out, then gave up. They were on their own.

"Look around," she said. "Press things. There's gotta be a way out."

Panic was in Zoe's voice as she said, "What if there isn't?"

"There will be. Henry put the book down here; he would have had a way back up."

"Maybe he used a ladder? Pulled it out after he was done?"

Chase had been thinking the same thing but had hoped Zoe wouldn't have a similar thought. She slipped the contents of the box into a zipped compartment in her messenger bag. The bag was waxed, and the compartment had a thin plastic lining. It would hold back the water for a short time. And if they didn't find a way out, then it didn't really matter if the journal got wet.

They started moving around the circular chamber, pressing their hands to the markings on the wall. Chase still couldn't decipher them. She handed the bag to Zoe, sucked in air, and stooped down beneath the water, looking around in the murky half-light for any signs of a hatch or a drainage control in the floor. She came back up for air with no further clues.

"What do these marking's mean?" Zoe called out.

"I don't know."

"Are they Egyptian?"

"I still don't know."

"Have you tried figuring it out?"

"Not helping." Chase looked around again, desperate. "It would be down here, before we float up. It would be easy to get to."

"Well, you're the expert in getting out of things."

"Oh, really? We're doing this now?" Chase turned away from the argument. She was looking for a lever. A switch. A ladder. Anything. There had to be something down here as an escape option. "There's got to be . . ."

"Walk away again," Zoe called out. The anger in her voice was mixed with panic. "It's your favorite trick."

Chase felt her own anger build. "Is that what makes it easier for you? Tell yourself it was all me? Maybe if you'd cared that much about what I thought back then—"

"What's that supposed to mean?"

"So caught up in what everyone else thought about you, like you could get something from everyone else that you couldn't get from the person who . . ." Chase's words trailed off. She didn't want to finish the sentence.

"Go on," Zoe pushed, the water rising around them both. "Let me hear it." "Look, I really don't think now is the time to go back over . . ." Back.

Chase waded over to the shelf and saw a small round switch where the metal box had been. It was the same color as the stone around it; Chase wouldn't have seen it if she wasn't on the lookout. She placed the box back over the switch, but it had no weight. She took the messenger bag back from

Zoe and lifted out the book, placing it back in the box. There was a quiet click.

"I think . . . " Zoe paused, waiting a few beats. "I think the water has stopped."

She was right. They stood for a moment and watched the level. It wasn't rising.

"Okay, we need something that weighs the same as the book."

Chase rummaged in her bag. She had a notebook, but it was smaller. Zoe slipped off her wet jacket, and the combined weight was enough to replace Forrester's journal. Chase swapped them in and put the journal back into her bag.

That was the first problem solved. Now for problems two and three: raising the floor back up and moving the grille above them. She felt around inside the alcove, but there were no more switches. Scanning the walls again, her eyes fell on something that didn't belong. Among the illegible markings, she saw one that was familiar. A small shape, like an arrowhead or a stubby T. It was the old symbol for Thor's hammer, worn as pendants at a time when people had to keep their beliefs secret. The hammer was made of the same metal as the disc in the chamber above.

Saint Mark was Christian. Anubis, Egyptian. The Minotaur, Greek. And now Thor, a Norse god. Throw in Aten, an Egyptian sun god. Nothing fit. Was this whole thing one big practical joke by a crazy old man?

Chase pressed the hammer. The floor and grille both started to rise, and Zoe cheered. The floor stopped when it reached its original level, and there was a loud metallic click, like the latches slipping back into place.

They wasted no time in stepping out into the night air. Their clothes were heavy with water. Chase's Vans squelched with each step, and she felt liquid moving between her toes. Zoe started to shiver.

"That was intense," Zoe said. "Look, I'm sorry I—"

Chase put a finger to her lips. Her senses were on edge, still heightened by the adrenaline. She'd heard something.

Chase spun on her heels at the next sound, and a fist knocked her off her feet.

TWENTY-THREE

C hase rolled onto her side, feeling the gravel biting into her jacket. Zoe bent down over her, reaching out to see if she was okay, and looked up at someone behind Chase. Chase coughed, pulled in some air, and started to climb back to her feet.

"I suggest you don't."

The voice sounded like malts and money. Where had she heard it before?

The light from the mausoleum was spilling out onto the path, casting shadows around them. One of the shadows moved, and two polished brogues stepped in front of Chase. She followed them up to a tweed suit and the man who'd given her directions to Zoe's shop. He still had the newspaper tucked under his arm. Chase felt movement behind her, and a second figure stepped onto the path from the direction the punch had come from. It was the younger man she'd seen earlier, dressed all in black.

Great. She'd been taken down by a kid.

"Who are you?" Chase asked, doing her best not to sound like she was still in pain.

"Believe it or not," the old man said, "we're friends. We're here to do you a small favor."

"You're going to introduce me to Mary Poppins?" Chase heard the kid stifle a snigger.

"See," she said. "He gets it."

The older man shot the kid a look that said, never do that again. He reached inside his jacket, in a movement that managed not to ruin any of the lines of the suit. He pulled out a black wallet and dropped it onto the path in front of Chase.

"We don't have the same resources as your employer," he said. "But we would very much like to give you the opportunity to walk away from this endeavor."

Chase picked up the wallet. It was an old-school leather billfold. She opened it and ran a thumb across the twenty-pound notes inside, counting ten of them. "You're right, this is nothing like my employer. I'd think Visitologists could afford more than this."

There was a hesitation before the man answered. His eyebrow twitched. "Is that who you think we are?"

If they weren't Visitologists, then who were they? Had he thought she was working for the Visitologists?

"Who the hell are you?" Zoe sounded remarkably composed. Chase could imagine her taking that tone with rude customers in the bookshop.

The older man gave Zoe his full focus. "My name is Stanley. My young friend there is Youssef. Let's just say we're old friends of the Forrester family."

"Cut the crap." Chase's own patience had worn out. "Is all of this supposed to be enigmatic? It's just annoying. If you really want to be our friends, tell us who you work for."

Stanley nodded to the wallet in Chase's hand. "That's a down payment. I don't know how much you're being paid at present, and, as I say, we don't have the pockets to match. But you need to stop looking for Alexander. I can arrange for a similar amount for your friend here."

Chase threw the wallet at his feet. "That's your best offer?"

"I thought it might be a better offer than the alternative."

"Which is?"

Stanley's head twitched to the side. It was a small gesture, but enough for Youssef to move in closer to Chase. "We kill you."

Chase looked at the wallet again. She picked it up and climbed to her feet. This time, Stanley didn't tell her to stay down. Zoe followed her lead. Chase hoped her ex was switched on and ready for whatever happened next.

Chase held the wallet out toward Stanley, then changed direction, swinging it toward Youssef, with the leather folded over to form a solid lump. The blow connected with Youssef's face, and he hit the ground.

Chase turned to Zoe. "Run."

They broke into a sprint, but Chase was far quicker on her feet, and she quickly began to pull away. Chase looked over her shoulder to check on Zoe and saw Stanley alone on the path.

Where was Youssef?

She turned back in time to see the answer. Youssef grabbed her from the side, pulling her toward him by the arm as he swung another punch at her head.

In the second before blacking out, Chase thought how much stronger he was than he looked.

When Chase regained consciousness, she was lying on her back in total darkness. The air felt close around her. Confined. She lifted her hands and hit wood a few inches above her. She ran her hands across the smooth surface and then down along more wood on either side of her.

A box.

No, a coffin.

Chase's childhood fear of the dark came out to play and found fuel with a more adult worry about being buried too soon. She swallowed and closed her eyes, focusing on her breathing.

In,

One,

Two,

Three.

Out,

One,

Two,

Three.

Chase calmed down. Her rational brain took control and started to weigh her options. She couldn't fight, and she couldn't fly. What was left?

The temperature was increasing. The air was growing hot and stuffy, and Chase could feel heat coming through the wood. After a moment she heard a loud whoosh.

The good news was she wasn't being buried alive.

The bad news? She was being cremated.

TWENTY-FOUR

T he get-out-of-jail-free card worked both ways. Mason said it was an urgent matter, and Cullis backed her up. If he'd been suspicious of her activities before, he would be expecting a full explanation now. On the way out, he whispered that he would try to pressure the committee to leave it there. He also insisted that the two of them needed to talk. Her gut said to trust him. But she also trusted Lonnen, and he'd said to keep quiet.

Mason got out without committing to anything either way, but the clock was ticking.

The call had been a tip-off. Parish had left his hotel room.

Mason headed to the hotel on foot. It took thirty minutes, cutting through St. James's Park and Green Park. The concierge greeted Mason with a subtle nod and pointed her in the right direction. The Grill at the Dorchester was always busy. The mood lighting left the room feeling like it was in a permanent state of eight o'clock. White cloths covered the tables where businesspeople spent someone else's money on designer food. The bar was stocked with spirits on glass shelves, bartenders standing ready to make the current hip cocktail.

Parish was sitting at a corner table, eating a club sandwich and drinking what looked to be a straight whisky. Mason started a conversation with the bartender. That would buy her a few seconds, enough to scope out the room and pick a play. Six men had checked her out as she walked in, including Parish and the bartender. Mason didn't have much time to get control of the situation. Tradecraft was different for women. For men, this would be about opening up a conversation with anybody other than Parish. It didn't matter who, as long as they weren't a distraction. For women, it was about spotting the right person to talk to. The guy who wasn't drunk or entitled, the one who wouldn't cause a problem. If she spent too long choosing, some loud guy would step in and make things difficult. A rookie mistake would be to find another woman to talk to. That attracted more attention. Straight men were wired a certain way, even the good ones. For her, the goal was to give them a reason to stop looking.

There was an older man at the end of the bar. He had a round face and thinning hair. He looked to have about fifteen years on Mason, maybe in his early forties. Not old enough to be her father, but enough of a gap that people might think he was an uncle or a boss. Enough to put up the buffer. He didn't look sure of himself. He'd been one of the six to check her out, but he'd been the first to stop doing it, scared to be caught.

Mason placed her drink by the empty seat next to him and said, "Busy today."

He nodded, trying not to look like an internal monologue was saying *Oh god, she's talking to me.* "Yeah."

"You drink here often? I haven't seen you."

"Me? Uh, no. I'm here for a meeting."

"Oh, I'm sorry." Mason picked up her glass and started to push back out of the chair.

"Oh no, not now." He grinned. A little confidence came into his face. Now that he was over the nerves, he could hold a conversation. "I'm in town for it, staying here."

Mason settled back down. Now she had his permission to stay; that was the cover in place. They slipped into an easy conversation. His name was Rob, and he was down from the Midlands for work. Mason leaned on one of her go-to legends for drinking in the city. She kept her eyes on Parish in the mirror behind the bar. He was reading something on his phone and taking occasional bites of food. A few times, he looked up as someone approached. Mason figured he was waiting for someone.

After twenty minutes, Parish was joined by a BBC executive. Mason recognized him. The Visitologists were in the middle of an aggressive media campaign to improve their image, and Mason guessed that included trying to win over senior media figures. Mason and Rob bought each other a couple of drinks while the meeting went on. After it was over, Parish gathered together his things and headed out onto the street.

Mason made a quick apology to Rob, putting her phone to her ear and saying she needed to take an imaginary call, and followed Parish out. Out in the fresh air Mason paused to check her phone and let him build up a lead. Parish turned onto Curzon Street, and Mason started to follow. As she rounded the corner, he was already half a mile along the narrow road. There were a number of embassies in this part of town, and Mason knew he could be visiting any one of them.

He headed down Bolton Street and onto Piccadilly. He was hesitant, looking down at his own phone every few hundred yards. Mason guessed he was following a map. That made him easy to follow but also meant she would be easier to spot. Everyone else on the street was walking at speed, with purpose, and Mason would stand out as someone taking her time. She took a gamble the next time he turned and kept going, taking the next turn. She picked up her pace, hoping to come out ahead of him. At the end of the road, she turned left and then right, which led her to Pall Mall.

Mason stopped on the corner, hoping to see Parish step out onto the street farther down. For a couple of nervous minutes, she thought she'd lost him, that he'd turned off somewhere else. But then he appeared. Still consulting his phone and looking at the road signs around him.

Mason hung back and let him pass. He didn't give any indication of noticing her. He walked down Pall Mall to the junction with Waterloo Place. He turned into a large white building, with Greek styling and columns out front.

It was one of the few places in London Mason wouldn't be able to follow. Parish had entered the Avalon members-only gentleman's club. Bankers and politicians. Secret handshakes and silly suits.

Mason continued down the pavement to stand in the shadow cast by the Duke of York's statue, watching the front of the club. A black cab pulled up in front of the columns.

Mason watched as Douglas Buchan climbed from the cab and entered the club.

TWENTY-FIVE

The temptation to panic was almost overpowering. Chase could feel how easy it would be to give in to the surge of animal fear that was building inside.

Trapped in a coffin. Being burned alive. Right there, she was a child again, lying in her bed the first night after her parents died, crying and alone. There were monsters in the closet and under her bed, crawling around her in the dark, and nobody was going to come and save her.

Panic.

Hide.

Wake up.

Chase kicked at the wood beneath her feet and punched at the lid above her. Neither would give. The chipping sound grew louder and began to surround her. The heat was intense, and she could feel her body trying to give in to it. She screamed in frustration and kicked harder, but nothing changed.

From what little she understood of cremation, she knew the chamber wasn't at its hottest. The heat at which a body is cremated would have killed her by now. And Zoe had said the oven was out of use. It might not work properly. That gave her a few seconds to play with.

Her back began to feel like it was burning. The flames beneath the coffin were almost through the wood, but more important the wood was absorbing the heat. Steam was rising off her damp clothes.

With the last energy that she could manage, she aimed four kicks at the foot of the casket. With her final kick, and with the flames now burning through the wood above and behind her, the bottom of the coffin gave, slightly, with a crack. The sound of the splintering wood gave her a new burst of energy, enough to kick again, and again, until her foot broke through.

The air that met her leg as it broke through was colder than the air around her. Chase wriggled toward it, her back scorching each time it touched hot wood. She slid out onto a metal surface but had the presence of mind to place her feet down first, so the soles of her shoes took the heat. She shuffled forward, arching her back to keep from touching the metal. As she came free of the casket, Chase knew there was no way out of this without pain. She needed to use her hands. She used her fingers to grab at the cuffs of her leather jacket and pulled the sleeves up around her palms. Using the lambskin as gloves, she gripped the edge of the wooden hole she had made in the coffin and braced herself to kick outward at the air, leaping free through the open door of the incinerator.

Chase didn't quite make it. Her shoulders landed on the doorframe, jolting pain along her spine. She slid forward and hit the back of her head on the way down to the floor.

After landing in a heap on the tile, Chase let herself rest for a moment. Her head slowly stopped pulsing, and the pain in her shoulders faded to a throb. Her shoes were almost beyond repair. The soles had melted. The cuffs of the jacket were singed and smelled like cooked meat.

Chase looked up at the incinerator. She heard another large whoosh and watched as the casket was destroyed. She slammed the door shut to keep the heat inside, but it bounced back open. The latch was faulty. A broken lock had saved her life.

Chase looked around for Zoe.

She wasn't there.
They've taken her.

TWENTY-SIX

C hase rounded the corner in time to see Zoe's red MG peeling away down Fulham Road. Stanley was driving, and Youssef was in the passenger seat.

Who were they?

Why had they tried to kill her?

Why had they tried to buy her off?

Zoe was in the back seat, her head slumped to the side, unconscious. Chase felt a moment of panic. In the field, she was used to processing fear for herself, and she worked with people like Wallace, who knew the rules. But now she'd led someone else into danger, someone who wasn't part of the game.

And more than that.

It was Zoe.

Chase couldn't let that happen. She had noticed a motorbike on the private street and ran for it now. It was on the other side of a traffic barrier, so the owner hadn't felt the need to chain it to anything. Hotwiring a bike in the middle of London was easy once you'd done the same in the Syrian desert. She roared out onto the road and accelerated toward the MG.

Stanley turned at the sound of the bike and made eye contact with Chase. The engine roared, and the car pulled away, swerving around a red double-decker bus that had pulled to the side to pick up passengers. A white van coming in the other direction mounted the curb on the opposite side of the street, blaring the horn before turning back into the road, blocking Chase's route around the bus. She turned the other way, up onto the sidewalk. She was racing blind around the bus shelter, praying to anyone who listened that no pedestrians would be on the other side.

The MG ran a red light at a crossing, and Chase followed, waving for people to get out of the way. She got close enough for a look into the back seat and saw Zoe still slumped across the leather. She wasn't moving. Chase's chest felt tight. She became more aware of her heartbeat. She swallowed back the sensation and found a little more speed, risking a head-on collision with oncoming traffic to pull out into the next lane. The bike started to draw level with the MG. The engine made a pained noise.

Stanley swerved toward Chase to drive her off the road, but Chase mounted the curb to avoid him. Stanley then pulled across the lane into a sharp right turn, headed toward the river. There were cars parked on either side of the narrow road, leaving only enough room for the MG. Chase stayed on the sidewalk, keeping level with the car but unable to get any closer with all the stationary vehicles between them.

There was a pub on the other side of the street, and men stood and cheered them on as they passed, holding up drinks in a mock toast. The sound of police sirens cut through above the engine.

Chase turned back onto the road at the next junction, where a silver Mini screeched to a halt as it turned onto the street in front of her. Chase rounded the small car, waving at the panicked driver.

The MG swerved left onto King's Road, and Chase mounted the curb again to cut the corner, accelerating straight at the side of the turning car. She pulled the handlebars sharply to the side and let go, airborne for a moment as the momentum carried her toward the car. She hit the rounded edge of the back bumper, and the air was knocked out of her lungs. Chase reached out with both hands and took hold of the frame for the convertible roof, behind the back seat. That was strong enough for her to pull herself forward, across the trunk. There was a loud crash as the bike slammed into a tree.

Stanley started swerving, trying to shake Chase off, and Youssef climbed over the front seat toward her with a knife in his hand. Chase threw herself from side to side across the small trunk, dodging the blade. She tightened her grip on the roof's folding frame with her left hand and swatted at the blade with her right. Youssef paused for a second and locked eyes with Chase as a dark grin spread across his face. He nodded at her left hand and slammed the knife down toward it. Chase let go at the last instant and grabbed his wrist, pulling him toward her. Youssef slammed into the seat cushion. He tried angling the knife down to stab at Chase's arm, but her grip was too tight. She reached toward him with her spare hand and only managed to grab a handful of his black shirt.

The fabric of Youssef's sleeve ripped, loosening Chase's hold. Youssef braced his free arm on the cushion and pushed back, tearing off the sleeve and finally getting free of Chase. She grabbed again onto the frame of the folded roof.

She saw a tattoo on Youssef's exposed forearm: the winged lion of Saint Mark.

What the hell?

Youssef swung the blade again, and Chase was forced to let go to dodge it. She braced herself to hit the road as she slid across the trunk, but a hand grabbed her.

Zoe.

She was awake and pulling Chase into the car. Youssef grunted and looked between the two of them, momentarily unsure who to target. Chase aimed a punch at him as she fell forward into the MG. Her momentum gave the blow extra weight, and he slumped back into the seat. His knife dropped to the floor and skidded away. Zoe's box of books had been tipped over, with the contents spilled across the seat and floor. Chase picked up a small hardback book, a Rider Haggard, and started hitting Youssef with the spine. Stanley was shouting for Chase to stop, but she landed another blow on Youssef's swollen face. His nose cracked and began to leak blood, a dark stain in the dim light.

"Where's my bag?" Chase threw another punch, and Youssef's eyes took on the glaze of concussion.

Stanley pulled the wheel hard to the right and took them the wrong direction down a one-way street to the sound of car horns. The police sirens were louder now, closing in from more than one direction.

Chase pulled a Zippo lighter from her pocket and pressed the cold tip to the base of Stanley's neck.

"I won't hesitate," she said. "I will shoot if you don't stop this car."

Stanley gulped. He shook his head and looked at her in the rearview mirror, his eyes flitting briefly to the front passenger seat, where Chase's messenger bag lay. Zoe reached past Chase to grab the bag.

But Youssef had regained enough sense to lunge across the seat, pushing Chase hard into the car's metal frame and sending a sharp pain down her right side. He clawed at her face, but she blocked his reach with her right arm and elbowed him hard in the face. He fell back, and she kicked him in the solar plexus, watching as the blood drained from his face. Stanley, free from the supposed gun to his head, was now trying to pull the bag back from Zoe with his free hand. He was the stronger of the two, and Zoe was being tugged forward, across the seat.

Chase saw one of the tins of lighter fluid.

She popped open the plastic lid and squirted the contents over Youssef's coat before letting the tin fall to the floor where the fluid ran out across the car. Chase grabbed Youssef's coat and held her lighter close to it.

"Who are you?" she asked.

He stared back at her with dazed eyes. She made a mental note that, in the future, she should ask the questions before concussing the enemy. She shook him and tried again. This time she saw some life in his eyes, but he still wasn't answering. A second later, he snapped back into focus and tried to head-butt Chase. She dodged, but he lunged straight into the flame of her lighter. His hair caught fire instantly, and as he batted at it with his hands, the flames spread to the arms of his coat, and then down the material toward the car seat.

Stanley was now swearing at a panicked pitch. He'd forgotten all about the bag, which Zoe clutched to her chest. Stanley tried to tamp down the approaching flames, unaware that the lighter fluid was spreading across the floor of the car below him. His tweed jacket caught fire, and he screamed, trying to shrug the jacket loose. The car shot out across Cheyne Walk, heading straight for the low concrete wall that separated the road from the Thames.

"I owe you one," Chase said to Stanley. She turned to Zoe. "Jump."

"You think?"

Chase and Zoe leapt clear.

They hit the grass verge hard and rolled with the impact. Chase turned in time to see the fireball arc through the air and into the river, where it broke the surface with a lot of fuss and then sank from sight.

In the darkness, Chase lay on her back and stared at the stars, sucking in air and waiting for the adrenaline to wear off and the pain to kick in.

Zoe rolled over and looked toward the river. "My car."

Three police cars screeched to a stop around them. Chase climbed to her feet, bracing herself for yet another jail cell.

TWENTY-SEVEN

B efore Mason had had time to decide what to do about seeing Douglas
Buchan, another call had come through. Chase had been arrested. In
London. When Mason had given her the card in Israel, she hadn't expected
it to be used so close to home. Yet there she was, waiting in the large
reception area at Belgravia Police Station. After she'd run out of a meeting
meant to decide whether she was a threat to national security, she was now
springing a known smuggler from jail.

Mason thought back to the first lesson Lonnen had given her. Governments don't have friends, he'd said, adapting an old line. They have
interests. He'd followed that up with, Spies don't have coincidences.

Buchan was meeting with Parish; the heir apparent to Downing Street
breaking bread with a Visitologist. The good news was that Lonnen's plan
was working. The enemy was being drawn out into the open. The bad news
was that this went way higher than either of them had expected. Mason was
playing with fire.

There was no greater reminder of the trouble she was bringing on herself
than sitting in a police station. Belgravia was a large redbrick building
to the south of Victoria. It was part of a collection of modern buildings
surrounded by older town houses. It looked to have been dropped into the
city from above, with no thought to blending in. Each police station in

London had a different ethos, reflecting the area around it. Belgravia was the Waitrose of cop shops. There were posters about how to report tax avoidance and warnings about a local car thief who specialized in BMWs.

The Asian desk sergeant hadn't seemed all that fussed about hospitality at first, but his manner had improved when she'd produced government ID. Legoland agents were required to carry their identification at all times on the mainland UK. Her credentials earned a second greeting and an offer of coffee.

"Instant, I'm afraid," the sergeant said.

Mason nodded that that would be fine. He left her with the drink and headed through a secured door to go get the prisoners. Mason sat on a padded seat. The legs scraped the carpet as she settled in.

She took two sips of the drink and then ditched the cup on the desk. Warm piss. Maybe it was time to become a coffee snob. The secured door at the back of the room opened, and the sergeant stepped back in, followed by Marah Chase and Zoe Forrester.

Mason recognized Forrester from her file. She looked tired and rattled. Chase looked bruised and grubby, which was now becoming routine for their meetings. Mason hadn't expected to feel awkward. She was coming here to get Chase out of trouble and send her back out into the field, nothing more. But as she stood and put a hand out to greet them, she couldn't help but be aware that Forrester and Chase had once been an item.

And what were Mason and Chase? They were one night in a foreign hotel. Nothing, really.

That kind of thing was an occupational hazard, part of the reason Mason had held something back from her fiancé. But she'd never brought any of it home, until now. She was used to holding important information back from an asset in the field, but it ate away at her to be keeping something from Chase on home soil.

Chase must have read the moment, because she faltered in their greeting. There was a pause as they both seemed to be stuck somewhere between a hug and a handshake. Mason realized Chase probably didn't know the correct way to introduce her.

She offered Forrester her hand. "Jane Bradley," she said, slipping into one of her go-to aliases.

Forrester's smile suggested she understood the tension between Chase and Mason.

"Thanks for coming," Chase said. There was an edge to it, like she'd taken it for granted that Mason would come when she called. Acting like this was just how things worked for her. It was the same confidence she had shown back when they first met, sitting in an Israeli jail cell as if it was a minor inconvenience.

It was annoying.

It was sexy.

It was not the time.

The sergeant placed a plastic box on the desk and started handing Chase and Forrester their possessions back, one by one. Keys. Money. Phones. He refused to give Chase back a small selection of tools and knives, and Mason waved for Chase to let it go.

There was an old battered notebook and some faded documents, and Mason saw both Chase and Forrester make a grab for them. Chase got there first, and she shared an odd look with her ex before dropping them into the messenger bag.

Mason thanked the sergeant and complimented his barista skills before reminding him that he'd seen nothing, and none of this had happened. Chase and Forrester were wiped from the computer file at the station, and Mason took the paperwork.

Forrester insisted on going home. Despite warnings from both Chase and Mason that it might not be safe, she wanted to head back to her own bed. Mason stood on the corner to give Chase and Forrester some space. She looked up at the security cameras dotted about. London was the most heavily monitored city in the world, and Mason felt exposed.

The conversation between Chase and Forrester seemed to have turned into a controlled argument. Neither voice was raised, but they were both showing small signs of aggression. They both had a hand on Chase's messenger bag. After another moment, it looked like Chase said fine and handed Forrester the notebook and papers.

Chase flagged down a black cab for Zoe and waved her off before turning back to Mason. "So, that government ID of yours can make problems go away?" she asked.

"Usually."

"Perfect." Chase hailed another cab. "We have work to do."

TWENTY-EIGHT

The cab dropped them off in front of the Embankment tube station. They walked past Victoria Embankment Gardens, and Chase noticed Mason was avoiding looking at the tents lined up behind the black railings. There was a noticeable increase in homelessness on the streets since the last time Chase had been in London. Was Mason ignoring it? And was that any different from Chase wanting to get into Syria by river, to ignore the damage in the cities?

They crossed the road and the bike lane, both of them busy, even at this time of night, and walked along the river.

Chase was glad Zoe had chosen to go home for the night. She needed some distance from the memories that hit her every time she looked at Zoe. Chase didn't know what she was feeling, and that scared her. She'd worked so hard to lock all that away. And now she could feel all the old doubts and fears bubbling up, wrapped in the same old excitement. Chase didn't like opening herself to the kind of pain that came with those emotions.

Chase knew Mason was dwelling on something, too. She'd been silent for the whole taxi ride. She hoped there wasn't going to be any drama with the spook.

After the car was gone, Mason said, "She knows, you know. Zoe."

"About what?"

"Nice try."

Chase shrugged. "Zoe gave up any say in who I fuck a long time ago."

A look crossed Mason's face. It was brief. A tell, easy to miss, signaling some kind of emotion that Mason had pushed away.

"I don't know who they were," Chase said. "They mentioned the Forrester family. One of them had a tattoo, the winged lion."

"What's that mean?"

"Well, the lion is the symbol of Saint Mark and Alexandria. Henry Forrester adopted it for the logo of the foundation that paid for me to go to

Oxford."

"Saint Mark? That's the name you mentioned in Israel."

"Yes. Patron saint of Alexandria. There's a link, I just don't know what it is."

Mason pursed her lips in thought, then said, "I'll look into it from my end. Known terrorist groups with that symbol, things like that. How have you got on so far?"

"I've found Henry Forrester's journal."

"That's great. What's it say?"

"I haven't read it yet." Chase paused. Sighed. "I had to let Zoe take the first look." Mason started to object, but Chase spoke over her. "It's her family. What am I going to do, turn up after a million years away and demand to read her great-grandfather's journal before she does? She has it tonight. Then she'll meet me tomorrow and I can take a look. From there, I'll try to put together the trail."

"And that other name you mentioned before? The Egyptian one?"

"Aten. A sun god. Forrester excavated Amarna, which was a city dedicated to Aten. But the Visitologists bought Forrester's journal for that dig, so if there is a connection between Aten and Alexander, they already have it."

Up ahead, Chase could see the shadowy tip of an ancient Egyptian obelisk sticking out above the trees. Twenty-one meters of red granite, inscribed with ancient hieroglyphs. As they drew near, she could also make out two bronze sphynxes on either side of the monument. They had been commissioned to guard the monument but erected the wrong way, facing toward it. "What's this?" Mason said, as they came to a stop in front of the monument.

Chase made the kind of disappointed tut she'd heard Turner give her on too many occasions. "What is it with you Brits? You live on the doorstep of all this history but know nothing about it. This is the oldest man-made structure in London. There's one in New York, too. They used to stand together in Alexandria, outside a temple built by Cleopatra."

"All by herself? Must've taken her a while."

Chase smiled. "Overachiever. Thing is, Henry Forrester believed the two needles used to point the way to Alexander's tomb, when they were standing together. And I had a lot of time to think, with you leaving me in jail for three hours."

Mason smiled. "I was busy."

"Uh-huh." Chase looked up at the large black plaque halfway up the plinth, then ran her hand along a small one, near the base. "Well, when this thing was put here, they buried a time capsule with it. Things from the day, newspapers, a Bible, some coins, and photographs of the best-looking women in England, because that's a thing. So what I really want to know is, do you have a knife?"

"What?"

"Well, I had a tool kit, but someone let the nice policeman confiscate it."

Mason felt around in her pockets and pulled out her house keys. There were two metal self-defense tools on the key ring. One was a short cylinder with a point on the end, the other a thin piece of metal that was just rounded enough to not technically be a knife. She handed the blade to Chase, who worked the edge under the side of the smaller plaque, trying to ease it loose.

Mason pointed to a tall building on the opposite bank of the river, on the other side of Hungerford Bridge. "That's the new Visitologist place. Right here. Daring us."

"This whole area was hit by a German bomb in the Second World War.

The needle, and the lions, were damaged by the shrapnel. Henry Forrester paid for the restoration work."

"So you think he might have taken the chance to hide something with the time capsule?"

"Maybe." Chase grunted with effort, but it was paying off. The metal was starting to move. "Or maybe I just want to look at the hot women."

Police lights bounced off the Needle as a cruiser pulled to the side of the road. They sounded the siren once as a warning. Mason walked over to meet the officers as they climbed out of the car and held a muted conversation, flashing her ID a few times. Chase kept working. The plaque came loose, and she took its weight, lifting the large sign down onto the ground. There was a small hollow section in the stone plinth behind it, and the metal box inside contained the time-capsule items she'd read about. Bibles, newspapers, trinkets. There were no photographs. Forrester must have taken them.

Dirty old man.

There was a smaller box at the back of the alcove, pressed against the wall. It was the same as the one Chase had found in the tomb. She lifted it out and released the latch to open it. Inside were two large folded pieces of paper and a small stone object. Chase didn't want to unfold the paper while the cops were around. It would only attract attention. But she couldn't help examining the stone. It was around five inches long, with the thickness of a Sharpie. The bottom half, or what she guessed to be the bottom half, was octagonal. The top half was cylindrical. The cylinder was covered in grooves that looked like ancient symbols scratched into the side. The markings were similar to the ones on the outside of Henry's tomb. The surface looked to be stone but felt more like metal.

Chase heard car doors shutting and looked up to see the cops pulling away. Mason walked back over. "I think we should go," she said. "That might not last long, and I don't want my name linked to anything."

Chase nodded but didn't move. With the police gone, she took the opportunity to unfold the paper, using the flashlight on her phone to examine the details. Both documents were annotated with a neat hand. They both bore an insignia of a small square and compass in the top corner.

This was the Freemason connection. Forrester had found what he was looking for.

The first document was unlabeled. It showed basic plans for a building that looked similar to Henry Forrester's tomb but seemed to be a much larger structure. There were notes in three distinct sets of handwriting beside the drawings, speculating on measurements for the walls and roof.

Mason must have read the excitement in Chase's face, because she said, "What?"

"I think . . ." Chase paused. Looked again. "I think this was the Soma. Alexander's tomb."

"You sound excited."

"Nobody's ever seen this. Well, I mean, the people who had it. But officially, nobody. Historians don't know what the tomb looked like. If the Freemasons could do this, they must have had some original plan or carving to base it off. This, this is history right here."

The second sheet of paper was a map. It looked similar to the Mahmoud Bey map that Turner had shown Chase earlier, but the walls were circular, and there was no coastline to place the streets in context on the modern city. The map was annotated in the same way as the tomb.

"Why wouldn't Forrester just destroy all of these?" Mason said. "If he was so keen to stop people finding them, why leave a trail?"

"I keep trying to figure that out. I think history was his life's work. He couldn't destroy these. He almost says it in that journal entry—he talks about hiding history."

Chase stopped short of saying the next thought that crossed her mind.

Because he was better than you, Chase. He respected history.

Chase slipped the plans and the stone into her messenger bag. Mason helped her lift the plaque back into place and press it back in. They walked along the river in silence for a moment, watching as a couple of late joggers headed away from them into the shadows beneath the Hungerford Bridge.

"I have a friend who can get me into Egypt," Chase said. "Zoe wants to come. I think it's fair, given her family connection."

Mason didn't say anything. Chase felt it was a very deliberate silence, and she wasn't sure what she wanted Mason to say. Did she want approval? Permission? Or something else, like jealousy? Chase didn't even know how she felt about it herself. Too many questions. Too many emotions.

Chase turned to Mason. "I have a hotel room tonight, and I'm open to suggestions."

TWENTY-NINE

W rapped up in each other's limbs, Chase and Mason both relaxed onto the bed. Mason could feel the thin layer of sweat starting. The good kind, the one earned in pleasure.

"I've never let anybody do that," Mason laughed.

"I like to improvise," Chase said, before slipping loose from their entanglement and putting a few inches between them on the bed. Mason had noticed the same thing on their first night, back in Israel. Chase very much present in the moment, in the heat of it, but putting a wall up as soon as they were done. Mason had been the one to make that move in every other relationship. But for some reason, with Chase, she behaved differently.

What she'd said was true. She'd never given over control to someone as completely as she'd just done, and rather than feel excited or new, she felt scared. Giving up any inch of control was terrifying to her. She lived for it. Set her compass by it. All of her darkest fears, all of her most powerful nightmares, revolved around the idea of being helpless or losing control. And yet here, for an hour in a London hotel, she'd handed it over completely to a woman she'd known for not much more than twenty-four hours.

Chase stood and walked over to the cheap desk mounted to the wall, sipping from a glass of water before saying, "Your people wanted me to be a decoy, didn't they?"

Mason didn't answer, and Chase turned back to face her. Mason thought again about the weird feelings rushing around her, tieing her usual priorities up in knots.

"It's okay," Chase said with a resigned smile. "I know you can't answer that. I'm just letting you know that I know. I've seen it before."

Mason didn't move, not an inch. She'd fought the urge to nod, but knew any gesture would be taken one way or another, an admission of guilt or a denial, which itself would be a lie.

For a moment she entertained the fantasy of opening up and telling the truth.

Yes of course you were a decoy. A secret weapon buried for thousands of years? A tomb nobody has ever been able to find, and the ramblings of an old crank from nearly a century ago?

Except now...

Well, now Mason was starting to believe. In the tomb, at least. There seemed to be enough of a trail, and one that Forrester had worked hard enough to hide. Maybe there was something out there. Alexander waiting to be found.

She propped herself up on her elbows. "I think finding the tomb of Alexander the Great would be a hell of a decoy."

Mason holding back on the full truth, that it wasn't her people who were behind this mission. It was just her and Lonnen. Making it up as they went.

Chase nodded. "Yep."

"I read you full file. You know, the firm looked at you, at Oxford."

Chase laughed. "They did not."

"Not for long," Mason bobbed her head once in admission. "But you were there on their list as a potential."

"A girl into punk rock, hair dye, history, archaeology and folklore. Not exactly James Bond material."

"History is a good indicator. Someone with a mind for understanding the past can be turned to good use when it comes to propoganda."

"But I look bad in a tux."

Mason smiled. "I bet that's not true." She breathed out to show how much exertion they'd put into the last hour. "You came alive back there."

"I should hope-"

"I mean at the needle. When you found the map, when you were talking about history, preserving it. You really came alive, I could see how much you love the job."

Chase snorted quietly, a sound more like blowing out a hair from her face, and sat on the edge of the bed. "Not this job. Relic Running. The trade. This is...just the trap I fell into. It's not archaeology."

Mason could see sadness rolling in behind Chase's eyes. The same deep melancholy she'd picked up on when they met, hidden beneath layers of armour and bravado. "You miss it."

"All I ever wanted to do. It's the coolest job."

"Really?" Mason rolled onto her side to free up one of her arms, pointing at herself for comedic effect. "Because, you know, spy."

Chase shrugged. "Paperwork and following orders. Archaeology is all about digging up cool shit. That's it. Sitting in a field and digging up cool shit. Forging a connection across hundreds or thousands of years between you and the last person to touch whatever it is you've found."

"Okay that does sound cool."

"I guarantee," Chase leaned in closer. "I've gotten laid way more by saying I'm an archaeologist than you have by...whatever it is you say."

"HR, usually." Mason laughed at herself. "But what if I were to tell you right now that I'm an archaeologist?"

Adam Parish turned off Gloucester Road and into the sleepy narrow street of Stanhope Mews South. This place cracked him up. Tiny little white houses, squished into a narrow lane. Hanging baskets and garden benches out front of each one. It was like something out of Harry Potter. Hell, everywhere he went in London looked like some kind of film. A different genre around every corner.Crime. Comedy. Action. Horror. Sci-Fi.

The Avalon Gentleman's club had been a whole movie unto itself. All Greek-looking from the outside, marble and columns, but obsessed with Arthurian myth and medieval chivalry on the inside. His meeting had taken place around a large wooden round table, which his hosts claimed dated back to Edward the Confessor.

He loved this city. More than he'd ever expected to. He was already planning on moving here once the mission was over, finding a movie location all of his own.

In the new age.

Of the Old Ones.

After the dark times.

He stopped outside number 6, a shiny black door with a brass knocker and no visible signs of extra security, though he knew this was the most protected building in the street. He waited, not bothering to announce his presence. It took a little under a minute for the door to open, with the person on the other side having waited to check security footage to see if Parish was being followed into the Mews.

The door swung in, and Camilla Worthington leaned against it, leaving just enough space to make the suggestive invitation. She was wearing a dark silk robe and an even darker smile.

"Nobody followed me," Parish said.

"Oh, I know." Worthington leaned her head against the wood, matching the relaxed pose of her body. "I've been tracking you for the last mile."

"How?"

"I'll show you later," she looked down at the two bottles he held, one in each hand. "Couldn't decide?"

Parish raised the bottles and shrugged, "I didn't know which one you posh types prefer." He grinned. "That's the right word, right?"

Worthington rolled her eyes dramatically and reached out to take the red wine. "I promise you, us posh types don't choose between red wine and bourbon." She straightened and stepped back, nodding for him to come in. "Would a bottle of gin killed you?"

She led him right, past a set of narrow stairs and into a dining room area that was deceptively large. A laptop was open on the table, and Parish couldn't help but notice it seemed to be showing a live satellite view of this very street. Worthington noticed his gaze and stepped over to shut the computer's lid.

"Later," she said again. "How did the meeting go?" She motioned for him to take a seat at the table and walked around behind him and through a door at the back of the room. "It's okay," she called through. "I can hear you."

Parish heard her opening cupboards, clinking glasses.

"Well. It went...perfect. Our friends from the Avalon club will stand down, let us do what we want."

"Good. Speaking of friends, the spy just bailed the relic runner out of jail."

"We already knew about that?"

"No." He could hear her frustration. "Again. Bailed her out again. Here. London."

That changed things. He hadn't expected them back in the UK so soon.

Worthington walked in behind him. He felt her in close, then her arm reached in past him to place a glass of red on the table in front of him. "Are you sure we picked the right relic runner? You've invested a lot in the Wallace one."

"He's the Alexander expert," Parish sipped from the red, pretending to like it. "She doesn't know anything. But I'm worried about this spy. Are you sure we shouldn't just kill her?"

"Not yet. We have eyes on them, and I have a plan for her tomorrow." Worthington stepped into sight beside Parish. She'd let the robe fall open, revealing she wasn't wearing anything underneath. She hitched herself backwards up onto the table, shuffling backwards to get comfortable, and then opened her legs wide. She grabbed his chin and pulled him forwards. "But I have a plan for you right now."

THIRTY

Fell's Landing was on the south bank of the Thames Estuary. It had grown up around a small cove, and legend held that the name had been inspired by a local smuggler. London had banking, Sheffield had steel, and Fell's Landing had the black market. Smuggling was arguably the world's oldest profession. The south coast of England had been built on it. And at Fell's Landing, they wore that history -discreetly- with honor. Everyone who lived in the town was associated with illegal activities in some form, whether it was the people bringing in the goods or the shopkeepers taking money they knew to be dirty. The authorities knew about it, but since smuggling had always been part of the country's economy, the law had a long tradition of looking the other way. There was an old, unwritten code that both sides honored: Human trafficking was out of bounds, and everyone had to be discreet. Occasionally, some idiot would bring in too much or publicly flaunt their success, and they would be offered up as a legal sacrifice.

Fool's Landing was a pub on the edge of town. The main bar looked just like any other modern chain pub, with a large open space, bright colors, and brand-name beers on tap. Chase led Zoe down a flight of stairs, into the basement bar, which had been carved out of rock. The low ceiling and chiseled walls gave the impression that drinkers were deep in the bowels of the earth. Anyone was welcome in the main bar upstairs, but only people in the trade were allowed downstairs. If you needed to book a discreet journey, by boat or by plane, this was the best place to come..

Chase was looking for an old friend, Chuy Guerrero. Born in Mexicali and raised in California, Jesús Eduardo Guerrero Marín was the best smuggler in Europe. He was wiry and strong, with a beard and permanent Ray-Ban sunglasses, even in the dark.

He somehow slipped goods past border controls in spite of being the most noticeable person in any crowd. If Guerrero was in a room, you would hear him before seeing him. He could hold court in any company, telling tall tales and dirty jokes. Chase usually only needed to follow the sound of laughter.

But it was now ten a.m., and even the hardiest of drinkers had turned in for the night. Guerrero was sitting alone at a corner table, nursing a coffee. He grinned when he saw Chase and stood up for a warm embrace.

"I don't want to worry you," Guerrero said, "but you're dead."

Chase played along. "That what people are saying?"

"Yeah, something about ISIS and Syria. But you're not dumb enough to—" Guerrero read her face as he spoke and changed tack. "Okay."

Guerrero waved for them to take a seat. Chase introduced Zoe, and Guerrero gave her a well-practiced look, one that said, Is she with you, or . . . ? Chase shrugged.

"So, you're some kind of smuggler?" Zoe said, after Guerrero was done getting her life story.

"I prefer freebooter," Guerrero said. "I like to free booty."

Chase had heard the line too many times to pretend it was funny. She cut to the point. "I've got a job."

"Good for you."

"A job for you, Chuy."

"No thanks."

"You don't know what it is yet."

"Sure, I do," he said. "It's dangerous."

"My jobs aren't always—"

A newcomer stepped into the room and made to walk toward them, but Guerrero gave a quick shake of his head. Not now. "I refer you back to the whole your-being-dead-in-Syria thing. And I'm still paying off the damage from last time."

"Really, as if that was even—"

"They shot holes in my plane."

"Why is that my fault?"

"They were aiming at you."

Chase grinned and slipped her hands into her pockets. She rocked back in her seat, playfully.

Guerrero saw what she was doing and put his hands up between them. "That's not going to work. No favors, no smiles, none of your little winks. I don't like being in trouble. My mother says it's bad for me."

"You love being in trouble. Besides, we'll pay."

That hit home. They'd both known that it would. His refusal was just theater, a version of a script they went through every time. Guerrero had been given a choice as a teenager: Join the military, or go to prison. He'd joined the air force but went AWOL when he realized there was more fun to be had on the private market. In all the years Chase had known Guerrero, he'd never turned down a job.

"How much?"

"A hundred grand. To start. More, if I pull it off."

"Oh. It's Nazi gold, right? There's a secret hoard in a cave, under a lake, guarded by beautiful Aryan ladies, and you want us to get to it before anyone else?"

Chase shook her head.

"So, okay, it's some magic fountain that's going to make me young forever and tastes like pulque?"

She shook her head again, and his shoulders dropped.

"You're going after a big lump of rock buried in some dirt, aren't you?"

"Now you're getting it." She leaned in close and Zoe followed suit. "The Visitologists are looking for something. I need to find it first. I need you to get me into Alexandria, then stick around to help. I want to keep this low-key. No team, just the three of us."

"Alexandria will be tricky. You know how crazy things are in Egypt right now. And aren't you on their watch list?"

"That's why I've come to the best."

"Is it worth it?"

"Fortune and glory, kid." Chase smiled. "Plus, we might get to stop World War Three."

"Will I get a medal?"

"I'll make you one."

THIRTY-ONE

MI6 had picked up the Legoland nickname when they moved into the custom-built modern building on the bank of the Thames. With its stepped design, people had been quick to point out the resemblance to the children's toy.

Mason checked in at the front desk and handed over her mobile phone. This was the second of the many security gates between the street and her office. The first was the armed police officer at the front gate. Once inside, a uniformed guard in the main reception performed a check of people's ID and confiscated phones. The third check was an automated metal gate that swung open once Mason swiped her card. All MI6 staff would see that stage. Analysts, assistants, secretaries, even the caterers. There was a fourth step, where Mason again swiped her pass and a large glass door would slide open. Only the classified members of staff saw that point, the people MI6 and the government tended not to admit to publicly.

The heightened security had forced a few changes to the way the organization operated. It took so long to get in and out of the building that staff didn't have time to go out for a smoke on their coffee breaks. The data analysts, buried away at computer desks in the basement, had complained it took so long to get to the street that they were losing most of their lunch hour. As a result, a floor had been given over to a food court, just like in a shopping mall, and there were several rooms that had been refit as smoking areas, with large extractor fans pulling the smoke outside. The downside to all this was that people who worked in those departments would go all day without getting fresh air or seeing daylight. "Lego sickness" was a phrase staff had come up with to describe the resultant stir-crazy feeling.

Mason took the lift to her own floor and smiled at Charlie the security guard on the way past. He was the fifth, and final, checkpoint. She pointed to the ID on her lapel, but it was only a formality. Charlie had been with the firm for thirty years, and he knew each and every one of the agents who had operated out of Mason's section. Her ID badge said she worked for Department B. There were no Departments A or C. The title was simply a bland way of filing away a team that nobody wanted to admit to. Up until recently, they were known in intelligence circles as the Scalphunters. The name had been discarded when cultural sensitivity finally made its way into the corridors of SIS. The members of the team rotated in and out of active duty and had become known as the Activists.

Mason stepped into the outer room of Department B, a small space not unlike the reception area of a law firm. In the old days there would have been a full-time receptionist there, but budget cuts had put a stop to that. Rumors had been flying that they would soon streamline from six Activists to three, with the rotation system changed. They'd been joking there would have to be some kind of Hunger Games–style tournament to decide who went.

Cullis's office door was closed. Mason was glad. She knew he was going to have questions about why she'd left the meeting in such a hurry, and she wasn't ready to answer them. She was technically still on leave, so she had left it late in the working day before checking in, in the hope that Cullis wouldn't be around. Only two members of Department B had remained on active duty during the stand-down. Cullis, as the head of operations, had stayed in place because there was an ongoing mission. Tan Bashir, the senior Activist, was already undercover in Syria and couldn't be recalled.

Mason's office was a small space, just big enough for three glass desks—her desk and two others that currently stood empty—and a filing cabinet, though Mason had never filed anything in all her time there. She logged on to her computer and spent twenty minutes sifting through her inbox. She was coming due for her physical, and the FCO had ordered an extra round of psych evaluations. She could deal with those later. She turned her attention to the information Chase had given her last night.

A tattoo of Saint Mark. Did that mean anything?

She searched the terrorism database, with tattoo, saint, and Mark as the keywords. She got half a dozen hits.

Most of them were crime reports. Suspicious activity in London and Egypt. Violence. Threats. Robberies. Arrests during the Egyptian uprising. Mostly small crimes, nothing that suggested a pattern. The tattoo was the only obvious link between the reports.

The other entries were older, dating back to the Second World War. Many of the files from back then weren't on the database in full. There would be a title, a date, and just a few keyword links. They were simply a record that the files existed, in hard copy, and weren't deemed important enough to have been scanned in.

Mason paused. There were three reports from Ian Fleming's team.

One was labeled "The Knights of Saint Mark." The other two both contained that phrase in the keyword listing. Who were the Knights of Saint Mark? Mason made a note to locate the hard-copy files.

She moved on to what she'd seen herself, the previous night: Parish meeting with Douglas Buchan, a senior Visitologist meeting with the rising star of British politics. In private.

Every keystroke in the system was logged. With the Church being such a political hot topic, Mason had been hesitant to put her name to a search.

But as Lonnen had said, they needed to be ready.

She typed in "Church of Ancient Science" and "Douglas Buchan." A security message popped up: Restricted Access.

Then a second one read: File 8921 Location Secured.

That meant the file was in the Box, a large room deep beneath the building that housed hard copies of classified files and banks of computers that held a database on a closed loop. The Box was used for files that were too classified or sensitive to be accessed from the mainframe. Mason didn't have clearance to access the Box. It was above top secret and needed someone on the level of Cullis, Lonnen, or the director of MI6 to enter.

What was going on?

Her intercom buzzed. It was Cullis.

"Mase. My office."

THIRTY-TWO

Guerrero was making good time with the flights. They'd stopped twice for fuel at small airstrips along the smuggler routes. The plane was a heavily modified Antonov An-2 named Molly. Antonovs were mostly used for short-range agricultural work and so weren't built with comfort in mind. This model wasn't manufactured anymore, and they were cheap to buy. Guerrero claimed he'd won Molly in a card game, but Chase knew he'd bought her for next to nothing off eBay. He'd refitted her with extra fuel tanks, a small sleeping area, and hidden compartments for smuggling.

Guerrero had secured clearance for a private charter to Egypt under the pretense of flying in bedsheets from Harrods for a millionaire staying at a hotel in Alexandria. Chase and Guerrero both knew night managers in hotels across the Mediterranean, and requests like this were easy to organize. Guerrero had recently flown a fedora from Ireland to Italy for a rock star who preached about environmentalism.

The flight mostly consisted of Guerrero trying to impress Zoe with exaggerated tales of previous jobs he'd taken with Chase. Between the first and second fuel stops, Chase settled into one of the padded car seats Guerrero had fitted in the rear of the plane. She pulled the journal out of her messenger bag and looked it over for any water damage. It had survived intact, though the book fell open to pages Zoe must have been reading. There were slips of paper, thin receipts from Zoe's shop, used as bookmarks. Somewhere in here, Chase knew, had to be a trail.

The journal started in 1920. Forrester gave overwritten summaries of his findings, talked about his time in the war and the stories he'd heard about the Freemasons having a stash of old maps. He detailed a theory, matching what Turner had said, that someone must have been working to keep Alexander hidden. Chase followed as he met with the Freemasons in New York, where they handed over the plans. His contact confirmed they were copies from an original but said the Freemasons had only been interested in the architecture. They weren't the ones who had been trying to hide the tomb. Forrester had learned what the Soma looked like but not where it was. And the Freemasons' plan of the original city was wrong, he'd noted. The wrong shape.

Chase paused to compare the Freemason map to the Mahmoud Bey version. The Freemason version was rounder, almost like a large walled city. It reminded her of a stretched-out version of the ancient city of Troy, a ruin that Alexander had visited to pay tribute to the gods, and was said to have stolen a weapon from Achilles tomb. The Bey map was more sprawling, matching the modern coastline. The walls of the oldest part of the city were highlighted on Bey's map in bold lines. Chase couldn't help but think the walls of the old city looked like the profile of a cartoon dog's head. There was a large rectangle around the west of the city, with a smaller rectangle jutting out toward the east, ending in a rounded snout.

She turned back to Forrester's book. A full page was taken up with drawings of the winged lion. Chase figured they must have been reproductions of carvings or paintings he'd seen in Alexandria, the start of his obsession with that image.

From there, Forrester started writing about ancient cults and speculated that Alexander had chosen to found the city of Alexandria on top of an old religious site. That made sense, up to a point. The first thing an invading force did in those times was take charge of the water supply, but the second move would be to seize the places of worship.

By 1922, the subject was back to Alexander and the missing tomb. Forrester's accounts of that final expedition were dry, short on the kind of flowery writing Chase had grown used to and long on weather details. She could sense tension in Forrester's words. He started to write about tunnels beneath the city. One of the first things the architect Dinocrates had done was dig channels down into the rock, an early version of plumbing, to bring drinkable water across from the Nile. Why all that effort, when they could have just built the city closer to the Nile? Why did Alexandria need to be here?

Chase compared the diagrams of the tunnels to the two maps she'd found with the journal. One was of the ancient city, with lines drawn over it that seemed to indicate these water channels. The second was a map of how the city was laid out by Forrester's time, over which he had marked a few extra lines, noting that they were the places where the original tunnels were still accessible. He recorded that they were used by smugglers. But Alexandria had been extensively modernized and rebuilt since then, and Chase doubted many of the tunnels from 1922 would still exist today. They would have been dug out to become foundations. If they had been a route to the tomb, they were probably long gone.

Chase reached the torn-out stub of the missing page. After that, Forrester stopped writing about the Soma and Alexander, completely.

They were off the coast of Italy when the problems started. As they took off from the second refuelling, at a small smuggler strip to the north of Tropea, Zoe came back to join her.

"So did you really do that thing with the—"

"No."

"But he said that—"

"Does he look like a man who would be sober enough to remember all of that?"

Zoe nodded at the book. "Anything?" Chase shook her head.

"Me neither. He liked to use flowery words, didn't he? What I don't get is, why go to such lengths to protect the journal if there was nothing in it? There has to be something in there we can use."

Chase made a show of stretching out in the chair, using it as cover to nudge her messenger bag closed. She hadn't told Zoe about the items she'd found at the Needle. She liked to keep things close to her chest, which had always been one of their points of argument. Zoe wanted to know her every thought, but Chase liked to ration out information about herself.

"Those people last night . . . Stanley said he was an old friend of your family. Have you heard of a Stanley?"

"No, doesn't ring any bells. But we didn't always share much, you know? We didn't always talk."

"The younger one, he had a tattoo. It was the lion Henry liked so much."

Zoe pulled a face but didn't speak. When she could see Chase was waiting for an answer, she said, "Nope. Nothing."

Guerrero broke into their thoughts to announce, "We've got company, ladies."

Chase climbed up into the cockpit. Guerrero pointed off to the right, where Chase could make out two helicopters on an intercept course.

Guerrero tapped the earphones of his radio headset. "They're asking for you," he said.

"By name?"

Guerrero passed her a headset and pointed to the empty seat beside him. He flipped a switch on the controls beside him and then started addressing the helicopters. "This is private charter 6932, over."

Radio crackle, then, "Hello there." The voice was gritted-teeth friendly. Was that a German accent? "Could I speak to Marah Chase, please?"

He'd mispronounced her name. Marr-ah. It was a common mistake for an uncommon name, and usually Chase took it in stride. Both pronunciations were correct for the word, but only one of them was her name. Today she wanted to believe it was deliberate. She shook her head at Guerrero.

"You must be mistaken, friend," Guerrero said. "No such passenger."

"That's unfortunate," the voice said. "Because she might have been able to talk us out of shooting you down."

Chase reached over and flipped the switch to mute the microphones.

"Can you outrun them? Planes are faster than helicopters, right?"

"Well, sure. Usually."

"Usually?"

"This thing ain't all that fast to begin with, and I'm carrying a bigger tank than she's built for. I never really had speed in mind when I was fixing her up."

"They're a ways off—we've got time before they reach us."

"Not really. They're on a course to cut us off, right after we cross the line."

"What line?"

"In about ten miles we'll leave Italian airspace and enter international territory."

Zoe leaned between them. "Would that be bad?"

"Well, it makes it easier for them to shoot at us. And I need to keep Molly off watch lists. Can't afford to replace her."

Chase flipped the switch again. "This is Chase."

"Marah." The name mangled again. "My name is Wilhelm. We took a trip to the hospital together in Syria."

"What do you want?"

"We want the book and the maps. And we are willing to pay for them."

Guerrero flipped the mute switch. "How much?"

Chase shook her head. "They'll shoot us the minute we land."

Guerrero pursed his lips and nodded. He'd known that already, really, but the mention of money always got the better of him. "But if they want a book off you, they won't shoot us down. The water would destroy it."

"There's a waterproof compartment in my bag."

"Do they know that?"

The helicopters were closing in. Chase could see the outlines of pilots but couldn't make out any features. The helicopters themselves looked ex-military. Black market. They were gray and black, and each one had a gun mounted on its side.

She flipped the switch again. "We're on a private charter to Alexandria. Dropping off linen. You can check the paperwork with the authorities if you don't believe us."

Laughter came back through her earphones. "If you want to keep playing that, it's okay by me."

Zoe didn't have a headset and so hadn't heard the conversation. "What's going on?" she asked.

Chase turned to her. "Go strap in."

"We just crossed the line," Guerrero called out.

The shooting started.

THIRTY-THREE

M ason knocked on Cullis's door and walked in before he could respond. His office was the same size as hers, but he was the sole occupant. His desk was in front of a large screen mounted on the wall. Sometimes it was switched to an outside view, like a digital window, but today it was showing an in-house news feed.

Cullis turned from watching the news to nod at Mason. He didn't invite her to sit down.

"Toby Schlamme was found dead this morning."

Mason's skull hummed. She felt numb. For a moment, she was keenly aware of her toes twitching. Part of her had already known he was dead, but it had been something that could be pushed away, not thought about.

Now it was a cold fact.

"What happened?" Her voice was hoarse.

"Looks like he was tortured and shot. And the weapon might be one of ours."

Oh, shit.

Mason had left her gun along with the Reinheit goons for Schlamme to clear up. Someone had used it on him. What information had they gotten from him before the end? He didn't know all the details of her secret mission, but he knew enough to cause problems.

Cullis knew she'd been in Israel. If he hadn't already known she'd met with Schlamme, he would have confirmed it by now. Mason braced herself for the questions that were about to follow and began lining up her lies and defenses.

"Camilla Worthington is after your blood," Cullis said. "After you left the meeting, she made that pretty clear."

"I thought she'd be on our side of this."

"She's looking to build a career in politics. You've been around enough to know what that means."

He pressed a button on his computer, and the screen behind him changed. Now it was showing a shaky video, something recorded on a phone. "A copy of this was found with his body."

The clip was a close-up of Tan Bashir. A gloved hand was pressed against his head, and he was answering questions in an eerie monotone. He gave his name and rank, then confirmed he worked for MI6 and had been working undercover in Syria. The video stopped.

"That's all there was," Cullis said. "But we don't know what else he gave away. We don't know who has it or what they intend to do it with."

"And Tan?"

He shook his head slowly. "We haven't found him, and we don't expect to."

They sat in silence. Mason was trying to get a grip of her new reality. It felt like only yesterday that she and Tan had shared a coffee in Westminster before his deployment. She had said things were looking bad with Sean, and Tan had told her not to make any big decisions until he got back. Now he was never coming home. Cullis was watching her. Mason knew what was coming next. He knew she was up to something. The rug was about to be pulled out from under her. Cullis's phone started to ring. He looked down at the display and sighed. That was unusual. He wasn't given to dramatic gestures.

"I need to take this," he said. "It's Worthington. Why don't you go for a smoke?"

Mason didn't move straightaway. She wasn't a smoker. Like most people in her line of work, she would sometimes do it in the field, as a prop or a conversation starter with an asset. But she never smoked on home turf, and Cullis knew that.

Mason didn't pause any longer. She agreed and turned on her heel as he answered the call.

Back in her own office, she walked around the desk to pick her jacket off the back of her chair. The computer beeped, and a small black window opened on the screen. It had a white blinking cursor that started typing a message.

They're onto you. you're going to be set up. get out.

She started to type a response, but the cursor started to move again on its own.

Leave now.

Mason pulled on her jacket and headed back out into the reception area. She stepped quietly past Cullis's door, hearing a muffled conversation, and out into the corridor. She smiled at Charlie on the way past and mumbled something about Lego sickness. She took the lift down to the ground floor. Mason's heart was pounding. This was worse than being in the field. At least out there, she had a sense of right and wrong and knew she was acting on orders from back home. But here, now, waiting for this lift . . . back home wasn't a guarantee of anything.

Mason felt nauseated.

She swiped her card through the first security point. The glass door opened, and she stepped through. She walked briskly to the end of the next corridor and pressed her card to the scanner at the metal gate. The light went green, and it swung open.

Now the final hurdle was the front desk, where the uniformed guard checked her ID. Mason smiled at the beefy guy behind the desk, who paused for a second and looked down at a screen out of Mason's sight.

A moment later, he looked up at her and nodded, handing over her ID, then turned to look for her phone in the drawer. He was taking his time. Mason could feel the seconds ticking away, but to hurry him up would arouse suspicion. She played it cool in perilous situations all the time out in the field, but this felt different.

Finally, the guard turned back and handed Mason the phone. She took it and stepped quickly toward the door.

She heard shouting from behind. Someone called her name. The phone vibrated in her hand, and she looked down to see a message on the screen.

Leave the building. don't look back.

THIRTY-FOUR

C hase asked, "You got any guns on this thing?"

Guerrero was well known for his distaste of firearms. It was a survival tactic more than anything else. Everyone in his trade was tense and suspicious, and a lot of people had been shot over misunderstandings. It defused tense meetings if everyone knew he hated guns.

But Guerrero wasn't a fool. He turned in his seat to point to a metal plate in the floor behind them. Chase climbed out of her chair and grabbed hold of the handle in the center. She started to lift, and Zoe bent down to help as the metal came clear of the hole beneath it. There was a selection of handguns, a crate of grenades, and one machine gun.The shots from outside were getting closer. The first few volleys had only been for show, but soon they would be within range.

"They're going to try to flank us," Guerrero said. "Get us on both sides."

"It's a bluff," Chase said. "They're just playing chicken." She watched the choppers for a second. One had now maneuvered beside them, keeping pace. The other had dropped down low and was out of sight beneath them.

"They'll try something else."

Molly began to shake. They bounced around in sudden turbulence.

"The rotors," Guerrero said. "Next to us, below us. They want me to lose control."

The helicopter beside them moved forward, and Chase saw someone lean out with a handgun and start taking shots at the propeller on Molly's nose.

"Aw, shit," Guerrero said. "That might work."

The window next to Guerrero had a latch on it. Chase picked up a grenade and leaned over him to open the window. She pulled the pin and then tossed the grenade underarm toward the chopper. The midair explosion sent the helicopter swerving away but also forced Guerrero to bank sharply, throwing Chase to the floor.

He shut the window. "What the fuck?"

Chase rubbed her shoulder. "I don't know. Making this up as I go."

A volley of gunfire came again from the chopper as it veered back toward them. The bullets ripped into Molly's side. Chase grabbed the machine gun. "Could you get close enough to use this?"

"This isn't a fighter. If I try to move like one, we'll rip apart."

"I never thought I'd see the day you turned into a coward."

Guerrero grunted something that sounded like fuck it. He narrowed his eyes, his jaw set in concentration. "Strap in."

Chase climbed back into the front passenger seat and buckled up. She turned to check on Zoe, who had already done the same in the rear. Guerrero pulled hard to one side. Molly banked, but Guerrero kept going. Chase felt her guts heave as Molly arced in a slow, awkward corkscrew. Chase looked out the window to her right as the chopper below them came into view. The pilot panicked and tried to move out of the way, but Molly's wing swiped through the blades. The plane shook, and the sound of tearing metal filled the air around them, but Molly kept going.

They were completely upside down, and the shaking stopped. Chase watched as the damaged helicopter plummeted toward the ocean above their heads.

Guerrero was fighting hard against the control and letting out a low growl. Molly continued her arc. As she righted, Guerrero let out a whoop.

"That was not in the manual."

Wilhelm spoke again in their ears. Clearly he was in the surviving chopper. "That was a brave move. Maybe we should have hired your pilot."

"I'm not for sale," Guerrero said. He muted the mic and turned to Chase. "Well, I am, but you know what I mean."

"You won't be able to do that a second time," Wilhelm said. "So why not just give in now?"

Chase unbuckled and stood up. Her legs were wobbly.

She knew her lunch was about ready to revisit. She picked up the machine gun and opened the window again. Pushing the weapon out as far as she could, she squeezed the trigger. The bullets fired into the space between the plane and the chopper, with a force that pushed Chase backward into the plane. She almost lost her grip on the gun.

Wilhelm swerved out of reach. Chase stopped firing and waited another moment. The helicopter came back closer, and Chase pulled hard on the trigger again. The new volley of bullets ripped into the chopper's cockpit, sending it on a long tumble down to earth. Wilhelm screamed in their ears. Chase lost the grip on the gun as it rattled through the ammunition, and it slipped out the window, following the falling helicopter.

Molly's engine sounded like a dying horse. The plane was bouncing along on the air like a stone skipping across water. Chase looked out at the wing to see torn metal. Then the plane rocked to the side, and Guerrero swore. He was fighting with the controls, but Molly wasn't listening.

Guerrero lost control completely, and they lurched forward into a dive straight toward the water. Molly started looping in a spiral as she went down, throwing Chase to the floor again. Guerrero let go of the controls and closed his eyes, breathing in deep. The plane shook more violently as gravity took hold without any fight.

"What the hell are you doing?" Zoe had unbuckled and rushed forward, but Chase blocked her.

She trusted Guerrero.

He sat still. With his eyes closed, he reached out and put his hands around the controls without gripping them. After a moment, he tightened his grip again and then eased the plane into the spiral, flying with the spin instead of away from it. They spun around in midair, like a metal ballerina, before straightening out with relative ease and regaining control.

"Just have to listen to what gravity's telling you," he said. "Go with the pull. If you ignore it, it'll slap you."

"You learn that in the air force?"

"From my first girlfriend."

THIRTY-FIVE

M ason paused on the corner, stepping back out of the bicycle lane
as a cyclist rounded her with a glare. The entrance to Legoland
was covered by a green gate and an armed police officer. He hadn't stopped
Mason from leaving, but she could see he was watching her. His head was
tilted slightly, listening to instructions in an earpiece. The phone buzzed in
Mason's hand.

turn right. now.

The message wasn't coming through any of the messenger apps. It appeared directly on her screen.

Turning right would take Mason toward Vauxhall Bridge and alongside
the building she had just left. Every bit of tradecraft told her that walking
past Legoland was a mistake. It's hard to evade people when they can just
look out the window and see you.

A new message flashed.

trust Me.

Mason went all in. She set out across the bridge.

It was the height of rush hour. The bridge was full of traffic and pedestrians, but Mason's instincts were honed enough to pick out the people tailing her. In the reflection of a passing double-decker bus she spotted two people behind her. To the untrained eye they were just part of the crowd, but their movements gave them away. It was the small gestures that added up. The way they were working hard not to look at her. The twitch of their heads as they listened to instructions in their earpieces. It didn't take much to make out a third tail on the other side of the road.

Legoland had a secret tunnel joining up with the Victoria line as it ran beneath the river, and Mason knew they could have people waiting for her on the other side if they mobilized fast enough. She also knew her bosses would want to handle this discreetly, without informing MI5. This was still unofficial.

"This is a bad idea," she said out loud.

i know what i'M doing.

Mason paused for half a step. "Who is this? How did you . . . ?"

MagiC. (only kidding.) it's Martyn.

"Asshole."

i Can hear you thru the phone MiC.

Mason was ready to give him plenty to hear. He was up for treason. And now—great—so was she. How would she explain this away? Sorry, I didn't know the strange messages on my phone were from Martyn. I thought they were from some other conspirator. Whatever level of trouble she'd been in before, she was past the point of no return now. "What the hell are you doing?"

keep Moving.

Mason was halfway across the bridge and could see that her tails had fallen back. This wasn't a quick grab. They wanted to see what she was doing, where she was going.

She was curious about both of those things herself.

Mason put the phone to her ear and started to speak. "Start talking.Ty ping. Whatever."

She felt the device buzz in her hand and pulled it away to look.

i Can't talk baCk to you. it's one way. long story.

follow My instruCtions. get ready to spring when i say.

Mason kept moving at an even pace. She touched her side, feeling the wound that had been stitched tight. "I don't know if I can run. I'm hurt."

Might need to.

At the end of the bridge, she reached a large circular tower block that managed to evoke both the future and 1960s ugliness. Those who ignored the past were doomed to redesign it.

down the steps.

A staircase between the building and the bridge led down to the path beside the Thames. Mason turned and started down them.

now run.

Mason broke into a flat-out sprint. She always wore dark slip-on trainers that were smart enough to pass as office wear. If Mason had been fully fit, she could have pulled away from them easily, but already she could feel the tightness in her side and a pain just beneath her lungs that tugged at each breath.

She was also drawing attention. People in the city were used to ignoring joggers. Especially at this time of day, they were intent on getting home, not paying any attention to those around them. But a woman running at high speed in office clothes? That was memorable.

The longer this carried on, the more likely it was that witnesses would be able to piece together a solid trail of her movements. And that was the best-case scenario. Mason didn't know how long she could keep it up.

two following you. one broken off. it's a net.

They would be trying to predict her movements, to get ahead of her to close in, or hang back and observe. left.

Cross the road.

Mason ran between the traffic, dodging cars that were moving in both directions. The other side of the street was lined with white town houses. At the end of the row of buildings was a small alleyway. Mason had been running at full burn for two hundred meters and needed to slow down.

turn in here.

Mason ran into the alley. It was a dead end, closed off by a brown brick wall.

CliMb the wall.

"Motherf—"

now.

She took a couple of seconds to control her breathing, then ran at the wall and launched herself just high enough to grab the top and pull up. She lowered down the other side, onto the grounds of the Chelsea College of Art. Her side felt raw, and the nerve endings were reenacting the stab with each breath. Mason pressed her hand to the pain, and her blouse stained r ed.

straight ahead. walk. fast.

London was the worst city in the world for tradecraft. CCTV covered every square inch, and the security services had access to satellites that could follow a person's every move. If Mason stuck close to the sides of buildings, she would be picked up on private security cameras in the shops and other businesses that lined the street. If she kept closer to the traffic, there was no cover from the satellites and state surveillance. Many of the surveillance systems would go down to minimum at quieter times, needing fewer resources to track people, but now, at rush hour, everything was operating at full capacity.

The training course for Mason's department included making it from the Tower of London to Wembley Stadium without being caught, all while being hunted by agents from both Legoland and Thames House. The training exercise was just about the only time the two agencies showed any unity, and the only circumstance—short of a declared state of emergency—in which Legoland was permitted to deploy agents on the British mainland.

Mason hadn't made it to Wembley. No agent was expected to get there. Passing marks came in the methods used to avoid detection and how long one lasted. Mason came within one mile of the stadium before being caught by two MI6 agents. It had been a source of pride in the department that Thames House hadn't been the ones to do it. Only two people had ever made it farther than she did, and they were the ones responsible for stopping her.

Tan Bashir had lasted an additional thirty minutes on the test and came within a hundred yards of Wembley. The second spoilsport had been Peter Cullis. He'd made it all the way into the stadium during his own test. His pursuers had eventually found him sitting with his feet up in the royal box, drinking a cup of coffee and eating a Cornish pasty. To this day nobody knew how he'd done it.

But now Mason was on the run for real. Wood's instructions led her in a loop around Erasmus Street and across to the junction of Rampayne Street and Vauxhall Bridge Road. He told her when to pause, when to pick up the pace, and when to change direction. Mason did as she was told each time, but with growing frustration. She was trained for this, while Wood was more used to sitting behind a desk. If he would just tell her the destination, Mason could handle it herself.

At the junction, he told her to stop and wait. Mason was only a few blocks up from where she had turned off at the river.

"You're using the cameras."

Cameras. phones. saturdays.

satellites.

"All that tech, and you don't have predictive text?"

shut it. get to the City bikes.

There was a docking station across the road. The traffic lights changed, and the cars came to a stop. Had Wood done that? Mason was now seeing signs of his interference in everything.

She couldn't tell if it was paranoia or common sense.

She crossed the street, hoping that none of the drivers was on the lookout for her.

i need to plan you a route. interferenCe on line. brb.

Mason took in her surroundings. The circular building she had mocked earlier provided cover from Legoland, so there was no direct line of sight to where she stood. The agents who had chased her weren't following. They must have taken a different route. But Mason saw two new spooks in her peripheral vision. They were walking away, up Vauxhall Bridge Road, and gave no indication of having seen her. So far, so good.

As she reached the row of city bikes, another message came through. third bike unloCked. working on a route. bear with.

As the words disappeared from the screen, a call came through. The number was unlisted, but Mason had an idea who it would be. She swiped to answer and put the receiver to her ear.

"What's going on?" Cullis's tone was calm. Measured. The tension was audible. "What are you up to?"

That answered one of Mason's questions. Cullis might have warned her to leave the building, but he wasn't working with Wood.

"If I knew what I was up to, I'd be a genius."

"Mase." She could picture him rubbing the bridge of his nose. "Buchan and Worthington have both called. Downing Street has already been told about the video. After Wood . . ." He paused. "Worthington wants you treated as hostile now. She's pushing for us to put Activists into the field after you. I can give you ten minutes to get back here before I make the call. You know what that means."

Mason killed the call. Her hand was shaking. If Department B was to be deployed on mainland Britain, that meant the prime minister had issued a terror alert. The Activists would be coming with instructions to take her dead or alive.

And if Downing Street had been called in during the time it had taken to leave the office and get here, that meant the situation had already been escalating to this point before she ran.

Lonnen had been right. The enemy was already making their move. This went right to the top, and Mason couldn't trust anyone. But how was Wood involved? Which side was he on? Either way, she needed to get to him. That was the best lead she had.

Wood came back on the screen.

soMeone trying to haCk.

will blaCk out CaMeras at your junCtion for five Minutes, but they Might be readin this. turn phone off for two hours.

Great. Mason was on the run from her own government, in the center of London, and she had no backup.

THIRTY-SIX

A lexandria teemed with life. The city reminded Chase of New York. It had been the original melting pot, where the ancient world met the dawn of the new age. The cultures of the Egyptians, Greeks, and Romans had fused into something that still informed modern life. Since the 2011 uprising, it had become the central hub of the illegal trade in stolen artifacts. Chase explained the city's history to Zoe as they traveled from the airport to the hotel, mostly to fill the silence between arguments.

Egypt had always had a problem with grave robbers. But over the past decade, the black market had exploded. Normal people took to the cities and deserts with digging equipment in order to support themselves and their families. Many of the country's most famous sites were now littered with fresh holes, and people were carrying out dangerous excavations in many towns and cities, risking the collapse of the buildings above.

In a worrying mirror of what had led to the civil war in Syria, Alexandria was now becoming crowded with people desperate for jobs, food, and safety. As Chase led Zoe down El-Nasr toward their hotel, they passed people speaking French, German, Arabic, and English. Cars old and new slipped past at high speeds. The air was filled with horns and exhaust fumes.

They heard music as they walked, drifting in from the waterfront. A regular rhythmic beat, with whistles and chanting. It sounded like a street party. But for Chase, it was always safer to find out what a crowd was celebrating before joining in.

Between stories, Chase watched Zoe for any sign of shock or stress. For Chase, a certain level of craziness had become normal. Her life fluctuated between boredom and excitement, with little in between. But even for her, shooting down helicopters with a machine gun was new, and she was rattled. She kept a lid on her inner turmoil to set a calm example for Zoe, but so far, her ex-girlfriend had shown no signs of worry. They were locked into the same cycle of silences and arguments they'd maintained ever since the shop, building toward something. Chase could feel it.

But the flight didn't seem to have changed Zoe's attitude at all. There was no concession, no pause to examine what they'd been through in the time since Chase walked back into her life. Zoe had taken it all in stride. Chase couldn't be sure how much of that was Zoe and how much was her own baggage.

Guerrero had stayed at the airport. He would meet them at the hotel after arranging for repairs to Molly. Her engines had cut out as the wheels touched down, and the wings were missing large chunks of metal. The chassis had been warped out of shape when Guerrero flipped her over. The bullet marks had been difficult to explain, though Guerrero had told the engineers that birds had started packing heat.

They turned off El-Nasr onto a narrow lane and came to a stop in front of a faded and cracked sandstone building. It didn't have any signs out front. They had walked past countless chain hotels, and Chase knew the night managers in many of them, but this was where she always stayed when she visited the city. Like Fell's Landing back in England, the Alexandria Royale was part of a network of restaurants, bars, and hotels across the world that was supportive of relic runners. The staff were discreet and knew how to keep the authorities at arm's length, and the hotel bar had become an unofficial neutral zone, a place where people on Chase's side of the law met to share trade secrets. Spooks and police would turn up to make deals and get information from the black market.

Chase checked them in and flirted with Ali, the elderly manager. He'd spent twenty years working for the Mukhabarat, Egypt's answer to the CIA, before deciding he could make more money by using his contacts to become a smuggler. He'd stayed in the trade until his knees and hips had given out. Now he ran the Royale and supplied accommodation, weapons, and information at reasonable prices. He knew Chase's flirting was just for show. They both pretended Chase hadn't fooled around with his daughter the last time she was in town.

"You here for dig?" Ali could speak flawless English, but he always made an act of a broken, stumbling version in front of newcomers like Zoe. Old training died hard, and he liked to be underestimated. "Wallace here yesterday. They hire everybody. Big, big team."

"Here for the same thing, but I'm not working for them. Have they found anything?"

"Rumors." He pursed his lips. "They think something beneath the church, maybe."

"Have they hired anybody who might talk to me?"

"Everyone nervous. Even in here, people think they're being watched, don't like to talk."

"What's the street party for?"

Ali grinned. "Music festival. Big idea. Try to help city's image. Show we big in the world again."

Chase showed him one of the drawings in Forrester's journal. "Do you know anything about people who have this tattoo?"

Ali's smile vanished. "Criminals," he said. "Not the good kind. Stay away from them."

Chase and Zoe made their way to separate rooms.

The accommodations at the hotel were like stepping back in time. Chase half expected Humphrey Bogart to walk in and start talking about beans. As soon as she'd dropped her bag on the bed, she stripped and stepped beneath the warm spray of the shower. The water came on in the staccato bursts of old plumbing.

She took her mind off the spray by thinking about Zoe. They were blowing hot and cold. There was a tension building, and the release had to come soon. Where would it stop?

Was Zoe waiting for Chase to make a move?

Did Chase want to make that move?

Back out in the room, Chase found a gift from Ali. He'd left a box on the bed, along with a note that read, Care package. It contained two Ruger Blackhawks, four boxes of ammunition, flares, and a few small explosive charges. Ali knew Chase's tastes. She was old-fashioned when it came to guns. A semi could carry more rounds, but she could see the moving parts on a revolver and trusted them to work in extreme conditions. She'd never been let down by a Ruger, and she liked the action on the Blackhawk.

Chase unfolded Forrester's maps onto the bed and studied each one closely. She loaded a specialist app on her cell phone, designed for smugglers and relic runners. Whereas standard trackers are only as good as their signal, this one gathered all GPS data for the city in advance and used the phone's built-in sensors, combined with Chase's adapted fitness watch, to track her movements and place her on the map. Chase wanted to find the entrances to the old tunnels, if any of them had survived. The music festival would give them the cover they needed.

Chase and Zoe took the twenty-minute walk to the bay. Under the clear night sky, the lights of the boats danced on the water in front of them. At the far end of the bay, jutting out into the water, was Fort Quaitbey, standing against the waves like a storybook castle. Quaitbey had been built on the ruins of the Pharos lighthouse. Farther along the Corniche was the site where Cleopatra's Needles had once stood. The traffic was congested here from dawn until dusk, but it wasn't difficult to imagine the waterfront as it would have been more than a thousand years before, with traders and fishermen coming in off the water, mingling with the locals, and visitors coming to pay respects at the temple.

There had been a time when sites like these had filled Chase with child-like excitement. Now they just served to remind her of how far she had strayed from the path.

The festival was in two public squares, fenced off from the near-constant traffic jams of the Corniche and Salah Salem. El Gondy El Maghool Square sat on the waterfront and led, via a long strip of grass and paving stones, to a second square, El Tahrir, forming a large T junction. The space was filled with tents, stalls, and a happy, dancing crowd. Chase led Zoe through the throng, dancing occasionally to the music and stopping at stalls. While Zoe tried on a selection of handcrafted hats, Chase scouted out a spot behind the tent.

Chase found what she was looking for, but there a new problem: They were being followed.

THIRTY-SEVEN

There was an art to being followed. In Mason's experience, most people got it wrong. They made stupid choices and got caught. As with every other part of the spy game, it was really pretty simple. The difference between those who lasted and those who didn't was how quickly people embraced the simplicity.

When being followed, a rookie mistake was to try to lose the tail straightaway. Deep down, there was an assumption that if you can't see them, they can't see you. That was almost never true. The best working principle was to think that they could always see you. It paid to level the odds and keep an eye on them.

She had taken Cullis's call on Vauxhall Bridge Road, on the corner of Rampayne Street. Pimlico tube station was at the other end of the road. Pimlico was known as Spook Station in the trade, hosting the entrance to a tunnel that ran parallel to the Victoria line and accessed both the basement of Legoland to the south and a few government buildings to the north. Anyone walking past Pimlico on foot could see a tunnel leading to a large car park beneath the station building. Most would assume it was for the nearby office block rather than for MI6.

Mason knew this street could be crawling with spies within seconds. The first thing she did was back away from the corner. She wheeled the bike along to a row of parked cars. Most of them were nondescript: Vauxhalls, Fords, Toyotas. She stopped at the most expensive one in the row, a shiny blue BMW convertible with the roof up. Mason used an electronic multi-tool from the equipment department to disable the alarm and unlock the doors. She put the bike across the back seat and settled in up front.

Within seconds, she watched both MI5 and MI6 staff converge on where she'd spoken to Cullis. A police car pulled up, and two officers got out, listening to orders from the spooks. Mason felt a brief swell of pride. She counted eight staff from the two agencies, some who would have been pulled back onto active duty just for this. And the cops would be relaying orders out across two police forces.

All this trouble for her.

The pride helped edge out the fear. The dark side of this, of course, was that she didn't know who could be trusted. The Visitologists had people in both the government and Legoland. It was safe to guess they'd worked their way into Thames House, maybe even the police. At this point, Mason was working on the assumption that the entire security establishment was compromised. That meant it was her versus the city of London.

Mason was fewer than a hundred yards from them, and nobody had noticed. Even as they looked at the road, trying to figure out which way she'd gone, they filtered out the expensive car right in front of them. People would look at a flashy car, like a Ferrari or an Aston Martin, but in London, BMWs were the cars of bankers and middle managers. The agents held a quick conference. A couple of them stepped to the bike station and touched the stand from which she'd taken her bike. They would be trying to trace it.

Mason used the tool to start the BMW's electronic ignition and pulled out, driving past them and turning down toward the river. Everything now was a game of minutes and seconds. Martyn's block on the cameras would have ended by now. She had maybe three minutes before facial recognition spotted her at a traffic light. It would cut down to seconds if she had to stop at a red.

Mason got the run of the lights for a mile along the river, then turned right, up into the private residential streets between the Thames and Victoria. She crossed Ebury Bridge, where she finally hit a red. It was time to change.

She pulled the BMW to the side of the road and kept the engine running. She left her jacket on the passenger seat, trading it for a baseball cap and tasteless mirrored sunglasses she found in the glove box. From there, she set off on foot into the small streets and mews to the west of Victoria.

Mason wanted to draw out the people who would be following her, to spend some time watching them. She'd be able to spot their tactics and get a feel for the personalities. She'd be able to guess who was calling the shots from the choices they made. And with that, she could guess at their blind spots.

As she walked in fast but random circuits of Ebury Mews, Chester Row, and Eaton Terrace, she took the chance to spot the people who were trying not to be spotted. They hung back at street corners and rotated regularly. Whoever was calling the shots, they were going through the playbook one page at a time. They were building a perimeter. It was called casting the net.

Let the subject walk, get a feel for the route they were taking, then throw the net over them from all sides. They were seeing their target stick to a small area. And she was making a show of looking for something, as if waiting for a rendezvous. The perimeter was slowly drawing in around her.

Once Mason was confident she had a feel for their numbers, it was time to lose them. And for this, she had to thank her ex. Sean had a few quirks. One of them was that he was obsessed with old London and hidden tunnels. He would regularly point out the site of a closed tube station or an abandoned air-raid shelter. A by-product of spending so long with him was that Mason knew the only routes in the whole of London that wouldn't be covered by surveillance. She took a couple of turns, ending up in Graham Terrace, where she scouted something out without stopping. At the end of the road, she looped back towards Sloane Square Station.

Mason bought a plastic bottle of water and two chocolate bars, paying the extra for two plastic bags, then stepped out onto the street and stood in front of the entrance to the subway station.

She turned on her phone.

"Can you still hear me?"

The reply popped up on screen:

yes. so Can they.

"Can you see where I am?"

yes.

Mistake.

That was good. Martyn was buying into the same assumption she wanted the authorities to make, that she was looking for cover to enter the subway system.

"Can you block the cameras?"

Mistake.

"I know. But do it."

three Minutes.

Mason had hoped for five but could do what she needed in three. It would just mean a little improvising. She cut into a small alley next to the station's entrance and climbed the metal gate. That would give her a few seconds out of sight of her followers, which was all she needed to lose them. At the end of the lane, she climbed a wall and ran along the top. On one side was a row of gardens; on the other was a long drop down to the uncovered subway platform. And that wasn't even the craziest part of her plan.

At the end of the wall, she lowered herself down into another lane and then ran out onto Whittaker Street. She took a quick look around. Nobody was on her yet. The trick with the wall had bought her time. Everyone would be looking at the map, trying to figure out which route she was taking, and she'd opted for one that wouldn't be on there.

One block over, she turned into Graham Terrace, where she had been a few moments before. At the end of the road was a manhole. It was different than the others, but only if you knew what you were looking for. This wasn't for a sewer or water pipe, and it wasn't for an electrical outlet. This was for something older that didn't show up on Google Maps.

London had several old rivers that had been diverted below ground and covered over. Some, like the Tyburn and Fleet, were still famous. There were many others that were now known only to geeks and surveyors, including the River Westbourne.

High tide was a couple of hours away. The level would already be dangerously high, but it was a risk Mason was willing to take to travel a few miles north without worrying about cameras. She took a look around, confirming nobody was on her. From her training, she knew the net had most likely closed in around Sloane Square, two blocks away. She lifted the manhole cover and climbed down the rusted rungs of the ladder set into the wall. The cover slipped back into place easily.

She undressed in the darkness, holding onto the ladder. After stripping down to her underwear, she slipped her clothes into the two plastic bags along with her electronic devices and purse and tied them closed at the top. Mason climbed down the rest of the way, through layers of metal, brick, and stone, into the cold water. She began swimming north, completely off grid, in the world's most on-grid city.

THIRTY-EIGHT

C hase had been keeping an eye on their tail for ten minutes. The foursome may have been following since the hotel, but she'd only seen them since joining the festival crowd. On a normal sidewalk they would have been able to blend in, but they stood out amid the dancing and celebration, moving along the edges, in tailored suits, with cropped hair.

Braun, and two men Chase took to be Visitologist security.

And there was a fourth: Youssef.

He was closer to Chase and Zoe than the others, flitting through the crowd. Chase caught sight of a bandage sticking up above his collar. There was a slight limp in his step. He always kept a few people between himself and Chase but never strayed too far away.

Nobody had made any aggressive moves yet.

The Visitology excavations were top secret, but the religion had made Alexandria its new home, and she knew they had established a large presence in the city. It was safe to assume they had already lined the right pockets and greased the right palms, making all the connections needed to get away with murder. She made her way back to Zoe.

"What's wrong?" Zoe asked, noticing Chase's tension.

"What? Nothing." Chase changed the subject. "This was where they killed Hypatia," she said.

Zoe looked around them again, as if taking in the area with fresh eyes. "Right here?"

"Right here."

Hypatia had been one of Chase's obsessions when she was studying on the Forrester scholarship. It had been understood that everyone who received the funding would publish work based on the history of Alexandria.

Most people chose Alexander himself, or the Ptolemies, maybe the dramatic stories of Anthony and Cleopatra. Kings. Pharaohs. Wars.

Chase had chosen the life and death of a teacher.

Hypatia had been one of the greatest minds of her age, a mathematician, philosopher, and astronomer who was largely responsible for keeping alive the traditions of Plato and advancing early ideas about the solar system. She was murdered in 415 ad, dragged out in front of the Caesareum and beaten to death by a mob of Christian fundamentalists. Chase hadn't made many friends in academia with her published piece, which had criticized not only the way history had treated some of its greatest women but also the way modern historians tended to write about them. It had been a subject she had spent many hours preaching to Zoe about.

"Feels like there should be a plaque or something," Zoe said, before adding with a sly smile, "With your name on it."

They had veered into their past. The next step would be another argument. She didn't have time for that.

"There used to be tunnels running all over the city," Chase said, avoiding the bait. "Most of them are gone, dug out for foundations or sewers. But there was one right beneath this square, and it might still be here. Forrester marked the entrance on a map."

Zoe started to ask a question, but Chase kept talking. "Don't look up. Don't react. We're being followed. But they don't have our map. When I say when, we're going to split up. I want you to stay in the crowd, but do two or three random circuits of the square. Keep changing direction. Then meet me inside the hat stall." Chase could see Zoe was already formulating a new question to ask. She didn't give her the chance, stepping away into the crowd and mouthing, "Go."

Chase pushed through the crowd in the opposite direction, heading for the end of the fenced-off area and the waterfront beyond. She could see Braun and one of the suits were still on her. That meant Zoe had the other two. But none of them had the advantage of knowing the exact spot where they would meet.

Chase picked up speed as she reached the barrier. The crowd parted to let her through.

"Magic."

Ryan Wallace was waiting.

He held two white plastic cups filled with dark liquid.

"I love this country," Wallace said. He offered Chase one of the cups.

"Everywhere you go, people say there's no alcohol, then offer you a drink."

Chase was aware of movement on either side of her. Braun and his goon had taken up positions but weren't closing in. Chase took the alcohol. She hoped the gesture would buy her some time to think, make it look like she was open to whatever they had to say. She raised the brim to her nose and sniffed. Smelled like rum. It would be enough to cover poison.

Wallace raised his own drink in toast. When Chase didn't match his gesture, he took a sip, then offered his own drink to Chase and reached out for hers with his other hand. They exchanged. Chase was still wary.

"It's just Morgan's. I'm not trying to kill you," Wallace said with a smile.

"You tried to kill me in Syria."

"Well, yes."

"Tried to shoot me down with helicopters."

"Okay, okay." Wallace put up a hand in mock surrender. "We've tried to kill you a few times, I agree. But my boss has noticed it isn't working. Let's just take a break, have a drink."

Chase put the cup to her lips, mimed enough of a sip to keep Braun and Goon thinking she was buying into what Wallace was saying. Wallace took a large swig of his own.

Chase indicated his drink. "Conscience bothering you?"

He downed the rum and sighed. He bent down to pick up a large thermos resting at his feet and poured himself another measure. "We want you on our side, Magic. The thing in Syria was my fault. Parish wanted both of us, but I was pissed at you."

"I don't work for terrorists."

He snorted. "No need to go to an extreme."

"I agree."

"They're not terrorists. They're believers. On the level. I've spent time with them, and they believe everything they say—the ancient science, the visitation. They're just doing what they think is right, to bring in some new age. Anyway, since when do we care about where our money comes from?"

Chase sipped the drink. The rum carried the odd taste that always comes with drinking from plastic, but the alcohol felt good. She took another pull. Wallace was right. She'd taken money from plenty of shady people. There was no moral high ground for her to climb up on.

"We're going to make history, Magic. Can you feel it? We're right here. He's right here."

"Alexander."

"Yes. He's right here, and we're going to find him. That statue? The one we took from Palmyra? It was from Alexander's tomb."

"That's not possible."

"I've seen it myself, the place they found out there. It's a temple. A shrine." He grinned, then pulled a small leather notebook from his jacket. Chase recognized it as another of Forrester's journals. "You could read this. If you're with us."

"The Visitologists stole the books."

"Well, it was that or let the Knights of Saint Mark get them."

Wallace smiled as he said it. He knew he was saying something Chase didn't understand, taunting her with knowledge.

"Knights?"

"The people who attacked you in London. That's what they call themselves. I think they just want to sound important. But we have this journal, and all the others. We have both sides of that torn page from the one you have. Come work with me, Magic. Put the band back together."

Both sides? The photocopy from Mason had only one side. Up until now, Chase hadn't given any thought to what was on the back. Did they have a map?

"What's on the table?" Chase drained half the rum and forced herself to relax, like the alcohol was kicking in. "How much they offering you?"

"Three million. Plus, my name goes on the discovery of the tomb, and I get media and book rights. They'll offer you the same money. The rights and the dig are mine, naturally."

"Naturally. And the weapon?"

He rolled his shoulders and leaned back on the barricade. "Their and went aliens stuff? Even if there's a thing down there, and even if it still works after two thousand years in the ground, they get it. We forget it exists. Just get our faces in front of the cameras and talk about the tomb, while they slip away with whatever we found."

"And when they use it?"

He shrugged. "We'll be far away from it, looking at our bank balances."

Chase finished her drink and held the cup out for a refill. Wallace smiled and nodded. He bent down for the thermos. As his head neared Chase's knee, she kicked him in the face. He fell back against the barricade, groaning. Chase saw Braun and Goon start to move, but they were too late. She vaulted the barrier out onto the Corniche and crossed the road, zigzagging between the near-stationary traffic.

Once Braun and Goon were halfway across the road, Chase ran back in the other direction, waving at drivers who slowed and shouting at those who didn't. Once she hit the sidewalk, she ran away from the festival. She hurried past the courthouse, and then left onto the next street. She sprinted down three blocks before taking another left, which led her back to the festival. Chase vaulted the barrier and slipped back into the dancing mass of people. Her gut tightened at the thought she would be too late.

Chase made it to the hat stall and saw Zoe dithering outside, looking around. Somehow, she'd evaded them. Her eyes were alive with the same spark Chase had fallen for all those years ago. The fun version of Zoe. The excitement. The danger. Chase grabbed her elbow and guided her through a gap between the stalls. They came out onto a patch of grass with a park bench. Next to the bench was an old rusted grille.

Chase pulled, and it lifted up. It gave way to reveal a hole. The entrance Forrester had marked, to whatever was left of the tunnels beneath the city.

There was nothing but blackness in the hole.

Great.

THIRTY-NINE

Chase swallowed back her fear. Not for the first time, her need to show off in front of somebody else was going to help keep her phobia in check.

She had a small collection of flares in her messenger bag, but they gave off too much light and would draw Braun to them. Instead, she pulled out a rubberized, battery-powered flashlight. She switched it on to its highest setting, and then let it fall into the hole. As it went, she caught glimpses of a rock wall, with hand- and footholds carved into the side.

There was a splash as the flashlight hit the floor of the tunnel.

Chase nodded for Zoe to go first, relying on her ex's own desire to look strong. After Zoe was in the hole, Chase took one last look around for Braun and then followed, bringing the grate back down over her. She climbed down hand over hand, foot over foot, telling herself that the darkness would only be temporary and focusing on the sound of Zoe moving beneath her.

She heard splashing as Zoe found the floor. A few seconds later, Chase's own feet touched down into a few inches of water. She prepared for the smell of sewage, but it didn't come. The water must have just been collected rain from the entrance above them. Chase also remembered Turner saying that many of the older remains had subsided down to the water table. This whole passage probably flooded on a regular basis.

Zoe had already switched on the flashlight setting of her phone, and Chase picked up her own flashlight. She focused on getting her bearings instead of on the darkness that lay at the edges of the beams. They were one hundred feet down. The walls around them were carved from solid rock. Chase pointed for them to head south. The ground inclined slightly, just enough to get clear of the water, and then the tunnel veered left after a few hundred yards. They passed a section that looked to have caved in, replaced by the large bricks of a building's foundation.

The air was growing warm and damp. A familiar foul odor filled their nostrils and forced them to close their mouths. The passage narrowed slightly. They came to the end of the tunnel, where it opened onto a modern sewage pipe.

Zoe shot Chase a look. "Is this a metaphor for our relationship?"

Chase smiled. "Be careful where you step."

"Just know, if I slip in here, I'm pulling you in after me."

They shined their flashlights around, and Chase saw that the passage continued on the other side of the sewer. There was a plank of wood at their feet, leaning lengthwise along the wall. With Zoe helping to take the weight, they pushed it out across the sewer, connecting with the entrance on the other side. They made their way across the makeshift bridge and then pulled the plank in after them. The passage turned left again and narrowed further. In a few places, they saw more brick walls beneath the stone, the foundations of a new building partially destroying the old network.

After a few hundred yards, Chase loaded up the map on her phone. She wasn't surprised to find she didn't have a signal, but she didn't need one. The app had been tracking her steps the whole time. It knew where she was, though it couldn't place her on a modern street. She swiped the city map to the right, which loaded an image of the next layer down, subway and sewer pipes.

The app couldn't find her there, either. They weren't in any passage known to the maps of Alexandria.

The pulsating blue dot placed them somewhere beneath a short lane called San Mark—a variation of Saint Mark. There was that name again.

Chase thought of what Wallace had said, that the statue in Syria had come from Alexander's tomb. Another lion. It was possible that the road above them was the remnant of a much-older street. If it bore the saint's name, it may well have led to an important site.

Sounds came from the direction they had just walked. There was the unmistakable scuffing of boots on stone, followed by a splash. Someone had

slipped into the sewage.

They weren't alone in the tunnel.

Chase pushed Zoe to move. They hurried along the tunnel, trying to put distance between themselves and whoever was wading through the muck. They came to a dead end, where the passageway had been closed off with a wall. It was made not of modern brick but of something older. Maybe sandstone. Someone had decided to block off this tunnel a long time ago.

Why?

Chase turned back to face the way they had come. She didn't know how long they had, but their pursuers would soon have them cornered. They couldn't run; they'd need to fight. She reached into her messenger bag for one of the revolvers. Its grip in her hand was a brief comfort.

Chase heard a scraping sound coming from behind her. Zoe let out a startled gasp. One of the large sandstone blocks was sliding backward, into the wall. After a few seconds it was gone, leaving a small opening low down.

It was big enough for Chase and Zoe to crawl through.

A face appeared in the hole.

Georgie Turner.

"Come with me," she said.

FORTY

C hase had a million questions, but Turner disappeared back into the hole.

Zoe made the decision for both of them, getting down on her knees to follow Turner. Chase brought up the rear, taking one last look behind. The distant glow of flashlights was bouncing off walls farther down the tunnel. The Visitologists were closing in.

Chase crawled through into a cramped space. The roof of the old tunnel was gone here, replaced with metal girders and wooden beams at shoulder height. The light of a halogen lamp filled the chamber around them. Zoe was pressed against one wall, glaring at Turner, who was crouched on the opposite side. Turner was dressed in long dark robes, a semiautomatic strapped to her side. Youssef was next to her, carrying the same weapon.

Zoe started to speak, but Turner put a finger to her lips and then nodded at Youssef. He began pushing the large stone back into place. He grunted and pulled one arm back, and Chase saw bandages sticking out beneath the cuff. She helped him push the stone back into place, and then they stayed silent in the small space and listened.

Voices approached the wall. Chase could hear a muffled argument between Braun and Wallace.

"No other way—"

"Well, there has to be, doesn't there?"

"I don't understand."

"That's my job. You're the bloodhound."

The voices faded as they went back along the tunnel, looking for the turn they assumed they'd missed. Once they were gone, Chase turned back to face Turner, but Zoe got in first.

"What—"

"Long story." The old woman smiled. She was probably aiming for enigmatic but only managed annoying. "Sound carries down here; we should stay quiet until we're safe. Youssef will lead the way."

Youssef set off down the tunnel in a crouch. His injured arm hung down at his side, used only occasionally to steady himself against the wall. Turner went next. Zoe didn't move straightaway. She paused, composing herself. Chase touched her arm and could feel the anger radiating off her. For the first time, Chase really understood that Zoe's emotional stake in all this was just as raw as her own, maybe more so. Chase had a million questions to ask Turner, but for Zoe, this was about family. Had Turner betrayed the Forrester Foundation?

Chase touched Zoe's arm a second time, offering support. Zoe nodded, swallowed something back, and set off after the old professor.

The journey was like an obstacle course. In some places, they had to climb over water pipes that shot through the walls; in others they had to crawl under beams. There was a second sewer crossing, but this one had a metal bridge rather than the makeshift wooden one. They took a sharp left into a new tunnel, narrow with modern brick walls on either side. They had to turn sideways to squeeze through. Once the passage opened out again into one of the old water tunnels, they were able to stand up fully.

Chase checked on her map and saw they were heading straight for the church.

They came to a stop at a dead end. Turner held up the halogen lamp above her head. There was a hole in the ceiling. Youssef pointed with his good arm to a metal ladder sticking out over the hole. Chase jumped up and grabbed the end, pulling the ladder down into the tunnel. Youssef braced it with his foot while Turner, Zoe, and then Chase climbed up.

He didn't follow them.

They emerged in a tight room with a low ceiling and plain stone walls. There was a crawl space low down in the wall ahead of them.

"There are two other entrances to the tunnel," Turner said. "Youssef'll watch our backs."

"I'm not sure that's a good idea," Chase said.

"Because you set him on fire?"

"Well, yeah . . ."

"He's loyal to me, and I'm protecting you. But I wouldn't get too close to him." Turner looked around the small chamber. "We can talk here, but we should keep it low."

"You mean you don't want me to shout at you."

Turner smiled. "Just do it quietly."

"Start talking," Zoe said. She managed to fit in all the anger and intent of a shout without raising her voice.

"We protect this place. Keep it secret."

Chase leaned in closer. "Who is we?"

Turner pulled up the black sleeve on her robe. On the inside of her forearm, about halfway up, was a tattoo of a winged lion.

"The Knights of Saint Mark."

Zoe looked caught off guard by that. "They have female Knights?"

Turner smiled. "We're an equal opportunity secret society." She dropped the humorous tone. "The head of the order is usually a woman." She made eye contact with Chase. "Including Hypatia. That's the real reason she was killed."

"What?"

"We've been in the city since 323 BCE, passing the mantle down to each generation, but there aren't many of us left. Two world wars, the thing with Israel, the 2011 uprising. We're down to the last few bodies. The Forrester Foundation was our life support, but that's gone."

"That's where the money went," Zoe said. Her tone was the same as when she and Chase had discussed the foundation in the cemetery—the old resentment.

Chase saw Zoe's side of the foundation debate for the first time. Before, it had felt personal, like the Forresters resented Chase and the other students. Now Chase could see it ran deeper. Henry Forrester had been pouring his money into some secret that even the family didn't know about. It must have felt like he didn't care about them. What could that kind of deep hurt do to a family?

Turner nodded at Zoe. "The real purpose of the Forrester Foundation was to find people worthy of recruiting for the Knights. They found me, and then I started looking for the next generation." She let that hang a beat, staring at Chase. "You."

All of Turner's anger toward Chase over the last decade made even more sense now. It wasn't just disappointment at her career choices. She would have been next in line.

Turner continued. "So, you can imagine, when you started selling history off to the highest bidder, I knew it was only a matter of time."

"When you were trying to warn me off doing this . . ."

"I was actually warning you off, yes."

"And the attack at Brompton. Stanley and Youssef."

"I'm sorry for the way that went. Stanley and I, we haven't always agreed on how to handle things. I set up camp across from Cleopatra's Needle. I knew if you figured that bit out, you'd end up here. When I saw you with that other woman, I caught the next flight."

Chase could feel Zoe staring at her. Chase's trip to the Needle, along with the idea that she'd found anything there, came as news. Or was it just the bit about the other woman?

"Did you know about Stanley's plan?" she asked. The real question was, Did you let me walk into the trap?

Turner paused before saying, "I'd hoped you'd drop it." The real answer was, Yes, I left you to die.

"They tried to burn me alive." Chase took a step back. She put her hands on her hips and stared at the dusty floor, controlling her breathing. She fought back her next thought. Then again, a second time. By the third, she couldn't. "You tried to burn me alive."

Turner's face crumpled. She seemed to lose an inch in height. "I'm sorry, that wasn't— That wasn't right. Stanley can be overzealous. I wouldn't have okayed that if I'd been there. Never in a million years, I wouldn't."

"You just wanted them to kill me nicely?"

Turner didn't reply. Chase wanted to lash out and boil over. But the same part of her brain that kept her alive told her now that they needed to focus on why they were all there.

She pushed through the anger to find pedantry. "Saint Mark established Christianity in Egypt. So he can't have had Knights here in 323 bC."

"This is not our original name. We changed it when Christianity arrived, to hide away in plain sight. But we were here, keeping the secrets—by force, if we had to."

"And what, exactly, is the secret you're protecting?"

Turner pointed to the crawl space. "After you."

FORTY-ONE

T he crawl space led to a large chamber the size of a church. There were engravings and hieroglyphs lining the walls, along with large chunks of stone that seemed to have been moved from somewhere else. A metal ladder in the center of the room led up to a hole in the ceiling. Beyond the ladder, in front of the far wall at the end of the chamber, was a large stone altar.

Chase down set her messenger bag on the altar and studied the room. There was an archway behind the trio, which had been filled with rocks during a cave-in. Chase figured it must have been the original entrance. On the pillars to either side of the arch, she could make out the cracked and broken remains of two statues. On one side was Anubis, and on the other was the Minotaur.

"They don't belong together," Chase said. "They're from two different cultures. Different centuries."

Turner didn't reply. She was apparently waiting to see what Chase could put together herself. On either side of the broken statues, carved into the wall, were the same markings that surrounded Forrester's tomb. Chase followed them around to the right and found two large scenes etched into the wall, surrounded by more of the unknown glyphs. Two figures with human proportions fought each other; one was holding a bolt of lightning.

"The Titanomachy. War of the Gods. That's Greek, too."

"Not necessarily," Turner corrected gently. "All of the ancient religions had wars between gods as part of their foundational myths. Even in the bible, God refers to other gods early in Genesis, before Babel."

Chase turned to the next wall, which ran the length of the chamber. The writing continued. Halfway along, the markings changed to Egyptian hieroglyphs.

There was a figure she recognized: Akhenaten, the Heretic King. He stood beneath a large disc.

"Aten," Chase said.

"That's right." Turner smiled.

Zoe sighed. "In English?"

Chase jumped at the chance to explain. She forgot all her anger at Turner with the opportunity to impress her mentor and show off for her ex. "Egypt was a polytheistic culture. They believed in a pantheon of gods. Different cities would give tribute to different gods, and they all came together under the worship of the Pharoah's approved deity, Ra, Amun, etc. Then, around 1350 BCE, Akhenaten came to the throne." Chase looked for a nod of approval from Turner over the date. "He announced that all the older gods were dead and founded a new state religion, based around one god, Aten. He demanded that the whole country convert to the new beliefs."

"That never goes well," Zoe said.

"It didn't. Akhenaten's reign lasted for around twenty years. His religion, Atenism, died with him. After he was gone, the priests of the older gods pushed back, and the country returned to polytheism. Akhenaten's temples and statues were defaced in an attempt to wipe him from history. Even

Akhenaten's son changed his name. From Tutankhaten, to Tutankhamun." Zoe's eyes flashed with recognition of the last name.

"Well summed up." Turner said. "That's the pop culture version. The truth is different, of course. Akhenaten didn't wipe away the other gods. At least not right away. He didn't change his name to incorporate Aten until the fourth or fifth year of his reign, and all the other gods were still tolerated until his later years. It was more of a gradual process. At first he simply changed the one that the state officially prayed to. And it wasn't really monotheism, not as we know it. He prayed to one god, but the people of Egypt had to pray to Akhenaten. Like a middle man. So it was as much a political power grab as a religious reformation, he took the power away from all the priests and temples. And, as this temple shows, Atenism didn't start with Akhenaten, and it didn't end with him. His reign was just a short period when an existing religious cult managed to grab political power."

Turner walked to the first wall, beside the archway. Chase followed. Teacher and student, falling back into a familiar pattern.

Turner touched the markings. "We don't really know what this is. Or, rather, who. It looks a lot like Linear A, with a little bit of hieratic, but also both Henry and myself trace some Hurrian. Here also," she touched a section, tracing the inscriptions, "almost Proto-Hebrew, the language that existed in the Sinai and Negev areas before the emergence of Hebrew."

"Not possible," Chase said. "Not all of those languages are even related."

"That we know of," Turner shrugged. "But even in the bible, there are countless names of tribes or people we don't know other than a passing mention. We don't even really know where Abraham came from, except educated guesses. And we don't know where Linear A came from, or the language that came before it."

Chase breathed the information in for a moment before looking back at the text. "How old is it?"

"No idea. Five thousand years old, maybe. Forrester thought it was double that."

Chase began to say not possible a second time, but the words died in her throat with a sigh.

Turner gave a patient nod that seemed to say, I know. "Atenists believed it was the language of the gods. The Visitologists would probably say it was aliens. If we accept the dates for a moment, this is the oldest written myth." She pointed to the image of the god holding lightning, and then to a small glyph beneath it. Stepping across to the wall that showed Akhenaten, she pointed to an Egyptian symbol. The two were close enough to be related. "We can see this word being adapted into Egyptian. It's the symbol for Aten."

Zoe stepped forward to touch the first image, running her finger along the lightning. "So you're saying this Atenism is the oldest religion?"

"Not really. It's old, we know that. But is it a religion in the way we think of today?" Turner moved back to stand beside Zoe. She touched the symbol for Aten. "This isn't the name of the god. This is the name of the lightning." She led them to the stones that were arranged around the room. "We've brought most of these here, hiding them away."

Two of the stones showed Akhenaten ruling over people. In the first, the pharaoh was holding a bolt of lightning. In the third, he was holding a different object. It looked like an arrowhead and matched the symbol from Forrester's tomb, the one Chase had taken for Thor's hammer. A third was painted, rather than engraved. It showed a fairly standard depiction of Alexander, with a sword in one hand and two horns in his hair. He was also holding a bolt of lightning. Chase had seen that image many times, and historians believed it showed Alexander to be aligned with Zeus. But in this new context, Chase could see it meant a whole lot more.

"Pop culture steps in again. Aten is mistranslated as a sun god, when, really, it was an aspect of god. An element. A power." Turner pointed to a fourth stone. This one was a different color, more like sandstone. It showed a bearded figure holding a large staff. "This is Sumerian. They believed in a god called Ninurta, and he held a weapon—a mace—that could level mountains."

"Sharur," Chase said, naming the weapon. She was familiar with the legend. "Translates as smasher of thousands."

"Yes," Turner said. "And it's a pattern that runs through the ancient cultures. The Germanic pagans had Thor. The Celts had Taranis. The Hittites had Pirwa. The Romans sometimes gave Hercules a magic club. All of them show the same idea, a weapon that holds great power."

"You're saying they all trace back to this?"

"Possibly. But that's just our speculation. Different cultures can come to similar ideas independently. Pyramids. Magic swords." Turner waved at the statues in the archway. "I look at those things and see the same as you. Anubis and Minotaur. Egyptian and Greek. But we don't know what the people who carved them saw. What we do know is that Atenism at its heart was idolatry, they worshipped an item, their god was the item, not a higher being represented by statues."

Turner moved along the wall again, to a collection of red-hued rocks that had clearly been moved here from somewhere else. They were engraved, in pale white lines, with the same root language as the archway.

"We found these in the Sinai," she said. "There's still so much we don't know about the religions of that region. How many older gods and cults were wiped out by Egyptian invasion, or assimilated into Israel. There seems to have been a strong presence of Aten worship there, in and around what later became the copper mines, and the range of mountains in the Timna Valley. Further north and east, these inscriptions vanish. It seems like Atenism couldn't get past a wall of cults dedicated to early Yahwism. But it was able to spread this way instead, across the lakes and delta, taking hold here."

"And you said they worshipped an idol? An actual Aten?"

"Yes. The Aten is a real object. Alexander found it when he came to Egypt. Hidden here, on the coast, in a buried temple. He said that to touch it was to bond with it. Become one with the gods, and draw on their knowledge and power. He claimed this knowledge helped him rule. Would have swept clean through India and on to China."

"What stopped him?"

"His sister. Thessalonike. She was the first of us, the founder of the Knights. She recognized that the Aten was corrupting Alexander's mind, poisoning him. She stole it, hid it away, and without it Alexander grew sick and died."

"Why just hide it? If it's so bad, destroy it."

"She tried. But it couldn't bend, break or melt. It was made of an unbreakable material. Something like stone."

"So she hid it."

"Not just her. Us. She gathered together a trusted group, from his family and lieutenants, and swore them to an oath to guard the Aten and to keep humans from destroying themselves with it."

"A relic of mass destruction." Chase laughed.

Even to her own ears, the laughter was nervous and hollow. Up until that moment, Chase hadn't really had any belief in the idea that Alexander had been buried with some ancient weapon. Finding the journal and maps had given her enough to think the tomb could be found, but she'd only been expecting to find a corpse. Now, this seemed all too real.

Turner ignored Chase's joke. "We've been here ever since. At first, we hid the Aten, but we couldn't stop people from visiting Alexander's grave. He was too famous. We kept the Aten safe from invaders, like Zenobia, who came looking for it." Zenobia was a Syrian queen who had ruled from Palmyra around six hundred years after Alexander's time. The last piece of a larger puzzle fell into place. That was what Al-Salif had been digging up in the desert. They'd found a link between Zenobia, Alexander, and the Aten.

"Alexander had become a pagan god," Turner continued. "The lion was one of his symbols. When Christianity came in, Alexander's worshippers adapted their customs. They adopted Saint Mark as a cover, a way to continue worshipping their own god while appearing to be Christian. We did the same. We buried ourselves away in the Coptic Church. After the tsunami in the fourth century, we took the chance to bury the Aten with Alexander and hide the entrance to the tomb. We started a game of telephone with travellers, giving different locations for the tomb, editing the legends, and never mentioning the Aten. Over the years, we had people in control of city planning. We designed the sewers, the new roads."

"And the Atenists? Were they still around?"

"We've never been sure." Turner pointed to a section of wall near the altar. "The inscriptions there are Demotic, the language that came after the hieroglyphs. So we know they were still here near to the time of Alexander. But this temple was abandoned when we found it."

Zoe cut in. "Why not just let people know? Explain why you've been doing it? You're hiding history from people."

"We believe in history. We believe in preserving people's faiths and customs, and especially their knowledge. But we believe they all belong to the people who believe in them, nobody else. Islam belongs to Muslims. Christianity belongs to Christians." She looked at Chase directly. "Judaism to the Jews. And more than that, Yahwism in its original form, belongs to the tribes of the Sinai and Negev, who no longer exist. And here, we believe that the ancient customs and beliefs of Egypt belong to the people of the past, it's not our place to steal them, co-opt them, or put them in museums." Turner gestured again at the ancient language. "Whoever they were. Whether you want to see them as the gods, or as aliens, or as ancient humans. Whatever your belief of choice, it doesn't hold a greater importance than their own beliefs."

"None of what you're saying makes sense." Chase found a kernel of anger beneath the confusion. "You have to know that. None of *this*," she waved around the chamber, "is *history*. It's certainly not archaeology. There's no context here. You have tablets dragged from somewhere else. Vague ideas of a weapon and some lost cult. There's nothing here to work with. I don't see anything that proves all of this belongs together, or that it wasn't just an ancient form of hoax. People cobbling disparate myths together after the fact."

Zoe wasn't ready to give up on her own line of thinking. "But this thing. This Aten. Whatever it really is. Maybe it can help people. If it has power, maybe modern technology could control it better than Alexander could. You could be sitting on something that could change the world, for the better."

Turner shook her head, just once. "If scientists hadn't split the atom yet, and you found plans for a nuclear bomb, would you hand them over to the world? If the Chinese hadn't found the formula for gunpowder, would you want to uncover it? We're not talking about something that can be used for good. The Aten has poisoned the soul and body of everyone who's tried to control it. No human should be allowed to have it. Nobody. If the Visitologists get close, we'll kill them." She paused. There was a hesitation in her words. "But I thought you deserved an explanation first."

Turner raised her gun.

She pointed it at Chase and squeezed the trigger.

FORTY-TWO

Mason felt another swell of pride. In all, she had counted ten members of MI6 staff and eleven from MI5. She believed there had also been five plainclothes police officers, but that was a guess.

She sipped a coffee and looked out across the concourse at Paddington Station. So far, so good. She was going unnoticed in one of London's busiest train stations. That would have been something to put on her next performance appraisal form, if she had been likely to get one.

She hadn't stayed in the river long. The Westbourne was mostly contained in culverts beneath the city streets, and in a few places, she had needed to go beneath the water and swim on ahead, blind, in the hope there would be headroom farther on. That wasn't a risk she was willing to keep taking. Swimming against the current was tiring, and the stab wound was hurting, both from the exertion and possibly from bacteria in the water.

After a mile and a half, she came to the place she'd been looking for.

Originally, the Westbourne had been connected to the Serpentine, a lake in Hyde Park. More recently it had been diverted, but there were still manhole access points in the park. Mason climbed out beneath the shade of a tree, next to a monument that marked the site of the river. There was a restaurant overlooking the lake. It had been closed for a couple of hours, and Mason let herself in through the back door. In the bathroom, she used paper towels to dry off. There was an assortment of clothes left in the staff room. Mason found an oversize jumper that would change her shape and a pair of jeans that must have belonged to the skinniest person in human existence. She squeezed into them, but they weren't comfortable.

The parks were one of the best places to hide in London, as there wasn't the same volume of cameras. She helped herself to food from the kitchen and relaxed onto a sofa, waiting until it was time to switch her phone back on.

When the specified time passed, she took a deep breath and powered up the device. This would put her back on the grid. She could get messages from Martyn, but Legoland would also be able to track her location. She would have a few minutes at most before they would be in the park.

The screen loaded. Mason watched as the phone searched for a network connection.

A message appeared:

> speak when you're baCk on.

"I'm here," Mason said.

After a few seconds, Martyn responded.

> i have a bloCk on the phone now that will last three Minutes. but they will have pinged your loCation when you switChed on. here's the plan.

Martyn's plan had been a bad one. He'd wanted her to incapacitate a police officer, swap clothes, and use their radio to listen in on the chatter and avoid capture. From there, she could head out to the East End, where there were fewer cameras and more ways to stay hidden. It sounded like something out of a spy movie. Mason had talked him around to the Paddington idea. Time was on her side, because they couldn't afford to argue the point in the few seconds they had. The station was close to the park and the last place anyone would suspect. What kind of spy would choose one of the most secure places in London to try to lose someone?

Only a fool. Or Mason.

She'd left the phone resting on a bench by the lake. On her way out of the park, she had seen four men entering, heading straight toward it. On the short walk to Paddington, she had spotted the rest of the team. Sitting in vans, walking dogs, pretending to be in arguments. The advantage of the security services being stood down from operations was that many of their best staff were out of town. She was the one with the edge.

Inside the station, Mason bought a coffee from a kiosk by a ticket machine and a Cornish pasty from the stall beneath the departures board. She looked directly at security cameras a couple of times, happy to be seen. Let them start building a new net. Mason wasn't hungry, but the pasty came in a brown paper bag, which would be useful. She settled in next to the stall and watched the entrances.

Most office workers had already gone home for the evening. At this time, it was the stragglers waiting for the lonely commute and people coming back into the city for a night out. As she watched the security services file into the station, Mason knew she'd made the right choice. Two men in suits headed for the manned ticket desk to speak to the manager and find a list of all tickets that had been sold in the last hour. Next, they needed two people for each platform, covering all bets. Mason saw one person take up each exit and imagined there would be more outside. Each of the lifts and escalators needed to be covered. Mason held back a smile as everything went to plan. Their resources were spread thin across the station, with no idea of what she was intending to do.

A train pulled slowly into platform seven, directly in front of Mason. She let everyone see her watching it, but didn't make a move. The doors opened on the left side of the train, and a handful of passengers stepped down and started filing out through the ticket barriers. Mason stepped forward, as if to head for the train, then turned away again, keeping her watchers guessing. She avoided eye contact with them, adding to their guessing games.

A PA announcement heralded the arrival of a second train on platform eight. The lights were already visible, growing larger. Two people started slowly making their way toward her from each side. She recognized one as Mark Bowen, MI5's chief field officer. The other was a woman; she looked new, and nervous. The new train slid in beside the previous arrival and the doors opened on the right side, onto the platform. A large crowd started to pour out and make their way towards the barrier, wearing football colors and singing loud, drunken songs.

A young man was moving fast ahead of the crowd. Mason read him as nervous, wanting to put distance between himself and the rowdy fans. He looked to be a tourist, carrying a plastic shopping bag and pulling a wheeled suitcase behind him.

Mason could see Bowen and the security staff hesitate, now needing to worry about the football crowd.

She stepped forward and grabbed the hand of the tourist as he stepped out through the gate. He smiled, but Mason could see panic in his eyes. An animal in the headlights. Was it the fear of being grabbed by a stranger, or the thought of holding a conversation with a woman? She leaned in and whispered a bad joke to him, too quiet for the security staff to hear. Mason let the security staff see her drop the brown paper bundle into the shopping bag before setting the tourist loose. That split her tails' attention further. Was this a drop-off? A rendezvous? Was this tourist an enemy spy?

Mason could feel the younger spook pause. The hesitation was telling— she would be looking for a cue from Bowen. When it didn't come immediately, Mason vaulted the ticket barrier onto platform eight, almost falling on the other side. The jeans were more restrictive than she'd thought. After landing on her heels on the other side, she sprinted toward the train. She heard two agents hitting the floor behind her. Shoes squeaked on tile, and she didn't need to look back to know she was being chased.

Mason pushed through the football crowd, drawing tuts and shouts and a couple of attempted grabs, but it also made it more difficult for the agents to follow. One of them slowed, blocked by the people who'd stopped to stare at Mason. The second had been smart. He'd gone wide and was now outpacing Mason along the platform.

Mason checked her run and jumped through an open train door and moved quickly along the carriageway. At the next exit, she turned away from the open door, and pulled the emergency exit lever on the one opposite, beside the other train. The mechanism engaged with a hydraulic hiss, and she bent down to find the same controls on the outside of the next train. Once she had that door open, she stepped across, and then through, and down to platform seven.

She had a clear run now, but it wouldn't be for long.

Mason got her head down and ran back toward the barriers. In the mess of shouts and confusion, she had a few seconds before people would spot what she'd done and regroup. She vaulted the barriers again, this time allowing for the lack of give in the jeans, and sprinted flat-out for the side door. Two agents tried to grab at her, but she was already up to speed, and neither would be able to catch her in the short distance she needed.

Mason turned onto Eastbourne Terrace and looked for the car Martyn had promised. She could see a hack cab farther along the road, overtaking a bus and heading in her direction. It was driving too recklessly to be on normal duty. This was her ride.

Mason heard a familiar voice from behind. "Mase."

She turned to see Cullis. He was leaning against the black railing. He wasn't out of breath; he'd been waiting here. He stepped toward her, holding a gun.

"You need to listen to me," he said. "I can help. Lonnen hasn't been telling you—"

The cab pulled in. Both Cullis and Mason looked at the black vehicle. Mason reacted quicker, pulling Cullis's gun hand toward her and turning into the move, hitting him with her left elbow. He fell back, and Mason dove into the cab through the open door.

"Stay down," a muffled voice called out from the front seat. She heard the engine gun and fingers tapping on an electronic device. There was a series of beeps. Then a computer voice said, "Active."

Mason stayed out of sight. The driver swerved left, then right. She heard car horns and shouting, then something that sounded suspiciously like a bullet. Someone would be in trouble when they got back to HQ. After that, there were sirens and even more car horns. They banked hard to the left. Mason guessed it was onto Edgeware Road.

Then a right. Where were they? Cabbell Street? What were the others? Mason tried to remember the maps she had studied during her training. Another right. Hard. The sirens were distant now. Then a left. They went up some kind of ramp, with the sound of metal beneath the wheels, then came to a stop in darkness.

Mason sat up. They were parked in a narrow container. The back of a lorry?

The driver got out and stepped to her door.

He opened it, and leaned in.

Mason looked up into the face of Adam Parish.

Parish sprayed something into her face. Mason felt instantly lightheaded, then dizzy. Her throat was tight. Her lungs were shutting down. Mason's arms seemed to fade away, and her face hit the floor of the cab.

Mason heard Parish in the distance, before everything went black, saying, "Thanks for your help." Then something else, which sounded like,

"For the old ones."

FORTY-THREE

"Wait," Chase called out in the second before Turner pulled the trigger.

It was just enough to throw off Turner's aim. Chase pitched to the right, and the semiautomatic fired high and wide to the left. The sound of gunfire bounced around the room, drowning out all other noise. Chase had thrown herself off balance and couldn't stop from hitting the floor. As she rolled, she heard a gasp of pain. Chase turned to see Zoe clutching her leg. One of the bullets had ricocheted off the ancient stone wall and hit her. Chase didn't have time to check the wound. She concentrated on the problem at hand.

Where were her own guns?

In the messenger bag . . .

Where was the bag?

She'd put it down.

Before Chase could reach for her guns, Turner spun to aim the gun at Zoe, the fallen target and easiest shot. Chase leapt to her feet and threw herself into Turner. The old woman had surprising strength and didn't go down. Chase and Turner grappled with each other, fighting for control of the gun. They fell together into the sharp edge of the stone altar. Turner spun as she fell and grunted when her shoulder took the impact.

The turn had thrown Chase into the stone first, and she hit her head. She slumped to the floor. Her head swam as she looked up at the gun

Turner was aiming directly at her face. Chase heard the bang, but then Turner staggered and fell to the floor. She dropped the semiautomatic weapon.

Zoe was standing behind her, with one of Chase's revolvers. She'd shot Turner in the back. Her hands were shaking, and the color had drained from her face; early signs of shock. Chase climbed to her feet and gently took the gun from Zoe, then made eye contact, smiling at her and saying, "It's okay."

Chase looked down at Zoe's leg. There was a large bloodstain on her pants, but it didn't seem to be slowing her down. That was a problem that could wait. Chase looked down at Turner. The old woman's breath was coming in jagged, staccato bursts. Her hands were twitching, but her legs weren't moving.

Chase bent over her. Before she could speak, her head cleared, and she realized she could still hear gunfire. It was coming from the tunnel, where Youssef had been standing guard.

"They're coming," Chase said. She handed her messenger bag to Zoe and pointed to the ladders, waving for her to start climbing.

Turner coughed. Chase could see the older woman didn't have long. She found herself rooted to the spot, feeling as though she was watching the scene from a distance, trying to figure out how to feel about it. Grief was the most powerful of the emotions pulling at her insides. Through the shock and the betrayal, there was still pain.

How differently would things have gone if Chase had never strayed from the honest path? If she hadn't started to sell off history, piece by piece? Turner could have trusted her with this secret, maybe even initiated her into the Knights of Saint Mark.

Though Chase had never been one for club membership.

"They can't." Turner coughed. "They can't find . . ." Her eyes turned to focus on Chase. "You've got to stop . . . I'm sorry."

Tears welled in Turner's eyes, even as the light went out behind them. Chase held her dead teacher for a moment. Then she heard a pained scream drift through the tunnel, and the gunfire stopped. Youssef was done.

Chase touched Turner's forehead in a brief goodbye, picked up the automatic rifle, and climbed the ladder.

Zoe was waiting for her at the top. They were in a modern sewer system. Someone had built up a low brick wall around the hole, like a well, to keep the water and sludge from dripping down. There was a metal lid resting against the side of the tunnel, which Chase guessed Turner and Youssef must have moved when they came in that way. Chase and Zoe worked together to lift the metal into place.

Zoe's eyes were distant. Her face was neutral. Chase knew she needed to get Zoe somewhere quiet and warm, to deal with what she'd just done. Chase pulled her along the tunnel, stopping at the first metal ladder they came to. At the top was a small metal sewer grate that lifted easily out of the way. Chase climbed out onto the street and helped Zoe up after her.

They were next to the Church of Saint Mark, on the north side of the building, closer to the harbor. Walking to the edge of the church, Chase could see the wooden hoarding and cranes of the building site on the south side. The Visitologists' secret excavation.

Chase hadn't been sure whether the sound of gunfire carried up to the street, but she got her answer in the form of approaching police sirens. She turned to make sure Zoe was following, and then set off running across the city. She cut down an alleyway that would keep them away from the main roads. Washing lines hung high above between the windows, and there were broken stones at their feet. More police sirens sounded, accompanied by shouting, but nobody was following them.

They made it back to the hotel. Guerrero was in the bar, telling tall tales and entertaining the crowd, but Chase needed to make sure Zoe was okay.

In Zoe's room, they stripped off her pants to check the wound. It was little more than a graze. The blood made it look worse than it was. Chase washed and dressed it, using a first aid kit she picked up from Ali at reception.

Chase sat on the bed with Zoe, each of them nursing a beer in silence. She felt a swell of emotions. She wanted to grieve for her mentor but didn't really know how. She'd never figured it out when her parents died and hadn't done it for the relationship with Zoe. Life was a thing best experienced in the moment. She didn't have the tools for dealing with regrets.

But she wanted to.

Zoe had taken a life to save her, and it would come at a cost. The thought that remained unspoken, the single thing Chase didn't want to say, was that all this was her own fault. She'd been the one to force the issue that broke them up, and led to Chase's career change, and to Turner not trusting her.

"You didn't tell me you'd found anything else," Zoe said quietly. "You didn't tell me you'd been to the Needle."

"No," Chase said quietly. "I should have."

"You never trusted me," Zoe said. "Never let me in. You burned us down. We were getting too close, and you got scared of opening up. You picked a fight you knew would burn us down." Chase said nothing.

At the bottom of the bottle, Zoe said, without looking up, "I'd like to be alone."

FORTY-FOUR

C hase stepped into the bar and saw everyone gathered into a corner, near a table full of condiments for the bar food. Guerrero was holding court, using a ketchup packet as a prop in whatever story he was telling. Chase took a step toward the group and froze. If she joined them, there would be half a dozen stories Guerrero could tell about scrapes they'd gotten into together. But that would involve talking, laughing, smiling, and Chase's battery felt empty.

She headed for the barman instead and ordered a bourbon. She pounded it straight down and ordered another. She was on her third by the time Guerrero touched her shoulder and nodded toward an empty table in the corner. They settled down away from the noise and chatter.

Guerrero didn't say a word. For all his bravado in a crowd, he knew when to be quiet. He read people better than anyone Chase had ever met. It was part of why he was so good at his job. A survival instinct.

"Weird day," Chase said, when she was ready.

"Want to talk about it?"

Chase stared down into her empty glass. Guerrero waved at the barman, who carried over two bottles. One was the bourbon Chase had been drinking; the other was red wine for Guerrero. He drank it straight from the bottle and licked his lips.

"It's not pulque," he said with a sly grin. "But it'll do."

Chase pulled a face. Guerrero had made her drink pulque once on a trip into Mexico. "I can still taste it. Alcohol shouldn't be that color. Or thickness."

"Alcohol can be anything it wants."

Guerrero took another swig and settled back into the chair. The wood creaked.

"An old friend of mine died," Chase said. "In my arms. Like, one minute she's there, the next, I'm holding something, but it's not a person. And you realize, their lips are never going to move again. They're never going to tell you everything will be okay. Never hold your hand. You're on your own."

Chase paused. She hadn't meant to let go of any of that. Guerrero stayed silent. He sipped at his wine and watched her. He nodded his chin upward, encouraging her to speak, or not to. Whichever she needed to do.

At length, she said, "Did I ever tell you about my parents?"

"You told me your mama was Scottish, and I've seen after a few drinks how you think that makes you William Wallace. I know your dad was American. Worked on a farm."

"Military, then farm." Chase smiled at the memory. "Well, farm, then military, then farm again. He'd never wanted to be a farmer. His whole family did it, and he wanted something else. Enlisted to see the world, saw a crazy woman in Glasgow. Still ended up on the farm."

"Your mother moved over?"

"Yeah. Glasgow at the time, it wasn't in great shape. She said she moved to Washington State to get away from the rain."

"The way people in Washington talk, they like to say they're the ones who know all about rain."

Chase played with her glass, pushing it in a small circle around the table. She picked up the bottle and poured herself a refill, then stared at it another second before drinking.

"They died in a mudslide," she said. "On the farm."

"Ay mierda, I'm sorry, I didn't mean—"

"No, it's okay. I'm not mad."

Too busy thinking, Chase thought. Your parents were killed by the ground, and you spend your life digging down, looking for things.

Some of the crowd broke off and started to move toward them, calling Guerrero's name. He waved them off, and they saw from his face that he meant it. They turned away and went straight back into laughing about something else.

"My friend, the one who died, she didn't trust me. She used to. She said now I sell off history 'to the highest bidder.'" Any other time, Chase knew Guerrero would have raised a toast to that, aimed for the joke, but he let her keep going. "And earlier, I saw Wallace. He offered me money to join them. The Visitologists."

"Did you take it?"

Chase set down her glass and shook her head.

Guerrero smiled, like the question had just been a formality. Never in doubt. "I didn't know your friend, but I do know you. And I know Wallace. And I think all that matters is you didn't take his money."

Chase looked down at her glass to avoid eye contact. The moment had been too earnest, too sincere. Zoe had managed to rattle her. The comments about Chase never trusting her, about Chase deliberately ruining the relationship, to avoid committing. But Chase trusted Guerrero. They'd been in more scrapes than she could count, had enough dirt on each other to collect on a dozen rewards, and saved each other's lives many times over. Why was it so easy for her to trust him and so hard for her to trust Zoe?

And how serious had Wallace's offer been? Did he really expect she would switch sides if the money was high enough? And why did they even need her if—

The penny dropped. Teasing her with the other journal. Offering clues about Palmyra, along with a last-ditch attempt at hiring her.

Chase smiled. Regardless of whatever they had on the back of the page, and having Forrester's books, Wallace had still coming fishing for information.

"They still don't know," Chase said. She turned to face Guerrero. "They still don't know where the tomb is. And they think I might."

FORTY-FIVE

C hase and Guerrero huddled around the notebook on Chase's bed. She'd wanted to do this alone, but Guerrero had picked up on her excitement and followed her upstairs. Chase flicked through the faded pages between the battered leather covers.

"Don't make them like that anymore," Guerrero noted.

"I don't think they ever did," Chase said.

Chase turned to the page before the tear.

The entry was full of observations on the expansion of the modern Alexandria. Modern for the twenties, anyway. Forrester wrote about sections of the ancient city walls that were still visible in a public park to the east. He commented on Strabo, the first-century traveler who had made mention of the layout of Alexandria at the time. Strabo, Forrester said, had described entering Alexandria from a gate in the eastern wall, and then walking through a second wall inside the city. Forrester noted that Alexandria had famously been separated into quarters and speculated that each one had been a distinct walled district. That idea still placed the Soma on the crossroads in the oldest part of the city.

Chase looked again at the Mahmoud Bey map, which was unfolded on the bed next to them. The ancient grid, over which Bey had marked the walls of the older city; the dog's head that Chase had noticed on the ride over, with the snout in the east; the church, and the old crossroads, in the western section.

Chase flipped past the missing page. There were no references to the Soma beyond that point, at least nothing that would explain where the tomb was. She turned back to the pages immediately leading up to the tear and kept track of the opening word of each sentence and the first letter of each line on the page. She was looking for some kind of code, but there was nothing that she could see.

Next, she opened the book and looked down the spine, where messages used to be hidden in the old spy adventures of Henry Forrester's time. Nothing. She ran her fingers along the inside of the leather, feeling for any signs of a flap or pocket.

Nothing.

Chase threw the book back down on the bed. "There has to be something in this book. Wallace mentioned the back of the missing page. There might be a clue on there."

"But why would there be?" Guerrero shrugged. "Look, if the missing page was about this old guy realizing he needed to keep the place a secret, then he wouldn't have written the location when he turned it over."

"Good point." Chase felt something click into place. "Anything there would be a misdirection."

Chase looked down at the book. It had landed spine down and fallen open. A few of the pages were still raised, deciding which way to fall. Chase noticed the natural divide seemed to be the torn-out page. That was where the spine settled as the middle of the book, even though the missing page was closer to the end.

Chase picked up the book and examined the spine along the remains of the missing page. She leafed forward and back, and then settled again on the same spot.

"There was an extra page here," she said.

Guerrero leaned in closer. "What?"

"You can see the tear here from the page they have. That was clumsy. But look closer, on this side, before we get to the tear. See there? It's small, but it looks like someone used a knife to remove a page. The blade scored the spine, so it falls open here."

Chase ran her fingers across the paper, feeling the indents left by the nib of Forrester's pen. Some would be there long after the ink had faded away. She pulled a pencil from her bag and started shading over the page, lightly at first, then a little heavier.

Guerrero said, "This is why I got into smuggling. For the art projects."

As the page filled with the lead, the grooves and scratches started to stand out. Most of them were in line with the words on the page, and the pencil was spelling out what was already there. But in a few places, they started to see other markings—the contents of the missing pages.

They were faint. Chase wasn't expert enough to be able to piece together a whole page of text, but the markings seemed to be adding up to something else.

The top half was taken up with a drawing of a walled city. It was the same loose circle as the one on the Freemason map. That was no use. Without extra reference, there was no way to compare the circular city to modern Alexandria.

The bottom half of the page was a crude reproduction of the Bey map. There wasn't enough detail visible from the faint lines to see if Forrester had annotated any sections of the city, but Chase recognized the outline.

Right at the top of the page, above the walled city, was another small drawing, a curved line with a couple of dots at a right angle. Maybe they were punctuation from a missing piece of text. She couldn't make out what it was.

So much for the big moment of discovery.

Chase held back a sigh. The room was tense. Guerrero was watching what she was doing, waiting for an announcement of some kind. Chase rummaged in her bag for the Freemason map. As she placed it on the bed next to the Bey map, the stone rolled out onto the duvet.

Guerrero picked it up and turned it over in the light. "What's this?"

"No idea," Chase said. "Paperweight."

With the two maps next to each other on the bed, Chase placed the journal between them, and started letting her gaze drift between them. The circular city. The Bey city. Forrester's drawings. The circular city. The Bey city . . .

A thought unwrapped itself. More a memory of a thought. On the flight over, when she'd thought of Troy. An ancient city with a walled royal center, and a sprawling mass of people living outside those walls.

Chase grinned.

"What is it?" Guerrero said. "What?"

Chase pointed at the dots. "These here? Cleopatra's Needles. We always assume they were square on to the coastline. But here"—Chase traced the curved line of the drawing—"is the coast. The two needles point southeast, I think, to the city. The first city. The one founded by Alexander. Look here." Chase ran her finger around the circular wall of the first drawing. "I thought that doesn't fit into what we know. But then, look."

Chase moved down to the bottom of the page, the map like Bey's. "This is the wall of the ancient city. Or what Bey thought of as all one wall. But people also talked about Alexandria having many sections. Like ancient Troy. So, how about this?" She moved to the eastern section, the dog's snout, and drew her hand in a loose circle. "This whole bit here was the oldest part. The original part. The *royal* part. After Alexander died, it was completed as his monument. The city expanded out around it."

"So that whole bit there?"

"The whole thing. It's the Soma. It wasn't one building; it was a district. That's why his tomb wasn't on the list of seven wonders. It wasn't, like, a statue or mausoleum. You don't pay tribute to him by building one thing. You do it by building a new Troy. Something that will last longer, be talked about wider. That whole section of the city was his monument. And you can still see it."

Chase bought up the aerial satellite map of the modern city on her phone. The dog's snout was still visible from the air, if you knew what you were looking for. It was a densely built-up area contained within a main road that looped around in a shape that closely matched the walls on both the Bey map and the drawing of the old, circular city. Chase looked at the Bey map again. She put her finger on the crossroads where the Visitologists were digging and ran along the large road eastward, to a second major junction. This one was inside the dog's snout, within the walls of the Soma. Chase looked at the modern city again on her phone, following that road along from the current excavation sites, toward where she now believed the tomb would really have been.

She checked the spot against the old water tunnels on the maps she'd found with the journal. Then, using the phone app to bring up the modern network of waterworks and electrical cables, she spotted a pattern. A small square in the east of the city had no sewers and no electric conduits. The buildings in that part of town were fed from the side, with small inlets and junction boxes.

Someone had gone to great care to avoid digging in that one small part of town.

Chase thought back to Turner's words: *We controlled city planning, designed the sewers.*

Gotcha.

"Right there," Chase said. "I know where he is."

FORTY-SIX

C hase stepped out of the shower when she heard someone knocking on her door. Guerrero had left to settle in for the night, ready for an early start, and Ali wouldn't bother her this late. Chase already knew who to expect when she opened the door. Zoe was standing outside, wearing the same style of faded hotel bathrobe. She looked tired and sheepish and was holding a bottle of wine and two glasses.

Zoe offered a conciliatory smile and raised the bottle. "Nightcap?"

Chase looked at the wine. Her head swam at the thought of more alcohol. There was already half a bottle of bourbon floating around her system, and Chase wasn't that hard of a drinker.

But some other part of her wanted to say yes, to invite Zoe in and try to open up. To get over whatever it was that kept her holding back. Her stomach knotted at the thought of it.

Chase opened the door wider but didn't step aside. "We've got an early start tomorrow."

"Chuy told me," Zoe said. "You know where the tomb is. I think we should celebrate."

Chase turned back toward the bed, leaving the door open for Zoe to follow. Zoe sat next to her and opened the screw-top wine. She poured two glasses and handed one to Chase, raising a silent toast.

Chase was willing herself to speak, but the words kept dying in her throat. She drank the wine and waited to see where Zoe wanted to go.

Zoe laughed at herself, shaking her head at whatever she'd been thinking. "The two of us."

"Yeah."

"I'm sorry. I was too hard on you before. It's . . . it's been a day."

"How are you doing? What happened in the temple, the thing you . . ."

Zoe nodded, paused before answering. "It's weird. Having . . . Have you ever killed anyone?"

Chase wished she could say no, so she didn't say anything at all.

Zoe waited a beat, then started again. "It didn't take any effort. And I didn't think about it. It was just the thing I did in the moment. Doesn't feel like it was really me. That sounds crazy."

"No, it doesn't. You did it to save me. It doesn't mean anything deeper about you."

Zoe leaned forward. She had a smile on her face that Chase hadn't seen in more than a decade, the same as the night they'd first met, stealing art. Chase shuffled back. She knew this would be a mistake, but it was hard to say no to memories. She felt a flush of something old and new.

The knot in her gut eased a little. It was time to push through, get it all out.

"You were right," she said. "Everything you said was right. It was my fault. I was scared, so I burned us down. I pushed you too far with your family, because I knew you weren't ready."

Zoe almost whispered; her voice cracked. "It's okay. You were right, too. Some guy on the street could say something, and that meant more to me than you or my family. Until you outed me to them. That was the first time I really stopped to care what they thought."

Chase opened her mouth to apologize again, but Zoe kept talking. "You were always so sure of yourself, you know?" she said. "You knew what you wanted. It was sexy. I'd never known. I was still trying to figure it out, and

I think I piled it all onto you."

"I thought the same about you. You had a family, a big home."

"You had love," Zoe said quietly. "This sounds horrible, I know. But you knew how your parents felt about you. You lost something. I felt like I never had it."

Zoe placed her own hand on top of Chase's on the bed. Chase felt the spark. Zoe touched Chase's wrist, where the bathrobe's sleeve had ridden up, and the first of Chase's tattoos was visible. Zoe touched the ink. She had the same symbol on her own wrist. Something they'd both done as a dare, in the first flush of their relationship. A small squiggle that the man in the tattoo shop had insisted was Sanskrit for fate. Chase learned many years later that it didn't mean anything.

Zoe's fingers traced upward, along the rest of the ink on Chase's arm, lifting the sleeve as she went.

"Do they all mean something?"

"Memories," Chase said, letting Zoe take the lead.

"Has it been that long?"

"That long, that far."

When the sleeve wouldn't move up any farther, Zoe stopped. She held it in place for a moment, then met Chase's eyes. The spark came again.

Zoe swallowed a couple of times, sniffed, and looked over at the maps laid out on the desk. "So, where is it?"

Glad of the distraction, Chase leaned toward the maps and placed her finger on a junction. "Right there."

Zoe moved in close to look where she was pointing. She put her own hand down over Chase's, and there was a spark as they touched. Chase turned to gently push Zoe away.

"Early start," she said again.

Zoe didn't move. Their mouths were inches apart. Zoe's brown eyes looked larger without her glasses. She touched Chase's cheek, and the spark came again. Chase's breathing was picking up in time with her heartbeat, and she could feel Zoe's doing the same. Chase's fingers slipped in through the opening of Zoe's bathrobe and found skin. She ran her hand down Zoe's side; Zoe gasped and closed her eyes. Her lips parted slightly, and Chase kissed her. Softly, at first, tentative. Then harder, as they both reached back into their past for something fiercer.

Chase closed her own eyes, and for a moment she was kissing Mason, before she was back in the moment with Zoe.

FORTY-SEVEN

L ights.

Noises.

The world came back to Mason in drips, one piece at a time. Her breathing was deep. Slow. She could feel her hands, with a tingling sensation in her fingers. Her wrists felt odd. There was something else. Handcuffs. Her arms were above her.

Was she floating?

No.

Hanging.

What the—

A pipe. Okay. Her wrists had been cuffed together over a pipe. She was hanging from it. Her toes just about touched the floor. Her arms ached.

Her side, the knife wound, felt raw, stretched.

Where was she?

A room. It was dark. No windows. No light. Nothing.

No, one light. Small, red, blinking occasionally, high up. A camera? Someone watching her? Mason could make out a shape in front of her. Someone else was trussed up the same way, suspended from the same pipe.

She swallowed. Her throat was dry. Sore. There was a bad taste in her mouth. Chemical, too clean. She'd been drugged.

There was a blackout in her memory. A gap. She remembered Padding-ton. Cullis. Had Cullis done something? No. She'd hit him. So what— The cab. The chase. Parish.

What had he said? Thanks for your help. But how had she helped? And how had Parish been there? Was he working with Martyn? Mason had been annoyed at Martyn. There was a part of her that thought of him as a traitor, for leaking the secrets. But she'd never had him down as someone who would work with the enemy.

There was a foul smell, getting stronger. Or was she becoming more aware of it? That made more sense. She felt cold. There was no heat down here. Or up here. Or wherever here was.

That smell again.

Mason recognized it.

Death. Someone had died in here. Close by.

It was the person in front of her. A dead body, strung up like a piece of meat.

Mason relaxed and waited. It was best to get used to the surroundings and push out any excess thoughts, to let the room tell her as much as it could. She was used to the poor light she would sometimes encounter in the field, on late-night operations. She let her eyes becomes accustomed to the shadows and the lack of definition. The red light gave her something to lock on to. Between the small red glow and the shape in front of her, Mason could get a feel for the size of the room. The body started to take more shape as her eyes adjusted. She could just about make out the features on the face.

Martyn Wood.

With a bullet hole in his head.

Mason stared at her dead friend. Something cold spread across her gut. She wanted to cry, but she couldn't afford for them to win. Martyn could be mourned later. First, she needed to stay alive.

Mason focused her attention back on her wrists. She interlocked her fingers and pulled her hands down over the pipe, taking her weight. Pulling up and down, she felt a slight amount of give.

Could it be pulled loose? Maybe. She needed time.

Right now, that didn't seem to be a problem.

FORTY-EIGHT

It was just before five a.m. when Ali drove Chase, Guerrero, and Zoe across the city in the predawn light. Alexandria was only quiet for a few brief hours each morning, the calm before the storm of traffic, smoke, and noise.

It had been hard for Chase to get any sleep. After Zoe had left for her own room, Chase had thought she would be asleep as soon as her head hit the pillow. But every switch in her brain flipped on at the same time. The tomb. The Visitologists. The Knights of Saint Mark. The Aten.

Zoe.

Mason.

Zoe.

At some point she finally drifted off, but her dreams had been an exhausting mix of all the same thoughts.

Ali had taken the long way around, making a number of deliberate wrong turns and doubling back a few times to weed out anybody tailing them. He pulled away with a string of Arabic well wishes and promised to be back later to pick them up.

They walked to El Shalalat Park. On the outer edge of the dog's nose from Mahmoud Bey's map, the park would have sat just outside the walls of the Soma. There were a few ruined remains of an ancient wall there, and tourists visited them as relics of the ancient city. Chase knew now they were what was left of the Soma, the district that contained Alexander's tomb. She noticed that some of the bricks had a slight pink hue. The Lighthouse had been said to have the same coloring. The trip to the park had given Chase a chance to confirm her theory about the wall, but it also gave them another chance to spot any tails.

They crossed over from the park at a large junction, which Chase believed would have been the original city gate. The traffic was still sparse, but they had only a few minutes before sunrise started to break across the sky and this stretch of road filled with bumper-to-bumper traffic.

Chase led her companions down El-Horeya, the modern version of the road that ran across Mahmoud Bey's map. Two blocks in from the junction was a large white building that resembled a mansion from colonial America.

"The museum?" Zoe asked.

Guerrero gave it a second look. "That's a museum?"

The white building had originally been the home of a wealthy businessman, who sold it to the American government. It had housed the embassy for more than seventy years. At the turn of the millennium, the Egyptian government had bought it back and converted it into a museum. That was all available on the Wikipedia page. What the entry failed to mention was that the mansion had been built on the site of Alexander's tomb.

Zoe looked confused. "I thought you'd said it was farther south, by the football field."

"I worked it out wrong," Chase said. "Took another look at it this morning."

Chase pulled out the map of the water tunnels and compared it to a spot marked on her phone app. She led Guerrero and Zoe back toward the junction. Out in the middle of the road, between the buildings and the park, was a small manhole cover. Chase pulled a tool that looked like an oversize Swiss Army knife from her jacket and used it to lift the metal lid. She waved for them to climb down, and to hurry.

Guerrero went first, then Zoe. Chase went last, pulling the manhole cover back into place as she descended the metal ladder. The heat was close around them. For a few seconds, Chase was wrapped in darkness. She froze. Her heart was pounding. She focused in on the rungs in front of her: the metal, the feel of it in her hands. She took them one at a time.

Guerrero and Zoe put on the flashlights on their phones, lighting the ground beneath Chase. Zoe was rummaging in her bag as Chase reached the bottom and switched on her own light. Zoe pulled out a video camera, switching on a high beam on the front.

Chase reached out as if to grab it. "You packed that?"

"I want to record all of this," Zoe said, taking a defensive step back.

"Right now, it's just evidence of us committing a crime," Chase said.

"It's a liability."

"Henry poured all my family's money into this. It means something. We should document it properly."

"You can't use your phone?"

"What if we want to show it? Like a documentary? We need good quality, and the light on this is better."

Chase didn't want there to be any proof of what was about to happen. She was having a hard enough time dealing with the idea of destroying whatever they found without there being video evidence of her doing it. But she hadn't told Zoe or Guerrero about Mason's order. Neither of them knew her plan to destroy whatever she found. It would be easy enough to lose the tape later. It could have an accident on the flight home, or the camera could go missing along the way. She let it go.

The passageway was almost as wide as the road above, with dark brick-work lining each side. Small archways appeared in the walls at regular intervals, the drainage from smaller systems. They were standing on a raised concrete walkway that kept them above the sludge.

"I take it back," Guerrero said. "This is why I got into smuggling."

Chase pulled the two revolvers out of her messenger bag. She slipped the first into her waistband. She hesitated a moment before holding the second out to Zoe. "Do you want it?" she offered gently.

"Will I need it?" Zoe said, taking it after a brief hesitation.

Chase turned away as she answered, looking down the tunnel. "Rats grow big down here."

"People, too," Guerrero said, his voice low. "We should be quick. Last time I was here, I heard stories that people had moved down here after the uprising."

"Down here?" Zoe sounded every bit the London bookshop owner.

Guerrero let the tone pass. "They lost everything."

Chase took them along the walkway heading back in the direction of the city. After two hundred yards, she stopped and shined her light across the channel of sewage, to a small ledge on the other side. There was an outlet archway next to it, but it looked dry and was at a different angle than the others. She compared it to both her map app and the water tunnel map. This was the spot.

They needed to cross a gap of maybe five feet. There were a series of small pipes running along the ceiling, over the sludge. Guerrero reached up and gripped the pipes first, going hand over hand across the gap like an army cadet.

Chase turned to Zoe, ready for an argument, but Zoe slung the camera's strap over her shoulder, gripped the pipes, and started across after Guerrero. Chase could already see Zoe's arms shaking. Chase caught Guerrero's eyes on the far side and could tell he'd seen it, too.

"Come toward me," Guerrero called out to Zoe. "Keep your eyes on me."

Chase reached out for the next pipe with her right hand, and then with her left. Zoe came with her, her face taut, trying not to look as though she was panicking. Chase reached out again, for the third pipe. Zoe froze, unwilling to move forward.

"The next one," Guerrero called. "The next one, then I can reach you."

Zoe reached across with one hand and tentatively gripped the copper tubing. But Chase could see that Zoe's grip wasn't strong enough. Zoe herself didn't seem to have realized this as she pulled her left hand free.

Chase called out, "Guerrero," but he'd seen it, and he reached out toward Zoe, grabbing at the camera strap and using that to pull her toward him. He threw his own weight backward, forcing himself to fall against the wall, and pulled Zoe down on top of him. She stood up and started dusting herself down in a hurry, yammering in the most English way imaginable. In the light, Chase could see Zoe's face blush red. Guerrero tried to hide his amusement. That was about the only thing he couldn't smuggle past p eople.

Chase joined them on the other side. They climbed up into the alcove.

There were sleeping bags, tinned goods, and plastic bags full of junk.

"Where are they?" Zoe said.

"On their way to work," Guerrero said. "A lot of the people who live down here have jobs; they just don't have homes."

They crawled past the makeshift dwelling, and Chase was surprised to find that the shaft angled down. This definitely wasn't a water runoff. At the end of the short passageway, they came to a brick wall. There was no mortar, and Chase pulled out the bricks carefully, one by one, until there was a hole big enough for them to slip through.

Chase's heart pounded, and blood rushed in her ears. A panic attack threatened to take hold at the thought of how dark it would be on the other side. She closed her eyes and swallowed. Once, twice. After a few more breaths, she was back in control.

She opened her eyes to see Guerrero giving her a knowing smile. He slipped through the gap before her, and she saw his beam light up the space. He waved for her to follow on through, and again Chase saw that look, like they were in on something together. Did he know? She'd always kept the phobia hidden. Or she thought she had.

Chase crawled through, followed by Zoe. The bright light of Zoe's camera filled the chamber around them. They were in a narrow passage cut from the rock, identical to the one they'd been in the day before. As they walked, the wall to the left changed. It was made of large bricks with a pink hue. Most of the bricks were sealed tight with an ancient mortar. But in the center, Chase could see a section where the mortar had been removed. The wall had been opened up and then pieced back together.

This was it.

Guerrero stopped beside Chase and looked from her to the wall a couple of times, at first not seeing what had caught her attention. He laughed when he spotted it.

Chase ran her fingers along the edges of the bricks. One pushed inward with very little pressure. Zoe and Guerrero both joined in, and they worked quickly and silently, finding purchase on the edges of the bricks and working them loose, piling them against the opposite side of the passage. Once they had a gap large enough to climb through, Chase pulled out a flair and tossed it through.

"I thought you'd do that," Guerrero said, with his easy smile.

"I like to see where I'm going."

Chase climbed through the hole and found herself on a stone staircase. The broad steps ran down into the darkness, with a flat ramp running down the middle, perfect for sliding a large sarcophagus up and down, with people taking the weight on the steps on either side. The way up was blocked. The ceiling was too flat and smooth to have been a cave-in. Someone had sealed the entrance.

The flare was burning a few steps down. Chase lit another and threw it, following the fluorescent glow downward. Guerrero and Zoe came after her. Zoe's steps were becoming bolder, as she grew surer of herself in her new role of adventurer. At the foot of the stairs the flare's light bounced off a wall five feet to the right. There were ancient torches affixed to the wall. When Chase reached them, she dipped a finger inside one and found a thick, dark liquid. It had the color of oil but felt like molasses. She lit each one with her battered Zippo and stood back as the light spread. Zoe turned off the camera's light. They could see the opposite wall now. There were more torches, and Guerrero lit them.

Zoe gasped. It was a sound of wonder and excitement, something Chase wished she could still feel. For a moment, Chase felt resentment building, a jealousy at something she'd lost. Then she tried to embrace the chance to live through Zoe's reactions, to see her world through new eyes.

The chamber was large. The walls were engraved with a mix of Greek and Egyptian characters, the two cultures merged under Alexander.

The king himself, with the two horns on his head, was shown on one wall, standing beneath a large sun. At the far end of the chamber was a stone plinth, engraved with battle images and Alexander holding the Aten above his head as armies fell. On the wall behind the plinth was a large disc, like the metal sun in Forrester's mausoleum.

On either side of the disc were engravings of Anubis and the Minotaur. The floor sloped at an odd angle, and there were cracks in the slabs beneath their feet.

"I think this is from the earthquake," Chase said, pointing to the damage.

"Step carefully—we don't know how sturdy this place is."

"And if it breaks?" Zoe said.

Chase shrugged. "The city will come down on us."

Zoe took a step back toward the stairs.

Guerrero laughed and slapped her shoulder, spurring her forward again. "If it's stood for two thousand years, we're not going to break it."

Silence settled again, and Chase felt the enormity of the discovery settle on her. "This is it," she whispered, as if saying the words too loud would change the facts. "Alexander's tomb."

"I notice an absence of Alexander," Guerrero said. "Did you forget to invite him?"

"That the best you can do?"

"This is a lot to take in." Guerrero shrugged. "Give me a minute."

Chase started walking along the walls, looking for a hidden door. Turner had said Alexander had been displayed to the public but brought below ground into the tomb. Maybe this was an outer chamber, where dignitaries and priests could visit him in private. There might still be a third chamber, where the sarcophagus could be stored.

Zoe must have figured out what Chase was doing, because she began running her hands along the opposite wall, filming as she went.

"He's late for his own funeral," Guerrero said.

"Getting better."

"He's so dearly departed, he's not even in his own tomb."

"You can stop now."

Chase and Zoe met in the middle, by the large disc. They shared a look. They both remembered how badly it had gone the last time. But Chase couldn't see any other way. She tried pressing the disc. It didn't budge. The surface was smooth and cold but felt different from the stone of the walls.

It was almost metal.

Just like the stone in her bag.

Chase pulled out the stone, running her fingers over its surface.

"What's that?" Zoe stepped in closer for a look.

Chase had done it again. Another secret. Something else she'd kept from Zoe.

"It was Henry's," she said, noticing the old doubts crossing Zoe's face. "I found it at the Needle."

Zoe tilted up her head in acknowledgment but didn't say anything. Another small lesion in the scar tissue of their relationship.

Chase focused on the stone. It was the same material as the large disc on the wall. Chase touched the engravings, thinking of them just as grooves instead of symbols, and it hit her. The disc had a small hole in the center. It was the same size as the tip of the stone.

She thought of Forrester's journal entry: I have been entrusted with the key.

He had meant it literally.

Chase slid the key into the hole. The narrow part slipped straight in, leaving only the base for her to grip as a handle. It turned ninety degrees with a simple click, and behind the walls to either side of them they could hear the movement of some ancient mechanism. The floor rumbled in time, making a sound like a large pestle and mortar. After a moment, the disc began to pull backward into the wall, leaving a stone archway in its place. Damp, warm air rushed out to meet them. The light from the chamber spilled in through the new archway, penetrating several feet into the darkness. Chase could make out stone pillars and a high ceiling. The disc stopped moving at the edge of the light.

The dampness of the air was a bad sign. They were down near the water table, and if the earthquake had caused the tomb to sink, then anything inside might have been ruined long ago.

"Let's go meet him," Chase said.

Chase and Guerrero switched off their flashlights to preserve the batteries and lifted the flaming torches off the wall. Zoe switched the camera's beam back on and raised the viewfinder to her eye.

Chase swallowed back the fear and stepped into the darkness beyond the arch. Zoe and Guerrero followed. Chase felt the surface beneath her feet change as she walked. The floor tilted even more steeply downward here. She saw that the paved floor of the outer chamber had given way to something more natural. They were in ancient cave.

"This was here long before Alexander. Whoever built the tomb, they would have known this was already here, building that outer chamber in front of it."

"Blocking it?"

Chase stepped to where the large disc had stopped moving. Walking around the other side, she could see it was a large, free-standing machine of some kind. There was a clockwork housing contained within a dusty, crystal outer shell. Chase had no frame of reference for a machine as large as this coming from Alexander's era. But Alexandria had been known as a hub of invention, with legends of statues that poured water, and mechanisms that lifted weights.

She turned the key in the disc again and found there were three settings. When turned to the right, the machine moved farther into the cave. When turned to the left, it reversed back toward the entrance. Chase chose the middle setting, which turned off the device, and slipped the key into her pocket. Up ahead, the cave forked into three different tunnels. The walls were covered with the same language as the Atenist temple and Forrester's mausoleum. The old man had definitely been here to see this.

"What's this?" Guerrero asked.

"The language of the gods," Chase said.

"Or aliens." Zoe added.

"How...old is it?"

"At least five thousand years," Chase said. "Forrester believed it was double that." She paused in front of the three paths and said, "We should split up. We don't want to take too much time, in case anyone follows us down."

Guerrero took the tunnel to the right. Zoe paused for a second, giving Chase an unreadable look, then stepped into the entrance to the left. Chase headed into the one straight ahead of her. Even with the light of the torch, the darkness crept in around her like a hand. It felt oily and unnatural.

There was a grinding sound, like gears. It was distant, somewhere to the left. Chase felt herself about to lose control to a full panic attack. She reasoned with it, pleaded with it:

Not now.

It's nothing.

Keep moving.

She focused on the torch in her hand. The ground at her feet. The things she could see and feel. Not the things she couldn't control.

She walked a few more feet, and the light played upon a face. It was all Chase could do not to yelp. It was a statue, set into an alcove in the tunnel.

A large, free-standing representation of Anubis, with jewels set into the eye sockets.

Chase reached up to touch the jewels and guessed the statue was around seven feet tall. Its head almost touched the ceiling.

That was when the grinding sound started again.

This time, it was followed by Zoe's scream.

FORTY-NINE

Mason didn't know how long she'd been awake. She was usually good at keeping time in her head. One of the most important skills in the field was keeping track of where, and when, you were. But the drugs had thrown her off. It felt like maybe an hour had passed, but it could have been two.

Mason's hands kept going numb, the cuffs cutting off circulation when she let herself hang from them. It took a lot of effort to push through that, knowing the pain that would come when she pulled herself up. It was a tough spot. In order to rest her hands, she needed to use her hands.

Mason heard new sounds. The turning of a lock? It was muffled, which told her the room was soundproofed. Mason was slowly putting together an idea of where she was and how to get out.

A door opened behind her, spilling light into the room in a narrow beam. There was a click, and overhead halogens blinked on. Mason winced and blinked a few times, waiting for her eyes to adjust. The room was covered in white tiles. She was hung from what looked to be a metal gas pipe running across the low ceiling.

Martyn had been dead for some time. His skin was gray, with marbled streaks running across the surface. A pool of congealed blood lay on the floor beneath him. A fresh wave of grief washed over her. This time, it came with more ammunition: self-doubt, failure. Martyn couldn't have been the one guiding her out of Legoland on the phone, which meant Mason had walked right into a trap. More, she'd run into it, letting them play her for a fool.

Why was she so off her game?

Ever since Martyn.

Ever since Sean.

No. More recently.

Since that night with Chase.

Mason heard footsteps on the tiles behind her and closed her eyes to pretend she was still out.

"No need, Joanna," Parish said, his accent now a strange transatlantic hybrid. "I know you've been awake for three hours."

He stepped in front of her with his hands behind his back and nodded to the small camera mounted on the wall behind Martyn. The red light blinked.

Mason tried to speak, but her throat was too tight. She coughed, which only made it worse, but it helped to get the words out. "You like filming women as they sleep?"

Parish tipped back his head and laughed. That annoyed Mason, because the line hadn't been that funny. Did he have a bad sense of humor, on top of being a white supremacist and religious fundamentalist?

"That was good," he said. "Funnier than him." He nodded at Martyn.

"He mostly just cried."

Mason ignored the dig at Martyn. Don't let him play you any further.

"It was you," she managed. "The messages."

He smiled. "Of course."

Mason coughed again. She wasn't sure what drug he'd used, but it must have had some kind of paralysis effect. "When did you get to him?"

Parish brought his hands around in front of him. Mason noticed he was wearing the same metal glove she had seen in Tan Bashir's interrogation video. He looked at Martyn's body in silence for a moment, with an expression that suggested fond memories.

"He never defected, if it helps." Parish said. "We played you on that one, too. Kept him alive long enough to make sure we knew how to access—then work— the surveillance grid. All the leaks were down to us." He had a small tablet device in his other hand. He raised it to show Mason. The screen showed a street map of a city she didn't recognize.

"Alexandria," he supplied. "I've been watching a friend of yours. There aren't as many cameras over there, but I think maybe she's found something."

Mason could worry about Chase later. There was something more important in what he'd just shown her. First, the tablet was showing a live signal. The room wasn't a Faraday cage. Second, the screen had a clock in the top right. It was coming up on five a.m.

If she could get her hands on that device . . .

She needed more time to find a way to get loose.

"What do you think is out there?" she asked.

Parish smiled. Bringing up the tablet again, he swiped to a new screen. An image showed carvings on stone tablets that appeared to depict a man holding up a staff and some kind of large explosion radiating outward. "This was in a temple we found in Syria." Next he showed her a barren desert, with a few man-made lines in the sand, looking like the foundations of old ruins. "This is the Thar Desert, in India. Something like an atomic bomb was detonated there twelve thousand years ago. The sand still carries traces of radiation." He swiped again to a satellite image of Africa. He circled his finger around the top third. "The Sahara is the bottom edge of a blast radius that would have covered the Mediterranean. All of this is real. It all happened. And soon, we'll have the weapon that caused it."

"And then what?"

"Then? We use it."

He clicked on a video. It was the Bashir interrogation.

Are you a British spy?

Yes.

And you were sent to work with Al-Salif?

Yes.

Mason noticed that Parish had framed the questions in such a way as to make it sound as though MI6 was working with Al-Salif. Parish flicked to a second video. This showed Mason getting Chase out of Belgravia. A third video showed them at the Needle, with Mason turning the cops away.

"What we seem to have here," Parish said, in a very punchable tone, "is evidence of a coup organized by MI6. British spies are organizing Islamist extremists in the desert and then hiring a known international criminal to dig up an ancient weapon. You've orchestrated an attack on London to bring down your own government. And, when the world finds out that ancient science exists, they'll come running to us for help."

"Why?"

Parish stared into Mason's eyes for a moment, confused by the question. "You know why," he said. "So we can show we're ready. So we can take control—be given control—by countries finally able to see that we've been right all along. And then"—he beamed—"we'll be ready for the new age. The next visitation can happen."

Mason's stomach lurched. Parish was a believer. She'd assumed he was just playing a role, using the religion as a cover for something else. Now, she realized, he meant it. And that filled her with dread. Because belief couldn't be bribed or reasoned with.

"These aliens, the visitation you're hoping for. They're white, right? All these sad little half-baked ideas you're clinging to, to make yourself important."

"Aren't you tired?" Parish was clearly warming to his subject. "War. Recession. Poverty." He stepped in close. "We've been here the whole time, trying to stop it. Trying to take us all to the next level. The Aten is the key. The Aten is the way."

"You sound nuts."

"You sound scared. I know the feeling. I was like you. Scared, angry—all the time. Waking up every day and worrying about money, or work, or people. It never ended. And then she saved me. Showed me the way."

"She?"

Parish held up the gloved hand. "I don't really know how this works.

Something about controlling the flow of electric impulses in your brain. Makes it impossible for you to lie to me. Using it for any more than three minutes will fry your mind." He wiggled his fingers. "I always go over three minutes."

He pressed the glove to Mason's head.

Her skull started to vibrate.

The glove grew warm, and Mason's skin tingled. Her vision flashed. The room went away, replaced by a wall of bright white light that wrapped around the inside of her head.

Mason could hear Parish talking, but he sounded far away.

"Let's see what else you know."

FIFTY

C hase slammed into Guerrero at the junction. They'd both had the same instinct to run toward Zoe. They dropped their torches in the collision. Guerrero's went out as it hit the floor, and Chase scrambled to relight it from her own.

Another grinding sound echoed around the chamber, emanating from the tunnel Chase had just left. She and Guerrero ran in the direction Zoe had gone. Chase tripped on the cracked floor but caught herself before she fell over. Zoe's camera lay on the floor just beside her, suggesting she'd tripped at the same spot.

A few feet farther on, they found drops of blood.

Chase opened the camera's video screen and rewound. Something large moved across the shot. She pressed play. The image on-screen showed that Zoe had walked down the corridor they were standing in now. The camera moved side to side, the light throwing a bright circle onto the walls. Then the beam caught something else, and Zoe froze. She moved the camera back, slowly, and lit up a large statue. It was similar to the one Chase had seen in her own tunnel, but this one was a Minotaur. It was the same height as Anubis, with large, powerful shoulders and the bull's head set into the body without a neck.

The camera moved in closer as Zoe examined the statue.

Then the Minotaur moved.

Chase jumped and almost dropped the camera. She tightened her grip, and they watched as the Minotaur's fist filled the frame, followed by Zoe's scream. That was the end of the video.

The grinding sound came again, moving toward them from behind.

"Uh, Chase?" Guerrero called out.

Chase turned. Thirty feet down the tunnel, she could see the outline of the Anubis statue at the edge of Guerrero's torchlight.

It had followed them.

"Plan?" Guerrero asked.

"Run," Chase replied.

They bolted deeper into the tunnel. It was difficult to run on the uneven floor. Chase almost twisted her ankle as a stone gave way, and she stumbled and hit the wall shoulder-first. Guerrero stopped to help, and she saw something in his eyes she'd never seen before. Pure fear.

The sound came from up ahead now, too. They were trapped. Going back to back, Guerrero looked out the way they had come, and Chase waited to see what was coming toward them.

The sounds stopped. In some ways, the silence was worse. They stood on alert, their hearts pounding, expecting an attack that didn't seem to be coming. Slowly, still back to back, they started to move down the passageway again. The torchlight illuminated something solid.

The Minotaur.

Chase felt the panic bubble up again, unsure she'd be able to reason with it this time. Because now, it wasn't irrational. She couldn't tell herself there was nothing there, in the dark, because it was right in front of her.

Chase and Guerrero each paced backward until they were touching each other, each of them still facing one of the statues. Neither of the creatures moved.

An idea whispered at the back of Chase's mind. She took a few steps toward the Minotaur, then a couple of more. There were no signs of life.

Slowly, she reached out to touch it with her shaking hand. Then, when it still didn't move, she tapped it and ran her hand over the smooth surface.

It was the same material as the key.

She peered up into the red eyes, and the idea whispered again, louder. The sum of all her old fears, about the darkness that rushed in around her bed at night, suffocating her, and the creatures that she'd been sure were moving within it. Monsters that couldn't hurt her in the light.

Chase set the torch on the floor and went up on her toes to cover the creature's eyes with her hands. For one brief second, as her hands covered the jewels, she felt the Minotaur start to move. Guerrero must have seen it, too, because he called out from behind her. Chase pulled her hands away and tried to step back. It had been only a couple of seconds, but already the large arms had reached around behind her. They hadn't closed in, so Chase was able to wriggle free. She didn't want to think about what could have happened if she'd waited longer.

"Light sensors," she said. "Or motion. Or both. I have no idea how. Seriously, like, this isn't . . . this isn't a thing."

"No," Guerrero agreed.

"But it's a thing."

"Yes," Guerrero agreed.

"Whatever this is, it can't move in the light."

"But Zoe's camera had the light on."

Chase looked down at the camera in her hand, then at the flames flicking from the torch at her feet. "Fire, sunlight, they're natural," she said. "Our phones and cameras are LEDs. Maybe there's a difference in the light."

"So they're robots?"

Chase paused, realising she knew what this was.

Or thought she did.

"Talos," she said.

"What?"

"In Greek myth, Tal0s was a moving statue, a guardian. Created by Hephaestus, the blacksmith of the gods."

"Throwing that G word around so much, you're seriously messing with my cool."

"I know."

"This is nuts."

"No argument. But if we know how to stop it, it's not a threat."

They left Chase's fire on the floor, keeping the two statues frozen in place, then stepped around the Minotaur and pressed on in search of Zoe.

Chase could feel that they were heading down, deeper into the earth and further from any version of history she'd ever read in a book. After another hundred yards there was more humidity in the air. They stepped in a few small puddles. Soon, the passage opened out into a cavern, where the other two tunnels also converged. The torches didn't give off enough light to see the size of the chamber, but Chase could feel it spread out and away from them. In front of them was a large metal bowl filled with dark liquid.

Guerrero dipped the torch into the dark ooze and it ignited, filling the bowl with flame and spreading light across the chamber.

A ceiling came into view above them, lined with stalactites that danced in the light of the flickering flames. The darkness at the edges of the cave looked to take on a more solid shape, giving the impression of walls just out of sight. The floor around them was damp and covered with slippery moss. The source of the water was a river at the far end of the large cave. At the river's edge, covered in moss, mold and other signs of moisture damage, was a large crystal sarcophagus.

Exactly as Turner had described.

The final resting place of Alexander the Great.

Standing between Chase, Guerrero, and the dead king was a third statue. It had the body of a man but the head of a lion and large bronze wings. Zoe lay at its feet. Her face was covered in blood.

Chase knelt over Zoe. She was breathing, and her pulse was strong. Chase wiped away the blood, looking for the wound, and found a thin cut across Zoe's forehead. It looked worse than it was. She would need to be checked for any lasting head injuries, but that was beyond Chase's abilities.

Guerrero stood a few feet away, apparently unwilling to come closer to the statue. "This is not why I got into smuggling," he said. "How is she?"

"I think she's okay. Just out cold."

"What do we do? I can carry her out."

Chase opened her mouth to say yes but stopped. She could feel the pull of history. Alexander was right here. In this room. Had Forrester made it this far? Chase found it hard to believe he could have found the tomb without wanting to see it through.

She stepped around the lion statue to look at the sarcophagus. It was much larger than she had expected, about the size of Zoe's car. Its sides were smooth and flat, with a heavy lid on top. The crystal flickered in the light. Even through the centuries of growth, Chase could make out inscriptions etched into the surface. Scenes of battle. Legends in the languages of ancient Greece and Egypt.

Chase dropped to her knees.

She was filled with the sense of awe and wonder that she'd resented in Zoe back in the outer chamber. She felt a rush of something pure and exciting, better than any drug. This was history. More than the pots and pans, the small statues, all the trinkets she had sold over the past decade. This was the reason people got into archeology. She could reach out and touch something that was truly unique, something that had played a part in the founding of the modern world. The sarcophagus had been hidden from the world for more than two thousand years. How many people had seen it in that time? Chase and Guerrero, possibly Forrester. Maybe the Knights of Saint Mark had checked on it. Chase was in a position that only a handful had ever been in.

She knew in that moment that she couldn't destroy it. She understood why Forrester had gone to such lengths to hide all the proof, rather than dispose of it. This was history. It was sacred.

She turned to see Guerrero had followed her lead. He was on his knees, as if in prayer. He shrugged.

They climbed to their feet and approached the sarcophagus. Chase raised the camera and started to film. There was a wax seal around the lid. The water damage had obscured the view, but Chase could now make out the shape of a human inside. But there didn't seem to be any mold. Based on what Turner had said, Chase guessed the seal must have been added when the Knights hid the Aten, which would have been around 365 a.d. It had remained unbroken since then. Not even Henry Forrester had tried to open it.

Chase pulled a knife from her pocket and paused as another wave of emotion hit her. It wasn't her place to open this. Finding it was archaeology. But the minute she opened it, the moment she removed the context of the finding, she was a vandal.But she needed to secure whatever was inside, to protect it from Wallace and the Visitologists. She pressed the blade into the seal and ran it all the way around. There was a soft hiss.

Chase set down the camera, still filming, while she and Guerrero worked their fingers under the lid on each side, nodded to each other, and then lifted it away. They placed the large piece of crystal gently on the ground. Chase picked up the camera and aimed it into the coffin.

The body inside was shriveled down to the bone, like a mummy. If the timeline was right, Alexander would have been on show for more than five hundred years before the tomb was lost. He was wearing a helmet and armor but no chest plate. Chase half remembered reading that one of the Roman emperors had stolen it to wear himself.

There was a sword resting beside the body on one side, and a shield on the other. A small assortment of trinkets and coins lined the edges. There was a bundle next to Alexander, wrapped in animal hide, about a yard in length. Guerrero picked up the camera and started filming as she lifted the bundle out. Chase took her time unwrapping the layers, until the hide fell away to reveal a staff.

It was a similar color as the key and statues, but now she was seeing them all in a different context. This object looked like ataxite, a form of crystalised meteorite rock she'd seen in a Cairo museaum, but cut through with something else, a metalic element she didn't recognise. The shaft was as thick as a guitar neck, tapering to a thinner point at the bottom. The top had a narrow cross section, like a hammer or an arrowhead.

This was it. The Aten.

Chase gripped the handle. She felt a hum running through her hands, and then a voice in her head, cracked and hoarse, whispering to her in a language she didn't understand. What had Turner said? To touch it was to bond with it. Alexander's thoughts were in her head. She could see his memories. Feel them. His emotions. Ambition. Anger. As she drew on them, she could feel the Aten doing the same. Images popped into her head. She was there, in each memory, living them. Armies fell. She stood, with Alexander, in front of the a tower. He lifted the Aten above his head. Black clouds rolled in, and energy shot down from the sky, destroying the tower. She turned to look to the side, and with that, she moved into someone else. Akhenaten. She watched as he issued orders, as a city was built. She witnessed the birth of his son. All the Heretic King's emotions flowed through her. Resentment. Nerves. He wanted to be loved. Why wouldn't his people embrace him? Another change, more people, more minds and ideas and emotions. Other men and women, going back through history. Names that were familiar, names that were unknown. Images danced in her mind. Where was this? Ancient cities burned. She saw...salt? Salt filling the air? The buildings weren't familiar. Wars. She saw more of the statues, the Anubis, the Minotaur, other variations.

Then another war.

The war.

The war of the gods.

Armies ran at each other. Fury. Aggression. Pure anger and hate. It ran through her, around her, and the Aten wanted more. The sky exploded above the army, a white wall of energy that engulfed everyone. Chase felt the heat on her face and started to give in to the emotions, to the purity of the feelings. Now she was in space. Falling to earth. Crashing into the desert. Bonding with the ground, forming into something new.

The voice in her head changed. It was speaking English now. Close to her own voice.

Use me.

Use me.

Guerrero was calling her name, but she couldn't focus on his words.

Then he was easing the Aten from her, wrapping it back up in the animal hide without touching the smooth surface.

"Where did you go?" he asked.

"I felt . . . amazing."

"You looked angry."

Chase breathed in and out. Every sense was heightened. Her heart was pounding. Hands shaking. She could feel the pull to pick up the Aten again, to hear that voice and feel the power. Chase closed her eyes and swallowed, trying to flush the influence from her mind.

"It's dangerous," she said, keeping her eyes closed. "They were right. It's too dangerous."

When Chase opened her eyes, Zoe was sitting up. She wiped the blood from her face with her sleeve and climbed to her feet. She swayed unsteadily where she stood, her eyes locked on the bundle.

"Is that it? That's the Aten?"

"And the dead guy," Guerrero said, trying for a nervous joke. "Alex, meet Zoe. Zoe, meet Alex." Guerrero turned to the dead king. "No need to get u p."

Zoe reached out a hand. There was an odd look in her eyes. It was more than the glassy stare of a concussion; there was a purpose to the expression, even a darkness. Instinctively, Guerrero put the bundle behind him. He looked at Chase. Chase turned to glance back into the coffin as the voice spoke in her head.

Use me.

Use me.

And a different voice now. An echo, a memory of what Zoe had said back at the bookshop: "I could have used you."

A gun cocked. Chase knew what she was going to see before she turned. Zoe was holding the Ruger in both hands, aiming it squarely at Guerrero.

Guerrero made a strangled noise of surprise.

"Give it to me," Zoe said.

"When did they get to you?" Chase took a slow step forward.

Guerrero asked, "What's going on?"

"She's with the Visitologists." Chase took another step toward Zoe.

"When was it?"

Zoe's mouth turned into a cruel smile. "You'd like it to be because of us, wouldn't you? Like the only thing I could replace you with was religion. What right did you have, to eat, travel, live off my family's fortune? And then you, you, living off my money, decided to change the rules? Before I was ready?"

Zoe's words were thick and slightly slurred. The head injury was slowing her movements, but that made her dangerous. She was holding the gun, but was she really in control of it?

"They don't lie to me," Zoe continued. "Never have. Never will."

Chase took a final step toward the gun. "And how is this supposed to work? You shoot us and claim the tomb for the church?"

Zoe's hands tightened around the grip. She didn't look comfortable with the feel of it, but Chase couldn't judge that now. Zoe had killed Turner, and who knew who else? How much blood did she have on her hands, to get to this point?

"You think I care about a tomb? We want the Aten."

"To do what?" Chase shot back. "Prove you're right? Put your god above everyone else's? You'll start a war."

"We're stopping a war. Don't you see it? We're right. All the years, the centuries, we've always been right. The needless wars over other gods, the murder, the genocide. We just need to be listened to. Trusted. And once we prove it, once it's our time, we will be ready for the next level. No more war. No more hunger, famine. No more pain. We're bringing in the new age. Bringing back the Old Ones."

Chase focused on only the one thing she believed in the middle of all that. Centuries? The Visitologists dated back to the fifties. But there was another explanation that made all too much sense. If the Knights of Saint Mark had been here the whole time, then . . .

"Atenists," Chase said. "You're Atenists."

"Of course. We just rebrand. Change the name, hide away in plain sight, just like Henry's little pet army. But now we've won." Zoe's eyes met Chase's. Something mean flashed behind them. "I killed the last of them. You helped me."

Chase remembered seeing the light go out in Georgie Turner. She felt the anger swell but bit back on it. She needed to stay calm. "But why? She could have told you everything."

"An accident. I was aiming for her shoulder. Still needed you alive." She smiled. "Back then."

"And what was last night?"

Zoe laughed. "Nothing."

She pulled the trigger.

FIFTY-ONE

For just a few seconds, Mason couldn't remember anything. Then the room came back in around her. This wasn't like waking up from the drug. Her body was already alert, but her mind felt distant. Fragmented. The glove.

Parish.

He'd stepped back and was talking into a phone.

"...right here. Yeah, knows about Douglas Buchan. No, not you, I don't think. I'll ask. After that, can I? Perfect." He paused, putting a hand over the phone to talk to Mason. "I'll murder you momentarily."

Mason was piecing her own mind back together at the same time she was trying to follow the conversation. Buchan was in on it. And somebody else. More important, Parish was asking for permission to kill her. He wasn't the one calling the shots. Mason needed to find out who was behind this.

What did she know about Parish?

Purely from his file? Nothing—the file was useless. Mason thought instead of the people she had spoken to. She had told Chase that he "loved conspiracy theories, hated grammar." That had been a direct quote from someone. She couldn't remember who, but it didn't matter. If the same angry kid was still in there behind Parish's bravado, Mason had a weapon. She could use his ego and his paranoia against him.

"Really?" Parish sounded excited. "Found it? We should step up the pace. Is she— Okay." He hung up and turned to Mason. "Where were we?"

"I think you were about to explain the rest of your plan to me."

Parish smiled. "Oh, you'll be part of it. Don't worry."

Mason laughed. It sounded as genuine as she could manage.

"What's so funny?"

"Nothing," she said. "Get on with it."

Parish stepped toward her and raised the glove. He paused again when he saw the sly smile at the corner of her mouth. "What?"

"You don't get it, do you?" Mason said, like she was about to explain how the moon landings were obviously faked. "You don't know what's really going on here?"

Parish cocked his head to one side. "I know we're winning."

Mason's wrists were rubbed raw. Her hands were numb, and her shoulder muscles were at the tearing point. The move needed to be now.

"Really." She laughed under her breath, enough to make him angry. "That's what they want you to think. You don't get it? You're just part of the game. We are so much bigger than you know. And now it's too late. You didn't see it in time."

Parish stepped in close. Mason could read the confusion in his eyes. That little boy prone to paranoia, seeking answers in conspiracy, now had one to latch on to. He opened his mouth to speak, and Mason made her move.

She head-butted Parish. As he rocked back on his heels, Mason pulled herself up and wrapped her thighs around his torso, pulling him in tight. She locked her feet together behind him and squeezed. Parish tried to pull away, but Mason held on. His arms were loose, and first he tried pushing at Mason's legs, trying to pry himself free. When that didn't work, he started aiming punches at her gut, chest, and face.

Mason had expected the blows, but that didn't make them any less painful. She took each one, trying to block out the pain. If Parish had been a more experienced fighter, he would have relaxed, making it easier to wriggle free, or aimed gouges at Mason's weak spots, like her eyes, mouth,

or armpits. Instead he fought back, twisting and turning, pulling and pu
shing.

Mason's wrists were pulling on the metal of the cuffs, and she felt blood
running down her arms. Her shoulders felt like they were being ripped
from her body.

But now it wasn't just Mason's weight on the pipe, along with Martyn's
corpse—it was also the struggling Parish.

Mason felt the pipe bounce. It moved down a couple of inches but didn't
break. She didn't have much strength left.

She looked at the security camera, wondering if anyone had noticed yet.
If they had, armed guards would be in here at any moment, and she would
be done. Mason felt the stab wound in her side tear open. Parish must have
noticed the blood, because he aimed a punch directly into the tender flesh.
One. Two. Three.

Mason yelped in pain and relaxed her grip. Parish pulled free.

He hit the wound again.

Mason's vision blurred.

Pain and exhaustion were overpowering her, and she felt unconscious-
ness calling, promising to ease the hurt. Mason knew if she closed her eyes,
she might never open them again. She heard the lock being turned in the
door behind her.

Now.

Something had to happen now.

Parish stepped in for another hit. Mason put everything she had into
pulling herself up, screaming at the pain of it, and wrapping her thighs
around his neck.

He pulled, pushed, rocked. Clawed at her legs and tried pressing into her
side. Mason held on, yelling again and again. She heard the door open but
blocked out any other sounds. Parish's movements slowed as he gasped for
air. She felt him weaken, and then go limp. He slumped over, dead weight.
Mason kept him in her grip, and as he dropped, the pipe broke loose.

Mason fell to the floor and landed on top of Parish. She rolled free and tried to stand up, but her legs gave out. The room was filling with the smell of gas. She looked up as someone stepped into the room toward her.

Peter Cullis, holding a gun, with blood on his arm.

He lowered the weapon when he smelled the gas. "I guess you don't need rescued, then?"

Mason raised her hands, gesturing for him to come and help her up. An overweight security guard stepped into the doorway as Cullis stooped to help Mason to her feet, his weapon trained on the older spy's back. "Freeze," he shouted, just like he'd probably seen in the movies. He was clearly about to shoot, ignoring the gas filling the room.

Cullis turned and punched the guard in the throat. He hit the wall, then fell to the floor.

Cullis took the gun off the slumped guard and handed it to Mason. She slipped it into the waistband of her stolen jeans. Cullis pulled a radio off the guard's belt and started searching the channels. Mason checked Parish's pulse. It was faint, but he was alive. She slipped the metal glove off his hand and put it on. They could learn a lot from taking Parish with them, but Mason wasn't in any shape to carry or drag him, and Cullis would need to concentrate on leading her out.

"Where are we?" she asked.

Cullis looked out through the doorway, checking that the path was clear, before turning to Mason. "The Visitology building. New one." That made sense. Mason should have guessed that herself.

She heard a beeping sound and pulled the tablet from Parish's pocket. The screen announced there was a message. Mason tapped to load the video, and Zoe Forrester's face filled the screen.

"We have it. Marah is dead. I'll send the footage for you to edit." Zoe paused to look at someone just out of shot. "Gotta go." The message ended.

Mason was exhausted. She ached all over, and her mind still felt scrambled from whatever Parish's glove had done. Still, she felt her heart drop at hearing Chase was dead. A feeling she'd been trying hard not to acknowledge now felt like the most obvious thing in the world. She wanted to cry, but they didn't have the time.

Mason and Cullis shared a look. It was down to them now.

Cullis nodded for her to follow and headed through the open door. Mason stepped out into a large room with three desks piled high with electrical equipment and used coffee cups and a number of computers. On one of the screens, she could see the live feed from the security camera that had been trained on her in the room. In this room, there were three guards on the floor, all dead.

Cullis had been busy.

"Still got it," he said with a smile.

He led the way to a stairwell, and they started to climb as fast as Mason could manage. Adrenaline could only do so much against her injuries. She was well past a second and third wind, hoping to find a fourth.

Cullis talked her through each move. "You can do it, yes, and again. That's it."

"How did you find me?"

Cullis apologized before slipping his hand into the back pocket of her stolen jeans. He pulled out a small metal device, the size of a credit card. It had small wires across the surface and a microchip in the center.

"Planted that on you at Paddington," Cullis said.

Another guard stepped into the stairwell as they reached the next level. Cullis slammed his fist into the guard's throat and let him crumple to the floor.

"It's a coup." Mason groaned in pain as she started down the next flight of stairs. "They're going to attack London, blame us."

They stepped out into the lobby. Mason recognized it from her time sitting across the street. There were three more guards on the floor, stacked neatly, next to a trail of blood. They had been stripped down to their underwear.

Guy Lonnen was behind the security desk, watching monitors. He twitched a gun in their direction before he saw it was them. He looked nervous. Shaken. Holding the gun like he'd only ever used one in training. He was dressed in a security uniform, and the other two were piled next to him on the desk.

Cullis passed one of the piles to Mason and took the other for himself.

"I thought you two hated each other," Mason grunted as she knelt behind the desk and started pulling the stolen clothes off.

"We do," Cullis said. "But we're on the same side. And we hate losing even more."

"I've never shot anybody before," Lonnen said, his voice carrying his nerves.

"You still haven't." Cullis turned away from him. "Everyone here was mine."

Before Mason could button up the large men's security shirt, Cullis knelt to look at her open wound. "Needs a real doctor. I think it's infected."

They could hear police sirens now. Still a couple of minutes off, but closing in. Mason doubted they'd be friendly. Soon the front of the building would be crawling with cops. Cullis helped Mason back to her feet, and the three of them walked out to a black van parked outside. Mason lay down across the back seat, with Lonnen and Cullis sitting in front. They pulled out into Belvedere Road and turned right, toward Waterloo Bridge.

Mason felt tiredness wash over her.

Zoe Forrester was a traitor. Chase was dead. The Visitologists had the weapon, and they seemed to have people in every level of the system. They could use the weapon to destroy London, which would kick-start the last stage of the takeover.

And, as far as Mason could see, the only people standing in the way of that happening were her and two broken-down old spies.

No pressure.

FIFTY-TWO

T he Ruger clicked on an empty chamber.

Again. Again. Again.

Chase moved in fast and grabbed the gun. She punched Zoe hard on the nose. Zoe's knees buckled, and her legs went out from under her. She fell into a sitting position, clutching her face. There was a sluggishness to her movements, the head injury exacerbated by the punch.

Chase cracked open the revolver to show there were no rounds in any of the chambers. "You really think I'm that stupid?"

Zoe spat blood on the floor, then wiped her lips, leaving a dark smear across her mouth. "When did you know?"

A smile framed Chase's words. "Like you always said, I've never trusted you enough. Turns out? Not a character flaw. As soon as you knew I'd figured out the location, you wanted to play nice."

"You lied to me," Zoe said. She sounded sleepy. "You showed me the wrong place on the map."

"Of course I did."

Guerrero said. "Hey, next time you have a really cool plan or know that we're working with a loco, could you tell me about it in advance?"

"She doesn't do that," Zoe said. "Character flaw."

They heard footsteps on stone. Someone was walking toward them through the central tunnel. Flashlight beams filled the entrance as Wallace and Braun stepped out into the open. They were both armed. Chase didn't recognize the make, but the guns looked to be semiautomatic.

Chase had one loaded Ruger. Guerrero wasn't carrying. They were outgunned and outnumbered. Unless she counted the Aten.

Even at the thought of it, the voice filled her head. Could she try it? Could she control it?

Wallace made straight for the sarcophagus. He looked inside with a child's glee on his face. "I'm going to be so famous." Then to Chase, pretending it was an afterthought, he said, "Oh, we built a tracer into the camera. Lost her when you entered the sewers, but it wasn't hard to follow your trail."

Braun helped Zoe to her feet. She swayed for a moment, then seemed to regain her composure. Braun pulled the camera from Guerrero and started recording. Zoe waved for him to keep her out of the shot. He filmed the contents of the coffin, then turned to scan across Guerrero, Chase, and Wallace.

Zoe turned to Wallace. "Go for it."

Wallace stepped to the sarcophagus. Braun followed him.

"Here we, uh. This is Alexander the Great. The last resting place of the legendary king," Wallace narrated. He sounded as though he were trying to remember a script he'd rehearsed before that were running away from him in the moment. "See his armor and the sarcophagus that is said to have replaced the original, which was made of gold."

Braun was moving as Wallace talked, focusing the camera on the target. Zoe swayed, as though she were zoning out for a second, then shook her head. She leaned in closer to Braun and pulled a gun from his belt, pressing it to Guerrero's gut. He let her take the bundle. Her focus became more intense as she unwrapped the layers, taking the weight on the arm that was training the gun on Guerrero. Zoe placed her hand on the smooth surface.

Her features became dark and ferocious, taken by the power of the Aten.

In that instant, Chase was struck by a less intense version of the whole experience all over again. She could feel the Aten in her head, drawing out her emotions. But more than that, Chase could feel Zoe. They were connected. For the first time, Chase really saw Zoe. She could sense her anger and resentment. A great well of bitterness flowed between them.

Through it all, there was something else, a deeper need. Loneliness. A need to be heard, to be seen, to belong.

Chase recognized what she'd been fighting in herself for as long as she could remember.

And more visions. Or the same visions, but through a different perspective. Where Chase had seen history, and meteorites and gods, now Zoe was seeing flying machines, skyscrapers, aliens.

The Aten was showing people what they wanted to see.

Zoe pulled her hand away sharply.

"Oh, wow," she said. "Yes."

Her voice was back to normal now. Any effects of the head injury seemed to have been purged by the power of the Aten. Keeping the bundle wrapped in the hide, she turned toward Braun, who filmed it in her hands, keeping her face out of the shot.

Wallace started again, in his most BBC voice. "And here we have what I believe is called the Aten. It's an ancient weapon. Left over from a time we don't remember, from before written records. It's the root behind many later myths, like Thor's hammer, Mjölnir, and Ninurta's mace, Sharur. Maybe it's also what Moses used to part the Red Sea. I'm sure further studies will prove . . ."

Wallace trailed off as Braun lowered the camera.

"That's all we need," Zoe said. "That'll edit together nicely."

"But I haven't finished." Wallace's voice came out in a whine. "I've got a whole—"

Zoe shot him in the gut. His knees buckled, and he stumbled forward before falling to the floor, clutching both hands to the wound and groaning. Chase rocked back on her heels. The last few days had dulled her to the shock of hearing gunfire, even at such close quarters, but nothing could stop her feeling sick at the sound of a bullet hitting flesh. She hated Wallace, but they'd been friends for a long time. Just as when she'd watched Turner die, the biggest thing she felt was a lack of knowing how to feel. She didn't have the tools for processing death or grief.

Zoe looked down at Wallace as he took jagged, wet-sounding breaths. "You didn't even find it," she said to the struggling man. She turned to look up at the statue. She tapped it, then touched her own blood on the large hand. "These are interesting. Machines, I take it? Something to do with light or movement?"

Zoe raised the gun to Chase's face. She leaned in close and pulled at the clasp of Chase's messenger bag. With no other choice, Chase let her take it.

There was a numbness spreading out around her mind, down her neck and into her joints. Every problem she'd ever had with trust, every time she'd pushed someone away or kept something secret, it all wrapped around her, as she watched the grinning monster.

Zoe winked and stepped back, ready to shoot. Chase wasn't going to close her eyes. Zoe would have to stare her down as she did it.

But then, as her finger tightened on the trigger, Zoe paused. She looked again at the statue. While Braun kept his weapon trained on Chase and Guerrero, Zoe slipped hers into her waistband. She lifted the shield out of the sarcophagus and walked back toward the tunnels. Braun followed. At the bowl of burning oil, Zoe told Braun to pick up the torches that Chase and Guerrero had left on the ground.

Zoe looked straight at Chase one last time. "I see you now. You've always been so scared of being abandoned. So fast to run away. And you're so scared of the dark, like a little girl. This is your own version of hell, isn't it?"

She lowered Alexander's shield over the oil, extinguishing the flames. The light shrank back from the edges of the cavern. Zoe and Braun were illuminated in the electronic glow of their flashlights. The statue started to move. As Zoe and Braun disappeared from the site, the chamber was flooded with inky darkness. The fragile lock Chase had placed over them was ripped away.

Zoe had scored a direct hit.

Abandoned.

With the darkness came the loneliness and fear. Panic rose up. She heard grinding as the statue moved nearby.

Wallace grunted. He called out, "No." Then his voice turned into a scream. There was a sickening tearing sound. A spray of warm blood hit Chase's face, and Wallace was silenced.

Chase's heart and lungs were trying to break out of her chest. She felt as if she were sinking into iced water. Shock was setting in. Some fears were irrational, unfounded. But now she was trapped in darkness, with a monster she couldn't see. It was every nightmare she'd ever had.

Breathe.

Breathe.

Her parents were gone, and it got dark.

Chase was waiting for the cold logic of survival to kick in, but it wouldn't come. The creature moved close by. She could feel its presence right in front of her. It reached out and wrapped a hand around her shoulder, starting to squeeze, and lifted her off her feet. Chase screamed in pain as the statue's free hand reached back, balled into a fist. Chase knew the blow would take her head clean off.

This time, she closed her eyes.

There was a click, a small, metallic sound.

Chase realized it was a Zippo lighter. A small spark lit up over her shoulder, followed by a tiny flame. The creature froze as Guerrero held his lighter in its face. He held the flickering light out with one hand as he helped Chase pull free of the grip with the other.

"Don't worry," Guerrero said. "You're not alone."

"How did you know?"

"Güey, how long have I known you? Don't worry. I'm a pilot who's scared of heights. Shit happens."

Chase felt her knees buckle but stopped herself from falling. She took deep breaths, focusing on the ground, and the flame from the Zippo, and having a friend next to her.

"Take your time," Guerrero said. "And by 'take your time,' I mean, 'hurry it up, will you?'"

Chase laughed and stepped closer to the Zippo. Together, they turned toward the entrance. But as Guerrero stepped between the statue and the lighter, he blocked the light. They heard the creature turn.

Guerrero was punched off his feet. The Zippo fell from his hand and went out, plunging them into darkness. Chase was knocked to the ground, then heard the grinding above her. She rolled away as a foot stomped into the place where she'd been.

Chase climbed to her feet and stepped away again as she felt the statue's bulk move toward her. She brushed past what must have been the metal dish, then felt it rock and tip over as the creature followed her. She turned again and ran until she felt her feet splashing into water at the edge of the river.

Chase heard the creature turn and move toward where Guerrero had been. She could hear Guerrero patting at the ground, looking for the Zippo. She flicked the flashlight setting on her phone and shined it at the creature's back as it paced toward Guerrero, giving him the light he needed to find the Zippo.

Chase was about to call out for him to light the oil when she saw it had tipped out across the floor, soaking her shoes and the bottom of her jeans. If Guerrero lit the oil, Chase might burn.

The creature aimed a kick at Guerrero, but he rolled out of the way. It started after him again.

Chase lifted Alexander's sword out of the casket and charged. She swung it at the creature's back. It bounced off, and the rebound threw her to the ground. She splashed down into more oil and wondered which part of the "sword plan" had seemed like a good idea. The statue turned and bent down toward Chase. She looked up into its red eyes.

Something tugged at the back of her mind. A thought, an idea that needed a few more seconds.

She heard the chink of the lighter again, and the creature froze as Guerrero's flame sparked into life. The light was small and timid. It danced before flickering out.

Chase's fears welled up again. But she felt something else spreading beneath them: confidence. She knew now that the world really did have monsters waiting in the darkness. She took comfort in knowing this was no longer an irrational fear. And if it was rational, she could control it. These statues were just another threat to be faced down.

And with that, the thought at the back of her mind was fully formed.

Eyes.

Light sensors.

Blind it.

She called out to Guerrero, "Give me the—"

A large hand closed around her shoulder and lifted her from the ground. She tried to wriggle free, but the other hand closed on her hip, squeezing hard against the bone.

She heard the Zippo click. Guerrero was at her side, holding the flame out ahead of them. The creature's head was twisted around, with its teeth inches away from biting into Chase's neck. Chase pulled out her knife and pressed it to the edges of the creature's right eye, working the blade beneath it. She applied more pressure and the jewel slowly worked loose. Hissing steam escaped from the eye socket. Warm, damp. Chase ignored the pain, the lesser of two evils, as she pried the second eye loose. More steam shot out from the hole. The statues grip on Chase loosened. It seemed to shrivel in slightly, as if deflated. It stood motionless, with a faint clicking coming from somewhere deep inside, along with what sounded like liquid settling to a lower point.

Guerrero dropped to his knees and picked up the jewels, turning them over in his hand and whistling.

Chase stared back at the dark shape of the sarcophagus. Guerrero's celebrations died down when he saw she wasn't joining in.

"What do you want to do with him?" he asked.

Chase breathed in deep, then let it all out. "He's not going anywhere. We can come back when this is done."

They headed back along the passageway. The two torches were still on the floor where they'd left them. Guerrero picked up one. Chase prized the eyes out of the two statues. They each made a slightly different noise as they deactivated. The Minotaur sounded more like a broken clock, a machine with faulty cogs. Anubis sounded, if anything, more electrical. Chase wondered what secrets they hid inside, what could be harnessed and adapted by modern science.

She handed the jewels to Guerrero. "Free booty," she said.

Back at the junction, they found the entrance had been sealed. The metal disc was back in place. Chase paused to look at the glyphs on the wall. She ran her fingers across the markings.

She was stunned. "I can read this," she said.

Taking a step back, she looked around the chamber, focusing on the inscriptions with fresh eyes. She understood the language. Touching the Aten had changed things. She'd shared memories, and emotions, with the people who had held it before her.

"What does it say?"

"It's a warning," she said. "People dug down too deep. In the Sinai, I think, from the description. The mines. They found bad things. Basically, it says they found the gateway to hell."

"This is why I got into smuggling," Guerrero said with a grim smile. "And…who is they?"

"They don't say…" Chase's words died off in frustration. "There's no declaration of who is writing this, nobody signed it by name. I can remember things though. It's hard to explain. Some of them are here, in my head, but when I try to focus on who they are, it fades away."

Chase turned to look again at the machine covering the doorway. There were inscriptions covering the crystal. She followed them around the side. There was a small depression in the surface, almost unnoticeable. Chase saw it now only because the writing was telling her where to look. She let out a small laugh. Guerrero raised an eyebrow, and Chase pointed to the spot. "It says, In case of emergency, press here."

She pushed the hidden button, and the machine rumbled into life, moving backward into the chamber and uncovering the archway. Stepping back into the outer chamber, Chase could smell eggs and damp fireworks. Gunfire. Blood was pooled on the floor and led in a drip-drip-drip up the stairs. At the hole in the wall, Chase found a dead body. It was a middle-aged man, dressed in the same black robes as Turner. He bore the winged-lion tattoo on the inside of his forearm.

The Knights had tried to stop Zoe from leaving with the Aten.

There were two more Knights in the tunnel. One of them was Stanley. He was still breathing. He grabbed Chase's hand and said, "Stop them. You must stop them."

Chase promised that she would. She hesitated before taking his hand. He'd tried to burn her alive but somehow they'd ended up on the same side. Brompton felt like another lifetime. The Aten had changed everything.

His grip was strong for one final moment, before his fingers relaxed and he slipped away.

Guerrero crossed himself and whispered a prayer under his breath. Then they climbed back out into the sewer, where Chase realized Guerrero had left the flaming torch down in the outer chamber of the tomb. She had come the rest of the way in darkness, with only the occasional dim light from his cell phone as their guide.

She wasn't afraid of the dark anymore.

FIFTY-THREE

Chase and Guerrero climbed out of the manhole. Cars were already swerving to avoid the opening with the cover resting beside it. Zoe and Braun hadn't bothered to put in back in place. There had been blood on the ladder rungs and more on the edge of the manhole. Either Zoe or Braun had been hit. Maybe both.

But they were gone.

Chase turned at the sound of a car horn and saw Ali pulling out from the curb, where he'd probably been illegally parked. He skidded to a stop beside them and leaned over to push the door open. Chase took the front passenger seat; Guerrero slid into the back.

"They went in a taxi," Ali said, "heading to the airport."

Guerrero leaned across the seat to whisper in Chase's ear. "Say it. You gotta say it."

"Follow that cab."

Ali floored the pedal. Drivers pulled across the lane to get out of the way, their horns and swearing filling the early-morning air. Ali pulled the wheel hard to the right, then back to the left, swerving between a truck and a car coming in the opposite direction. He took the on-ramp for the Cairo-Alexandria Road, the wide, modern highway that led south into the country. It would take them most of the way to the airport.

"Where are they going?" Guerrero said. "With that thing."

Chase thought back to the moment Zoe had touched the Aten and their thoughts had been connected.

"London," Chase said. "They're going to use it on London. As soon as they land."

"What do we do?"

Chase's voice was flat. Calm. "We stop them."

"This is why I got into smuggling," Guerrero said. "For the big damn heroism."

Chase had seen Zoe as she really was. And beneath the posturing and anger, there had been some small trace of someone hurt, someone scared. Someone who needed to matter. Chase was banking on that, hoping she could still reach Zoe.

There was a box on the back seat next to Guerrero, full of weaponry. Chase pointed to what she needed. Three grenades, a knife, and two revolvers. She loaded the guns with ease.

Guerrero shook his head. "Remind me never to piss you off."

"You need reminding?"

Ali laughed. He was switching lanes every few hundred yards, weaving between traffic. He turned onto the Tanta-Alexandria Highway, now a straight shot to the airport. Chase saw the towers and departure lounges rising up above them, with planes coming in to land. There was a small jet sitting on the tarmac, with people climbing the stairs. Chase recognized Zoe from behind. She was carrying the wrapped bundle.

Chase pointed at the jet, but Ali shrugged.

"They rich," he said.

Since the uprising, the country's security forces were stretched thin, and everything was available to the highest bidder—even airport security.

Chase had planned for this. She had cash back at the hotel, ready to bribe their way out when needed. But they'd left in a hurry and, like most of Chase's attempts at a plan, they were now making it up as they went.

Guerrero leaned across the seat and held up one of the jewels. "This will get us in the private gate."

"Will Molly be ready to fly?" asked Chase.

"Really don't know. She was in a bad way, and they haven't had much time to fix her up."

At the private gate, Ali bartered with the guards in a mix of dialects. He was going too slow for Chase's liking, playing the game of pretending to have nothing, working his way up to revealing the jewel. He needed to get the maximum value for it, and Chase had to sit and wait.

At the end, Ali had bought an armed escort out onto the tarmac. The guard rode on ahead of them on a cheap motorcycle, leading them in the direction of the Visitologists' jet.

The plane's door was already closed, and the engines had started. Chase watched as it began taxiing to the runway. There was no way to stop it now, short of a rocket launcher.

Guerrero pointed across the field. Molly stood in the far corner, in front of a hangar, with large pieces of her hull hanging off and wires trailing from the engine.

"Doesn't look good," Guerrero said.

The sound of the jet's engines increased to a roar, and the plane shot down the runway, lifting up into the sky with speed and grace. There was a bright flash from the direction of the hangar, followed a second later by a thunderclap and a wall of heat. Molly exploded into a ball of flames.

Guerrero climbed out of the car and took a few steps toward the burning wreck of his plane before letting out an anguished yelp and falling to his knees. Chase knew he'd loved Molly in the way middle-aged men love a sports car, but she didn't have time to let him grieve.

There was another plane poking its nose out from the hangar. Chase didn't know much about planes, but this one looked to be newer and larger than Molly. She knelt down next to Guerrero and placed a hand on his shoulder.

"Feel like a joyride?"

FIFTY-FOUR

The safe house was on the top floor of a new building on Cosser Street.

Across the road was a backpackers' hostel, full of European students and burned-out hippies. Mason stood in the bedroom window and watched as they left in groups, shouting greetings and farewells to one another in a variety of languages.

Mason was wearing clean clothes. Her wound was freshly dressed. There was a doctor three doors down, in one of the older houses, who specialized in back-door treatment for the travelers from the hostel. Cullis had brought him up to the apartment to see to Mason's injuries. The stab wound had indeed picked up an infection, but the doctor had cleaned it and applied an antibiotic ointment and a new dressing. Mason had hurt both shoulders, but the doctor couldn't tell whether they were strains or more serious muscle damage. He gave her a supply of painkillers to get her through the next few days.

Mason was used to pushing through pain. Ignoring it. She kept the drugs nearby but wouldn't take them unless things became unbearable. She needed to be alert for what was to come.

The safe house belonged to Lonnen. He'd bought it five years earlier through an alias. His paranoia may have been the butt of countless jokes in the service, but it had paid off. Nobody at Legoland knew about this place, or the four others he had dotted around the city. There were hundreds of cameras in the area, but they were all trained elsewhere. The hostel. A hotel at the bottom of the road. The police station just around the corner. A mosque half a mile away, which had never shown any signs of being a danger. Lonnen explained there were only six black spots like this in all of London, tiny dots on the map that had slipped through the cracks, and he knew each of them. Mason was willing to guess his other properties were in those places, but she didn't push the issue.

She walked through to the kitchen at the back. Cullis and Lonnen were sitting around a desk covered in computer monitors. Each one showed a different CCTV feed. There was also a satellite image of the whole city refreshing every few seconds and what looked to be updates from a police network, showing the locations of units and popping up boxes full of information on emergency calls.

Through the window, Mason could see the Visitologist building, rising up less than a mile away. They were sitting in the shadow of the enemy, and nobody knew where they were.

Mason poured herself a coffee from a pot on the counter and pulled up a chair next to her two mentors.

"So this is what Parish was using?"

Lonnen nodded, but it was Cullis who answered. "Yes."

"I'm hacked into the security grid through a backdoor," Lonnen said. "I can watch everything they're doing."

"When Parish was talking to me on the phone, when I thought it was Martyn, and he said someone was trying to hack him—"

Lonnen nodded again. "Me. But I have to be careful with it. Each time they notice me, they try to track the line back here. I'm running out of lives."

"Were you using me all along, like Chase? Just a decoy to draw them out?" Mason kept her voice controlled, not letting her anger show.

Cullis looked down at the drink on the desk in front of him. Mason could see his jaw flexing. He looked to be fighting himself about the best way to reply.

"Sorry," Lonnen said. He paused to wipe his nose. "I didn't like it. Neither of us did. But desperate measures."

"It was rough," Cullis agreed. "I'm sorry, Mase."

Mason felt heat flush on her cheeks. She didn't like being used. By anybody. Trust wasn't something she gave out lightly, and two of the only people she trusted in the world had lied to her. But through it all, Mason was a professional. She lied to people all the time. Those were the rules of the game. She'd lost a fiancé to it. She'd been willing to manipulate Chase, believing the ends to justify the means. She felt like a hypocrite for being angry at Lonnen and Cullis for doing the same thing, but they'd done it to her .

And thinking of Chase was enough to bring down her emotions. Another casualty to the game. Someone who had put her faith in Mason and died because of it.

She pushed through it all, getting back on topic. One of the windows on the screen was showing a small plane, a sleek jet, in the air over a layer of clouds. "What's that?"

"The Visitologist jet." Lonnen clicked the mouse and brought up information about the plane, its takeoff time and expected arrival at Heathrow.

"They're on the way here from Egypt, with whatever they found."

"How long do we have?"

"It's due to land in two hours and six minutes." He dragged the flight details across the screen to show a separate window beneath it, with a live feed of BBC News 24. "And that's not all."

Lonnen clicked on the small speaker icon, and the reporter's voice filled the room.

"—details of a foiled terror attack on the London Eye this morning. The security services haven't released any details, but I'm just hearing that

Douglas Buchan has called for the new National Security bill to be brought forward to an emergency session. If agreed, then government could be—"

Lonnen muted the sound. "The prime minister has agreed. Parliament will be meeting in three hours."

"They labeled you rescuing me as a terrorist attack?"

Cullis nodded. "And they're bringing a weapon in. Parliament will be sitting ducks."

"We need to do something," Mason said. The urgency in her voice, with an edge of panic, was a shock to her own ears.

"I am." Lonnen brought up another window. "You think your friend might know how to deactivate the weapon?"

A second plane.

Smaller. Slower. Mason's heart bounced when she realized what it meant.

Chase was alive.

FIFTY-FIVE

S tealing a plane turned out to be easy.

One of Guerrero's jewels was enough to convince the security team to take a coffee break. A second jewel paid the fire crew to ignore the foreigners creeping around behind them. Two more were enough to bribe the mechanics to fuel up the plane and hand over all the paperwork.

That left Guerrero with just one of the jewels he'd taken from the cave. He said he would guard it more closely than his own family. Chase didn't take much from that. She knew one of the reasons he'd enlisted in the air force was to get away from his parents.

Guerrero let out a childlike squeal when he got a look at his new ride. He turned to Chase to see if she'd heard him, and she busted his balls straightaway. He'd explained it was an Antonov, the same as Molly, but a model that hadn't been released yet. He listed a bunch of letters and numbers: AN-13-something. A transport plane designed specifically at the request of the Saudi royal family. It was larger than Molly—especially after the explosion. There was a small cockpit, with a door through to a long and luxurious passenger area, and a cargo section at the back. There was a large propeller on either wing.

Chase had never seen Guerrero so excited. He sat up front, in what he insisted on calling the captain's chair, and made Chase ask for permission to climb aboard. The engines fired up at the first attempt, which in itself was an improvement over Molly, and they eased into the sky with none of the previous plane's rattles or shakes.

They flew out low over the Mediterranean, before climbing high into the clouds as they approached the south of Italy. Guerrero tried to make radio contact with the Italian authorities to clear a flight route but couldn't find anybody.

"It's like we're not here," Guerrero said. "Everything is working fine, but there's no radio signal, no tracking from the authorities. Either we're not here, or they're not there. But we are here, and they are there."

"Is that a problem?"

"We'll find out. If they shoot at us."

"Is that likely?"

"We'd probably get a flyby first, if they're worried. It's kind of hard up here to pull over and show license and registration."

"And we're in a stolen plane."

"From the Saudi royal family, yeah. I think they might take issue with that."

"So as long as they don't notice us at all . . ."

"Well, there's also the chance of a crash."

"Up here?"

Guerrero shrugged. "I've got no flightpath information. And nobody on the ground is seeing us. There could be Boeings, jets, all sorts of things, heading up through the clouds straight for us. It'll be fun."

Chase leaned forward to look at the layer of clouds beneath them. "Is this your way of calming down a passenger?"

"We just fought messed-up robots from the dawn of time, and a bunch of crazy people have a weapon that can destroy London, but you're worried about my bedside manner?"

He started running his hands over the dials and controls in front of him, talking to the plane in a soothing voice and telling it to ignore whatever Chase said.

"What are you going to name her?" Chase asked over Guerrero's smooth talk.

"The I Hope It's Worth It, maybe?" He grinned. "I don't know. A name has to come naturally. We'll see what she is. It's in the way she handles, the way she talks."

"Right."

"And if she's a cien en el zapato, I can call her Marah."

"I think that's how my parents did it."

They stayed silent for a long time after that.

Chase heard a noise coming from the passenger section behind them, on the other side of the cockpit door. It could be nothing. Or it could be the door to the cargo bay opening. She looked at Guerrero, who nodded to say he'd heard it, too.

Chase unbuckled her seat belt and stood up, trying to make no sound as she moved. She walked slowly over to the door and pressed her ear against it. Nothing. She slid the lock to open, slowly, trying to make no noise, and gripped the handle ready to open it. The door pulled away from her, and she fell through. A fist hit her square in the jaw, knocking her backward into the cockpit.

Braun stepped in after her. He had a bandage wrapped around his head, and his jacket showed a deep bloodstain on the sleeve. Chase guessed he was the one who'd been hit in the gunfight with the Knights.

"My turn," he said.

Guerrero swore under his breath and stood up out of his seat. Braun pulled a gun and fired. Chase turned to see Guerrero fall backward against the controls. The jet tilted forward into a dive. Guerrero's shoulder was a mess of blood and pulp, his arm hanging at his side, but he was still breathing and started to wrestle with the controls. Braun took aim again, but Chase jumped at him before he could shoot. Braun caught her. He was still too strong for her weight to move him, but there was a grunt as he moved his injured arm.

He pulled her into a bear hug and started to squeeze. Chase pulled her right hand into a knuckles-out fist, forming a sharp point, and pressed it into the blood on Braun's arm. It took some searching, but she found the soft spot and dug in. Braun yelped like a wounded dog.

Braun spun around and threw Chase into the passenger section. Her head hit one of the seats, and she fell to the floor, stunned. She shook her head, trying to refocus, and shuffled backward as he walked toward her.

"Can you fly a plane?" Chase said, playing for time as she looked for something to use as a weapon. She neared the emergency exit over the wing. "Because you'll need to, if you kill Chuy."

He laughed. "For the new age."

It sounded like a dark motto. A phrase repeated between cult members.

Chase's gut turned over. This was a suicide mission for Braun. He wasn't going to worry about damaging the plane on his way to finishing the job.

Chase needed to hold him back. She needed the Antonov to stay in the air.

Braun smiled.

He pulled a gun and pointed it at the fuselage wall. Keeping his eyes on Chase, he pulled the trigger.

How are we watching this?" Mason asked, staring at the screen. Satellite images showed the plane's progress, updating every few seconds like a slow animation.

"Our surveillance system has a few . . . upgrades," Lonnen replied. "We can piggyback onto other European networks, watch their CCTV, hack the satellites. I'm keeping her plane off the reporting systems, but if I do any more than that, I'll break my cover."

"Do the other countries know we can do this?"

"Not exactly."

"They don't know," Cullis cut through Lonnen's vague answers. "But we're pretty sure they're doing the same to us."

Mason started to feel uneasy. She'd always known the security grid existed, and common sense told her how much they were capable of with modern technology. But to see it in front of her now, at the touch of a button, was different. She'd dedicated her life to spying on people and gathering information. Every day for her involved a moral compromise, an unspoken deal with her own conscience. But the job involved human interactions, speaking to people, judging their body language and honesty. It felt a world removed from using technology like this.

"I don't like this," she said.

"Neither do I," Cullis said. He was leaning back in his seat, as far away from the computer screen as possible, without moving the chair back across the room.

Lonnen shrugged. "Nothing has changed. The job has always been information. This is information."

Mason touched the screen. "Where's it controlled from?"

"Usually multiple terminals. Wherever authorized people are logged on. GCHQ have a whole team for it, Thames House has three terminals. We have one at Legoland."

Mason leaned closer. "I'm sensing a but..."

"When the security forces were put on stand-down, all but one of the terminals were closed. Locked up."

"So whoever is controlling all of this . . ."

"Is the person we need to go after, yes. We now have a target, but getting to them will be tough. They have access to every camera, every phone, every computer in London."

"How were you two able to come for me, if they can watch everything?"

Cullis held up a metal card, like the one he'd planted on Mason the night before. "Part of the backdoor Guy had built into the system. There's a signal that tells the computer not to pay attention to you, blocks out facial recognition. If someone sees you on the street, or a direct video feed, you're still toast, but if they're filtering it all through the system, they won't see you."

Cullis handed the card to Mason.

Lonnen typed a few commands into the computer. "You're activated."

"How did you do all this?"

"Martyn, mostly," Lonnen said. "He didn't know the full picture. Like you, he only knew his part of it. He'd been working on the last upgrade to the network and started building in these backdoors for us, but then he went missing. Next thing, he's in the news as a traitor."

Cullis tapped the image of the muted BBC channel. Douglas Buchan was giving a speech. Lonnen bought the sound up.

"—for far too long. The attack this morning shows how fragile our peace is. At a time when our trust in our own security forces, the very people sworn to protect us, is at an all-time low, what this country needs, what this world leads, is a strong and stable guiding hand. We need to put trust back into our politics and our security. Today's bill is vital to restoring our own control, to put security and freedom directly into the hands of the people you have elected—"

Lonnen muted it again. "I've heard enough."

"They want to put all of this"—Cullis waved at the screens—"in the hands of one person. Do away with judicial review, with oversight. We'll be a dictatorship overnight."

"But they don't need it," Mason said. "If this weapon does what they think, they don't need the law on their side; they can just attack."

"They always want the law on their side. That's how dictatorships happen. With a pen. With consent."

Lonnen added, "We should know. We've facilitated enough of them."

"But hang on." Mason paused a second. There was a piece she was missing. It was just out of reach. "Are we saying the prime minister is in on this? A Visitologist?"

"I don't believe so." Lonnen tapped Buchan's face on the screen. "I'm sure he's their man in government."

"So what good will it do to let the prime minister have control—"

Click.

The pieces fell into place.

It was almost audible, because all three of them seemed to realize it as the time.

They looked at one another, then to the images of the two planes.

Mason said what they were each thinking. "Parliament convenes, debates the new bill, maybe even passes it in an emergency vote, or at least gets it into the public's mind. Then the prime minister, and whoever else in government isn't in on this, gets taken out in a terrorist attack planned by rogue MI6 agents. So then a hero steps in—someone like Douglas Buchan—to reluctantly push the reforms through, take control of the country."

"And it's all legal," Cullis said. "All voted for. All agreed to."

"Then we need to bring in the experts, the only people who seem to understand this weapon and its power." They fell silent.

On the screens, Buchan finished his speech. The Visitologist jet inched closer.

Mason said, "We can warn the airports, close them down."

"That will give away our position. Whoever is monitoring the network could trace it back to here. And even if they don't, they can just override the command with the airports. Tell them it's a hoax."

"Or we broadcast a warning to the people, on the internet, television, radio."

Lonnen threw up his hands. "Same problem. While they're in control of this network, if we send out a message, they can just block us or contradict us. And they've got the video evidence that we are the enemy."

One problem at a time. The weapon hadn't yet arrived. Someone was controlling the security network. They had just under two hours to sort it out.

"How do we shut this down?" Mason asked.

Lonnen nodded as he answered. "Another part of the backdoor. There's a command, a hidden diagnostic program. It would lock the system up in running a permanent sweep."

Cullis raised a finger. "There's just one problem." "What's that?" Mason said.

"We can't run the program from here. It needs to be from one of the authorized terminals. And only one of those is currently running. In the Box. At Legoland."

The sound of the shot bounced around the cabin. The bullet left a small hole in the fuselage wall. Pure sunlight beamed in, leaving a bright dot on the opposite side. There was a sucking sound, and the temperature was dropping fast.

Otherwise, nothing changed.

Braun looked at the hole, and then at Chase. Childlike confusion was writ large across his face.

"Seen too many movies," Chase said, taking her own chance to smile.

Guerrero called from the cockpit, "Don't shoot holes in my plane."

He sounded drowsy. Chase needed to see how bad the gunshot wound was, but first there was this giant slab of Nazi to deal with. As Braun turned to aim his gun at Guerrero, Chase jumped on his back. She wrapped both arms around his neck and started to squeeze. He still got a shot off, but it went wide, hitting the controls. There was a fizz and a pop, followed by an electronic beeping sound, but the plane was still in the air. Chase needed to get the gun before Braun could do any permanent damage.

She loosened her grip with one arm and grabbed at the weapon. Braun was caught by surprise, and she was able to bat it from his grip. The pistol skidded along the floor, toward the back of the plane. Braun growled and spun around, throwing Chase off. She hit a seat and bounced, falling into the aisle.

Braun paced toward her. Chase knew she couldn't take him in a straight fight. He was too strong. Guerrero would stand a slightly better chance if he weren't bleeding out and trying to keep them airborne.

Chase scooted backward, toward the rear of the plane. Feeling the door to the cargo area behind her back, she reached for the handle and opened it, climbing to her feet and stepping through. She pressed the door shut. The room around her was bare. Empty shelves large enough for suitcases lined one wall, and there were straps and ties on the opposite side, next to the emergency exit.

She heard a grunt, followed by a bang. The door almost gave. It would break on the second attempt. Chase wrapped her right arm up in one of the cargo straps. As the door fell inward, she pulled on the release mechanism for the emergency exit. The handle turned upward and came out toward her.

Braun stepped into the room, and they locked eyes.

Chase pulled the release the rest of the way, and the outer door opened, shooting out into the air with more force than she had anticipated. The power of it nearly pulled Chase's arm from its socket as she was yanked out onto the side of the plane. She almost lost her grip on the strap.

Her ears popped. For a second, she couldn't hear anything at all, then nothing but wind and a sucking sound. Tears streamed down her face as the air inside the cabin was sucked out past her. She slammed into the plane's side, once, twice, three times. The air in her lungs felt heavy; she could feel them expanding, like she was drawing in a deep breath. She looked at her feet, her head swimming, and saw the tail of the plane beyond them, and then nothing but empty sky.

Braun slipped by, trying to grab hold of something to pull himself back in. His hands caught her legs with a violent jerk, nearly ripping her from the strap. Her arm and shoulder screamed in pain as they both hung from the side, flapping against the fuselage. Chase knew she didn't have the strength to hold on for long, and her hands were growing numb with cold.

The plane rocked and bounced, skipping through the air like a stone on a lake. Each jolt threatened to shake her loose. They flew down through the clouds, and Chase hoped it was deliberate, that Guerrero was trying to bring the plane under control at a lower altitude.

Breathe. She needed desperately to breathe.

Why couldn't she?

Chase pulled herself forward, along the strap, and wrapped both arms around it. She turned in the air, trying to focus on Braun and block out the pain and the sight of the mountains below.

Were they the Alps?

Maybe they were the Alps.

Best not to think about the Alps.

Chase squinted, the wind battering her eyes. She couldn't shake Braun free, but soon he'd pull them both loose. She needed to do the exact thing her instincts were telling her not to. Every muscle in her body was trying to seize up, telling her to hold on with everything she had. She relaxed her grip slightly, enough to get a little slack on the strap. She wrapped it around her right arm and then, with a prayer to anyone who was listening, she let go with her left.

Chase was pulled out farther and smacked into the side of the plane, hitting the back of her head. But she held on. Her right arm was now the most important thing in her whole life. With her left, she punched downward, into Braun's wound.

Again.

Again.

She saw his mouth open and close but couldn't hear anything. Again and again, she pressed the advantage. His grip loosened. Then, with one last shout, he let go and was gone from sight.

Chase tried to suck in a breath, but still she couldn't. Her lungs felt paralyzed. There was no oxygen around her to get. She turned back to the strap and started pulling herself in, inch by inch. She was moving but couldn't feel her hands. Some part of her brain was managing to control them, but it wasn't receiving signals back. She crawled all the way in and managed a few shallow breaths, sucking in the breathable air inside the cabin and flexing her fingers until feeling came back, followed by a deep burning sensation.

It took all her remaining strength to pull the door closed, and push down on the handle, engaging the lock. She lay on the floor, heaving, until she felt strong enough to stand. She failed at the first attempt and fell back to her knees, ready to throw up. After a few more deep breaths, she tried again and paced unsteadily to the cockpit.

Guerrero was in the captain's seat. His hands were firm on the controls, though one of them was slick with blood. He turned to look at her with heavy-lidded eyes.

"I'm definitely naming her after you," he said.

FIFTY-SIX

Mason and Cullis stood on Rampayne Street. Mason looked down the road, to where she had stolen the BMW while escaping MI6. That had been either the day before or a lifetime ago, depending on which model she used for keeping time. And now she was about to break into the same building she had been running from.

Pimlico tube station had been built into the foundation of an eight-story office building. It was the only station on the line that didn't officially interchange with any other routes, and also the one that never seemed to get any of the renovations rolled out across the city. To civilians, this was just an inconvenience, put down to bureaucracy and funding. In reality, Pimlico had more money spent on it than almost any other station in London. There was a light electric rail system running parallel to the tube line, which led straight into a purpose-built platform beneath Legoland.

The office building above the station, though officially home to a number of small businesses, was full of MI6 staff. The security services were largely exempt from health and safety laws and so didn't need to abide by legislation about access to emergency exits. In theory, they were able to refuse to allow staff out even in the event of a fire. Nevertheless, even MI6 had something of a heart. Many civilian staff, the paperwork pushers who

could be allowed to run screaming from flames without risk to national
security, were housed in Spook Station.

In the event of an evacuation, the disguised black doors lining the base
of

the building would open, and nonessential staff would file out to con-
gregate on the corner, waiting for the fire marshal in a high-vis jacket to
tick them off a list. If such an evacuation were to take place, there would
be a window of opportunity, a matter of about two minutes, for someone
to push in through the crowd, down the steps, and onto the light rail
system. The security barriers would be open. Electronic passes wouldn't be
needed. That would be a problem they would encounter at the other end of
the tunnel, where Legoland's doors would still be guarded and locked. The
staff guarding those doors would rather burn alive in a fire than abandon
their posts.

Mason and Cullis were waiting across the road, with high-vis jackets
hidden beneath their coats. They were silent, each one keeping time in their
heads. Lonnen was sitting back in the safe house, watching things unfold
from his desk. He was keeping track of the incoming jet and making sure
Chase's plane stayed off the system. He would be running interference for
them when needed. They wouldn't be able to communicate with him until
they were inside the Box. Lonnen needed to be careful not to do anything
obvious, nothing that could be noticed by whoever was at the terminal deep
within Legoland.

Sixty seconds.

In less than a minute, either everything would start to happen, or they
would be finished.

Cullis and Lonnen had planned for this eventuality. If not this exact
scenario, then one close enough to be useful. They had left smoke bombs
in their offices, set to trigger remotely. The command had already been
sent. If Lonnen had kept to the schedule, the bombs would have detonated
around the time Mason and Cullis took up their positions. Nonessential
staff would already be filing out of Legoland, on the other side of the

river, and running along the underground tunnel. The offices in front of them would trigger an alarm as a backup, to let the rest of the personnel out, and notifications would also be sent to Whitehall, GCHQ, and Thames House.

Thirty seconds.

Cullis looked at Mason with a smile.

She could read his expression.

There was an age-old contradiction in field agents. They were troublemakers. Disrupters. They loved nothing more than interrupting the normal flow of things and giving authority figures a bloody nose. And yet, at the same time, they were employed to protect the status quo. To channel their impulses at targets selected by the state.

Now they were getting to use their training against their own side. For the first time since the Wembley training exercise, the job felt pure. Simple.

Free of compromise.

Ten seconds.

The black doors opened. Men and women in business suits started spilling out onto the street. Mason and Cullis slipped the fire marshal gear on over their clothes and pushed into the crowd, moving through a mixture of confused and bored staff. Half of them seemed to assume this was a drill; the other half had clearly linked this to the news of the planned attack on the London Eye and wanted to get far away from the target. Nobody would be looking at the two fire marshals as they pushed into the building.

Mason turned to the left and Cullis to the right, letting the crowd separate them. Two people in high-vis might lodge in someone's mind. They slipped along the sides of the hallway and down the steps. The lifts and escalators were all deactivated as a precautionary measure, so they took the long way down. At the foot of the stairs, they turned to walk through the first of the security doors. An electronic pass would usually be needed to pass through, but for now they were open. That led to another short flight of stairs and a second door.

They were on the platform for the MI6 rail system. The stragglers from Legoland were still walking toward them along the footpath. Mason and Cullis dropped down onto the tracks and started to jog down the tunnel, out of sight of the pedestrians. There were cameras dotted along the ceiling above them, and they had passed several on the stairs down, but they trusted the guards would be busy monitoring the flow of staff walking past them, not looking at the screens.

At the other end of the tunnel they climbed back up onto the platform. A flashing light above the security door showed it was about to reactivate. They slipped through just as the door closed.

Two armed guards turned to face the newcomers. Mason had wondered if anyone would recognize them. Mason's role was top secret, and she didn't mix with many of the other MI6 staff. But Cullis was a legend in the service and held a senior position in the building.

Both guards recognized him. Mason watched as their faces went through the same split-second calculation of recognition, greeting, and then re-membering he was now the enemy. They started to pull their guns, but it was too late. Cullis stunned the first guard with two fast punches to the throat and eased him down into a chair.

Mason had planned ahead for an easier trick, one that wouldn't push her injuries. She slipped on the metal glove she'd taken from Parish and pressed her palm to the second guard's head. As he went limp, she helped him down into another chair.

Cullis injected each of them with a deep sedative and said, "Sorry, boys. We're the good guys. You'll see."

They locked the unconscious guards in a small storage cupboard be-neath the stairs. Mason and Cullis stripped off the high-vis jackets, and the heavy overcoats they'd worn beneath them, to show the same bland black suits that marked the uniform of the security staff in the building. They lifted the electronic passes from around the guards' necks and took their ID badges. They wouldn't pass a close inspection of the ID photographs—

mainly because Mason wasn't a muscular bald man named Rickards—but from a distance they'd be fine.

Together they swiped through the door from the security office and out onto the stairs leading up into Legoland.

They were in.

Lonnen stared at the screen. He wasn't sure what he'd seen. Chase's plane had lost altitude over Mont-Blanc, and it looked as if one of the emergency doors had opened. He'd lost the visual for a few seconds while they went down through the clouds. Before he lost them, there was something on the side of the plane. When he picked them up again, everything looked normal.

Eventually the plane started to climb again. What had he missed?

Lonnen needed to do something. The Visitologist jet was already over the English Channel. He could hear them securing a route to Heathrow and permission to land. Chase was an hour behind, and that was only if they didn't need to stop in France to refuel.

He flicked over to the security feeds from central London. Cullis and Mason had just entered Spook Station at Pimlico.

Or he assumed they had. They were both carrying the cards. The devices worked so well that he couldn't see either of them on the live feeds. Some of the cameras were picking up a disturbance, with flickering images and strange white spots on the screen. Others were simply failing to load fresh images, which someone would only notice if they checked the time stamps.

They were on the staircase down to the electric rail line.

They would be too late.

Mason and Cullis wouldn't be in control of the security network before the Visitologists had landed. And once that plane was on the ground, all bets were off. Lonnen needed a backup plan. Maybe Chase could head off the Visitologists before they got to London, but her plane was too far behind.

He needed to make some time. But how?

Lonnen was already pushing his luck by interfering with the EU air traffic. Each time he stepped in, he left a trail that someone in the Box would be able to follow if they were looking for it. His whole plan rested on the idea they wouldn't be paying attention. Focus would be on the Visitologist jet and on the security systems in central London. They would be looking at the clearest route to deliver the weapon, not at small glitches and irregularities over Europe.

They wouldn't be paying attention . . .

He stared at the screens from the security services.

It was going to come down to a gamble.

The cops, Thames House, and the Geeks, all sending one another signals. Bouncing reports to the train stations and airports. Hundreds of messages a minute, flowing through the system.

The security grid had already gone up several levels with the faked terrorist situation near the London Eye. The conspirators had been smart. Reporting it as a shootout at the Visitologist building would have lodged in people's memory the wrong way. Flagging it as an attack on the tourist attraction across the road, the London Eye, had made it easier to raise the panic. Thousands of alerts had been fired around the system since then.

Who would notice one more?

Lonnen hating taking these kinds of risks. He was a man of plans and backup plans. Contingencies. He'd already told Mason that contacting the airports would be a stupid idea, but here he was. He swore under his breath.

Go for it.

Lonnen flicked onto the border channel, the line for flagging security lockdowns at airports and train stations. He fired off a report of a suspicious package found in the baggage processing tunnel of Heathrow's Terminal 5. That system was huge; it would take them a minimum of thirty minutes to check everything, and longer if he sent a second report after the initial madness. He sat back and watched as, one by one, all of his screens came to life with security chatter.

Within five minutes, Heathrow was on lockdown. Two minutes later, every other airport in the greater London area followed suit, with all other UK airports placed on high alert.

Nobody would be getting permission to land any time soon.

Chase had a chance to catch up.

Mason knew the hardest part about storming a castle was usually getting past the outer wall. Once an invading force breached that initial defense, the rest was simple. Legoland's defenses were more sophisticated than a castle's, but the principle wasn't that much different.

The inner layers of the building were virtually impenetrable from above. All the security checks Mason went through on a daily basis, added to the blast shields, armed guards, and bulletproof barriers, would stop a small army from getting in off the street. Much less thought had been given to stopping people attacking from below.

To get in that way, the invaders would first need to know about Spook Station at Pimlico. They would then need to know about the rail system. They would have to have figured out a way past the six security doors. From there, the attackers would need to be skilled with hand-to-hand combat, to take out the six guards posted between the rail system and the Box. And they would need to have security passes to get through each automatic gate after that.

Basically, in order to break into MI6 and make it all the way to the most secured point, someone would need to be either Peter Cullis or Joanna Mason.

Lonnen turned back to the security feed from inside Legoland. He could guess where Mason and Cullis were, but only because he knew what he was looking for. The cameras in the train tunnel were glitching, the feed jumping slightly, crackling as if a wire was loose.

He checked the reports coming from inside the building. The smoke bombs had been carefully placed in the ventilation system. They were set to burn briefly, letting the smoke out, then stop completely while the air conditioning circulated it all. It would take them a long time to discover the origin of the smoke, but the alarm itself had already been stopped. They had figured out there was no fire and no immediate danger.

Lonnen watched as the security gates started to reactivate. Cullis and Mason needed to be on the inside of that gate when it closed. Otherwise the game was up.

He flicked the screens back to the air traffic information. The Visitologist jet had already been placed in a queue, told to wait until the security alert had been stepped down. He could see whoever was in control of the main terminal was trying to figure out what had happened. They were bringing up reports, pooling for traces of the emergency alert that had caused this.

Chase wouldn't be coming into Heathrow. She was with that smuggler, Guerrero, and he used the Fell's route.

Then he saw the Visitologist jet start to change course.

Mason and Cullis settled into an easy rhythm as they went through each security point. They would use the stolen passes to open the door, Mason would go straight for each guard's head with the glove, and Cullis would drug them up while they were neutralized. None of the guards were their enemies, unless proven otherwise, and they were going to do all they could to spare people.

The final door was a problem.

The Box.

The secured vault was circular, buried twenty feet below them, beneath layers of concrete, metal, and blast-proof defenses. It was a self-contained atmosphere, running on a separate electricity and air-conditioning unit than the rest of Legoland. The entrance was an elevator, just one small car that lowered into the middle of the Box. The door was secured by an automated scanner that required both the correct pass and a retinal scan. None of the security guards they had taken out had clearance to enter the Box, so their cards were useless.

Cullis was usually authorized to enter, but his credentials had been deactivated. He had tried his own card before knowing this and set off an alarm, which would bring all remaining armed guards down on their position. Mason had sealed the metal door they'd come through, the outer chamber for the vault, but it wouldn't hold for longer than a few minutes. Mason could hear the drilling coming from the other side.

This was the part of the plan they hadn't been able to figure out in advance. Neither Mason, nor Lonnen and Cullis, had known a way into the Box without the right card. Mason had been willing to press on anyway. Putting aside a lifetime of needing contingencies and backup plans, she'd decided to do what Marah Chase would have done.

Roll with it, and wait for the magic moment of inspiration when the final detail would slot into place.

Except here, it hadn't happened.

Mason and Cullis sat with their backs to the elevator door, listening to the sounds of the security guards working their way through the metal. Mason turned to look up at the plate where Cullis had tried his luck with his ID, then at each of the three cameras trained on them.

It couldn't end here.

She looked again at the console Cullis had used. Then at the cameras. She stood up and pulled out the small metal card from her back pocket. She raised it to show Cullis, then threw it across the room.

Now she would show up on the security network. But, more important, Lonnen would be able to see her, too, as he piggybacked the signal.

"Guy," Mason looked up at the cameras, hoping to hell that at least one of them had a microphone. "I bet you can see me now. They deactivated Peter's pass. But that means it's on the same grid as everything else. The security system isn't part of the Box's closed loop."

Cullis muttered something that sounded like, "Too right."

"So, if you reinstate him right now, even if they override it straightaway, that gives us a couple of seconds to access the Box."

Mason knew exactly what she was asking. It would open Lonnen up to attack. Whoever was controlling the system would see his location. But it was everything or nothing.

Cullis stood up. He groaned like an old man, and Mason remembered his age for the first time since they'd started the operation. He held his card against the screen. After a pause, the glass lit up green, and there was a soft, pleasing beep. He pressed his eyes against the retinal scanner, which immediately gave the same sound.

The elevator door opened.

"I'm getting the UK signals," Guerrero said. "We're back on the grid. Whatever happened, we're back."

They were somewhere over the English Channel, and the plane was running on fumes. They'd needed to stop a while back, but Chase didn't want to lose any more ground. Even on the smuggler routes they might get awkward questions about Guerrero's injury. It wasn't fatal, but he'd lost a lot of blood before Chase patched him up, and he'd need to rest as soon as they landed.

"Can't we go any faster?" she said, getting the feeling that Zoe might already be out of reach.

"I don't know if you noticed," Guerrero slurred, "but someone shot a hole in the plane. Then someone went and opened the door. And I got shot, you know. Right here."

"Faster, Chuy."

He affected the worst Scottish accent in history, filtered through Mexicali and Imperial Valley. "We cannae go much faster, Captain."

"So I'm the captain now?"

"I got shot, did I tell you?"

Chase looked at Guerrero's wounded shoulder. He was covering it with humor, but Chase knew he was in a bad way. It was a mess. His skin was pale, and Chase didn't know how he was holding off from going into shock. His bad arm looked close to useless, and he was doing everything one-handed.

Screens on the dashboard lit up and started showing numbers. Guerrero listened in, read the reports.

"There's a lockdown," he said. "All the airports. Nobody is landing."

"So, Zoe?"

"If the lockdown happened in time, yeah, they're still in the air. We caught up."

Chase looked at the dial Guerrero had tapped each time he'd referred to the fuel situation. "Do we have enough to stay up?"

"Not. One. Bit." Guerrero shook his head in an exaggerated fashion. "But it doesn't matter. We're not using the same system to come in. Fell's Landing isn't on the grid."

"At all? I thought they were on the grid, just ignored."

"The way I'm told it, the smugglers let the air force use the runways during the war—they weren't on the maps that the Germans had. And ever since then, it's been kept that way, like a tradition. So Fell's is a blind spot built into the UK air traffic zone. We can go straight in."

"You going to be able to land us one-handed?"

"I can do amazing things with this hand."

Guerrero adjusted course to take them around the southern tip of England, lining up a descent into Fell's Landing. The radio crackled again, and this time Chase heard someone say her name. She and Guerrero shared a look.

"Chase," the voice came again. It was distant. Electronic. "I'm working with Mason. Pick up."

Chase nodded, and Guerrero flipped the switch, filling both of their headsets with the voice.

"Who is this?" Chase asked.

"Lonnen. Guy Lonnen. Listen, I don't have much time."

"How are you—"

"Just listen, please. I've called the radio tower at Fell's Landing. They're holding the phone up to the radio, and I might not hear everything you say. So, the Visitologists figured out about Fell's and the jet has rerouted. They'll be going in right ahead of you. They've infiltrated the system, and we don't know who to trust. We have to assume nobody is on our side. I've been keeping you off the grid, but from here it's down to you. They can't reach London. They're going to use whatever you found. Going to attack Parliament."

"No. No. Listen, this is hard to explain . . ." Chase trailed off. She knew there was no quick way to describe the way she'd seen into Zoe's thoughts. She didn't really believe it herself. "Trust me. Parliament

isn't the real target."

Lonnen watched Mason and Cullis enter the vault. He knew what this meant. On the system in front of him, he could already see the security system tracking his exact location. Lights traced across a grid of telephone and broadband lines for the whole city, closing in on him. Numbers scrolled crazily across a smaller window, as they had since he'd used the system to override Legoland's security. On a third window, being controlled by whoever was at the desk in the Box, he could see a satellite image refreshing every few seconds, zooming in on where he was.

Lonnen was done. He hoped it was worth it.

On another screen, he saw the satellite image he'd been using to watch Fell's Landing. The plane had crashed, but he'd watched as Chase left on a motorbike. The chance was alive and well. They just needed a few lucky breaks.

The security network locked onto where he was.

Each of the windows on his screen went dark, one by one, as the person in the Box shut down his access routes.

Chase had been right. He'd known as soon as she'd said it. Of course Parliament wasn't the target. That's why they'd been willing to let the early terror alerts go out. Each wave of panic in the system suited their needs. Each time the police were put on a higher alert, it only helped the

Visitologists set the scene for their end game. Each of the computer screens filled with the same image. Lonnen was looking into the eyes of Camilla Worthington sitting in the Box. She was smiling at him.

"Game over," she said.

"It would be you."

Lonnen thought of one last thing he could try. He pressed a few keys on the computer and prayed the system was still listening.

The front door crashed in downstairs, and Lonnen heard boots on the stairs. The living room door burst inward, and he turned to face three armed men in black military gear. In the lead was Adam Parish.

Parish raised the gun. "For the new age," he said, and fired.

Mason and Cullis stepped out into the Box. The first thing Mason noticed was that it wasn't circular, as legend stated. The room was large and stretched out ahead of them like a warehouse. Metal shelves filled the space. There was a large metal desk next to the lift shaft. Cullis nodded at it and grabbed one end. Mason took the other, and they dragged it into the doorway, stopping the lift from going back up for the guards.

Cullis led the way. He'd been down here before. Mason looked at the shelves as they passed. Some were stacked high with papers and filing boxes. Others had every model of computer going back to the fifties. She saw two enigma machines.

At the end of the shelves they came upon a circular platform with steps leading up to it. There was a hatch in the floor with a wheel handle, like in old submarine movies. On the platform itself, Mason could see a bank of computer screens, all showing the same images Lonnen had been viewing at the safe house. A robed figure was sitting watching the live feed.

As Cullis and Mason climbed the steps, the figure turned to face them. A hand pulled the robe's hood back to reveal Camilla Worthington, the other member of the committee investigating MI6. Her face was twisted into a smile.

"You're too late." She pointed at one of the screens, where a small video feed showed Lonnen's dead body. "All you've done is help us."

The screens were changing. One by one, the windows were closing their video displays to be replaced by scrolling green numbers. This was how Lonnen had described his own shut-down program. He'd said they would know it was working when Big Brother switched over to numbers, running an internal scan that would lock it up. Worthington had beaten them to it. The computer was closing itself off, and they wouldn't be able to access whatever function Worthington had commanded it to follow.

"It's over," she said. "Welcome to the new age."

The gunfire started as soon as Guerrero touched the wheels down onto the tarmac.

Chase could see the jet. It had pulled to a stop outside a hangar. Three cars waited, nondescript Fiats. A line of hooded figures stood next to the runway, and they trained submachine guns at the landing gear of Guerrero's plane.

"Huevos."

Guerrero fought for control. The plane weaved across the surface of the runway. There was a crunching sound, and they tilted down, crashing onto the tarmac. The rotors bit into the ground. One cracked; the other lifted the wing, almost turning the plane over. They slid along, with the sound of metal on concrete filling the air.

"You'll need to jump," Guerrero said. He was holding the controls with both hands. Chase could see the pain on his face as he pushed through, despite the bullet wound. "Go."

Chase didn't move at first. She didn't want to leave him there. Through the window, she could see the end of the runway fast approaching, and beyond that, a small area of rocks, and the Thames Estuary. They were skidding toward the water.

"You've got to go." Guerrero shouted. "I'll distract them, try and keep her steady."

Chase knew he was right. Zoe needed to be stopped. She kissed his forehead and then stepped out into the cabin. Releasing the lock on the door, she swung it open. It banged back against her, pushed by the movement of the plane. She opened it again, then pulled the toggle that opened the emergency chute. The large slide inflated but dragged along the ground. Chase swallowed, then jumped.

She slid down and rolled onto the grass.

Chase turned over a couple of times before coming to a stop. She was on the edge of the field, in a ditch. The plane was slowing. At the end of the runway, it crashed through the low metal fence and tilted, sliding down into the rocks. Chase heard the impact of metal on stone as the cockpit touched down.

Two of the armed figures were running toward the plane. They didn't seem to have noticed Chase. She'd jumped off the opposite side from where they'd been standing, and Guerrero had kept the plane as straight as he could, providing cover. Chase recognized their fatigues and the black hoods. They were Al-Salif mercenaries. The last piece of the puzzle clicked into place, something that she hadn't seen in Zoe's thoughts. They would carry out the attack as Al-Salif. It was the perfect cover. Then, when the dust settled, the Visitologists could step in and save the day.

Chase looked back to the jet.

More of the Al-Salif goons were climbing into the Fiats. She recognized the shortest one as Zoe. Her head was wrapped up the same as the others, and she carried the bundled Aten. Zoe took a red car; the others were gray and blue. They pulled away from the hangar and headed toward the gate.

Chase crawled on all fours, staying out of sight of the two mercenaries inspecting the downed plane. Halfway along the runway, she came up with a plan. There was a motorbike outside the nearest hangar, a gleaming Triumph. It looked like it had a kick starter. It was someone's passion project of a restored bike, and, well, Chase had a passion for stealing them. She stood up and ran.

There were shouts from behind as the Al-Salif guards noticed her. Bullets hit the ground. She didn't stop to see how close they'd been. At the bike, she swung her leg over, took a hold of the handlebars, and kicked the engine into life. It responded straightaway—a real, old-school, rumbling engine. It sounded like it was talking to her. Chase grinned, forgetting the tension of the moment, as she turned it toward the gate and took off after the cars.

Out on the road, the Visitologists had a large lead. They were heading straight for London. Chase got her head down low to the front of the bike, trying to avoid the wind hitting her face, and pushed the throttle as far as it could go.

On the outskirts of London, the three cars split up. They had stayed together on the country roads, through Southfleet and Bexley, and then again as they neared Woolwich. Shortly after that was when they separated. The blue and gray Fiats, carrying the Al-Salif mercenaries, stayed on the same road, south of the river. The red car, with Zoe behind the wheel, turned right, heading toward the Blackwall Tunnel.

She was crossing the river.

Chase ignored the mercenaries. They weren't important right now. She knew what they were about to do and wished she could stop them. But if she didn't stay on Zoe's tail, every effort would be wasted.

Chase followed through the tunnel. She took the chance to gain ground on Zoe, weaving in and out of traffic as they hit a more congested area. She became aware of a detail that had been nagging at her all the way in. Every traffic light had gone green as the cars approached.

On the other side of the river, they both turned onto Aspen Way. Zoe was headed straight for the heart of London. Chase was following on a public highway with no motorcycle helmet. But there were no police anywhere.

As long as she was in Zoe's slipstream, she seemed to be invisible. The city seemed to be laying out a welcome mat for Zoe.

An invisible hand was guiding them toward the end game.

FIFTY-SEVEN

Worthington put up a fight, but it felt like a token effort. Against two trained spooks she didn't really stand a chance. She couldn't know one of them was seriously injured, and the other was suffering from arthritis.

She pushed past Mason to head for the steps, but Mason grabbed her and threw her back against the computer. Cullis stepped in and pulled her toward him, pinning both arms behind her.

"What have you done?" he demanded.

Worthington didn't answer.

"How do we stop it?"

Again, nothing.

Worthington relaxed. She wasn't going to fight them anymore. That made Mason's stomach turn over. She'd seen that kind of calm before, in suicide attackers who feel at peace in the moments before the end. Worthington had done her part, for whatever she felt her greater good was, and she was resigned to what happened next.

Mason looked at the computer and the screens full of numbers. Only three still worked.

On the first, Mason watched a red Fiat speed toward Westminster. A readout next to the image showed traffic lights being manipulated and the high security status being downgraded in each city grid as the car entered it.

The second screen showed two more cars, on the road south of the river, with the same route being opened up for them.

The third was BBC News 24, showing live coverage of the anti-terror debate in Parliament. The prime minister was at the dispatch box, fielding questions from the house.

Mason looked around the chamber. In the distance, she could hear banging, sawing.

The guards were breaking into the lift shaft. It wouldn't be long before they were down here. They needed a play. Fast.

She pulled out her phone and switched it on. When it had loaded, she opened the video camera. The Visitologist plan would only work if their lies held. No matter what else they managed to do, they couldn't take over if the truth was known.

Mason slipped on the glove and powered it up. Worthington looked worried for the first time. She tried to pull back as Mason pressed the glove to her head, but Cullis held her in place until she went limp. Mason started filming with her other hand.

"What's your name?"

"Camilla Denise Worthington."

"You're a member of the Church of Ancient Science?"

"Yes."

"The church is part of a conspiracy to take over the British government?"

"Yes."

"The conspiracy involves Douglas Buchan, Adam Parish, Ayman Musab Faraj, and a woman named Zoe Forrester?"

"Yes."

"Who is in charge?"

"We serve the new age."

"Who is running this operation?"

"My love."

"And who is that?|

"Zoe Forrester."

That caught Mason by surprise. She had expected it to be Buchan or Parish. What did that say about Chase's taste in women? What did that say about...

Not now.

"You've framed members of the security services and an American named Marah Chase for crimes against the British government?"

"Yes."

"And you're going to blow up the Houses of Parliament?"

"No."

Mason paused.

She looked at Cullis over Worthington's shoulder. He shook his head as if to say, Don't know.

On the screens, she saw the two cars come to a stop south of the river, near Westminster Bridge. The third car, the red one, was on Holborn, still heading west. On the news feed, the debate was in full swing. And Mason could see Douglas Buchan was sitting directly behind the prime minister.

They wouldn't be blowing up Parliament with him in it. What had she missed?

"Who is the target?"

"Prime Minister."

Mason pulled back the glove. Her eyes met Cullis's. That was why the Visitologists had allowed the escalation of the security alerts. They were using the government's own procedures against them. In the event of a security threat while Parliament was in session, the prime minister would be—

Cullis finished the thought out loud. "Evacuation."

Cullis sedated Worthington. He didn't bother easing her to the floor. She hit the metal with a solid thud.

On the screens, four armed men climbed out of the cars that had stopped at the end of Waterloo Bridge. Their heads were covered. They were dressed like Al-Salif mercenaries and carrying submachine guns. They started walking across the bridge, firing their weapons into the air at first, making people run. Then they lowered the guns to point at the fleeing tourists.

Within seconds of those shots being heard, the prime minister would be bundled out of the House of Commons. The security team would head straight for Downing Street in an armored car or, in the case of the highest alert possible, there would be a helicopter pickup from Parliament Square Garden. Either way, the prime minister would be exposed for a few seconds, out in the open, and then in a moving target.

If the Visitologist weapon was as powerful as they believed, the PM was a sitting duck.

Mason looked at the red car. It was setting a land speed record for making its way through the city, heading straight for Westminster.

The trap had already been sprung.

They heard a metal-on-metal sound as someone broke through the lift shaft and pulled the door aside.

The armed guards would be there in within seconds.

Cullis pointed to the hatch in the floor. "Emergency route."

Mason didn't hang around to argue. She took the metal steps two at a time and pulled on the handle, unsealing the hatch. She lifted it and climbed down the ladder beneath, into a dark tunnel. Cullis closed the hatch above her. In the seconds before it resealed, she heard shouting, followed by shooting.

Mason turned to face the tunnel and started to run.

The tunnel felt as though it had been dug diagonally across the river. Mason had heard the rumors of a system that connected Legoland to Whitehall but never believed them. After about five minutes of running flat-out along the tunnel, Mason stumbled. Her side screamed with pain. She couldn't move much more. She leaned against the wall and tried to breathe.

Come on. Just a little more.

Up ahead, she could see ladders illuminated by a dim bulb. Her shoulders ached. Mason knew she'd been asking her body for just a little more for two days now, and there was nothing left in the tank. She started to slide down the wall into a crouch.

Mason heard a loud crack, followed by a rumble, and then the walls shook. Something that big, it had to be an explosion. There was a second, similar sound, and this time the ground vibrated beneath her feet. From farther down the tunnel she heard stone hitting stone, and running water. The tunnel was flooding.

She climbed to her feet and started to pull herself up the ladder, one rung at a time. The metal was damp and clammy. At the top was another hatch, like the one in the Box, but with the handle on the underside. It could only be opened from below.

Mason turned the handle slowly, trying not to aggravate the wound in her side. The lid finally swung upward into a tall round chamber. Mason could hear screams and sirens. There was another ladder bolted to the wall, leading the way about a hundred feet up to a manhole cover. Mason took each step slowly. At the top, she eased the manhole aside. She was in Old Palace Yard, one of the car parks for the Houses of Parliament. The clouds overhead were like nothing Mason had ever seen. The air was thick with the smell of smoke and sulfur, and she could taste dust.

Mason looked into the cloud in St. James's Park. She could just about make out two figures standing in the center.

The doors to Parliament opened, and people started running into the car park. They were evacuating the building, fleeing something. Mason had no idea what explosion had been, but she guessed it was to do with Zoe's weapon and the dark cloud.

Mason was still dressed in the suit she'd used to blend in with security staff, and it did its job again, letting her slip out among the crowd onto the street, past the armed guards who were more worried about stopping someone getting in than checking who was running out.

Mason had to get a message to them: Don't bring the prime minister out.

But they were in defense mode. Mason didn't have her own ID and, even if she did, she had been declared a threat. They would shoot on sight.

The evacuation helicopter came in low, around the edges of the cloud. Mason caught sight of the pilot as he came in toward Parliament Square. There was a flash of bright white light, a thundercrack, and the helicopter exploded into a ball of flame, hitting the side of the parliament building like a firebomb.

Security guards and MPs were standing beneath it. Mason jumped forward, pulling three of them back before the rubble could hit. The rest were lost.

Armed police stood in the road in a circular defensive formation. The prime minister was in the center. They'd been on their way to meet the helicopter; now they were exposed. Mason could see the moment of hesitation. Protocol told them to evacuate the prime minister, but the ways out were gone. One of the armed officers turned inside the circle and pushed the prime minister down to the ground.

The tunnel. They could get the PM below ground, back the way Mason had come, and away from the weapon. But did they know the tunnel existed?

Mason knew they wouldn't listen to her. She'd be shot dead before she was anywhere near them.

But she had to try.

Mason put her arms out, showing she wasn't carrying a gun, held one of the many fake IDs she'd acquired in storming Legoland, and ran toward the police.

They raised their weapons and prepared to fire.

Chase ditched the bike at Villiers Street and started to run. She heard shooting in the distance. As the sounds continued, people paused, looked around, and tried to figure out in which direction they should head. Seeing Chase running past must have confused them. Was she running away from the danger? She hoped none of them followed her.

Chase stumbled as images flashed in her mind.

Zoe was holding the Aten, and they were connected again. Chase could see glimpses of Zoe's thoughts and knew Zoe could see hers.

The sky above was growing dark. Thick storm clouds were gathering. They didn't look natural. They were too dark, pulsing with electric energy. Chase knew she didn't have long.

Sprinting out across Trafalgar Square, she could see cops trying to herd people north, away from the attack on Westminster. Chase changed her course to avoid running into the police and headed up onto Pall Mall. Cutting between buildings, she made her way down to the Mall and into St. James's Park. She paused for a few deep, ragged breaths. The clouds were directly overhead, swirling. A funnel started to descend toward the park, like a tornado.

Chase ran toward it.

She spotted Zoe. She was facing away from Chase, striding across the grass with the Aten held aloft. She was still wrapped in the Al-Salif garb, but the wind had blown back her hood. Chase could feel Zoe's thoughts. She didn't care about the hood. Her skin seemed to glow with the power of the Aten.

Now she would be seen.

Now she would be felt.

Now she couldn't be ignored.

Chase headed straight for her. It was hard. The wind was whipping around, trying to throw her off balance. The tornado had almost touched down to surround Zoe.

I can't believe I'm doing this.

Chase rolled under the dark cloud, into the eye of the storm. She turned to look back as the whipping gray cloud touched the ground, sealing her in with Zoe.

The view out was clearer than the view in, so Chase could see what was happening on the other side of the swirling mass. Police were firing at them, but the bullets weren't getting through, sucked into the cloud and being pulled upward, into the crackling sparks of energy above them.

Zoe pointed the staff forward, and the cloud above broiled and crackled.

A bolt of red-blue lightning shot down. Chase saw a flash, and her feet rumbled a second later from the explosion as Big Ben was reduced to rubble.

More screams filled the air around them.

Zoe turned to her right. She pointed the Aten at Buckingham Palace. An unnatural lightning bolt came down from the sky, taking out half of the old building in an explosion of stone, glass, and wood. Chase was thrown to the ground by a shock wave of raw energy.

Sirens were all around them now, mingling with screams and falling rubble.

Zoe briefly turned to acknowledge Chase. Her eyes were dark. There was nothing human in them. Their thoughts mixed again, and Chase could hear not only Zoe but the many other people who had wielded the weapon in the past.

She could feel their anger.

Resentment.

Ambition.

Zoe smiled and turned her attention back to what was happening outside the cloud.

A helicopter flew in low, circling the edge of the cloud. It was coming in to land on a public square across the road from Parliament.

Zoe flicked the staff, and a bolt of lightning hit the helicopter.

Chase saw a circle of armed police. They'd been crossing the road toward where the helicopter was due to land. They were protecting someone in the center of the formation.

The prime minister.

Zoe took a step forward. She raised the staff.

Chase sucked in another breath, then charged. She pulled Zoe back by the shoulder. Energy crackled between them. It felt like a live current, running straight through Zoe.

Zoe turned to face Chase. Her black eyes lightened for a second, looking human again. They were filled with anger.

Chase looked into her face. She saw all her own weakness and fears. Was this who Zoe always was? Or had the issues grown in their years apart? Had they always been on this path? She felt a great swell of regret and something else. Was it love? Or was it something that had been love, before the betrayal? And which betrayal was she thinking of? The ones in a cave beneath Alexandria, or the one here in England, fourteen years earlier?

They were still connected. With Zoe holding the Aten, they had a bond. They were touching each other's thoughts, their memories, their ambitions. Chase could feel Zoe's emotions. She could feel sparks of each of them, pure and powerful.

And Chase knew that was it. The Aten was feeding on their emotions. Directing them. Giving them destructive form.

Chase grabbed the staff.

Her mind flashed white. She could feel Zoe's rawest hate, anger, resentment. Zoe had been scared and alone. Now she was powerful. She had followers, people willing to die for her cause.

What could Zoe feel of Chase's emotions?

They were feeding off each other now, or the Aten was drawing them both out. Chase fought to push down her own feelings, but she felt her grief overtake her for a moment, and Zoe read all the usual regrets. But then there was a change, and now they were feeling the grief for Michael, the one other person Zoe had trusted. Loved.

And there, in the center, Chase could feel Zoe had loved her. There had been a trust growing, for both of them. The same worries, the same hopes.

The same pain.

Chase could feel the cloud.

She could feel the lightning.

Most of all, she could feel the power.

Right then, right there, she could do anything.

Zoe's energy was aimed outward. She wanted to lash out. Chase was focused on herself, on the years of closing herself off, punishing herself for things that weren't her fault—and maybe for a few that were.

The cloud descended, enveloping them. Chase could see the lightning crackling in the air all around her. It touched the staff, and she felt a jolt.

The Aten was speaking to her. It was speaking to both of them.

Use me.

Let me loose.

Take control.

Chase pushed the voice away. She focused on her own power. She was sick of carrying all the fears, the anxieties, the pain. Zoe wanted it. Chase felt that. And she knew the Aten was looking to home in on the raw, jagged edges. The staff was searching, looking for pain to call its own, looking for flaws, looking for ego.

Zoe could have it. All of it.

Chase let Zoe take it all, pushing out through their connection. Zoe's power swelled, but she couldn't control it. She was overwhelmed. She was experiencing now not just her own lifetime's worth of pain but Chase's, too.

The cloud closed in.

Chase felt the electricity surging through both of them. It built up, ready to strike.

"For the new age." Zoe's words shook; her teeth rattled.

"For your mom's face," Chase called out, above the wind.

A bolt of the blue-red lightning surged down from the sky, hitting them both.

Mason sprinted across the road, toward the guns.

She called out, "Friendly. Legoland. I'm here to protect the prime minister."

The police radios squawked. Mason saw the head of every armed officer hesitate and tilt to listen to the command. Mason was only a few feet away now. If the kill shot was coming, it would have to be right then.

They lowered their weapons.

The officer in command said, "Are you Joanna Mason?"

Mason stopped running. She almost skidded. "What?"

"Mason?"

She nodded, then answered, "Yes."

He handed her the radio, along with his earpiece. Mason listened in. Cullis was issuing instructions. Directing the police and military to form a perimeter around the park. Mason tried to respond to him, but it was a one-way transmission. He was broadcasting across the security network.

The officer said, "He told us to do whatever you say."

Mason pointed back the way she had come. "There's a tunnel. We can get the PM below ground." Mason remembered the phone in her pocket. The video recording. She handed it to the prime minister. "And you need to see this."

Mason led them along the side of Parliament, around the rubble of the helicopter crash, and into Old Palace Yard.

"Down there."

The armed team lead the prime minister down into the tunnel. Mason took one of their guns and stayed topside, guarding the entrance. The radio went silent for a moment, before Cullis spoke again.

"Mase?"

"Here."

"I know, I can see you. I'm in control of the network. You know what? I think I'm getting the hang of it."

"What happened?"

"Lonnen. Seems like Worthington wanted him to see her face. To gloat, I guess. She started broadcasting from the terminal, to his hacked line. He rerouted the broadcast onto the emergency broadcast channels. Her confession was broadcast to the cops, GCHQ, probably a few stoned teenagers and conspiracy nuts."

"So we won."

"Almost. Hang on, something's happening . . ."

Mason turned toward the park. A bright column of pure energy rose up toward the sky. For a moment, Mason could see two figures lit up within the cloud.

Chase and Zoe.

They were glowing with the power of the lightning. The light became too bright, and Mason heard a scream before the light went out. The cloud rushed past her like wind, leaving the park a scorched wasteland, the smell of burning flesh hanging in the air.

Chase opened her eyes. She felt fried. Literally. Her fingers tingled with static. A wave of electricity passed through her. Her clothes were blackened, burned through in large patches. Chase realized she was half-naked in the middle of London. Her hair was standing on end.

The grass was dark. Burned to a crisp. A layer of thick salt was dusted all around her. Where Zoe had been, there was only a scorched imprint in the ground, a memory of where someone had stood. The Aten was lying in front of her.

It was dark, covered in ash and salt. But Chase could still hear its voice.

Use me.

Let me loose.

She pulled off what was left of her jacket and wrapped it around the staff before lifting it. Again, the Aten whispered to her, but the pull was fading. Chase had no interest in what it was offering.

A circle of police, wearing combat gear, with automatic rifles trained and ready, was closing in around her.

An officer tilted his head to the radio on his shoulder and held a muffled conversation.

He stepped forward. "Are you Marah Chase?"

FIFTY-EIGHT

A dam Parish heard a noise in the darkness outside the farmhouse. He jumped, then calmed down, laughed at himself. He took a look out the

window, just to be sure. There was nothing there.

It had been two days since the attack had failed.

Two days of hiding. Of remembering each of the security grid black spots. Recalling which streets and alleyways he could use, which ones he couldn't. He was holed up in a farm he'd rented under a fake name, a backup plan in case things didn't work. Parish never liked to walk into any situation unless he'd figured three ways out.

There were no security cameras here, in the middle of nowhere. No neighbors. Nobody to spy on him. A satellite would need to be pointed at this exact spot to find him, and who would know to do that?

Parish coughed. His throat still burned from where that bitch tried to kill him. He should have killed her when he had the chance. A sip of water soothed the raw edges of the pain.

The Church would come again. The Aten had only been the start. There was so much more out there, waiting to be found. They were right, and people would see—would be made to see—that he was right. They would listen to him.

He heard the sound again. A scraping. Something moving. But now it was inside the house. He picked up the rusted metal poker from the fireplace and turned toward the door. He took a step. Two. Three. The sound came again, from the hallway right ahead of him. He slowed down and stretched out his paces, taking long strides as he raised the poker above his head. He sprang into the hall, shouting, and bringing the weapon down to strike.

There was nobody there.

Parish laughed at himself and relaxed. His grip loosened on the metal.

A floorboard creaked behind him. He turned and saw the spy, the bitch, standing in the kitchen doorway.

Joanna Mason.

She was leaning against the frame. When she took a step into the room, Parish could see she was limping. Favoring her side. Injured.

Mason held something up. The glove. His glove.

"I used this. During the attack. Just for a few seconds, and it felt good. It's a trip, isn't it? I bet that's why you like it. Makes you feel big. Makes people listen to you."

Mason threw the glove at him. It landed at his feet, but he didn't bend down to pick it up. Why would she give him an advantage? He was already bigger than her, and stronger. He'd spent two days in hiding, recuperating. He squared his shoulders, making himself big.

He smiled. "You think you don't need that?"

"I don't want it."

"You here for a rematch?"

Mason lifted her other hand. She was holding a gun.

She pulled the trigger.

Parish's knee exploded. Pain jolted through him, everywhere except the knee, which didn't seem to be feeling anything at all. Lights danced in front of his eyes. He hit the floor, which sent a further wave of pain bouncing around.

Mason knelt over him.

"I'm here for Tan Bashir."

FIFTY-NINE

C hase sat in the bar of the Alexandria Royale. She sipped a bourbon and watched Guerrero work the crowd that had gathered around them, telling an edited version of their adventure. His arm was in a sling. MI6 had quietly paid for reconstructive surgery to his shoulder. As far as anyone else knew, he was as fit as ever, but in quiet moments Chase could see the pain in his eyes.

He left out details of the large-scale conspiracy to overthrow a government, and so far, that part of the story had been kept out of the news cycle, too. The attack on London was still being talked about on every channel, but Al-Salif had taken the blame. The usual debates were happening online. Far-right leaders using it as an excuse to attack Muslims, the left calling for tolerance. Nobody really talking about Al-Salif as a criminal organization, rather than ISIS.

Chase guessed the government was still figuring out the best way to spin it. A few wackos kept posting online about Visitologists and a confession that had been broadcast from a secret bunker—maybe from the same place where they kept the aliens and controlled the weather. The theory gained some traction online, but then, all theories did.

Guerrero's story also skipped over the cavern deep beneath the city and the ancient weapon that he and Chase had placed back down there just a few hours before.

Mason had been good to her word. The British government had paid Chase everything she'd been promised. Chase had given most of it to Tim Barron, with instructions to start up the Forrester Foundation again, finding more children like her and giving them opportunities to study at expensive universities. Chase trusted some of the money would find its way to the Knights of Saint Mark. Whatever was left of them. She didn't trust them yet, and maybe never would. But they'd been important to both Henry Forrester and Georgie Turner, and that was enough for now. Guerrero had used his one remaining jewel to fix up the new plane and add a few upgrades. After a few days' rest in a luxury hotel on MI6's expense account, they had flown back to Alexandria to return the Aten.

Mason had been good about the weapon so far. Helping Chase sell the idea to the authorities that it had been destroyed in the blast. Giving cover for Chase and Guerrero to smuggle it back out of the country. And being good enough never to ask where the tomb was, or where the Aten would be hidden. The tomb had been cleaned up. Someone had removed the bodies and put the bricks back in place. Chase and Guerrero replaced the bundled weapon in the sarcophagus next to the dead king. Chase said a few words. A memorial of sorts, for all the people who had been lost. She placed photographs of her parents in with Alexander. She'd taken some time on the walk back to read more of the inscriptions on the walls. The words were fading in her mind, the ability to read them not as clear as it had been. The surge of power in London had done something, lessened the connection she felt to the Aten and it's secrets.

On the way back to the surface, they had encountered four old men, each dressed in the familiar black robes of the Knights. They hadn't said a word, simply bowed their heads before letting Chase and Guerrero pass.

A part of Chase's mind was still down there, though. Even though the connection had faded, she could still hear the Aten, quiet at the back of her thoughts, saying *use me, use me.*

So many questions. The origin of the Aten and it's connection to mines in the Sinai. The identity of the people who buried it here, away from the world. Could they be a forgotten people, ten thousand years ago, as Forrester believed? Or simply a different version of the Aten cult, contemporary to the Eighteenth Dynasty? Even a more recent pious fraud?

But those questions could wait.

As Guerrero got the crowd warmed up to a big laugh, the punch line about how he'd named his new plane Marah, Mason walked into the bar. She locked eyes with Chase and nodded to an empty table in the corner.

Chase watched the spook limp. She was moving gingerly. Mason waved for the waitress and ordered a bottle of rum as Chase sat down.

"An archeologist and a spy walk into a bar," Mason said with a smile.

"Archeologist?" Chase said. "Is that what we're calling me?"

Mason pulled an envelope from her bag and slipped it across the table. Chase didn't pick it up. Instead, she reached for the bottle as the waitress set it down and poured a drink for each of them. She needed a few seconds to think. Why was Mason here, so soon after the Aten had been restored to the tomb? Had the spy followed them here? Was she keeping tabs on the location for a later date?

"Two job offers," Mason said. "One from the British Museum, one from the American Museum of Natural History. They're both willing to pay for you to get a doctorate. Oh—" She put a slip of paper down on top of the envelope. "And that's the number of a producer at the BBC. He'd like to talk about commissioning work from you."

"Options."

"Your life back." Mason sipped her drink. "I keep my promises."

"And how are you doing?"

"I've got some fun new scars." Mason's eyes twinkled. "And a lot of work to do."

"What's happening about the Visitologists?"

"Officially? Nothing yet." Mason shrugged. It was slow and cautious. "The politicians are playing politics. And the Church covered their tracks. Someone executed Parish, but there's a tape of him being interrogated before he died. They were clever. Zoe Forrester was the most senior Visitologist in the UK, and Parish never spoke to anybody higher. They have deniability, and they're using it. Saying Zoe went rogue. They're lawyering up to protect themselves, and of course they're offering to help pay for the damages, as a sign of goodwill. Ayman Musab Faraj has claimed Zoe was working with him and Al-Salif. And we still can't officially prove that Al-Salif are just a Visitologist front."

"So you can go after Faraj?"

"The order will come soon."

"What about the MP? Buchan?"

"He's hiding in an embassy toilet."

"They're still out there."

Mason nodded. "Yeah. And still inside, too. The new Permanent Under Secretary wants to give me a department of my own to root out the traitors in government. It's going to take a long time."

Chase knew this was all classified information. She shouldn't be hearing any of it—unless there was a catch.

"You could come work for me," Mason said. "Join the team."

"I've only just got clean. Taken me a long time to get legit again."

Mason leaned in close. "I'm not sure it'll suit you."

They kissed, slow and tender. Guerrero led the crowd in a cheer. Mason stood up and placed a room key on the table. She set it down far enough from the envelope to make it clear they were two separate options.

"Room 306," she said.

Mason left the room with a brief wave to Guerrero and an ironic bow to the crowd. Guerrero walked over to take the seat she'd just vacated. He tapped the envelope, and Chase nodded. They both knew what it was.

"My man over there," Guerrero said, "has this crazy story about a pirate ship in the Bermuda Triangle. Says he can show us the way, for a share of the gold."

"Free booty?"

"Freebooters."

Marah Chase watched a slow smile spread across Chuy Guerrero's face. She looked at the envelope, with its promise of a safe life, and then to the key, able to literally unlock an interesting one. Then she looked over at the smiling smuggler, a reminder of the dangerous life she'd been leading.

Chase had options. She was in control.

She felt her heart kick-start as she made a decision.

MARAH CHASE

WILL RETURN

A NOTE ON THIS EDITION

I don't like Director's Cuts.

The story you presented at the time is the story. Leave it be. Move on. Deckard is a human, dammit.

And yet.

The version you have just read contains a number of small differences to the book that was originally published by Pegasus in 2019. The truth is, Marah Chase has been a long labour of love. I first created the character over twenty years ago now, intending her to be my big break into creator-owned comic books.

This novel has existed in many forms, going back over a decade before it finally saw publication in 2019. The final form of the story – the one I consider 'canon'- was written sometime around 2017. It was a large, idea-filled, action thriller, with a lot of mythology, commentary, and subtext.

But traditional publishing is a team effort. A collaboration. First there were the long discussions with my agent to figure out how to make the story more commercial. We streamlined the plot. Cut down on some of the connections, distilled conversations and ideas. Then there was feedback from buying editors who ultimately did not buy.

By the time Pegasus acquired the book it was a much leaner story. More of a straight-ahead action movie. And, while I will always be proud of that version, it never fully represented the real story I set out to write. Key nuances and subversions were lost. Some of the attacks on 'Ancient Aliens' theories had been watered down to such a point that it was possible to read the book as subscribing to these theories.

For the sequel I endeavoured to put a lot of the depth, character-work and quirks back in, and readers did notice the difference in tone.

None of this is to be read as bitterness at people who suggested the changes. These are not sour grapes. Publishing is not an exact science and we make the choices we think are right in the moment. Each of the people involved in this long process made my writing better.

But for this edition I have restored many of the ideas that had been cut. This turned out to be fairly simple. The structure of the book didn't need to change, none of the characters were altered, though some of their motivations and connections are -to my mind- more interesting. In most cases, the restoration amounted to adding a few extra lines of dialogue back into a scene, or reverting back to the original version of a conversation. Think of a filmmaker having multiple takes to choose from. There are three instances of scenes being added back in. These were originally cut as part of an attempt to streamline the number of characters that readers needed to keep track of. But, with hindsight, I think the cut was a mistake.

If the 2019 version was the cinematic release, this is the Director's Cut.

And, as I'm in charge of the Chaseverse, this is now the official version moving forward.

2019 POST-SCRIPT.

I carried the character of Marah Chase around for a long time, waiting for the right moment. I owe a massive thank you to my agent, Stacia Decker, for encouraging this moody hardboiled crime writer to finally let loose with some explosions, big ideas, and car chases.

Jacque Ben-Zekry and Christa Faust helped me to figure out who Chase really is, and how she fits into the world. Chuck Wendig picked out the guns—if you don't like them, blame him.

Steve Weddle always listens, and both Johnny Shaw and Bart Lessard reminded me to be faster and funnier.

Chantelle Osman, Eva Dolan, Luca Veste, and Nick Quantrill always keep me sane during the writing process. Thanks also to Greg Rucka and Anthony Johnston, two cool people who make one of my dream jobs look easy.

You wouldn't be reading this right now without the faith and support of Katie McGuire and Pegasus Books. I'm happy to be working with people who get the idea so clearly. That's one of the most important things in publishing.

Special thanks to Dave White, who has been pushing for me to give Marah a book for a long time.

I owe everything else to the love, patience, and support of my wife, Lis.

JAY .

ABOUT JAY STRINGER

Jay Stringer was born in 1980, and he's not dead yet.

His crime fiction has been nominated for both Anthony and Derringer awards, and shortlisted for the McIlvanney Prize.

His stand-up comedy has been laughed at by at least three people. Jay is English by birth and Scottish by legend; born in the Black Country and claiming Glasgow as his hometown for the last 17 years.

Jay is dyslexic, and came to the written word as a second language, via comic books, music, and comedy. Jay won a gold medal in the Antwerp Olympics of 1920. He did not compete in the Helsinki Olympics of 1952, that was some other guy.

DID YOU LIKE THE COVER DESIGN AND TYPESETTING OF THIS BOOK?

Jay is a freelance artist available for hire to do either or both. Check out www.jaystringerbooks.com for more details, or email Jay at jay@jaystring erbooks.com

Ingram Content Group UK Ltd.
Milton Keynes UK
UKHW010646270723
425883UK00004B/228